THE EMPEROR'S FINEST

More Sandy Mitchell from the Black Library

• CIAPHAS CAIN •

CIAPHAS CAIN: HERO OF THE IMPERIUM
(Contains books 1-3 in the series – *For the Emperor, Caves of Ice* and
The Traitor's Hand)

CIAPHAS CAIN: DEFENDER OF THE IMPERIUM
(Contains books 4-6 in the series – *Death or Glory, Duty Calls* and
Cain's Last Stand)

Book 7 – THE EMPEROR'S FINEST

• DARK HERESY •

Book 1 – SCOURGE THE HERETIC
Book 2 – INNOCENCE PROVES NOTHING

Dan Abnett novels from the Black Library

• GAUNT'S GHOSTS •

*Colonel-Commissar Gaunt and his regiment, the Tanith
First-and-Only, struggle for survival on the battlefields
of the far future.*

The Founding
(Omnibus containing books 1-3 in the series: FIRST AND
ONLY, GHOSTMAKER and NECROPOLIS)

The Saint
(Omnibus containing books 4-7 in the series: HONOUR
GUARD, THE GUNS OF TANITH, STRAIGHT SILVER and
SABBAT MARTYR)

The Lost
(Omnibus containing books 8-11 in the series: TRAITOR
GENERAL, HIS LAST COMMAND, THE ARMOUR OF
CONTEMPT and ONLY IN DEATH)

Book 12 – BLOOD PACT

Also

DOUBLE EAGLE

SABBAT WORLDS
Anthology includes stories by Dan Abnett, Graham McNeill,
Sandy Mitchell and more.

A WARHAMMER 40,000 NOVEL

Ciaphas Cain

THE EMPEROR'S FINEST

Sandy Mitchell

BLACK LIBRARY

For Dave, for showing the rest of us how it ought to be done.

A BLACK LIBRARY PUBLICATION

First published in Great Britain in 2010 by
The Black Library,
Games Workshop Ltd.,
Willow Road, Nottingham,
NG7 2WS, UK.

10 9 8 7 6 5 4 3 2 1

Cover illustration by Clint Langley.

A CIP record for this book is available from the British Library.

UK ISBN13: 978 1 84416 890 3
US ISBN13: 978 1 84416 891 0

See the Black Library on the internet at
www.blacklibrary.com

Find out more about Games Workshop
and the world of Warhammer 40,000 at
www.games-workshop.com

Printed and bound in the UK.

IT IS THE 41st millennium. For more than a hundred
centuries the Emperor has sat immobile on the Golden
Throne of Earth. He is the master of mankind by the will
of the gods, and master of a million worlds by the might of
his inexhaustible armies. He is a rotting carcass writhing
invisibly with power from the Dark Age of Technology. He
is the Carrion Lord of the Imperium for whom a thousand
souls are sacrificed every day, so that he may never truly die.

YET EVEN IN his deathless state, the Emperor continues his
eternal vigilance. Mighty battlefleets cross the daemon–infested
miasma of the warp, the only route between distant stars,
their way lit by the Astronomican, the psychic
manifestation of the Emperor's will. Vast armies give battle in
his name on uncounted worlds. Greatest amongst his
soldiers are the Adeptus Astartes, the Space Marines,
bioengineered super–warriors. Their comrades in arms are
legion: the Imperial Guard and countless planetary defence
forces, the ever–vigilant Inquisition and the tech–priests of the
Adeptus Mechanicus to name only a few.
But for all their multitudes, they are barely enough to hold
off the ever–present threat from aliens, heretics,
mutants – and worse.

TO BE A man in such times is to be one amongst untold
billions. It is to live in the cruellest and most bloody regime
imaginable. These are the tales of those times. Forget the
power of technology and science, for so much has been forgotten, never to be relearned. Forget the promise of progress
and understanding, for in the grim dark future there is only
war. There is no peace amongst the stars, only an eternity of
carnage and slaughter, and the laughter
of thirsting gods.

Editorial Note:

This selection from the Cain Archive is taken from a relatively brief, but far from uneventful, period of Cain's life, when he was attached to the command staff at brigade headquarters as an independent commissar. Reviewing the records of these half-dozen years, it's not hard to see why he arranged to be reassigned to a regiment on active service at the earliest opportunity, as even this would have seemed relatively safe in comparison to some of the assignments which came his way, a consequence of his unwanted reputation for heroism which he seems to have found both natural and inconvenient in the extreme. (A reputation which, true to form, he continues to insist throughout the current extract is completely undeserved. Many of my readers have taken this claim at face value, and many others have construed it as a rather engaging blindness to his own virtues. Having known him personally, I tend to the view that the truth is a little more complicated than either postulation.)

I have already disseminated several of his subsequent exploits with the Valhallan 597th, and see no need to recapitulate the circumstances of his finally getting his wish. Instead, I've chosen to concentrate on what may have been the pivotal incident of that period of his life, the consequences of which were to reverberate for decades to come. With hindsight, too, we can discern the first faint breath of wind destined to become a storm which threatened to engulf the entire Eastern Arm by the turn of the millennium.

I was also influenced in my choice of material by the reflection that this selection answers a number of questions raised and left open by some of the previous extracts I've edited and circulated among my fellow inquisitors, not least of which is the nature of his connection to the Reclaimers Astartes Chapter, and the circumstances surrounding his involvement in their ill-advised boarding of the space hulk Spawn of Damnation. Since the details of his appointment as Imperial Guard liaison officer to the Chapter, and his eventful journey to meet them, have been covered in one of the short extracts I've already disseminated, I've chosen not to repeat the material here, but to begin Cain's account of events with the Viridia Campaign itself.

As always, I've endeavoured to clarify matters where appropriate, by the use of footnotes and the interpolation of additional information by other hands, especially where Cain's habit of concentrating on the relatively trivial incidents which affected him personally threatens to lose sight of the bigger picture. The bulk of what follows, however, is unadulterated Cain, and as idiosyncratic as ever.

Amberley Vail, Ordo Xenos.

ONE

IT'S NOT OFTEN I'm happy to find myself heading into a war zone as fast as the warp currents can carry me, but in the case of the Viridia Campaign I was prepared to make an exception. My journey there had been eventful, to say the least. Having taken passage on an Adeptus Mechanicus transport heading in roughly the right direction, I found myself fleeing for my life through a necron tomb world, which my hosts had been incautious enough to start poking around *en route*. If it hadn't been for the fortuitous arrival of a ship from the Reclaimers Astartes Chapter, there would have been no survivors of the affair at all. As it was, I'd escaped by the skin of my teeth, and more luck than anyone has a right to expect. I don't suppose anyone will believe a word of it, though,[1] so I'll get on with a tale I can prove. As I doubt anyone's ever going to read these ramblings of mine, it's all academic in any case.

---

1. *Which indicates that this portion of his memoirs was composed some time before he got round to recounting the Interitus Prime incident: a typical example of his cavalier approach to chronology.*

I can't say I remember much about my first few days aboard the strike cruiser *Revenant*,[1] but that's hardly surprising given the condition in which I boarded it. When I came to, it was to find myself in a spartan sanatorium, occupying a bed which seemed far too big for me, while faces I didn't recognise swam in and out of the mist which seemed to be hovering just in front of my eyeballs.

'Commissar,' a voice which sounded impossibly deep, rich, and resonant asked. 'Are you awake?'

For a moment I doubted that, still comfortably insulated from reality by the pharmaceuticals cluttering up my bloodstream. To my drug-addled mind, the voice sounded like that of the Emperor Himself, and I found myself wondering if I should have spent a bit more time in the temple, and a bit less in bars, gambling dens and bordellos, but it seemed a little late to be worrying about that now. If I had indeed arrived at the Golden Throne, I'd just have to hope its occupant was in a good mood, and try to steer the conversation on to safer ground at the earliest opportunity.[2] Then one of the indistinct faces swam close enough for me to focus on, and memory belatedly kicked in.

'I think so,' I husked, vaguely surprised by how thin my voice sounded. For a moment I wondered if it was due to disuse, and feared I'd been unconscious for weeks, but as my faculties began to trickle back, I realised that it simply sounded feeble in comparison to the one which had addressed me. Almost at once, memory followed, and I relived my desperate dive through the necron warp portal, and my arrival aboard their ship just in time to encounter a Space Marine boarding party. 'The metal creatures,' I asked urgently. 'Are they dead?'

'A debatable point,' one of the trio of giants surrounding me said, and smiled, in a somewhat unsettling manner. A mechanical claw, which looked as though it would have been more at home

---

1. *In his account of his escape from the necron tomb world Cain refers to the vessel as a battle-barge, which is hardly likely, given that these huge craft are only employed where a significant proportion of an Astartes Chapter's assets need to be transported between war zones. It's quite possible, however, that, given their rarity, he simply believed it to be a generic term for any Space Marine vessel.*

2. *He is, of course, joking here – or so I sincerely hope.*

attached to a power loader, hovered behind his shoulder, in the manner of a tech-priest's mechadendrites.

The one looming over me shot him a reproving look and turned back to the bed I was lying on. Though thinly padded, it seemed damnably hard for an infirmary. 'You'll have to excuse Drumon's sense of humour, commissar. It's not always appropriate.' A hand as broad as a dinner plate slipped behind my shoulders and helped me to rise to a sitting position, bringing more of my surroundings into view. Gleaming metal surfaces, burnished like a drill sergeant's boots, were everywhere, making the place feel more like a Mechanicus shrine than a place of healing. If it hadn't been for the pervasive aroma of counterseptics, and the icon of the Emperor, in His aspect of the Great Healer, gazing at me sternly from the wall opposite, I might never have realised I was in a sanatorium at all. Most of the equipment I'd expect to see in such a place was absent, perhaps tidied away in the featureless metal lockers ranged against the wall, and what little there was still visible meant nothing to me. 'I'm Apothecary Sholer, of the Reclaimers. And in answer to your question, their vessel was destroyed.'

Which didn't exactly answer the question, of course, but it sounded good enough to me at the time. (Knowing what I know now about the necrons, I wouldn't even have bothered to ask, but it was the first time I'd encountered them, don't forget. These days I wouldn't count them out if the entire planet they were standing on had been razed.[1])

'Ciaphas Cain,' I said, inclining my head courteously and immediately wishing I hadn't. 'I believe I'm your new Imperial Guard liaison officer.'

'That's my understanding too,' the third giant said, speaking for the first time. Like the others, he was dressed in ceramite armour of a dull, off-white colour, with yellow gauntlets, although his was inlaid with a great deal more ornamentation than the suits of his

---

1. *There have indeed been reports of necron warriors apparently surviving on worlds which have been subject to decrees of Exterminatus. Although, given their apparent mastery of the warp, it's equally possible that the 'survivors' merely arrived through an undetected portal deep below the surface after the firestorms abated.*

comrades. He bowed his head. 'Captain Gries, commanding the Viridian Expeditionary Force. It appears your reputation was less exaggerated than we believed.'

'Indeed,' the Techmarine Sholer had introduced as Drumon said, his mechanical claw flexing slightly as he spoke. 'Few men could have escaped unscathed from a necron tomb world.'

'Hardly unscathed,' I said, suddenly remembering two of my fingers being ripped away by a glancing shot from the metal killers' hideous weapons. Nerving myself for the sight, I lifted my right hand into view, and found myself staring at a formless bundle of bandages, so bloated with padding that no shape hinting at whatever they might conceal could be discerned. As if being reminded of its existence had flicked a switch, I suddenly found my entire hand itching abominably.

'The augmetics are knitting in well,' Sholer assured me, as if I had the faintest idea what he was talking about. Before I could ask him, Drumon cut in again.

'You alone survived,' he said, 'when scores of your fellows perished. Two fingers seems a small price to pay.'

'If you put it like that,' I said, 'I'm forced to agree. I didn't even notice they'd gone until I was waving goodbye to the creatures in the tunnel.' The jest was feeble enough, I'll admit, but I was hardly at my best under the circumstances, and it did the job, which was to convince my listeners that I was modest about my so-called heroism. Time and again, I've found, the more I appear to be trying to play down my unmerited reputation, the more people seem to believe it.

Drumon seemed surprised at my flippancy, but agreeably so. His broad face, seamed with a faint tracery of scar tissue, widened for an instant with a barely perceptible smile, before returning to its previous immobility.

Gries didn't react at all, but returned to the point as though no one else had even spoken, with the single-mindedness of a servitor attempting to follow a simple set of instructions. 'I would like a full report of your experiences on Interitus Prime at your earliest convenience,' he said.

Technically, I suppose, I could have told him to keep his thinly veiled orders to himself, as the only people I answered to were the Commissariat, but that would hardly have been polite, or politic. I was going to have to work with him, or the people who reported to him, for quite some time, and putting his back up before we'd even officially begun wouldn't exactly help matters. Besides, I'd have to come up with something for General Lokris and his staff back at brigade headquarters, to explain how I'd managed to mislay an entire starship, and since both it and the expedition it carried had belonged to the Adeptus Mechanicus, I was pretty sure they'd be taking a keen interest in whatever I might have to say about it too.

There certainly didn't seem any harm in letting the captain of the Reclaimers have a copy as well; the wider I could spread my version of events, the less likely it seemed that anyone would be able to claim I'd been somehow culpable. (Which, for once, I hadn't been, just in the wrong place at the wrong time, as seems to have happened inordinately often during my long and inglorious career.) So I simply nodded again and tried to ignore the firecrackers going off behind my eyes as a result of the incautious movement.

'If someone could find me a slate, I'll get right on it,' I said. 'It's not as if I've got much else to do while I'm in here.'

As JOBS OF makework go, reliving the nightmare I'd so recently been through was hardly the most congenial I might have chosen, but as I progressed, I found myself setting out events with greater ease and more fluency, recalling them in greater detail than I'd expected. No doubt it helped that I had an unexpected ally in this endeavour, Drumon having taken it upon himself to debrief me, and making several visits to the quarters I'd been assigned on leaving the sanatorium for the purpose. As I recounted my experiences, he would ask questions about the equipment the tech-priests had been using to probe the ruins, and such blasphemous artefacts as I remembered seeing in the depths of the tomb world. I had no illusions about the fact that his interest lay in whatever technotheological insights I was able to provide, rather than my company, but as the voyage progressed, our conversation gradually widened to encompass other topics, and I can't deny that he was rather more congenial than the other Astartes I'd so far encountered.

I wasn't the only unenhanced human aboard, of course: in fact, the few dozen Reclaimers[1] were outnumbered three or four to one by the Chapter serfs who crewed the vessel. I found these servants tedious company at best, however, even more so than the skitarii I'd met aboard the *Omnissiah's Bounty*. Their reverence for the Astartes they served seemed second only to their devotion to the Emperor, and, unused to the society of anyone outside their enclosed little world, they remained distantly polite, rebuffing any attempt at conversation with formal and strictly factual responses.

The one assigned to look after me, a youth named Gladden, was efficient, unobtrusive and unexceptionable, so much so that I found myself missing the presence of Jurgen more than I would have thought possible. True, my aide was a walking insult to the uniform of an Imperial Guardsman, who made the average ork seem fastidious and fragrant by comparison, but I'd learned to trust his dogged loyalty, and he'd become an invaluable bulwark against the more onerous aspects of my job. After some consideration, I'd decided to leave him back at brigade headquarters, however; partly because the notion of Jurgen in close proximity to the finest warriors the Imperium had ever produced made even my mind boggle, and partly because I'd got an inkling that Lokris had me earmarked for another assignment fit for the hero he fondly imagined me to be, and I wanted my aide in place to head it off with his usual obdurate refusal to deviate from protocol.

The upshot of which was that Drumon was the closest thing I was likely to find to a tolerable companion before we reached Viridia, and I found myself looking forward to his occasional visits. On the last occasion he dropped by my quarters he found me annotating a hardprint of my report with an inkstick, and the faint smile I'd seen a few times before drifted across his face.

---

1. *A typically vague statement: there seem to have been around forty or fifty in total, far fewer than a full-strength company, but still more than sufficient to deal with the kind of civil insurrection sweeping the Viridia System.*

'The new fingers appear to be satisfactory,' he said, a trace of pride entering his voice.

'They are indeed,' I agreed, laying the tedious job aside with a sense of relief and flexing my newly acquired augmetics. I still found their altered appearance a little disconcerting, but they'd started to feel like part of my own body at last, and I was able to grasp things again without looking to make sure I'd judged the distance correctly instead of over- or under-reaching by a millimetre or two. Drumon, it transpired, had constructed them himself, collaborating with Sholer on their installation, so it seemed I had a lot to thank the Techmarine for. I nodded at the pile of papers. 'At least I got this finished before we left the warp,' I added.

'The brother-captain will be pleased,' Drumon said. As usual he remained standing, and seemed perfectly comfortable doing so. In my time with the Reclaimers I seldom saw any of the Astartes sitting down, and when I did it was almost invariably for some practical reason, such as driving or riding in the back of a Rhino. 'There will be little time for paperwork when we reach Viridia.'

'I suppose not,' I agreed, pouring myself a much-needed measure of amasec. In actual fact I was planning to do as much file-shuffling as possible, in preference to visiting any of the battlefronts, but I wasn't about to admit that to one of the Emperor's finest.

As things were to turn out, though, the insurrection had continued to grow while we'd been transiting the warp, and by the time we arrived, notions like fronts and rear areas had ceased to have any military meaning at all. The entire system was one huge cauldron, seething with conflict, and we were about to drop into the middle of it.

'Have you found time to analyse the strategic review?' Drumon asked, and I nodded towards the data-slate on the desk beside me.

'I've skimmed it,' I admitted, which was the best anyone could have hoped for, and a great deal better than I normally managed with the briefing documents provided by the Munitorum. Usually,

I found far more pleasant ways of spending my time aboard ship than wading through the turgid prose of Administratum drones, whose conclusions would invariably turn out to have been overtaken by events while we were transiting the warp in any case, but the *Revenant* was conspicuously lacking in recreational opportunities. 'Pacifying Viridia looks simple enough.'

At the time my confidence seemed more than justified. Rebellions in backwater systems like this one tended to be sparked by grievances against the planetary government rather than the Imperium itself, and the arrival of a few Guard regiments was usually enough to bring both sides to heel. So far as I could see the situation hardly merited the deployment of the Astartes at all, and the Reclaimers would undoubtedly have found better uses for their time if it hadn't been for the fact that the Viridia System was a major supplier of food and raw materials to the hive-worlds of the sector: unless the flow of tithes was restored in pretty short order they'd begin to suffer socially and economically in turn, leading to a wave of instability which, left unchecked, would drag down a dozen worlds within a decade. The manpower and resources required to deal with that would be incalculable.

'I concur,' Drumon said, with all the confidence I would have expected from one of the Emperor's chosen, and I must admit that I considered it more than justified. The average insurrectionist rabble wouldn't last five minutes against a couple of dozen Guardsmen, let alone the genetically enhanced Space Marines. He might have been about to say more, but the familiar disorientating sensation of a starship slipping through the barrier separating the material universe from the warp swept over me at that point, leaving both of us disinclined to further conversation.

'I don't suppose I'll ever get used to that,' I said, little knowing at the time how far and frequent my travels were to become in the ensuing years, to the point where I was able to shrug off the lingering nausea almost at once. On this occasion, however, I was more than grateful for the amasec I'd poured a few moments before, and drained the goblet in a couple of swallows.

I was just beginning to feel relatively normal again when the lights flickered, and a faint tremor ran through the deck plates beneath my feet. Memories of my experience aboard the *Hand of Vengeance* a few years before sent my heart racing, and I was already reaching for my weapons when, after listening to the comm-bead in his ear for a moment, Drumon told me what I'd already deduced for myself. 'We appear to be under attack,' he said.

Editorial Note:

Since, as usual, Cain only gives the most cursory background to the events he's describing, here seems as good a place as any to insert a more objective overview of the Viridia Campaign at the point he entered it.

From *The Virus of Betrayal: The Cleansing of Viridia and its Aftermath* by Lady Ottaline Melmoth, 958.M41.

IT'S UNDOUBTEDLY FAIR to say that the first few months of what was to become the Viridian Insurrection gave few clues as to the scope of the chaos and carnage to come. What had begun as a wave of popular protest against the mooted imposition of a two per cent tax on incense and votive candles by the Administratum erupted into violence in several provinces almost simultaneously. With hindsight, of course, we can see how carefully events were orchestrated, from the moment an agent of the conspiracy first slipped the controversial measure into the fiscal projections for the following year. Despite the protestations of the planetary governor that he'd never seen the proposal, and certainly wouldn't have approved it if he had, a large section of the population laid the blame for it squarely at his door, some even going so far as to begin calling him 'Alaric the Heretic' (a nickname which the poor man remains saddled with even today, albeit now in jest).

How much of the Ecclesiarchy's predictable condemnation of the so-called 'tax on piety' was spontaneous, and how much the result of infiltration of their ranks, we can only conjecture, but there's no denying the outrage with which the average Viridian in the thoroughfare reacted. We've always been proud to call ourselves an Emperor-fearing folk, and the prospect of being unable to afford to maintain the tiny shrines which grace even the humblest hovel, or to do so only at the expense of starvation and destitution, a choice many of our poorest citizens would undoubtedly have made, was all but intolerable to most of the proletariat.

In vain, Governor DuPanya pledged that he personally would make sure that the proposed legislation was never enacted. By the beginning of 928, the 'piety tax' had become a rallying point for malcontents of all kinds, united only in their dislike of the planetary government. After the initial riots had been suppressed by the Guardians,[1] backed up by elements from the Planetary Defence Force in a few cases, the inevitable casualties among the civilian population became the focus of fresh resentment, and the wave of unrest intensified. With what seemed at the time to be astonishing rapidity, but which with hindsight is clearly the result of careful coordination by the shadowy enemy whose existence as yet no one even suspected, Viridia became all but ungovernable, and Governor DuPanya was left with no choice but to appeal to the Imperial Guard for help.

Help was not slow in coming, but the distance between stars is a vast one, and many agonising months were to pass before the vanguard of the relief force arrived in our system. To the joy and astonishment of all loyal Imperial citizens, the vessel was no Imperial Guard troopship, but a battle-barge[2] of the Astartes, bearing not only the matchless warriors of the Space Marines, but Commissar Cain, the hero whose exploits against the orkish invaders of Perlia had inspired billions across the sector.

---

1. *The local name for law enforcers.*

2. *Melmoth is clearly labouring under the same misapprehension as Cain here.*

As fate was to have it, however, no sooner had the *Revenant* re-entered the materium than it was treacherously attacked, the anarchy which had by then overwhelmed our home world having spread to engulf the void stations and mining habs scattered throughout the system.

TWO

HAVING NO BETTER plan in mind, I followed Drumon to the bridge. If necessary, I was prepared to argue that my position as liaison officer made it my business to remain abreast of any unexpected developments, although to be honest I just thought that would be the best place to find out what in the Throne's name was going on. I've been involved in a fair number of space battles in my time, far more than any Guardsman has a right to expect, and in all too many of them the only thing I could do was sit there and wait for the troopship to take a hit. At least on the bridge you can watch events unfolding in the hololith, which introduces a curious kind of detachment into the proceedings, as the contact icons go through their stately dance of life and death.

In the event, however, no one challenged my right to be there, which came as a welcome surprise. In fact, the only thing which surprised me more was that until Drumon arrived, there were no Astartes on the bridge at all.

'Techmarine.' The vessel's captain, who for some reason rejoiced in the title of shipmaster,[1] vacated his control throne and inclined

---

1. *Presumably because 'captain' is a Space Marine rank, and to confer it on a serf, even in a different context, might lead to confusion.*

his head respectfully. (Not something the Navy would appreciate, having the man in charge abandon his duty for the sake of proto-col in the middle of a battle, but the Space Marine Chapters, as I was already beginning to grasp, have a different perspective on things. Quite how different I wouldn't fully understand for a few more decades, however.)

'Carry on, shipmaster.' Drumon acknowledged the greeting with a barely perceptible nod of his own, and the shipmaster resumed his seat, absorbed again at once in the flurry of information blizzarding across his pict screen. One of the control stations ranged about the hushed and dimly lit chamber, through which the muted chanting and clouds of incense from the tech-adepts servicing the targeting systems drifted, remained vacant, and as the towering figure of the Techmarine took his place before it, I realised that it was placed higher than the others, where a standing man more than two metres tall could work at it comfortably. The other lecterns were manned by Chapter serfs in uniforms similar to those of the Imperial Navy, although their insignia were different, no doubt reflecting their affiliation and status in some manner I couldn't be bothered to enquire about at the moment.

'What's happening?' I asked, and Drumon glanced briefly in my direction as though surprised to be reminded of my presence, his gauntleted fingers continuing to rattle the keys of the data lectern. A blizzard of images, changing too rapidly for me to assimilate, danced across his face, reflected from the display in front of him.

'We have sustained only minimal damage,' he assured me, which came as a tremendous relief. The last time I'd been aboard a ves-sel under fire I'd ended up breathing vacuum, fortunately for no more than a handful of seconds, although it had seemed a great deal longer to Jurgen and I. The *Revenant* was made of sterner stuff than the venerable troopship which had delivered me to Perlia, however, being designed to be capable of holding her own against a ship of the line, and the voices around me were reassuringly calm.

'Who from?' I persisted, and if Drumon was irritated at all, he was too polite to show it. By way of reply he activated a nearby pict screen, and I found myself looking at a slightly blurred image of a System Defence corvette.

'Viridian vessel, this is the strike cruiser *Revenant*, of the Reclaimers Chapter of the Adeptus Astartes,' the shipmaster said, his voice clipped. 'Break off and surrender, or be destroyed in the name of the Emperor.'

'They're turning,' one of the vassals said, his voice equally matter-of-fact. 'Looks like another attack run.'

'Gunnery stations stand by,' the shipmaster said, then glanced at Drumon for approval.

The Techmarine nodded again. 'All weapon batteries charged and ready,' he assured the crew, his voice carrying easily to every corner of the bridge.

'Fire when ready,' the shipmaster said, his voice as calm as if he'd just ordered a mug of recaf. 'Wait for a positive lock.' The seconds stretched unbearably, the image of the attacking vessel growing ever larger on my screen, until I expected to see ravening beams of energy lancing out from it with every heartbeat.

'Target acquired,' another of the bridge crew said, seeming equally relaxed, and I finally realised that it was Drumon's presence which was making them so dispassionately efficient. Nobody wanted to be the one to let the crew down in front of their masters, so they were all doing it by the book, instead of cutting corners and giving way to impulsive profanity like the Guard troopers I was used to herding so often did when the las-bolts started flying.

A moment later the attacking corvette broke apart, like a seed-head on the wind, as our starboard batteries tore the guts out of it, to leave a slowly dissipating cloud of debris drifting apart in the void.

'Who were they, though?' I asked, not really expecting an answer, but the auspex man answered me anyway.

'The IFF beacon tagged it as the *Lady Helene*, one of the local System Defence boats.'[1]

'Then they ought to have been on our side,' I said, beginning to

---

1. *A generic term for all light warships incapable of warp travel.*

feel that matters weren't going to be quite so simple after all. If part of the SDF had mutinied, then the chances were that a substantial proportion of their counterparts in the PDF had followed suit (or, more likely, led by example).

'Acknowledged,' Drumon rumbled, and for a moment I thought he'd responded to my comment, before I realised that he'd probably been too busy listening to the voice in his comm-bead to have even heard it. 'I will inform the commissar.'

'Inform me of what?' I asked, already more than half-convinced that I didn't want to know. His first words were enough to tell me I was right about that.

'The situation has deteriorated significantly,' he said, with commendable restraint. 'According to our signal intercepts, a state of civil war now exists throughout the system.'

'Frakking great,' I said, seeing little need to restrain myself under the circumstances. 'Does Captain Gries have any suggestions for dealing with it?'

I'd got to know Drumon well enough by now to be fairly confident that the expression which ghosted across his face was one of faint surprise that I'd even bothered to ask. 'Intervene at once,' he said, then broke off to listen to a voice in his earpiece. 'He is embarking in the hangar deck as we speak, and extends an invitation for you to join him.'

Not, needless to say, an invitation I could even consider refusing. I was there to liaise with the Reclaimers' command staff, which basically meant Gries, so wherever he went, I had to go too. At least until the Imperial Guard forces turned up, and I could find some plausible excuse to go and bother them instead.

'I'd be delighted,' I said, hoping I sounded as though I meant it.

I'D ARRIVED ABOARD the *Revenant* by teleporter, and been unconscious at the time into the bargain, so this was my first sight of the warship's hangar bay. My immediate impression as I walked through the airtight hatch, which slid closed behind me with a squeal of metal against metal, was one of purposeful activity. The inevitable crowd of Chapter serfs was bustling about under the supervision of a handful whose bearing and demeanour betokened higher rank than their fellows, even though the iconography of their uniforms continued to be strange to me. A startling number of them had visible augmetics, which either indicated a fair degree of hazard in their occupations (even by the standards of serving aboard a warship), or the kind of willingness to voluntarily adopt whatever enhancements would assist their work I'd previously encountered only among the Adeptus Mechanicus. I suspected the latter, as I'd gathered from the skitarii aboard the *Omnissiah's Bounty* that some kind of pact existed between the Reclaimers and the acolytes of the Machine-God, but there was no time to think about that now. Gries and his entourage were clearly visible in the distance, towering over the surrounding crewmen, and I set off across the echoing metal plain between us as quickly as possible.

Like every hangar I'd ever been in, the chamber was vast, but the very scale of it felt curiously comforting; for the first time since coming aboard I felt a measure of relief from the nagging sense of strangeness I'd experienced everywhere else about the vessel, whose corridors and hatchways had been designed to accommodate the greater-than-human bulk of Space Marines, and left me feeling curiously shrunken. Unlike the docking bays I'd passed through while embarking and departing from troopships, however, the vast space felt clinically efficient. All the apparatus required to refuel and rearm the pair of Thunderhawks currently occupying it was neatly stowed, and there was a marked absence of cargo pallets and other detritus cluttering up the place.

The Thunderhawks were impressive enough, too, and I slowed my pace a little as I neared the closer of them. They weren't as large as the platoon-sized drop-ships the Guard routinely used, let alone the company-sized behemoths I'd ridden in on occasion, but their blocky solidity looked immediately reassuring. Their heavy armour could doubtless soak up a lot of incoming fire, and they seemed more than capable of dishing it out as well as taking it, judging by the amount of ordnance I could see hanging off their airframes. They were painted yellow and white, like the armour of the Astartes marching up the boarding ramp of the one I was approaching, their simultaneous footfalls echoing off the metal mesh like drumbeats, and looked as fresh as if they'd just been rolled out for the first time. Having gathered a little of how much tradition meant to a Space Marine Chapter, I had no doubt that they were considerably more venerable than they appeared, perhaps even centuries old, but their immaculate condition was a tribute to Drumon and the serf enginseers he supervised. It heartened me, too, I have to admit, as I found it hard to conceive of an enemy capable of standing against such a formidable vessel.

I trotted up the ramp in the wake of the power-armoured giants ahead of me, and found myself in a passenger compartment constructed on the same cyclopean lines as everything else sized for Astartes. Only about half of the seats were occupied, and I scrambled into one of the empty ones, feeling oddly like a child in an adult's armchair as I fumbled with the crash webbing. My feet hung awkwardly above the deck plates, and I was unable to draw the webbing quite as tight as I would have wished, but at least I had room for my chainsword without having to remove it from my belt, as would have been the case aboard an Imperial Guard landing barge.

'Commissar.' Gries's helmet turned in my direction, easy to identify, as it was as richly ornamented as his armour and surmounted by a crest of green and black. 'Are you prepared?'

'By the Emperor's grace,' I replied, falling back on one of the stock responses which I generally used to avoid committing myself, and feeling it wouldn't hurt to look a bit more pious than usual surrounded by so many paragons. There were fifteen of them in all: Gries's command squad, which I was pleased to see included Sholer, his narthecium ready for use on his left vambrace, and ten tactical troopers, already broken down into two combat squads. Most carried bolters, which I was more used to seeing mounted on armoured vehicles, as easily as a Guardsman handled his lasgun, while two of their comrades were equipped with heavy weapons it would have taken a team of ordinary troopers to use effectively on the battlefield. One carried a missile launcher, several reloads pouched at his waist, while another casually hefted the first man-portable lascannon I'd ever seen without a groundmount. The faceplates of their helmets were all the same yellow as their gauntlets, although the captain's shone with the lustre of gilding rather than pigment.

'May He watch over us all,' Gries intoned in response, although, to my surprise, he made the cogwheel gesture I generally associated with members of the Adeptus Mechanicus rather than the sign of the aquila.

I didn't have much time to think about that, though, because the boarding ramp was retracting, and the engines fired up to a pitch which left my ears ringing. It might have been fine for the Astartes, whose heads were cocooned inside their helmets, but it was distinctly uncomfortable for me. There was no point complaining about it, however, even if anyone could have heard me, so I just pulled my cap down as far as it would go, and quietly resolved to get hold of some earplugs before I accepted another lift in a Thunderhawk.

'Look in the locker to your left,' the nearest Reclaimer said, his words just about audible over the howling of the engines, even amplified by the vox built into his helmet. With some difficulty I followed his suggestion, since everything was laid out for far longer arms than mine, and discovered a comms headset with padded earpieces and a vox mic on a stalk. I donned it gratefully, and found the noise almost instantly reduced to a level I considered bearable.

'Thank you,' I responded, feeling faintly foolish.

'This is our primary objective,' Gries said, activating a pict screen. It seemed someone on his staff had been busy in the relatively short time since our arrival in-system, and had managed to gather a remarkable amount of information. 'Fidelis, the planetary capital, currently being fought over by three of the major rebel factions. The loyalist forces are dug in around the Administratum cloister, the cathedral precincts, the Mechanicus shrine and the governor's palace, no doubt hoping the rebels will whittle one another down for them.' The landmarks he'd indicated flared green on the map. 'We'll deploy from the palace. If we can assure the safety of the governor, then the Emperor's rule should be swiftly restored.'

I found myself nodding in agreement – always assuming the

man was still alive, of course. If he wasn't, and had been inconsiderate enough to expire without leaving a clear line of succession, the resulting confusion as conflicting claimants brawled for the throne would probably make things ten times worse.

'I take it you have good reason to believe he's still in charge,' I said, more to show I was paying attention than anything else. Gries's helmet dipped in almost imperceptible acknowledgement.

'He made a pictcast five hours ago, appealing for calm and promising retribution against all who continued to defy the Emperor's will. The rebels responded as one might expect.'

'Shelling the palace?' I asked, and the captain's helmet inclined again.

'Given the amount of damage the building has already sustained, we can infer that he managed to survive the latest bombardment with little difficulty.' He adjusted the image on the pict screen, and the palace and its grounds rushed towards us, filling the frame. Either the *Revenant* carried some of the most sophisticated long-range sensors I'd ever come across, or Drumon had managed to gain access to the PDF's orbital net, because according to the time stamp in the corner the image was a current one. The palace itself showed signs of extensive damage, an entire wing burned out and roofless, while the rest of the structure was pocked with the stigmata of heavy ordnance. The perimeter walls, which had been designed with this sort of contingency in mind, had evidently withstood several assaults already, and been shored up or strengthened in a few places, although, to my relief, I couldn't see any actual breaches. The muddy wasteland separating the two, which had presumably once been formal gardens, was criss-crossed with trenches and the tracks of armoured vehicles, several dozen of which could be seen parked around the place. That was good news, if nothing else, as it meant there would be a substantial garrison of PDF loyalists to hide behind if, by some inconceivable quirk of fate, I was to run out of Space Marines.

Gries highlighted an open area between the trench line and the building, which common sense and experience told me had to be covered by emplaced weapons from at least two directions. 'This is our landing zone,' he said. 'My team and the commissar will present our compliments to Governor DuPanya, while Sergeant Trosque's squad will move out at once to ensure the safety of the cathedral and the shrine of the Omnissiah.'

The sergeant, who I'd already picked out by virtue of the chainsword scabbarded at his hip, opposite the holster of his bolt pistol, made no visible sign of acknowledgement, but his voice responded at once. 'One combat squad should suffice for each objective. Mine will safeguard the shrine, Veren's the cathedral.'

'What about the Thunderhawk?' I asked, hoping the answer would be something to the effect of it staying on the ground with its engines running in case we needed a rapid dustoff, but knowing this was extremely unlikely.

'Seek and destroy,' Gries said, which made perfect sense. With the local loyalists dug in at four known enclaves, pretty much anything else that looked military would be renegade units, attached to one or other of the squabbling factions, and fair game for the circling gunship. 'Let the rebels know we've arrived.'

Given the amount of firepower I'd seen while boarding, that was hardly going to be difficult. I nodded, with every outward sign of approval. 'Might as well start as we mean to go on,' I agreed.

Gries manipulated the controls of the pict screen again, and the image changed to an external view, relayed from part of the fire control system judging by the targeting graphics superimposed on it. We were still at high altitude, but undeniably within the atmosphere.[1] As I watched, transfixed, the smoking ruins of Fidelis rolled over the horizon, and I found myself trying to pick out the landmarks Gries had highlighted during his briefing. The cathedral was the easiest, still dominating the quarter in which it stood, despite the tumbled ruins of most of its spires. With that to orientate me, I was soon able to pick out the blank-sided slabs of the Administratum ziggurat, and the burnished steel cladding of the Mechanicus shrine. The governor's palace was another matter,

---

1. *As he does so often in the course of his memoirs, Cain is clearly compressing events here for dramatic effect; even at maximum acceleration, the Thunderhawk would have taken several hours, or possibly longer, to reach Viridia from the* Revenant's *closest viable point of re-entry to the materium.*

however, less tall than the others and still some distance away, surrounded by a cluster of lesser mansions and their grounds, like a she-grox with young. As we grew closer, it became evident that many were burned out, and all had been pillaged, in a manner which put me in mind of mob violence rather than battle damage.

Then the pall of smoke cleared, and we skimmed over the outer wall of the palace grounds, too fast to be targeted by ground-to-air fire, the upturned faces of guards and besiegers alike identical masks of astonishment.[1] Abruptly, I found myself pressed hard against the crash webbing, as the pilot kicked in the retros, killing our forward momentum, then my stomach seemed to float free of my body as we dropped towards the ground. It was just as well Jurgen wasn't with me, I thought, as he was prone to airsickness at the best of times, and this was hardly one of those. Without warning, an ork-sized boot seemed to kick me in the fundament, and the noise of the engines died back to almost bearable levels. We were down.

'Prepare to disembark,' Gries said, as the ramp began to drop, letting in a swirl of damp air, lightly scented with burning vegetation from the heat of our landing thrusters. Trosque's fire-team[2] deployed first, jogging down the ramp and securing it; I was pleased to see that they were taking nothing for granted, even though we were supposed to be meeting allies. After a moment the sergeant assured us that all was well, and Gries and his command squad followed. Seeing no reason to delay any further, and convinced that if there was treachery afoot there could be no better place to discover the fact than from behind a solid wall of bolter-carrying ceramite, I trotted after them, trying to look as imposing as I could given that my head barely came up to the level of their pauldrons.

As my bootsoles hit solid ground, crunching a little on the ashes and baked mud which still smoked gently beneath the Thunderhawk, I got a lungful of smoke and tried to suppress the

---

1. *Clearly an exaggeration, as the Thunderhawk would have been past far too quickly, and at too great an altitude, to be able to make out facial expressions on the ground.*

2. *The Imperial Guard term for their equivalent of a Space Marine combat squad.*

reflex to cough. No one else was, and I didn't want to be the one to undermine the dignity of the occasion.

As Gries stepped off the bottom of the ramp, he paused for a moment, two of his companions at either shoulder and an exact pace behind. Taken briefly by surprise, I stopped too, just short of walking into the back of him, and level with the other four Astartes, completing the line, and, of course, completely invisible from the front.

'Welcome to Viridia,' someone said, and I shuffled sideways a little to get a better view. We were evidently expected, as a delegation had come to meet us: ceremonial troopers, their gaudy uniforms looking rather the worse for wear by now, who held their lasguns like men who'd recently discovered exactly what they were for, and were ready to employ them in an instant, surrounding a man in robes so ridiculously over-ornamented there could be little doubt as to who he was, even before he announced the fact. 'I'm Governor DuPanya.' Then, to my astonishment, he went down on one knee. 'You honour us by your presence.'

'Please rise,' Gries said, the vox system of his helmet, perhaps mercifully, purging any traces of surprise or amusement from his words. 'We have much to discuss, and little time to waste on ceremony.' He reached up, removing the helmet, and DuPanya relaxed visibly as the captain's face came into view. It wasn't exactly a hololith, consisting as it did mainly of augmetics and scar tissue, but it looked a great deal more friendly than a blank visage of pitted ceramite. 'I am Captain Gries of the Reclaimers Chapter, these are my battle-brothers and this...' he turned, apparently surprised to find me so close to hand, 'is Commissar Cain, our liaison with the Imperial Guard elements of the task force.'

'Imperial Guard?' DuPanya asked, standing up as he'd been bidden and giving me my first proper look at him. He appeared to be in early middle age – although I was too familiar with the nobility's fondness for juvenat treatments, even on a backwater world like this one, to put much faith in outward appearance – and running slightly to fat. His eyes, however, were keen and looked at me appraisingly. 'I was not informed of their arrival.'

'They're still in the warp,' I told him, reflecting somewhat

ruefully that I could have saved myself a considerable amount of
inconvenience if I'd delayed my departure to travel with them, and
whatever piece of gung-ho idiocy Lokris had been planning to
drag me into could hardly have turned out to be worse than the
metal abominations I'd barely escaped with my life from on
Interitus Prime. 'Emperor willing, they should be here within the
week.' In fact they should be there within the next couple of days,
if the warp currents hadn't shifted appreciably since the last
estimate I'd heard, but nothing to do with the Realm of Chaos
itself is ever certain, and I preferred to err on the side of caution. I
raised my voice a little, above the scream of the Thunderhawk's
engines, which were powering up again now that Veren's team had
disembarked behind us. 'But perhaps this isn't the best place to be
discussing operational matters.'

'Quite so,' Gries agreed, his voice cutting through the din as
though it were little more than the murmuring of wind through
the trees. 'Having come here to ensure your safety, it seems a little
unwise to be talking where the enemy could deny us our objective
with a lucky mortar round or a sniper's bullet.' This didn't seem to
have occurred to the governor, who, to his credit, seemed relatively
unconcerned at the possibility. Nevertheless, he turned and led the
way inside, his escort looking considerably relieved as they
regained a little hard cover. Gries and his entourage followed,
while I oscillated between the two parties, connected to both by
ties of protocol, but properly part of neither.

As we reached the heavy wooden doors of the palace and passed
inside, I glanced back at the Thunderhawk, which was rising from
the ground like a raptor in search of prey. Beneath it Trosque and
Veren were leading their sections towards the perimeter wall, in
diverging directions as each made for the gate closest to his objective, and I breathed silent thanks to the Throne that I'd be well
under cover before the serious shooting started. I had no doubt
that the Astartes would make short work of any traitors standing
between them and their targets, but the initial contact for both
teams would be close enough for us to attract any collateral damage that might be going.

Well, perhaps the Thunderhawk could help clear the path for

them. It circled lazily over our heads one final time, then roared away to find something to shoot at.

Watching it go, I felt a faint sense of unease, reflecting that, for better or worse, I was now committed to the defence of this beachhead, with nowhere to go unless it was through the enemy. Then reason kicked in, and reassured me that I must be as safe here as anywhere on Viridia. After all, the palace hadn't fallen yet, and it had now been reinforced by five of the most formidable fighters in the Imperium. Plus me. I should be able to avoid trouble here, surely.

Editorial Note:

Cain has alluded in passing to the subsector-wide importance of Viridia, but knowing a little more about the world, and the system of which it is a part, makes it abundantly clear why its pacification was important enough to warrant the deployment of an Astartes expeditionary force. The following extract is almost as idiosyncratic as Cain's own prose, but serves its purpose of filling in sufficient background to clarify much of what follows without sacrificing readability to pedantry. Anyone wanting greater detail is referred to the Compendium of Tithings of the Damocles Gulf and Bordering Regions (Abridged), Volume MCLXXIV, appendices 17, 2,378 and 3,452,691, which may be consulted at any Administratum archive, once the appropriate requests have been filed in triplicate. Eventually.

From *Interesting Places and Tedious People: A Wanderer's Waybook*, by Jerval Sekara, 145.M39.

THE AGRIWORLD OF Viridia lies a little to spinward of the more populous regions of the Damocles Gulf, but can be reached surprisingly easily, due to the large volume of traffic to and from the neighbouring hive-worlds. This makes it a useful stopover point, since passage there, and to whatever eventual destination the wayfarer may settle upon once its decidedly bucolic charms have begun to pall, may be easily obtained.

It is, however, worth a brief sojourn, as it manages to combine both rural simplicity and urban sophistication in a manner which, if not unique, is certainly uncommon in this part of the Imperium. In part this is due to the sheer volume of shipping, since enterprising grain barge captains compete energetically with one another to wring some kind of profit from the inward leg of their journeys, ensuring a steady supply of offworld merchandise of a variety almost unparalleled elsewhere in the subsector. As the local saying has it, if you can't find it on Viridia, it probably doesn't exist.

All of which has made the world itself tolerably prosperous, with a thriving mercantile class, who, in the manner of parvenus everywhere, fritter away their profits on grandiose architecture and philanthropic enterprises intended to better the lot of the artisans, whether they want it bettered or not. As a result, the planetary capital, Fidelis, is positively awash with grand public buildings, ornamented to within an inch of their lives and separated by a profuse scattering of parks and gardens. The local populace is hardworking and pious, to such an extent that almost every street contains a chapel or shrine to the Emperor. Notwithstanding, they throw themselves into any excuse for a celebration wholeheartedly, with the annual festivals dedicated to some aspect or other of the agricultural cycle being particularly popular. The epitome of ecclesiarchial architecture, however, must surely be the cathedral in Fidelis, which in size and splendour can rival those to be found on far more populous worlds, and which attracts pilgrims from all over the Viridia System.

For, unlike most other agriworlds, Viridia exports a great deal more than just foodstuffs. The rest of the planetary system of which it is a part is exceptionally rich in minerals, and millions of its citizens live offworld, in orbitals, void stations and mining habs, dedicated to harvesting this bounty as assiduously as their pitchfork-wielding cousins on the surface do theirs. In fact, it's no exaggeration to say that around half the total Viridian population have never set foot on the planet they nominally call home, and never will. The raw material they gather is dispatched to the manufactoria of the neighbouring systems in a never-ending stream, slaking the hunger of their production lines just as efficiently as the grain barges do the workers who labour thereon.

THREE

DuPanya and his bodyguard led us through the palace at a rapid pace, down carpeted corridors lined with tapestries and through wooden-floored galleries whose polished surface fared badly under the heavy stride of the Space Marines, the rich, warm sheen of generations of waxing scuffing and splintering wherever they set foot. The deathmasked faces of the governor's ancestors stared down disapprovingly from the walls at this casual vandalism, although DuPanya didn't seem to mind much, or even notice; after all, the damage was slight enough, compared to the devastation the rebel artillery had already wrought on his home.

The Astartes seemed equally indifferent, walking in the same synchronised fashion I'd noticed before among their comrades, each left foot striking the floor at exactly the same time, then the right, with the precision of servitors. Every time they took a step the floor shuddered under the combined impact, and I felt the shock of it travelling up my legs, to the point where I began to feel as though I was aboard some slightly unstable watercraft. Fortunately the sensation was relatively short-lived, as, before long, the wooden floor gave way to bare rockcrete, the walls roughly finished in the same material, and I realised we were now in a bunker beneath the palace itself. As we descended several levels, I found my unease diminishing; this hidden redoubt had survived innumerable artillery bombardments unscathed, and would undoubtedly continue to do so. It was, therefore, with something approaching a light heart that I stepped through a pair of reinforced blast doors, currently propped open by a brace of guards in the same comic opera uniforms as their compatriots, who at least had the grace to pull themselves into a semblance of attention as we passed them, to find myself in a reasonably well-equipped command centre.

Dragging my attention from the solid buttresses and thick ceiling protecting us, I caught intermittent glimpses of pict screens and data lecterns between the towering figures in power armour which blocked most of my view, but could make out little until they fanned out, indicating that we'd reached the operational area at last.

'Governor.' A middle-aged man in a rather more practical uniform than the ones we'd seen so far, resembling standard Imperial Guard fatigues, mottled in greys and mid-blues,[1] looked up from the hololith which dominated the centre of the space. A faintly flickering image of the city was being projected in it, spattered with icons I was fairly certain marked the positions of friendly and enemy troops. 'The Astartes are assaulting the enemy outside the east and north-western gates.' If he was surprised to see me or my companions, he gave no sign of the fact, merely nodding a preoccupied greeting in our direction, and I decided I liked him, whoever he was. Either he was keeping his mind on the business of defending our enclave, or he'd simply decided he was damned if he was going to look impressed by us, a game I knew well, and always enjoyed playing myself.

Gries nodded, no doubt being kept up to date with his men's progress by monitoring systems built into his armour, and I began to regret discarding the bulky headset I'd been wearing before we

---

1. *Though Cain doesn't say so explicitly, no doubt expecting his readers to be sufficiently au fait with matters military to recognise it, this is almost certainly some form of urban camouflage pattern suited to operations in Fidelis.*

left the Thunderhawk. It had been heavy and awkward, true, having been designed for a head far larger than mine, but I'd got so used to following the progress of a battle through the comm-bead I habitually wore that I found myself feeling cut off from events without it – a sensation no member of the Commissariat ever feels comfortable with, particularly one as paranoid as me. Well, I'd just have to make do with the hololith to follow what was going on. 'They are,' the Reclaimers captain confirmed, 'and proceeding to their objectives. Resistance is light.'

From where I was standing it looked like the enemy were throwing everything they could at the two combat squads, but I suppose from Gries's point of view, having just seen off a tomb world full of necrons, a rabble of rebellious PDF troopers afforded little more than a handy bit of target practice.

'Thank you, general.' DuPanya discarded his robe with evident relief, turning out, to my surprise, to be wearing a uniform similar to the officer who'd greeted him beneath it, but without the rank pins at the collar. 'That's better.' He handed the richly patterned material to the nearest guard, and smiled at me, in the manner of a man imparting a confidence. 'Can't stand the blasted thing,' he said. 'Makes me look like a sofa.'

I couldn't really argue with that, so I didn't try. Instead, I turned to the hololith and addressed the general. 'You no doubt know who we are,' I said, 'so I won't waste time with introductions.' Especially since I didn't have a clue who three of Gries's companions were in any case; with their helmets on they all looked alike to me, and I doubted that removing them would have left me much the wiser. 'What are we looking at here?'

'The dispositions of all the units we're currently aware of,' the man in blue and grey replied, apparently just as happy to dispense with the formalities as I was. 'Blue for loyalist, yellow, green and red for the different enemy factions. They've been gunning for one another as much as us, so we're happy to let them get on with it while we wait for the relief force to arrive.'

'It has arrived,' Gries reminded him, looming suddenly at my elbow and staring at the display with a thoughtful expression on his face. 'These deployments make no sense.'

I looked at the display more carefully, trying to see what he meant. The red, yellow and green icons were clustered around the blue enclaves like scum round an outfall, each encircling whichever Imperial redoubt fell in the sector of the city they controlled. One each, plus the palace, which seemed to be on the cusp of their zones of influence, and which was bordered on the south and east by red, yellow to the north, and green to the west.

'You're right,' I said after a moment. There were concentrations of colour along their mutual borders, but they weren't contiguous. This wasn't entirely unexpected, since the squabbling factions would need far more manpower to fortify an arbitrary line several kilometres long than any could conceivably bring to bear, but the positions they had dug in at didn't seem particularly strategic, and several potential weak points had been left completely undefended.

Gries reached for the control lectern, muttering the litanies the enginseers who maintained similar systems for the Guard seemed to employ while fiddling with the knobs. He must have hit on the right ones, because the three colours suddenly turned a uniform sickly purple, and the whole pattern fell into place.

'Throne on Earth,' I said, horrified. 'The whole city's a trap!'

'Clearly,' Gries said, as though it should have been obvious from the start – which, I suppose to him, it may well have been.

Only DuPanya looked confused. 'General Orten?' he asked, which at least answered the lingering question of the fellow's name. 'What does he mean?'

'He means we've been idiots,' Orten replied, looking about as happy as anyone would be after just being struck by that uncomfortable realisation. 'The internecine squabbling we've been counting on to whittle them down for us was just for show.' He sighed heavily. 'I'll remain in my quarters until you can convene the court martial.'

'You'll do no such thing,' I snapped. 'If this mess really is your fault, I'm damned if I'm going to let you weasel your way out of cleaning it up by jumping in front of a firing squad.' Orten and DuPanya gaped at me, and although the Astartes remained as impassive as ever, something about their attitude managed to convey a degree of surprise as well.[1]

'Commissar Cain is correct,' Gries agreed. 'This is no time to deprive ourselves of the most senior PDF officer.'

I nodded, following up on the unexpected show of support. 'Right now, we need your local knowledge. We can determine whose fault this all is once the rebels have been brought to heel.'

'I'm at your disposal, of course,' Orten said, with something of the air of a spirejack who's just hopped casually over a vent in the hive skin, before glancing back and realising it goes down to the sump.

'I'm afraid I still don't follow,' DuPanya said, a trifle apologetically, and Gries gestured at the hololith with a yellow-gauntleted hand.

'These troop dispositions make perfect sense if the rebels are acting as a single unified force. They can defend the city from outside attack extremely effectively, and hamper the movements of any Imperial assets attempting to deploy within it.'

'An Imperial Guard landing would have to take place at the aerodrome,' I added, pointing out the landing field on the outskirts of Fidelis where, in happier times, aircraft and orbital shuttles would arrive and depart. 'It's the only open area large enough to establish a beachhead. But once they're down, they'd be sitting waterfowl for a coordinated bombardment, from these Basilisk and Manticore units.'

Orten nodded. 'Which have been targeting one another up till now, or so we've been led to believe.'

'They can be neutralised,' Gries said calmly. 'Now we're aware of the scale of the deception, the stratagem will not succeed.'

'Not while the rebels think we're still fooled, anyway,' I said, wondering how they'd managed to pull off so huge a piece of sleight-of-hand. The degree of coordination required would have been immense, taxing the skills of even an experienced high

---

1. Quite understandably, as most of Cain's colleagues would at least have had the man arrested, pending an investigation, and many would simply have shot him on the spot without even the formality of an enquiry.

command, let alone a rabble of disaffected militia. My palms were itching again, but this time no sudden flood of insight made sense of my nagging disquiet, so I turned my mind to more immediate concerns. 'The trouble is, the moment we make a move to take out those positions, they'll realise we're on to them.'

'My assessment as well,' Gries agreed. 'Redirecting our combat squads would reveal our intention at once, as the enemy will certainly be aware of their intended destinations by now.' He studied the hololith again. 'The Manticore battery is close to the line of advance we would take to relieve the defenders of the Administratum cloister, however. If my battle-brothers and I make a third sally, the rebels should assume it to be our objective until it's too late.'

'Which only leaves the Basilisks,' I agreed, unable to fault his logic.

'Can the Thunderhawk take them out?' Orten asked, and I shook my head.

'I doubt it,' I told him. 'I've served with an artillery unit, and they're always prepared for an aerial attack. The minute it appears on their auspexes, the Basilisks will scatter. We'd get some, but there's no guarantee enough wouldn't survive to mount an effective bombardment of the aerodrome.'

'Then you'll just have to sneak up on them, won't you?' a new voice cut in, and I turned to find myself facing a young woman in an even more absurd version of the elaborate uniform most of the troopers in the bunker were wearing. The crimson fabric was festooned with silver braid, and the regimental crest was worked into her epaulettes in gold thread, which glittered under the luminators almost as brightly as the buttons on her tunic, the top couple of which had been left undone to expose a generous helping of cleavage. The whole ensemble had clearly come from a couturier rather than a quartermaster, although the laspistol holstered at her waist looked functional, even if nothing else did.

'Commissar, honoured Astartes, my daughter Mira,' DuPanya said, although the resemblance was so strong I'd already deduced that for myself. Mira DuPanya had obviously inherited her father's build, although so far the genetic tendency to chubbiness had got no further than a hint of lush ripeness around the face, and imparting a well-filled look to her tunic and trouser seat, which I would certainly have taken the time to appreciate under more relaxed circumstances. Her hair was blonde and elaborately tressed, green eyes gazing in our direction as though somehow faintly disappointed not to find us more entertaining.

'That might be a little easier said than done,' I replied, address-ing her directly, in a tone which, although formally polite, managed to convey the unspoken suffix *so run along and leave the soldiering to the professionals.* Unfortunately, Mira, as I was soon to discover, wouldn't recognise a hint if it was presented to her gift-wrapped, with a label saying '*Hint*' around its neck.

'Only if you're stupid enough to stay on the surface, where they can see you coming,' she said dismissively, and went to stand next to her father, who was beginning to look distinctly uncomfortable. I couldn't say I blamed him either, as he obviously had a much better idea of who we were and what we represented.

To my surprise, though, Orten was nodding thoughtfully. 'You mean go underground?' he asked, and Mira echoed the gesture.

'Of course I do,' she said, scorn and self-confidence mingling in her voice in a manner I was beginning to find quite irksome. 'We spent enough time booby-trapping the service tunnels to stop the rebels getting in, didn't we? Why can't your people get out the same way?'

'It sounds plausible,' I said, having spent enough time running around the undercities of various worlds to be well aware of the sprawling nature of the infrastructure almost certainly underpin-ning Fidelis. 'Are there any maps we can consult down here?'

'There should be,' Orten said, and went off to converse with a nearby aide.

I turned to Gries. 'I've been down service tunnels before,' I said, 'and they tend to be a bit on the cramped side.' I tried to picture him and his men squeezing through the conduits I used to play in as a child,[1] and failed dismally. 'Perhaps you'd better stick to your original proposal, and leave the Basilisks to a local strike.'

---

1. *Apparently in an underhive, although on which world remains a mystery.*

'Indeed,' Gries agreed. 'A two-pronged assault, underground and overground, would seem to be the best strategy. Once our forces are committed, the combat squads and the Thunderhawk can divert to back us up.'

'Sounds good,' I agreed.

'Then we can begin as soon as you've selected a team to accompany you,' Gries said, and I realised too late what I'd backed myself into. It goes without saying I'd never intended to lead the assault on the Basilisks in person, but knowing what Gries believed about me, which was essentially that my inflated reputation was justified, I could belatedly see why he'd made that assumption. Of course now I couldn't back out without alienating the Astartes I was supposed to be liaising with, and undermining my authority in front of the governor, so I'd just have to make the best of it. At least, I thought, things couldn't get any worse.

'I'll take care of that,' Mira said, butting in again with all the casual arrogance of a rich brat born to rule a planet. She nodded coolly at the Astartes captain. 'We'll be ready to move in half an hour.'

IN THE EVENT it was closer to an hour before the PDF were able to get themselves organised, by which time we'd received the encouraging news that both combat squads had reached their objectives without taking any casualties, and that the prowling Thunderhawk had got the rebels stirred up like a stick in an ants' nest. At which point I found myself in a thoroughly unwelcome conversation with the governor's daughter, who seemed unable to grasp the idea that anyone else's authority could exceed her own.

'I'm sorry, my lady,' I said, exerting all the diplomatic skills I possessed to suppress the impulse to say something far more direct, 'but I cannot in all conscience permit you to accompany us.'

Mira looked at me with the sort of expression I imagine she normally reserved for a ladies' maid who'd run her bath at the wrong temperature. 'I'm leading this expedition,' she said tartly. 'Live with it.'

'It's you continuing to live at all which concerns me,' I said, deciding that subtlety was clearly wasted on her. 'The battlefield is no place for a civilian.' Especially if their presence was liable to put me in any danger, which hers almost certainly would.

The governor's daughter drew herself up to her full height, which was roughly level with my chin, while still somehow contriving to look down her nose at me. 'I happen to be colonel-in-chief of the Household Regiment,' she said, waving a hand in the general direction of her embonpoint, which was jutting determinedly in my direction. 'Or can't you recognise a military uniform when you see one?'

'As a rule,' I said, biting back the obvious rejoinder about her garish costume. 'But the title of colonel-in-chief is generally considered an honorary one.'

A faint flush began to spread across her cheek, followed by a petulant frown. No doubt the sensation of not getting her own way without question was an unwelcome novelty. 'How much actual military training have you done?' I asked.

'My usual duties don't leave time for that sort of thing,' the girl admitted reluctantly. 'But I've been out on the walls a few times.' She hefted the lasgun she'd picked up from somewhere, with more confidence than I'd normally expect to see in a civilian, and I had to concede she handled it as though she knew what she was doing. 'And I've been using guns on hunting trips since I was a child.'

'In very few of which, I imagine, the game shot back,' I replied sarcastically. I turned to DuPanya, who was hovering nearby with the squad of troopers who'd escorted him to meet the Thunderhawk. Despite their ridiculous getup, they all looked as though they could handle themselves well enough, which was no more than I'd have expected: on most worlds, the household troops guarding the governor tend to be the cream of the PDF, or at least the curds left behind after the Guard tithes have been met. I'd have felt a lot happier undertaking this fool's errand with proper Guardsmen to hide behind, but at least this lot would be the best available. The majority were keeping their expressions studiedly neutral, but a few were making no secret of how much they were enjoying the spectacle of their colonel-in-chief meeting unexpected resistance. 'Can't you talk some sense into her?'

'Not often,' DuPanya admitted, sounding almost proud of the fact. 'And her rank might be honorary, as you say, but she does take it seriously. After all, it makes her the most senior officer in the regiment.'

'Fine,' I said, greatly cheered by the realisation that in that case I could legitimately shoot her if she got too annoying. 'But we're running out of time to debate this.' Gries and his Astartes had already left the command bunker, and would be halfway to the gate by now. If we were going to be in position before the enemy realised their artillery batteries were the Reclaimers' real objective, and be ready to launch our own assault at the same time, we'd have to get moving; otherwise we'd arrive to find our target on high alert, instead of having the advantage of surprise.

'Then stop wasting it,' Mira said. She turned and gestured to the troopers, most of whom were carrying satchel charges in addition to their usual weapons. 'Move out.'

'Stay where you are,' I snapped, freezing the squad's first shuffle of movement to instant immobility. I turned back to Mira, with my most intimidating commissarial expression on my face. 'You're staying behind. Live with it.' As I'd anticipated, having her own words thrown back at her didn't go down at all well.

'Correct me if I'm wrong, commissar,' she replied, pronouncing my title in tones which would have frozen helium, 'but I was under the impression that your position is purely an advisory one, outside the normal chain of command.'

'Technically, that's the case,' I admitted, masking my sudden unease. 'But our advice is generally heeded by the officers receiving it.' Because if it isn't we're entitled to shoot them, which inclines them to listen.

'Then consider me advised,' Mira said, turning to beckon to the soldiers once more. 'Move out.'

Well, I could hardly gun her down in front of her father and hope to continue a productive working relationship, and there seemed to be every possibility that the enemy would do the job for me in any case, so I simply shrugged with what I hoped looked like casual indifference. 'Duly noted, colonel,' I said dryly.

FOUR

AT FIRST, TO my carefully concealed surprise, things seemed to be going well after all. Too naive or arrogant to appreciate the dangers of taking point, Mira led from the front, which clearly sat well with the troopers accompanying us, striding confidently through the echoing underground labyrinth as though we were simply out for a stroll rather than heading deeper into enemy territory with every step. That was fine with me. Apart from the callipygian spectacle she presented from that angle, she was certain to draw the fire from any enemies who might be lurking down here, or trigger any booby traps they might have set, in good time to warn the rest of us.

Entering the warren of tunnels had turned out to be surprisingly easy, simply a matter of dropping through an access hatch set in the floor of a corridor near the palace kitchens, and as I'd straightened up after flexing my knees to absorb the impact of landing, I'd immediately felt more comfortable than at any time since my arrival on Viridia. Accompanied by an absurdly dressed fire magnet or not, this was an environment I felt at home in, all my old underhiver's instincts flooding back. I glanced round, noting with approval the burned-off stubs of metal in the wall which had once supported a ladder leading to the hatchway overhead.

Orten had assured me that all possible precautions had been taken to safeguard the palace and its environs from enemy infiltration, short of collapsing the tunnels completely with demo charges (which would have prevented DuPanya from fleeing if the palace fell to the besieging rebels, and was therefore unthinkable), and I was pleased to see that he appeared to be right about that. Apart from a regrettable tendency to believe intelligence assessments without asking too many questions, he seemed to be competent enough, and I felt a certain amount of satisfaction that my judgement about leaving him alive and in charge appeared to be sound.

Abruptly we were plunged into darkness, as the trapdoor above us was dropped back into place, and I felt my other senses reaching out as they always did in the absence of light. A faint current of air against my face provided a sense of direction, and the overlapping echoes of bootsoles against 'crete pinpointed the walls nicely. 'Close your eyes for a moment,' I advised. 'It'll help them to adjust.'

'Or we could just kindle the luminators,' Mira said, suiting the action to the word. A sudden flare of light made me squint, and a couple of the troopers followed her lead, filling the narrow corridor with dancing beams, which struck highlights from the pipes and cable runs fixed to the walls and depending from the ceiling. At least she'd had the sense to attach the thing to the bayonet lugs of her lasgun, leaving both hands free to handle the weapon, and the others weren't slow to do the same.

'Good idea, colonel,' I said, with heavy sarcasm. 'And how about a rousing chorus of "Soldiers of the Throne" while we're about it, so the enemy can hear us coming as well?'

'You're the one who said we're running out of time,' she rejoined, turning to lead the way at a brisk jog, which did interesting things to her over-filled uniform. 'We won't get anywhere stumbling along in the dark.'

Reluctant to admit that she had a point, I contented myself with hanging back enough to take advantage of the shadows, in the comforting certainty that my black greatcoat would be almost perfect camouflage in the dark, particularly against an enemy still dazzled after gunning down Mira.

After a few hundred metres, which by my estimate put us more or less beneath the outer wall, I was able to see the reason for her confidence. The corridor up ahead was blocked by a fresh rockcrete wall, into which a narrow iron door had been set, just wide enough for one man to pass through at a time. Mira stopped just ahead of it and slapped her palm down on the scanner plate of a genecode reader, which had evidently been wired into the locking plate by a tech-priest with rather more pressing concerns than doing a neat job. The device buzzed and hummed to itself for a moment, giving me time to catch up with her, then the latch clicked, and the door swung outwards. Unbelievably, I was the only one covering it.[1]

'How do you know the enemy aren't just waiting on the other side?' I asked, nettled by her smirk as she paused on the threshold to look back at me.

'Because none of the mines have gone off,' she answered. 'Better hurry, they'll be set again in thirty seconds.' Then she was gone, trotting off into the darkness beyond, her troopers pelting through the doorway in her wake.

I followed, the door booming back into place at my back, content to see by the relatively dim light from her luminator, and picked up my pace when I saw she hadn't been exaggerating about the mines. There was a big cluster of frag charges, fixed to the walls and ceiling, their curved casings designed to spread their deadly payload as widely as possible. In the open they'd be lethal enough, but in a space as confined as this, they'd quite simply shred anyone incautious enough to approach them into bloody mist.

I picked up my pace until I was sure I'd passed beyond the range of the lethal devices, hearing them rearm with a faint *click!* a second or two after I was through the choke point, and suppressed a shudder. 'Any more little surprises like that one?' I asked, keeping my voice steady nonetheless.

---

1. *Which means he must have drawn his laspistol, although he doesn't bother to mention the fact.*

'None we'll have to worry about,' Mira assured me. In my experience, statements like that are just tempting fate, and, sure enough, before the day was out, we were to be presented with a surprise greater and more deadly than either of us could possibly have imagined. But since I was still in blissful ignorance, I turned and followed her, instead of running in the opposite direction as hard as I could.

ANOTHER HOUR OR so of brisk walking got us to our destination. According to the map Orten had provided, and which I'd immediately loaded into my slate, it wasn't the most direct route; but it did avoid having to pass through any choke points where we'd have had to crawl, climb or negotiate obstacles, which Mira had neither the build nor the temperament to deal with. Since I didn't think we'd lost any appreciable time by the detour, which had taken us through the usual collection of utility ducts, watercourses and sewers (the last of which had clearly raised Mira's fastidious patrician hackles, to my carefully concealed amusement), I didn't bother to call her on it.

Despite my fears, her luminator didn't seem to have attracted any unwelcome attention, which, contrary to what you might expect, did nothing to relieve the tension I was feeling. The longer we remained undiscovered, the more I became certain that we were surely about to be, and I found myself listening out for any trace of sound which might betray ambushers lurking ahead of us in the darkness. I heard plenty, of course, but instinct and experience enabled me to identify most of the noises almost at once, and discount them as any kind of threat.

Most common was the scuttling of vermin, running for cover at the approach of light and noise, but occasionally the scuffling was louder, indicating a human presence. Invariably these would be fleeing too, however, rather than advancing to contact, which meant they were civilians, with an understandably cautious attitude to men with guns. Whether they were artisans, trying to keep the fractured infrastructure of the city from falling apart completely, or merely the luckless dispossessed endemic to large-scale civil disorder, desperate or fearful enough to attempt to find some kind of refuge down here, I had no idea. They weren't shooting at us, and that was all that mattered to me.

'We're here,' Mira said at last, and I checked my chronograph, wondering what sort of progress Gries and his squad were making. From what I'd seen of them, I'd have laid pretty fair odds that they'd reached their objective by now, and were making short work of it. Once again, I found myself reaching for the comm-bead which would normally have been sitting in my ear, and rueing its absence. It had, of course, occurred to me to scrounge one from the command bunker, but such refinements appeared to be lacking among the Viridian PDF. The best they could offer me was a bulky portable voxcaster, which was currently bouncing along on the back of its operator. Stopping to use the thing would have taken up time we could ill afford, however, so I'd had to resign myself to remaining out of touch for a while longer, and trying to ignore my misgivings as best I could.

'Good,' I responded, surreptitiously checking my slate to see where 'here' actually was. It turned out to be a sewer, running directly under the piazza the rebels had decided to use as an artillery park, and I began to get the first inkling of a battle plan. A little late for that, you may be thinking, and you'd probably be right, but I'd been bounced into this fool's errand by circumstance, not choice, and I hadn't had much of a chance to think about anything much, beyond the most immediate concern of ensuring my own survival. I beckoned the vox man forwards, and he came to join me, unclipping the bulky handset as he did so.

'Cain to Astartes,' I said, praying to the Emperor that the frequency I'd been given was correct, and keeping it short in case we were being monitored. 'In position. Query yours.'

'Engaging,' Gries responded, to my relief. 'Resistance light. The Thunderhawk will commence diversionary attacks in two minutes.'

'Thanks,' I replied, taking in the single squad of troopers accompanying me, and the distinctly unmartial figure of Mira, who was listening intently, but who, for once, seemed able to resist the temptation to shove her oar in, thank the Emperor. 'We're going to need all the help we can get.'

'Leave this channel open,' Gries said, then cut the link at his end.

'What did he mean by that?' Mira demanded, as if I knew the answer and was merely withholding it out of pique.

I shrugged. 'Probably wants an accurate position fix for the Thunderhawk, so we don't end up on the wrong end of some friendly fire,' I hazarded. Considering the amount of concentrated lethality that the gunship represented, it seemed a reasonable precaution to me. I turned to the sergeant in charge of the squad, whose name I didn't know. Mira hadn't bothered with introductions, if she'd even considered the men under her nominal command as individuals in the first place. 'We'll need to get up top and find out exactly where the artillery pieces are. With a bit of luck we can use the demo charges to collapse this tunnel underneath them, and cripple the battery without having to fight our way through the sentries.'

'If they're parked close enough to it,' the sergeant agreed, homing in on the weak spot of the plan without undermining my authority by actually stating it, like efficient noncoms[1] have been doing since humanity first swung down from the trees on Holy Terra and started hitting one another with rocks.

'Let's hope they are,' I said, 'or we'll just have to do this the hard way.'

From my time with the 12th Valhallan[2] I knew that each artillery piece would probably be fully crewed, plus a few sentries, logistical support personnel and a handful of junior officers and noncoms to make sure the conscripts shoved the shells in the breach the right way round. Given that we already knew, from the orbital picts, that there were five Basilisks in the battery, that meant anything from thirty to fifty men. Although I'd be happy enough taking on odds of three or five to one against mere PDF mutineers with proper Guardsmen behind me, the troops I had now were probably little better in quality than the ones we were facing. And that was without taking Mira into account, who was probably worth an extra squad to the enemy just on her own.

---

1. *Non-commissioned officers.*

2. *The artillery unit he was assigned to at the outset of his career.*

'Well there's only one way to find out,' she said, starting up the ladder leading to the manhole cover above our heads before I could stop her. Having already seen enough to know that remonstrating with her would be pointless, and shooting her would be out of the question close enough to the enemy for an alert sentry to hear, I'd just have to go along with it for now.

'Wait here,' I instructed the sergeant, who seemed more than happy to comply. 'Check the charges while I'm gone.' There was no point in having the whole squad blundering about up there, when I was sure Mira could attract the attention of the enemy perfectly well on her own. I could hardly leave her to her own devices, however, so I clambered up after her, having waited a moment to make sure that her emergence into daylight wouldn't be followed at once by a barrage of lasgun fire.

It wasn't, so I stuck my head cautiously out of the hole, finding myself in a street which looked much the worse for wear: the buildings on either side of it were pockmarked and perforated by the prolonged and indiscriminate use of heavy ordnance, while the carriageway a few metres ahead had been comprehensively blocked to traffic by the rusting hulk of a burned-out Chimera. Taking advantage of the cover it afforded, I popped up out of the hole like a sump rat scenting a fresh corpse, and scuttled into the lee of the derelict vehicle.

'Where are the others?' Mira asked, from roughly the level of my knees, having gone prone under the raised dozer blade for extra protection, the first sensible thing I'd ever seen her do. Her lasgun was unslung, aimed back at the manhole, evidently intended to cover my advance, and I breathed a silent prayer of thanks to the Golden Throne that she hadn't been spooked enough to pull the trigger.

'Down the hole,' I said quietly. 'I told them to stay put.'

'You did what?' She stood up and glared at me, the effect somewhat spoiled by the thick coating of grime now adhering to her jacket and the knees of her trousers; at least she'd blend into the background a little better now, which was something. 'We need them with us!'

'Did you ever go stalking on these hunting trips of yours?' I asked.

Mira nodded, sullenly. 'Of course,' she said, having the common sense to keep her voice down too, which was a welcome surprise.

'And did you have a demi-score of troopers crashing around the place while you did?' I asked reasonably.

Mira shook her head dismissively. 'Of course not, it would have frightened the game away...' Then the coin dropped. 'I see, of course. We're going to need to move quietly.'

I shook my head. 'I'm going to need to move quietly,' I said. 'You stay here, in case I need covering fire.'

I'd be the first to admit that taking the risk of scouting the enemy positions myself, instead of letting Mira get on with it, seems a little uncharacteristic, but I had sound enough reasons at the time. Firstly, I'd had more than enough practice at sneaking around in the immediate vicinity of the enemy without being spotted, whereas Mira's alleged stalking skills were an unknown quantity. Secondly, thanks to my time with the 12th Valhallan, I knew enough about artillery to assess just how big a threat the battery really was once I got a decent look at it, whereas the most useful thing Mira was likely to report was that the Basilisks were a horribly unfashionable colour. Thirdly, thanks to my innate affinity for underground environments, I'd know instantly, just by looking, how close they were to the sewer line, and where best to place the charges to cause the maximum amount of subsidence.

For a moment it looked as though Mira was about to argue the point, but before she got the chance the circling Thunderhawk pilot decided to provide the diversion Gries had promised me. Whatever she'd been going to say was abruptly swallowed by the muffled *crump!* of a distant detonation, and a plume of smoke nudged its way above the artificial horizon of the buildings surrounding us, followed a moment later by a faint tremor through the soles of my boots. It seemed he'd found an ammunition dump, or something equally combustible; at any rate, it was a pretty safe bet that the attention of the rebels had been effectively grabbed.

Taking advantage of the moment, I made a run for the nearest building, which seemed structurally sound, despite the number of holes blasted through its outer walls. It had evidently been an emporium of some kind, but what it used to sell I could only guess, as the looters had been there long before me and gutted the place. Entering through the long, wide gap where the window used to be, my feet crunching and slithering for a moment on the shattered glass, I made for the shadows at the rear of the shop, where, as in the tunnel, my sombre uniform would allow me to blend in more easily.

Luck, or the Emperor, was with me, and I found a staircase just the other side of a wooden door which had been kicked or rammed off its hinges. There was an elevator too, but I wouldn't have taken it even if the power was still on; the idea of being discovered by the enemy trapped in a small metal box was disturbing, to say the least. I took the stairs easily, five or six flights, before a chill draught arrested my progress, and I ventured out into what had evidently been one of the upper sales floors. Indeed, it seemed that irrespective of the number of storeys the emporium used to boast, this was now as high as it was possible to go. The ceiling was down across half the floor area, along with sufficient rubble to make me certain that whatever might remain of the original structure higher up, it was extremely unlikely to be able to bear my weight.

This storey was high enough for my purposes, though, as a quick glance was enough to assure me. The far wall was missing, the floor coming to an abrupt end about a metre from where it should be, affording a panoramic view across much of the city. I made for it cautiously, testing every footfall, but it all seemed solid enough, and within a minute or two I was close enough to the edge to look down into the rebels' artillery park, across the rubbled remains of the intervening building on the other side of the street. This had evidently fared far worse than the one I was occupying; though a few floors still remained, it had been reduced to about half the height of the shattered structure I was currently standing in.

The most cursory of glances was enough to tell me that my plan to collapse the sewer wouldn't cut it. Only one of the artillery pieces was in the right place to be disabled, the rest being dispersed around the square, backed into the remains of buildings for concealment and protection, and surrounded by sandbagged emplacements. No chance of being able to just run up and place a satchel charge either: we'd be cut down before we even got close. As the wind shifted, it brought with it the grumble of idling engines and the acrid tang of burned promethium; I'd been right about them being prepared to scatter if the Thunderhawk moved in their direction too. Perhaps if we mined the roads with the demo charges we'd brought with us we could bottle them up long enough for the gunship to take them out, but our chances of being able to place the explosives in the open without being spotted were minimal.

I was still musing over the problem when a las-bolt hissed past me, impacting against the stump of one of the columns which used to support the floor above. I turned, drawing my weapons and cursing myself for a fool. The very reason I'd chosen this spot to scout the enemy emplacement from also made it the perfect place to station sentries, and I should have anticipated an enemy presence here. Two men were running at me, lasguns in their hands, and firing as they came, but fortunately it's almost impossible to shoot accurately while on the move; if they'd had the sense to stand still and aim properly, they'd probably have dropped me before I'd even become aware of their presence.

Unfortunately for them, I wasn't so stupid, only taking a couple of strides to find refuge behind the sturdy pillar which had already stopped one of their las-bolts, before dropping to a crouch and cracking off a couple of rounds of my own. My aim was scarcely any better at first, one of the las-bolts from my pistol clipping the edge of the right-hand man's torso armour, but it was enough to make him hesitate. As he looked around for some cover I saved him the bother, putting a third and less hurried shot through the middle of his face. He went down hard, and beyond the usual reflexive spasms, didn't move again.

Which left the second man, who was going wide, towards the drop, hoping to flank me and get a shot in round the rockcrete pillar I was sheltering behind. I dodged back, trying to target him around the other side, but with a belated surge of common sense he switched to full auto, hosing my makeshift position down with a blizzard of fire too heavy for me to be able to risk popping out to take a crack at him.

Abruptly the firing ceased, and I seized the opportunity the momentary lull presented, lunging out to the side as I stood, my chainsword swinging to meet the anticipated charge, while my laspistol sought a target. To my surprise, however, he was already down, flat out on the rubble-strewn floor, deader than Horus. I approached the corpse warily, anticipating some kind of trick, but as I got closer I could see that the back of his head was missing, taken out by another las-bolt. From the angle of the wound, it had clearly come from somewhere down below, outside the building.

I edged cautiously to the brink of the drop and glanced down. Mira was still crouched in the lee of the burned-out Chimera, her lasgun raised and pointing in my direction. Seeing me, she lowered the weapon and waved, in a manner which, even at that distance, struck me as distinctly pleased with herself. Hard to resent that under the circumstances, though, so I returned the wave and turned back to the bodies of the late sentries. Neither had any vox gear on him, or anything else which might have provided some useful intelligence come to that, so I started to head back towards the stairs, intent on nothing more than getting back down the hole and out of sight before anyone got around to missing them.

I'd barely gone a pace or two, though, before the air seemed to thicken around me, the hairs on my arms bristling as if a thunderstorm was building, and a remarkably unpleasant sensation of pressure began to grow behind my eyes. It felt as if my sinuses were being packed with rockcrete, and I stumbled, my vision blurring. Then, as suddenly as it had begun, the feeling ended, leaving me almost giddy with relief.

I hurried back to the hole in the wall, looking outside, anxiously, just as a rumble of displaced air echoed between the buildings, like one of the distant explosions where the crew of the Thunderhawk were continuing to amuse themselves. The rebel artillery park was in a state of complete confusion, with people running everywhere, like rats in a room when someone turns on the lights, and as the firing started, I began to see why. Towering figures in white and yellow armour were plodding unhurriedly through the pandemonium, shrugging off the las-bolts and occasional grenade sleeting in their direction with magnificent disdain. They were larger and bulkier than the Astartes I'd seen before; although I was to become familiar with it later, this was the first time I'd ever seen Terminator armour in action, apart from a handful of seconds aboard the necron vessel before losing consciousness. Most of the Astartes wearing it seemed to be carrying twin-barrelled bolters, which put out a staggering amount of firepower, ripping all traces of resistance to shreds with contemptuous ease, and one had a pair of missile pods mounted above his shoulders.

As I watched, the Terminator fired one from each, taking out a Basilisk which had started to move away in an explosion which knocked many of the defenders from their feet, but left the Astartes striding grimly forwards, apparently unmoved. Another of his fellows approached the nearest artillery piece and began literally tearing it apart, the long metal claws attached to his gauntlets shearing through the thick metal as though it was no more substantial than mist and shadows, a faint nimbus of arcane energies crackling about them.[1] Panic-stricken crewmen bailed from it and ran in random directions, desperate to get away before those formidable talons found purchase in flesh.

Tearing my eyes reluctantly away from the spectacle, because it's not often I get so close to a battle without someone diverting my attention by trying to kill me, I glanced down to make sure Mira was all right. As it happened she was looking distinctly apprehensive, and who could blame her; apart from the disconcerting effect of being caught in the fringes of a teleport field, she'd be hearing all the noise without a clue as to what was going on. Catching her eye, I waved, as nonchalantly as I could manage, and started back down the stairs to reassure her. After all, annoying brat or not, she had just saved my life, which was always welcome, and she was

---

1. *Conventional practice would be for Terminators to be deployed in dedicated squads, equipped with either ranged or close-combat weaponry. It's unclear from what Cain says here whether this is in fact the case, and two full squads were sent in, or whether the Reclaimers had combined elements of both in a single unit, as they also appear to do later in his account. If the latter, this would be extremely unusual.*

considerably more decorative than Jurgen, whose job that usually was.

'What's going on?' she demanded, the minute I came within earshot.

'The Space Marines are taking out the artillery for us,' I told her, trying not to sound too pleased about it. 'That headache a few minutes ago was a bunch of Terminators teleporting in.' Which seemed a bit like overkill, given that a combat squad of ordinary Astartes could have taken out the rebels without breaking sweat, but only the Terminators had the training and experience to deploy by teleporter. A thought struck me, and I nodded in sudden understanding. 'No wonder Gries wanted the vox link kept open. They must have used it as a homing beacon.'

'Then we need to get the men up here,' she said, turning towards the manhole we'd first emerged from. 'The Astartes might need some backup.'

'I doubt it,' I said, keeping the relief from my voice with an effort. It could just have been the bulk of the intervening building, but it sounded to me like the firing was already reducing in both intensity and volume. 'But you're right about getting back under cover as fast as we can.' If I'd read the situation right, the few remaining rebels would give up trying to make a fight of it and start fleeing for their lives at any moment now, and that would be a bad time to get caught in the open. I fully expected Mira to argue about that, as she seemed to do more or less by reflex every time I tried to get her to be sensible, but if she was about to she never got the chance. Instead, she crouched behind the wrecked Chimera and raised her lasgun.

'Too late,' she said.

FIVE

A QUICK GLANCE round the Chimera's hull was all it took to confirm that Mira was right: there was no way we could get back to the tunnels now without being spotted. A full squad of rebel infantry, still wearing the remains of their old PDF uniforms, embellished by some paintstick scrawl in place of the unit patches which had been ripped away from the sleeves, was deploying further up the road in skirmish order. As I watched them come, the palms of my hands started to itch. Though I couldn't quite put my finger on it yet, something wasn't right.

'There are more up there,' Mira said, swinging her lasgun in the direction of the upper floor I'd been observing the enemy from, and where I'd left the two dead sentries a few moments before. She was rewarded by a flicker of movement, as whoever it was ducked back out of sight with almost indecent haste.

'Frak!' I said, heedless of the fact that there was a lady present. We'd be dead meat if anyone started shooting at us from up there, and even though Mira had picked off one man from this distance, I didn't imagine for a moment that she'd be able to repeat the trick with las-bolts bursting around her. 'There must have been a third man up there all the time.'

I didn't see how there could have been, though, or he would have surely intervened in the firefight. But the only other explanation I could think of didn't make sense either. Neither of the sentries we'd taken out had any vox gear, so how could they have called for help?

'I'm more worried about the ones down here,' Mira said, cracking off a couple of shots before I could stop her, which took one of the troopers advancing on us down and sent the rest scurrying for cover. She grinned exultantly at me, before returning her eye to the sights. 'I got one!'

'Instead of holding your fire long enough to be sure of several, when they got a bit closer,' I said, trying not to sound too hacked off about it. I readied my own weapons, hunkering down just as a las-bolt hit the discoloured metal above us, sending a brief rain of rust particles pattering off my hat. As I'd feared, the man on the building was targeting us too, although, thank the Emperor, he seemed to be an indifferent marksman.

'I think I'm doing pretty well, actually,' Mira snapped, turning to send a couple of retaliatory las-bolts back in the direction of the upper floor. She didn't seem to hit anything this time, but successfully discouraged whoever it was from trying again for a moment or two. 'At least I'm shooting at them, instead of just criticising all the time.'

Nothing in all my years as a commissar had prepared me for a response like that, but then I'd never encountered anyone quite like Mira before either; at least, not in a parody of a military uniform, and apparently trying to live up to it. My dealings with the daughters of the aristocracy had, up until that point, been confined to the kind of soirees my fraudulent reputation had attracted invitations to, generally as part of a delegation from an Imperial Guard contingent who'd either just arrived in-system to deal with some pressing threat, or were about to depart after having done so. I knew they were reasonably good dancers, moderately dull conversationalists and tolerably pleasant company for the night, but that was about all. There was little point in frittering our last few moments away on a pointless argument, though, so I bit back my instinctive response and peered round the Chimera's dozer blade again.

'Something's definitely wrong, here,' I said. These were no panic-stricken routers, fleeing the Astartes: they were advancing swiftly and purposefully from one piece of cover to the next, half of them moving while the rest kept their comrades covered. I pulled my head back behind the thick steel plate just ahead of a blizzard of las-bolts.

'You think?' Mira levelled her lasgun to retaliate, heedless of the state of her powerpack, and I cracked off a few shots of my own in the general direction of the upper floor, certain I'd seen movement up there again. The situation was getting more desperate by the second: it could only be a matter of time before the lurkers above us managed to line up a shot, or the advancing troopers moved round our flanks.

Looking back, we'd probably have been dead, or a great deal worse, in another handful of minutes, had it not been for the surviving rebels in the artillery park. By the grace of the Emperor, they chose that moment to break and run, pelting down the avenue in an inchoate, howling mob, any pretence of military discipline completely forgotten in the desperate rush to save themselves.

'Come on!' I said, grabbing Mira by the arm and making a dash for the open manhole before she had a chance to start arguing again. 'Now's our chance!'

To her credit, she seemed to get the idea, putting on a fair turn of speed for a woman whose usual idea of exercise was probably walking down the corridor to the dining room. Timing was crucial: it would have been ironic to say the least to have been shielded from the las-bolts of our enemies by the bodies of their comrades, only to be trampled to death by the hysterical mob.

As it was, we managed to make it to the hole in the road with no more difficulty than one might expect, despite the risk of twisting an ankle on the rubble-strewn carriageway, cracking off a couple of shots at our most visible enemies as we ran; not with any hope of hitting them, of course, but in the vague hope of preventing them from gunning us down as we emerged. Seeing no point in delaying any more than I had to, I raised my laspistol and chainsword above my head, to keep them from fouling on the manhole's rim, and jumped feet first into the darkness beneath. I was no stranger to this sort of thing, having grown up in the underhive, and was already flexing my knees to absorb the impact as I hit the rockcrete about three metres below. I don't mind admitting it jarred a lot more than I remembered it doing as a juvie, but I remained on my feet, and took a couple of cautious steps to check that my ankles were still where they belonged, instead of having been driven up through my shins like they felt.

'Are you mad?' Mira asked, scrambling down the ladder, the luminator still attached to her lasgun strobing round the narrow chamber, and I shrugged.

'How would I know?' I asked, not really caring to hear her answer. I'd already met enough head cases in the course of my career to have filled an asylum, and every single one of them had thought they were perfectly sane. To my relief, however, Mira disdained to reply, having found something else to get sniffy about.

'Sergeant!' she yelled, raising echoes which chased their way down the tunnels. 'Where are you?'

'Quiet!' I said, the absence of the squad we'd left here beginning to register for the first time. 'Something's very wrong.'

'I can see that,' she said pettishly, the beam of her luminator sweeping round the tunnel at random, which was no help at all. At least there were no visible signs of recent combat, which I supposed was something. 'They should have been waiting for us.' The full seriousness of the situation still seemed not to have registered with her; it was a minor annoyance, on a par with being kept waiting by a tardy chauffeur, that was all.

'We need to get moving,' I said. Whatever had happened to our companions was a mystery which could wait until later. 'That squad will be down here after us at any moment.' As if to punctuate my words, something rattled down the rungs of the ladder, and I started to run down the passageway without further thought. 'Grenade!' I called back over my shoulder.

Fortunately, Mira was fast enough on the uptake when it mattered, and was hard on my heels when the frag charge exploded, peppering the stonework around where we'd been standing a moment before. 'You just left me there!' she squeaked indignantly, once the echoes had died away enough to hear her.

'I warned you,' I snapped back. 'What more do you want? "Ladies first" doesn't count on the battlefield.' And a good thing too, if you ask me, otherwise we'd both have been shredded.

Mira stared at me, her mouth working, but stunned into silence for the first time since I'd met her. While my momentary advantage still lasted, I grabbed the barrel of the lasgun,[1] and doused the luminator. 'And keep that frakking thing turned off,' I added, 'if you want to get out of here alive.'

I braced myself for the argument I was certain would follow, but our adventures so far seemed to have convinced Mira that playing soldiers was a lot more dangerous than she'd bargained for, and she contented herself with muttering something that sounded like 'peasant'. All in all, I've been called a lot worse in my time, and could certainly live with that.

'Come on,' I said, taking her arm and leading her down a side passage which l could sense nearby from the altered pattern of echoes around it. I suppose it was possible that our pursuers might have given up after chucking their frag grenade down the manhole, but if I was as determined to see someone dead as they seemed to be, I certainly wouldn't be taking anything for granted at that point.

'Where to?' Mira asked, keeping her voice down at least.

'Wherever this leads,' I replied, resisting the temptation to shrug, which she couldn't have seen anyway. There was a faint current of air, which meant that it must come out in the open eventually, or at least connect to somewhere that did. Then I caught the unmistakable sound of running feet in the passage-way we'd just left behind us, and tightened my grip on her bicep. 'Freeze.'

At least she had the gumption to comply with that, and we remained immobile as the slapping bootsoles got louder, accompanied by a rising glow, which seeped into our refuge – though not, fortunately, far enough to reach our position. If any

---

1. *Which of his own weapons he stowed to do this we can only speculate.*

of the troopers chasing us had bothered to direct a beam along the side passage they would have nailed us for sure, but luckily they seemed convinced we'd stuck to the main tunnel, and could be caught up with if they just ran fast enough. As the glow and the hurrying footsteps faded away, Mira let out a sigh of relief and sagged against me.

'Who were those people?' she asked.

'I've no idea,' I told her, happy to let her remain there for a minute or two, while I got my bearings and my breath back. Sure we'd eluded our pursuers for the moment, I pulled the slate out of my pocket and checked Orten's map, being sure to keep my back between the passageway behind us and the faint glow of the pict screen. Mira's face shimmered out of the darkness, as she leaned forwards to look at it.

A few seconds' scrutiny was enough to identify the side passage we'd taken refuge in, and my spirits began to lift, at least a little. We hadn't come far, and if we could follow the draught I still felt against my face to the surface, we would come out close enough to the Astartes to link up with them.

'We have to go back,' Mira said, a worried frown just visible on her face as she studied the pictscreen. 'This passage is heading completely the wrong way.'

'It's the right way, if it's taking us away from those troopers,' I told her shortly. 'They'll realise we've given them the slip at any moment, then they'll double back.' This clearly hadn't occurred to her.

'But what about our own people?' she asked. 'Shouldn't we try to find them?'

I shook my head, forgetting the gesture couldn't be seen in the darkness. 'There's no point,' I told her bluntly. 'Something must have happened to them, or they'd still be waiting when we got back. Best case, they spotted some rebels trying to escape along the tunnels and are still trying to chase them down.'

'And worst case, the mutineers found them first,' Mira concluded.

'Right,' I said, not wanting to think too much about that. There was too big a contradiction here, between the disciplined, coordinated troopers who were pursuing us, and the disorganised rabble who'd fortuitously got in their way just when they had us cold.

'Then let's get on with it,' she agreed. 'Can we use the luminator again?'

After a moment, I agreed, reluctantly. We'd make precious little progress without it, the governor's daughter lacking my feel for the labyrinth we'd found ourselves in, and I didn't want to still be here when the squad we'd eluded came back to check the side tunnels. 'For the moment,' I said. 'But keep listening out. The moment we hear movement behind us, I want you to douse it. Clear?'

'Pellucid,' she said, and clicked it on again. The beam revealed the same age-worn brickwork that I'd seen in the main sewer, its surface moist and slick with lichen, although the branch passage we'd entered seemed to be a storm drain rather than a cloaca, to Mira's evident relief. The trickle of water under our boots was clear, and noticeably less odiferous than the stream we'd so recently left. 'What's that?'

'Nothing good,' I said, stopping to examine the patch of lichen she'd spotlighted. It had been scraped by something, which had left parallel grooves of visible brickwork. I spread my fingers, barely able to span them. 'Are there any stories of mutants living down in the tunnels here?'

'Of course.' Mira began to laugh, before realising I wasn't joking. 'There are always stories about the undercity. I doubt there's anywhere in the Imperium which doesn't have its folk tales.'

Well, she was right about that, which didn't mean there wasn't a germ of truth in at least some of them. There was no point worrying about it though: the soldiers behind us were real enough, and anything else we might run into was only a potential threat. I gestured ahead of us, into the darkness. 'After you,' I said.

'I thought you said "ladies first" didn't count on the battlefield,' Mira said, moving off, with a grin in my direction.

'It does when you're carrying the light,' I told her, making sure I hung back enough to take advantage of my black coat in the darkness. A faint alteration in the pattern of echoes tickled the edge of my awareness, and I urged her on, picking up my own pace as I did so. 'Better get moving. They're coming back.'

Mira needed no further encouragement and broke into a trot, her lasgun held ready for use. I followed, my own weapons readied, hoping I wouldn't need them, but rather suspecting I would before too much longer.

The faint current of air was growing a little stronger now, and I began to hope we'd make it back to the surface before the pursuing troopers picked up our trail again, but in this I was to be disappointed. 'Kill the light,' I murmured, just before the footsteps reached the junction behind us, and, to my relief, Mira did so at once, without arguing.

'I can see daylight,' she breathed, the relief in her voice palpable, and I must confess to feeling the same. A faint grey glow was seeping into the tunnel from somewhere up ahead, and we hurried towards it, certain that our pursuers must be gaining by now. The scuffling of bootsoles behind us suddenly became more resonant, telling me plainly that they'd entered the narrower passage behind us, and my shoulderblades began tingling, anticipating a las-bolt at any moment.

The glimmer up ahead began to grow brighter, but the yellower glow of luminators began to pervade the tunnel too, and I turned, loosing off a flurry of las-bolts from my pistol. I scarcely expected to hit anyone, but I was hoping it might take the edge off their enthusiasm at the very least.

'Are you sure you should be giving them ideas?' Mira asked waspishly, but I was too busy trying to listen to the commotion behind us to pay any attention to her. The bobbing light dimmed, and the rhythm of boot against brick was abruptly disrupted. The echoes made it hard to be sure, but it sounded to me as if the leading trooper had stumbled, or even been brought down if I was really lucky, and the others were either tripping over him or breaking stride to negotiate the sudden obstacle.

'I've just bought us a few more seconds,' I snapped. 'Don't waste them!' The light up ahead was bright enough to pick out our surroundings by now – more lichenous brick – and I could see the droplets of water thrown up by our feet as they slapped down in the thin film of moisture coating the tunnel floor. The air current was stronger too, and smelling fresher; we were almost out into the open air.

Abruptly we broke free of the tunnel, into a wide chamber, from which a number of passageways similar to the one we'd entered by led. Mira stopped, almost in the centre, illuminated by a wan shaft of sunlight, which struck highlights from the garish ornamentation on her tunic and her by now rather bedraggled coiffure. 'Frakking warp!' she said feelingly.

I was so surprised by the sudden barrack-room oath in the mouth of a lady of breeding that it took me a moment to register the reason for her outburst. When I did, I'm bound to confess, I felt like heartily endorsing it. Daylight and fresh air alike were coming from a metal grille in the ceiling, at least a metre above our heads, with no obvious method of getting to it, or through it even if we could.

'Up on my shoulders!' I said, stowing my weapons to free my hands and stooping to offer Mira a boost.

She looked at me as if I was deranged.

'I'm a chatelaine, not a carnival performer!' she snapped.

'You'll be a dead one if we can't get that grille open,' I retorted. 'Would you rather lift me up to it instead?'

Any verbal response to that being entirely unnecessary, she simply slung her lasgun across her back and clambered up to perch awkwardly on my shoulders, her legs dangling either side of my neck like an overstuffed scarf. I reached up to steady her, and she slapped my fingers away, almost overbalancing in the process.

'Keep your hands to yourself!' she squealed, in tones of outrage.

'I'm sure you're convinced you're the Emperor's gift to men,' I snarled, 'but believe me, a furtive fumble is the last thing on my mind at the moment. Get the frakking grille open!' The squad pursuing us was getting uncomfortably close by now, and although it was hard to make anything out with Mira's thighs clamped to my ears, I was suddenly convinced that I could hear movement down some of the other tunnels too.

'It won't move!' she called, an edge of panic entering her voice. 'It's been welded shut!'

'Oh, nads,' I said, the coin suddenly dropping as I looked up to see how she was doing, and picked out a couple of small stubs of metal on the rim of the grille. I'd seen identical protrusions not long before, where the ladder had been removed from beneath the trapdoor we'd entered the tunnels beneath the palace by, and I was suddenly prepared to bet a year's remuneration that a similar one had stood here not long before. 'We haven't been chased here, we've been herded.'

'What are you talking about?' Mira demanded, as I handed her down, with a considerable sense of relief. All that padding might be aesthetically pleasing, but it didn't exactly make her a lightweight.

'I mean we're trapped,' I said, with as much restraint as I could muster, and drew my weapons again. There was definitely movement in several of the tunnels, but I couldn't be sure which, and how great: the echoes were overlapping too much. If I could determine one that was clear, we might still be able to make a run for it, though...

Abruptly, that hope evaporated, as the rebel squad which had attacked us on the surface trotted into the chamber, their lasguns level. They were a couple of men short, though, which gave me a certain amount of vindictive satisfaction; if I was on my way to the Golden Throne, at least I'd be taking an honour guard with me.

Mira unslung her own weapon and brought it up, but I forestalled her with a hand on the barrel.

'Stand down,' I said. 'They obviously want us alive, but I'm sure they'll change their minds if you start shooting.'

'Quite right, commissar,' someone said behind us. The voice was vaguely familiar, but it wasn't until I turned and saw the sergeant of Mira's detail emerging from another of the tunnels that everything fell into place. He was carrying his lasgun too, with an easy confidence that told me he was perfectly willing to use it the moment he felt the need. There were another three or four familiar faces standing beside him, in the same ridiculous uniform, including our vox man, his backpack transceiver still in place. All were still carrying their guns, but the satchel charges had evidently been stashed somewhere else for safe keeping. Where the rest of the squad were, I had no idea, but strongly suspected they'd paid dearly for refusing to turn their coats. The sergeant and his cronies were looking decidedly the worse for wear, their flak armour scored and dented, their faces pained. 'Milady will be a great asset when she joins us, but you, in the heart of the Imperial war machine, will be a prize beyond value.'

'Dream on,' Mira said scornfully. 'If you think I'm going to betray my world and my father, you're even more stupid than you look.'

'You'll think differently when the brood takes you in,' the sergeant assured her, and a gush of ice water seemed to sluice down my spine. There were innumerable minor wounds among the turncoat soldiers, but all had sustained identical ones below the ribcage, marked by a trickle of blood, already clotting. I'd seen wounds like those before and searched the men's faces again. As I'd expected, they looked dazed and disorientated, but followed the lead of the sergeant. He alone seemed alert and in control, his own armour unmarred – a third-generation hybrid, then, or even later, able to pass fully for human.

Despite my mounting horror, I kept my voice steady, concealing the knowledge of what I'd deduced and looking desperately round the chamber for some avenue of escape. More people, or, to be more accurate, things that looked like people, were emerging into the light, from tunnel mouth after tunnel mouth, some armed, mostly not. Many bore visible traces of their inhuman heritage: some had an extra limb or two, tipped with razor-sharp talons, while others had skin thickened to natural armour, or were betrayed by nothing more than a subtle wrongness of posture, like Kamella, the joygirl who'd tried to bite my head off on Keffia.

'What are they?' Mira asked, curiosity and revulsion mingling on her face. 'Mutants?'

'The stories don't seem so far-fetched now, do they?' I asked, unwilling to reveal to the hybrids that I knew their true nature. I didn't know quite how concealing that knowledge would aid us, but I wasn't willing to concede any potential advantage, however small, over an enemy. One tunnel seemed to be open still, and I powered up my chainsword, nudging Mira towards it. Of course that was precisely what we were meant to do – I didn't need to be able to tap into the brood mind to know that – but pretending we were fooled, even if only for a few seconds, might just tip the balance back in our favour. It was an insanely slender chance, but it was only a few weeks since I'd taken a header through a necron warp portal, and compared to that, what I was contemplating looked positively sensible.

As I'd expected, the whole damned lot of them responded at once, taking a couple of steps forwards in eerie silence, tightening the cordon around Mira and me, while moving out of the tunnels and into the open space. Including, to my carefully concealed relief, the hybrid sergeant and his newly implanted squadmates.

'Follow my lead,' I murmured, certain that if I wasn't actually overheard, enough of the abhuman monstrosities would be able to read my lips and share the knowledge of what I'd said with their brood mates. 'Back towards that tunnel behind us. If any of them look like shooting, drop them first.'

Mira nodded, once, tightly, her posture stiff with nerves. 'Count on it,' she said, her voice hardly wavering at all.

'Good girl,' I said, keeping up the charade and feeling that a bit of quiet encouragement at this juncture would look appropriately commissarial. 'If they rush us, just hose them down on full auto.'

Which would probably be about as effective as giving them a severe talking to, if the mob I'd survived on Keffia was anything to go by. The brood mind doesn't care about a few losses, any more than a tyranid army does, but it's the sort of thing that would work against a mutant horde, and I was more interested in misdirecting the alien gestalt intellect facing us than giving sensible tactical advice.

It almost worked, too. We were just edging into position for my desperate gamble, the hybrid sergeant practically within reach of my humming chainblade, when I became aware of an ominous susurration in the depths of the tunnel behind us. I turned slowly to face it, Mira following suit, the pit of my stomach knotting. I knew that sound: a chitinous exoskeleton, moving fast.

I brought up my weapons, but before I could shoot, the ghastly form of a purestrain genestealer burst from the darkened portal and flung itself upon us.

SIX

As SHE GOT her first sight of the xenos monstrosity, Mira screamed, as well she might; if I hadn't had an image to maintain I'd probably have done the same, but as it was, I took an ineffectual cut at it with the chainsword, diving to one side to get out of its way. By great good fortune, the movement got me closer to my real objective, but there wasn't any time to exploit the fact, as the creature turned, all four arms reaching out to eviscerate me. Mira pulled the trigger of her lasgun, unleashing a burst, and I flinched, anticipating falling to friendly fire; but she was aiming down the tunnel, from which another 'stealer emerged, seconds later, bearing down on her like a Chimera at full throttle. How many more of the things there may have been lurking in the depths below the city I've no idea, but fortunately the brood mind seemed to think that one each would be more than enough to implant the two of us with its taint.[1]

'Drop your weapons,' the hybrid sergeant urged us. 'They won't harm you if you don't resist.'

---

1. Many of the hybrids probably had the ability to do this as well, but by now the brood mind had evidently concluded that Cain would be less easy meat than the PDF troopers, and deployed the most formidable of its assets accordingly.

'Yeah, right,' I said sarcastically, parrying the reaching limbs with my chainsword. It bit deep, shearing through chitin in a welter of flesh and ichor, which spattered liberally around the chamber, misting the faces of the nearest spectators. None reacted with the revulsion you'd normally expect, just continuing to watch in impassive silence, which in its own way was more unnerving than the creature in front of me. 'Just turn us into abominations like you.'[1]

The creature flinched, withdrawing the injured limb, and I rolled under another just as its fist closed in a grab, missing me by millimetres. The one closing in on Mira momentarily checked its charge too, as a rash of las-bolt craters erupted on its thorax, then came on again as her lasgun fell silent, its powerpack expended. With a shriek which all but ruptured my eardrums she flung the empty weapon at the onrushing monstrosity, hoping to achieve Emperor knows what. The 'stealer swatted the mass of metal aside in an eyeblink and it clattered to the floor nearby, where the watching hybrids ignored it.

'You couldn't just have reloaded?' I asked pettishly, finding myself close enough to slash at its leg as I tried to make distance from the one attacking me, and doing so with enthusiasm. Again, the blade bit deep, and it stumbled sideways, crashing into the other 'stealer, which was still lunging desperately in my direction.

'He's carrying the spare powerpacks!' Mira snapped back, taking advantage of the ensuing confusion to slip past the entangled creatures, and glowering at the sergeant as she did so. The crowd of hybrids began to close, moving forwards to narrow the arena we fought in, and I cracked off a couple of shots from the pistol in my hand, dropping the two nearest to the tunnel the 'stealers had emerged from.

Of course he was, I thought irritably. Nobles never carried anything for themselves; that's what servants were for. 'Pick the bloody gun up!' I shouted, as she almost tripped over the thing, and she scooped it into her hand again without slackening her

---

1. *I suspect a little exaggeration may be creeping in here, as close combat against a creature as formidable as a purestrain genestealer is hardly likely to leave enough time for defiant speeches.*

pace. If she'd been issued with it, she should damn well look after it, so far as I was concerned.[1]

The purestrains were sorting themselves out and looking seriously hacked off by now, even more so than their kind usually did.[2] As one, they turned to stare at me, the brood mind no doubt perceiving me as the greater threat. Well, it had got that right, I'd seen bath sponges more menacing than Mira looked at the moment, and with nothing left to lose I did the one thing I hoped they wouldn't expect: charged both creatures, bellowing 'WAAAAAAAAGHHHHH!' as loudly and enthusiastically as the orks I'd seen far too much of on Perlia. As I'd hoped, it focussed all the hybrids' attention on the purestrains, so when I veered aside, leaving the pair of them leaping to attack the spot where I suddenly wasn't, and shot the sergeant instead, none of the creatures reacted for a crucial second, taken completely by surprise.

By the time the sergeant hit the floor, I was among the crowd hemming us in, swinging my chainsword in defensive patterns years of drilling and duelling had made so instinctive I was barely aware of them, reaping a rich and repellent harvest of severed appendages and spouting ichor. The newly implanted PDF troopers were still too dazed to react, going down without even trying to resist, and I felt a small qualm at that point, tempered with the reflection that it was not only my duty to purge them but a merciful deliverance too. As the vox op folded, his head flying off in a random direction, I let my pistol fall unheeded to the sodden rockcrete beneath my feet and grabbed the handset, praying to the Throne that it was still tuned to the same frequency as I remembered.

'Astartes! Help!' I just had time to bellow, before being borne to

1. *Imperial Guard regulations are firm on this point, prescribing execution as the penalty for losing a weapon, unless it was an unavoidable consequence of action in the field. Which probably accounts for most Guard troopers' tendency to carry theirs everywhere when on duty, even to the latrines.*

2. *Cain might well have encountered purestrains on Keffia, although the short account of his activities there only mentions hybrids. He may also have seen them in one of the sporadic cleansing actions against the tyranid splinter fleets in which he was involved prior to this juncture.*

the moisture-slick floor by a tidal wave of malformed bodies. I did my best to resist, of course, kicking and flailing wildly with the chainsword until it was torn from my grasp, and probably biting too if anything came close enough, but it was hopeless; there were simply too many of them. For a moment I could see nothing but twisted faces, their expressions blank, still moving in eerie silence. No one screamed, shouted or swore at me, and that was the most disturbing thing of all. At least until they parted, and I found myself staring into the eyes of the genestealer I'd maimed.

There have been far too many times in my long and inglorious career when I've been convinced, with good reason, that my last moment had come, but few of them were accompanied by such a complete sensation of absolute helplessness. In almost every other instance I've at least had the illusion of being able to affect the outcome, seen some last, desperate gamble which ultimately paid off, but here there was nothing at all I could do, beyond writhing ineffectually and letting rip with a volley of profanity that would have made a Slaaneshi cultist blush. It didn't perturb the 'stealer, though; it just hissed through its thorax and opened its jaws unfeasibly wide, showing far too many teeth and adding a layer of sticky drool to the other unpleasant substances already ruining my coat.

Something moved in the back of its throat, and a thick, muscular tube emerged in place of a tongue. I flinched, anticipating the stabbing pain about to be inflicted on my chest, and, worse, the complete subversion of everything I was. Would I still feel like me at all in five minutes' time, and if I didn't, would I even care? I recalled the implanted troopers I'd known, and fought alongside, on Keffia. They'd seemed perfectly normal, giving no clue at all to their altered nature, until they'd revealed themselves by turning on us in the heat of battle against their brood mates. If I became like them, with the access I had to a Space Marine Chapter and the upper echelons of the Imperial Guard, the damage my altered self could do to the Imperium's interests would be incalculable. Rather more to the point though, I was perfectly happy with myself the way I was, and the prospect of being turned into a puppet of the tyranids by an overgrown cockroach was absolutely intolerable.

Abruptly, the creature looming over me jerked and shuddered, keening loudly, even over the stuttering crackle of a lasgun on full auto, as a rain of successive las-bolts chewed their way through its armoured carapace and began making an unholy mess of its innards. Taken by surprise once again, the brood mind lost its focus for a moment, and the myriad of hands and talons holding me slackened their grip.

That was the only chance I needed. Tearing free of them, I snatched up my weapons, which, praise the Emperor, still lay on the floor within easy reach, and turned to face my deliverer. I am, by nature, something of an optimist, but I'd never dared to hope that my message would be answered so quickly, if it even got through at all.

'What the hell are you still doing here?' I asked in astonishment, laying about me with the chainblade again and popping off random las-bolts, certain that in a crowd this dense they'd find some kind of mark.

Mira paused for a second, before ejecting the spent powerpack from her lasgun and snapping a fresh one in, whereupon she began firing short, precise bursts at the second 'stealer, presumably having discovered just how quickly staying on full auto would deplete it.

'Thank you for saving my neck, milady,' she said sarcastically. 'Oh, think nothing of it, commissar.' She was standing astride the sergeant's body, which at least explained where the reloads had come from. No doubt she'd carry her own from now on, if she still felt the urge to play soldiers.

'Run now, thanks later,' I said, cutting my way through to her side. 'But I'm definitely pleased to see you.'

'I'm flattered,' she said, backing towards the nearest tunnel mouth and continuing to pepper the purestrain with las-bolts. This one, however, was made of sterner stuff than its fellow and continued to advance inexorably, hopping awkwardly on its injured leg, no doubt aided by the fact that Mira kept having to shift her aim to keep the swarm of hybrids off our backs too. If the ones with weapons opened up we'd both be dead in seconds, but to my amazement and relief they continued to hold their fire, still believing that they had the advantage of numbers and could eventually take us alive, to become part of their conjoined mind. They were probably right about that too, closing in around us with a speed and precision I wouldn't have believed possible if I hadn't seen what they were capable of before, and as heedless of their own losses as the tyranids themselves. For every one that fell to our las-bolts and my whining chainblade, another would step in, and it could only be a matter of time before we were overwhelmed and brought down.

I shot another hybrid standing between us and the tunnel mouth, but even as I did so I could tell it was too late: that way out was blocked now, the silent crowd pressing in on all sides. For the second time in a handful of minutes, I was facing the imminent certainty of my own death – or at least the death of everything I defined myself by.

'It's been an honour to serve with you, colonel,' I said, feeling that my last act might as well be to boost Mira's morale. I'd hardly been a model commissar, Emperor only knows, but at least I could die like one.

'We both know that's a big fat lie,' she replied grimly, as her last powerpack ran dry despite her attempts to husband it, and she began to use the heavy lasgun as a club, 'but I appreciate the thought.'

'You're welcome,' I said, my laspistol giving up too, and swept the chainsword at the 'stealer. We only had seconds left now, but I was determined to take as many of the abominations with me as I could. Time slowed and stretched, as it generally seems to under this sort of circumstance, and I found myself suddenly aware of a rising shriek, which grew in intensity and volume. I flicked my gaze apprehensively at the nearest tunnel mouth, anticipating the sudden appearance of some fresh horror, a screamer-killer perhaps[1] – nothing would surprise me now... except for what actually happened next. With a rumble like thunder, and a sudden burst of ozone which left the hairs on my arms tingling upright,[2]

---

1. *A form of tyranid carnifex, so named for the sound it makes while spitting a ball of bio-plasma.*

2. *Clearly the result of air being ionised by the discharge of a turbo laser.*

the roof over our heads vaporised in a burst of light so dazzling I was left blinking after-images from my retina for several minutes. Shards of carbonised debris pattered around us, but fortunately nothing of any significant size actually hit; the turbo laser must have struck the ground above us full on, to leave nothing larger than a few handfuls of gravel behind.

'What the hell was that?' Mira yelled, as the noise suddenly redoubled without the intervening layer of brick, earth and rock-crete.

'It's the Thunderhawk!' I bellowed back, recognising the distinctive silhouette as it flashed past overhead, its shadow momentarily eclipsing the open pit we now found ourselves in. A second later the screaming of its engine was suddenly punctuated by the distinctive staccato rhythm of heavy bolter fire, and the hybrids scattered, racing for whatever refuge they might find in the surrounding tunnels, while the genestealer exploded messily just before closing to contact with us. 'And the Astartes!'

The unmistakable bulk of the Terminators I'd seen taking the heretic artillery position apart were lumbering into position around the rim of the pit, pouring fire from their storm bolters into it, while the hybrids fled and died in droves. This was hardly a comfortable position to be in, even given the phenomenal accuracy of the Space Marines, but they picked off their targets without even coming close to us, and in any case the firing died away about as quickly as you might expect, given how rapidly they ran out of targets.

Mira and I stared at one another, grinning like idiots, not quite able to believe how narrowly we'd escaped with our lives and souls intact.

'It seems I owe you an apology,' she said after a moment, her generous décolletage heaving with emotion. 'I should have listened to your advice and stayed behind.'

'Under the circumstances,' I conceded, 'I can only be grateful that you didn't.' Now they'd run out of things to kill the Terminators were advancing into the pit, mainly by the simple expedient of jumping, which was creating a series of minor tremors in the ground. How they were intending to get up again, I had no idea.[1]

Mira eyed me speculatively. 'I'm sure we can find some way of making it up to each other,' she said, in a manner which made it abundantly clear just what kind of reparation she had in mind. I nodded, the prospect seeming distinctly appealing at that point, and Emperor knows I felt I'd earned it.

'I'm sure we can,' I said, then turned to the Terminator in charge, easily recognisable by the powerblade he was carrying along with his storm bolter. 'Thank you, sergeant. Your intervention was most timely.'

'Your death while a guest of the Reclaimers would have been an affront to the honour of our Chapter,' he told me, the sepulchral tones of his kind issuing from the vox unit of his helmet. I was used to the timbre by this time, but Mira was clearly startled, flinching visibly as he began to speak. 'We made what haste we could to the source of your signal.'

'Then I'll do my best to keep your honour upheld,' I said, feeling oddly disconcerted by the dispassionate statement. The other Astartes were fanning out, weapons at the ready, poking at the fallen bodies of the genestealers and the hybrids. I gestured to the remains of the nearest, drawing the sergeant's attention to it, although I had no doubt that the voxes built into the Space Marines' helmets were already humming with the news. 'Especially now things have become a little more complicated.'

---

1. *Since they would probably have teleported back to the* Revenant *at the conclusion of their mission, this wouldn't have concerned them overmuch.*

Editorial Note:

The Reclaimers' arrival on Viridia had proven to be as brisk and decisive as intervention by an Astartes Chapter generally is, and news of their coming spread rapidly. Though, in those first few hours, their presence had been confined entirely to the planetary capital, the effect on the rest of the planet had been profound; something Cain, as usual, doesn't bother to mention, any more than he does the rest of the retaking of Fidelis.

Since my readers cannot be presumed to share his lack of interest in the bigger picture, the following extract has been appended.

From *The Virus of Betrayal: The Cleansing of Viridia and its Aftermath* by Lady Ottaline Melmoth, 958.M41.

THE ARRIVAL OF the Astartes was as welcome to the loyal servants of the Emperor as it was startling, many of the faithful taking their advent as a sign of His special interest in our blessed world. Indeed, many services of thanksgiving were begun in temples and chapels around the globe even before their first battle was concluded. Not that this made any difference to the fervour of the celebrants: for them, the coming battle to cleanse Viridia of heresy and worse seemed little more than a formality, since the

whole galaxy knows that His Space Marines are the strong right
hand of the Emperor Himself, and that once they embark on a
quest in His holy name, the task is as good as done.[1]

The Astartes made their first landing in Fidelis, at the palace of
Governor DuPanya, losing no time in breaking the heretical
siege lines which had kept the Emperor's anointed custodian of
the planet confined and powerless to intervene directly in the
constant turmoil of civil strife which had done so much to mar
the fair face of Viridia. This done, he immediately took up the
reins of his interrupted stewardship, while the Astartes swept on
to even greater victories. The cathedral, always a beacon of hope
in those desperate times, and therefore under constant threat
from the dissident elements, was liberated within the hour, as
was the shrine of the Omnissiah, freeing the tech-priests to begin
ministering to the city's wounded machine-spirits with the
utmost dispatch.

Perhaps the most desperate battles were those to eliminate the
artillery batteries which the rebels had set up to prevent a mass
landing of Imperial Guard troops, which, if left in place, would
have taken a terrible toll in lives and resources. The crucial
importance of this assignment can be deduced from the fact that
the mission to remove one was led by the commander of the
Astartes expeditionary force and his personal guard, while the
task of placing a beacon to guide the teleporting strike team
which destroyed the other was entrusted to none other than
Commissar Cain, accompanied by Colonel Mira DuPanya, the
governor's youngest daughter and a formidable warrior in her
own right.

It need hardly be said that both missions ended in unqualified
success, with the complete destruction of the designated targets,
although one was to have unexpected and serious consequences.
DuPanya and Cain's reconnaissance *en route* to their destination
had revealed the true nature of the enemy we were facing, and,

---

1. *Those of us who have had much to do with the Astartes, and found them rather more
concerned with the traditions of their Chapters than effective cooperation, may find
these sentiments ringing a little hollow...*

for the first time, the full extent of the hideous conspiracy gnawing away at the fabric of our society (quite literally, it seemed) became clear.

SEVEN

THE NEXT FEW days passed in a predictable blur of briefings, conferences and occasional bloodshed, as the full extent of the genestealer cult's reach became clear. Not to put too fine a point on it, the bloody things were everywhere, from the local Arbites[1] to the sanitation workers' guild, and winkling them out was a job I felt heartily glad hadn't landed in my lap. Fortunately the Guard troopships had arrived in-system on schedule, bringing a mixed bag of Tallarn, Vostroyan and Caledonian regiments with them, so there was no shortage of outsiders unquestionably free of the xenos taint to start rounding up suspects and begin the screening process.

'The trouble is,' Mira said, on one of her periodic social visits to my quarters, 'that means pretty much the entire population.' She shrugged, setting up interesting ripples in the fabric of the gown she was almost wearing, and leaned forwards to study the regicide board on the table between us, giving me the opportunity to fully appreciate the effect. She was an enthusiastic, if somewhat direct,

---

1. *Like many seasoned travellers, Cain uses the term to refer to law enforcers in general, rather than actual members of the Adeptus Arbites. As previously mentioned, they were known as 'Guardians' on Viridia.*

player, an attitude she seemed to bring to all her recreational activities, and despite us having got off on the wrong foot, a surprisingly congenial companion. At least for the short time I expected to remain on Viridia. I could see her innate self-centredness would grow wearying after a while,[1] although I suppose, given her upbringing, that was hardly her fault.

'The crucial thing is to purge the most influential institutions as quickly as possible,' I told her, drawing on what I remembered of the Keffia Campaign, in which all the policy stuff had taken place so far above my head it was practically in the stratosphere: in those relatively carefree days, all I'd had to worry about was rounding up the defaulters, watching our Earthshakers lob shells at an enemy too distant to shoot back, and avoiding Colonel Mostrue's occasional attempts to manoeuvre me into the firing line. (Apart from getting sucked into a stand-up fight with a horde of genestealer hybrids uncomfortably reminiscent of the one Mira and I had so recently faced together, of course.) 'Starting with the Guardians and the PDF.' Because the sooner the Viridians could begin cleaning up their own mess, the sooner I'd be able to get back to brigade headquarters and away from anything wanting to kill me; at least until General Lokris found another insanely risky errand to lob in my direction.

The Reclaimers would hardly want to hang around once the initial flurry of action had subsided, and the back of the rebellion had been pretty much broken already. There were still a few units of PDF mutineers out there, either composed of hybrids and implanted humans under the sway of the brood mind, or clinging to the ideological twaddle they'd been fed to get them to join the revolution in the first place and unwilling to admit they'd been duped by xenos, but they were hardly going to last long against Guardsmen, let alone the Emperor's chosen warriors. Gries had made no secret of the fact that he intended pulling out to look for a more interesting war as soon as the Reclaimers had finished cleansing the offworld habs, and when the Astartes left Viridia my

---

1. *The irony of this statement seems to have eluded Cain entirely, though not, I suspect, most of my readers.*

assignment would go with them, as there would hardly be any need for them to continue liaising with the Imperial Guard.

In the meantime, I was far more comfortable than I'd any right to expect. Mira had prevailed on her father to find me a guest room in the palace, citing the need to keep me on hand as a military advisor with experience of genestealer infestations, and if he was aware of her real motives the governor was enough of a gentleman to affect ignorance of them. In fact the accommodation was too luxurious, if anything, and I'd taken to sleeping on one of the couches, the bed being too soft for me, at least for its intended purpose.

'I suppose so.' She turned one of my ecclesiarchs, effectively surrounding the king with her own pieces, and sat back, looking smug. 'My game, I think.'

'It looks that way,' I said. In truth I could probably have turned it round again in a couple more moves, but the ensuing end game would have been tediously protracted, and Mira's inevitable sulk at being made to look foolish would have put a damper on the rest of the evening. Whereas resigning now would leave her in a good mood, and ready to move on to the more enjoyable pursuits we both knew were the real reason for her visit.

So it was with somewhat mixed feelings that I heard the door of my suite bang closed, followed by the unmistakable clatter of an overstuffed kitbag falling to the carpet. Mira's eyes widened, in much the same fashion as they had when she first caught sight of the genestealers, and even before a familiar odour drifted past my nostrils I would have put a considerable sum of money on what I'd find when I turned round.

'Jurgen,' I said, a degree of warmth which surprised me elbowing its way into my voice. 'How in Terra's name did you get here?' He looked just as unprepossessing as I remembered, as if a nurgling had somehow become entangled with a random collection of Guardsmen's kit, but I was delighted to see him again nevertheless.

'On one of the troopships,' my aide said, picking his nose thoughtfully, taking the rhetorical question as literally as he did everything else. 'Then I got on the first shuttle down. The general wasn't happy about it, but I told him I was with you, so they found room.'

'I'll bet he did,' I said, knowing all too well how obdurate Jurgen could be in pursuit of whatever he conceived to be his duty, irrespective of any difference in rank or status between him and the unfortunate target of his ire. I've no doubt that without the protection the quasi-commissarial credentials his position as my aide conferred, he would have been shot on the spot for insubordination innumerable times. I indicated my guest, who seemed even more astonished that I apparently knew this apparition than she had been by his original appearance. 'This is Milady DuPanya, daughter of his Excellency, and a senior officer in the PDF. Mira, my aide, Gunner Jurgen.'

'Pleased to meet you, miss,' Jurgen said, mercifully too distant to proffer a hand. Unable to reconcile her evident civilian status with what I'd told him about her military rank, he raised a hand to the straggle of lank hair escaping from under his helmet in something between a wave and a salute, before scratching his head in perplexity. 'I thought you were with the Astartes, sir.'

'Liaising with them,' I said. 'But the main PDF command centre's here, in the palace, which means it'll be the centre of the Guard operation as well.'

'I see,' Jurgen said, nodding judiciously. 'So you need to be here, really. For this liaison thing to work.'

'It's a lot more convenient,' Mira said, stifling giggles. 'For the liaison thing.'

'Yes, it is,' I said, a little more shortly than I'd intended. Jurgen and I had been through a lot together, and he'd already saved my life more times than I could count. I was used to people judging him by his unprepossessing exterior, but Mira's thinly veiled mockery raised my hackles. Perhaps fortunately, they were as thick-skinned as one another in their own fashion, and she remained as oblivious to my disapproval as Jurgen did to her amusement. 'We'll have to find you some quarters.'

'That won't be a problem,' Jurgen said, rummaging in his kitbag. 'I've got a bedroll.' He started looking round the lavishly appointed drawing room for somewhere to spread it out.

'I'm glad to see you're as prepared as ever,' I said, trying not to picture the shambles he'd reduce the elegant chamber to within a day of settling in, not to mention the disruption his presence would cause to my continuing to liaise as happily as I had with a particular honorary colonel of the Household Regiment. 'But I'm sure we can make you a little more comfortable than that.'

'Of course we can,' Mira said, rallying at last and recomposing her features. 'The guest suites in this wing have servants' quarters attached.' She indicated a locked door on an inner wall, which I'd assumed on moving in simply connected to an adjoining suite like my own, for the benefit of guests needing a bit more space to sprawl. 'You can use those.'

'I wouldn't want to put you to any trouble, miss,' Jurgen said, apparently under the impression she was proposing to take care of the matter herself.

Mira shook her head. 'It's no trouble,' she assured him, with a commendably straight face. 'The main door from the corridor should still be unlocked, for the cleaners.' For whom, though I'd never seen them, I felt a sudden pang of sympathy. 'And we can get the majordomo to open that one in the morning.'

She glanced a wordless question at me as she indicated the connecting door, and I nodded. Despite his slovenly appearance, and the miasma of ripe socks which hung about him, Jurgen's discretion was considerable; he wouldn't intrude without good reason. Not to mention that, with a genestealer cult lurking in the woodwork, I'd sleep a great deal more soundly knowing my aide and his lasgun were within earshot. I always kept my own weapons to hand, of course, but it was surprisingly comforting to know that once again I had back-up I could rely on completely. In fact it's hardly an exaggeration to say that I only fully appreciated how much I'd missed it once Jurgen materialised so unexpectedly in my quarters.

'Then, if there's nothing else, sir, I'll turn in,' my aide said, stooping to gather up his kit.

'Probably best,' I told him. 'Now the Guard have arrived, we're in for a busy day tomorrow.'

'Almost certainly,' Mira agreed, as the door clicked closed, leaving only the lingering trace of his presence hanging in the air like an odiferous phantom. She raised a speculative eyebrow at me. 'Perhaps we'd better get on with some liaising while we still can.'

WELL, I HADN'T been wrong about the effect the sudden arrival of a few score thousand Guardsmen was going to have on the planet, and my peace of mind. Now there was an actual Imperial Guard force in the system to coordinate things with, Gries began voxing me rather more frequently than once a day, and at greater length than the terse exchanges we'd grown used to, which had largely consisted of exchanging the tally of 'stealer spawn bagged by his Astartes (high) and Orten's PDF (pitifully low) since the last communiqué. Given how compromised the PDF were, Gries had decided to set up the Reclaimers' operational headquarters at the Adeptus Mechanicus shrine, where, I gathered, he and his men had been made as welcome as outsiders ever were by the disciples of the Omnissiah. As yet I hadn't ventured across the city to join them, feeling that my duty required me to stay as close as possible to the PDF command bunker, and the rather less spartan accommodation offered by the palace.

Within a couple of days of the Guard's arrival, however, I was beginning to find the prospect of a bit of Mechanicus austerity considerably more appealing. Governor DuPanya had kindly put the bunker under his home at the disposal of the expeditionary force,[1] which meant I was dealing with general staff matters pretty much non-stop. Predictably, everyone from regimental commanders and their commissars on up wanted to meet me, get my opinion on matters I'd never heard of and ask if I could perhaps suggest to the Astartes that they move these pressing concerns to the top of their To Do list. If it hadn't been for Jurgen deflecting the majority of these requests with his usual combination of stubbornness and literally minded adherence to protocol, I'd never have been off the vox to Gries at all. Even Mira's presence was starting to seem scant compensation for the never-ending litany of requests, complaints and data-shuffling.

---

1. *Probably to make sure he wasn't pushed out of the loop entirely.*

I had no doubt, from what I'd seen of the Astartes during our voyage here, that their patience with this kind of confusion would be limited at best, so you'll no doubt appreciate my surprise when Gries voxed one morning to request a meeting with the governor, and the senior Guard officers, at his earliest convenience. As it happened I was having breakfast with Mira at the time, and she looked at me quizzically over the plate she'd just stuffed with salt grox, coddled eggs and some local species of smoked fish.

'What do you suppose he wants?' she asked, and I shrugged, quietly fascinated as usual by the amount of food she seemed able to pack away without any noticeable ill-effects.

'I suppose we'll find out soon enough,' I said, sipping my cup of tanna[1] gratefully. Jurgen had brought a supply with him, and I hadn't realised quite how much I was missing the stuff until it was back. 'We needed to get him in for a joint strategy meeting anyway. Probably a lot easier if he thinks it was his idea in the first place.'

'Perhaps,' Mira agreed, slightly indistinctly. 'But why wouldn't he come if you asked him anyway? I thought we were all supposed to be cooperating.'

'Astartes like to cooperate on their terms,' I told her, punctuating my words with sips of the fragrant liquid. I had no doubt that they were zealous servants of Him on Earth, but whatever alchemy made them more than human undeniably set them apart. Perhaps if I hadn't been so affected, both physically and mentally, by my experiences on Interitus Prime, I might have interacted with them to a greater extent on our journey here, and found more common ground than I had, but somehow I doubted that. The closest thing to a personal connection I'd been able to forge was with Drumon, and he'd been more interested in the necrons and their infernal devices than anything approaching the social niceties.

'Who doesn't?' Mira asked, reasonably enough. I couldn't think of an answer to that which didn't sound trite, or smug, so I took refuge in my breakfast and simply shrugged.

* * *

1. *A Valhallan beverage, which Cain developed a taste for shortly after his first posting to a regiment from that world. Why, I have no idea.*

To GIVE THE governor his due, he lost no time in setting up the conference Gries had requested. As I entered the command bunker, the taste of tanna still fresh in my mouth, I was pleasantly surprised to see Orten there, apparently at DuPanya's invitation. Having him on hand as a source of local knowledge would be useful, and save us the bother of rebriefing him later in the unlikely event of us needing the forces he commanded for anything. I nodded an affable greeting and exchanged a few words, noting with quiet amusement how my friendliness towards him seemed to change the attitude of a number of the Guard officers present from indifference or barely concealed disdain to a slightly forced cordiality. They would have had little enough time for the PDF even if a fair proportion of it hadn't been shooting at their men, of course, but under the circumstances, I wouldn't have been all that surprised if at least some of them hadn't suspected Orten of being a hybrid himself.[1]

Rather more surprising was Mira's presence, wearing another of her wedding-cake uniforms, but at least this time she'd had enough sense to pack the cleavage away where it wouldn't distract anyone. She smiled at me as I came in, although if any of the assembled officers noticed, they had the good grace not to appear to take it for anything other than a perfectly natural infatuation with the dashing hero I was popularly supposed to be. I made my way over to the girl and her father, acknowledging the greetings of the Guard officers I was acquainted with, or who wished to foster the impression that I was.

'Governor,' I said, greeting him first, as protocol demanded, before nodding to Mira. 'Colonel. An unexpected pleasure.' Which it was. She'd said nothing about tagging along when she'd left my chambers an hour or so before, and must have got changed remarkably quickly, at least by her standards. Many of the Imperial officers milling around us seemed confused by her presence, as even if they accepted her military rank as real, which I doubted

---

1. *He was, of course, one of the first Viridians to be screened and declared free of the xenos taint. Otherwise he'd hardly still have been breathing, let alone given access to one of the most secure facilities on the planet.*

any of them did, it was by far the most junior in the room. She smiled again, but before she could reply, DuPanya cut in, as dextrously as I might have pinked an opponent with my chainsword.

'My daughter is here as my potential successor, commissar,'[1] he said. 'In these days of uncertainty, it's important for her to be kept abreast of policy matters, in case she has to take over the reins of government.'

'Of course,' I said, nodding gravely, as if there was any government worth a damn on Viridia at the moment other than jumpy Guardsmen with lasguns, who'd apply whichever fragments of the occupation code[2] they remembered so long as nothing or no one looked like threatening the safety of their squadmates, and use their weapons indiscriminately if their paranoia was sufficiently tweaked. (Which, under the right, or wrong, circumstances, wouldn't take much, as a rule.) 'But I'm sure we all hope it won't come to that.' I certainly would if I was a Viridian, anyway.

'Quite.' DuPanya glanced at his daughter, apparently picking up my implied meaning without effort, and moved the discussion on to safer topics. 'What do you think the Astartes want to discuss?'

'I've no idea,' I admitted, trying not to sound as though it rankled. We were, after all, supposed to be on the same side, but, as I've mentioned before, the Astartes were a law unto themselves, and confided as much or as little in their allies as seemed to suit them. At least, that was true of the Reclaimers, and I've no reason to suspect that it doesn't hold true for the other Chapters as well.[3] 'But I'm sure we'll find out soon enough.'

We didn't have long to wait, either. At the appointed hour, almost to the second, the synchronised clash of armoured feet

---

1. *Not strictly true, as she was the youngest of three siblings, but she was the only one present in Fidelis at the time.*

2. *Or, to give it its official title,* The Emergency Martial Law Regulations and Provisions for the Safeguarding of Civilian Populations in Areas Under the Protection of His Divine Majesty's Imperial Guard and Allied Forces *(CCXXXVIth revised edition, 759.M40).*

3. *The vast majority, certainly. Most, if not all, have their own traditions and secrets, sometimes to a degree which would seem positively heretical in less devoted servants of the Emperor.*

against rockcrete I'd come to associate with the Astartes echoed through the bunker, shaking a thin film of dust free of the support beams to sprinkle everyone lightly with synthetic dandruff, and all eyes turned to the main doorway. After a moment or two, in which the clattering and the vibration increased to levels just short of uncomfortable, Gries appeared, flanked by a couple of his companions from the squad which had accompanied him before.[1] A moment later, I had a real surprise. Drumon was trailing a pace or two behind them. Even if he'd still been wearing his helmet, which was hanging from a pouch-filled belt at his waist, next to a holstered plasma pistol, I would have recognised him instantly by the metal claw at his back, the jointed arm to which it was attached folded neatly away parallel to his spine. He was carrying a scabbarded sword on the opposite side to his pistol, with an activation rune of some kind in the pommel. He was evidently used to employing them in tandem, in the same fashion I used my chainsword and sidearm, and I smiled involuntarily, amused to have found another small thing which the towering Techmarine and I appeared to have in common.

Catching my eye, Drumon returned the smile and nodded a greeting, which clearly astonished those among the assembled officers who noticed it even more than it did me. In fact, I was so taken aback, I took a moment to register the red-robed tech-priest gliding smoothly in his wake, like a gretchin after an ork.[2] I had no idea what the tech-priest's presence portended, but I was pretty sure it was nothing good.

'Captain.' DuPanya stepped forwards to greet Gries, who glanced down at him, then removed his helmet, hanging it at his hip as Drumon had done. Seeing the two men together, I was put incongruously in mind of an adult, tilting his head to listen patiently to an importunate child. 'To what do we owe this unexpected pleasure?'

---

1. From which we can infer that they'd either removed their helmets, and Cain had seen them on some other occasion, or he recognised the personal heraldry on their armour; probably the latter.

2. Not, I suspect, an analogy the Techmarine would have appreciated.

'We have been conferring with the acolytes of the Omnissiah,' Gries explained, without preamble. 'Magos Yaffel believes he has identified the source of the genestealer taint.'

That got everyone's attention, as I'm sure you can imagine. The room, which had gone quiet enough when the Astartes appeared, stilled completely. I could hear little but the susurration of my own breathing, and I'm pretty sure a few of the others stopped even that for a moment. Fortunately, before anyone could turn blue, Drumon and the tech-priest commandeered the hololith, coaxing it into life with a few dextrous touches of their ceramite gauntlets and mechadendrites respectively, while murmuring the litany of activation. We all crowded round, trying to look as though we weren't using our elbows on purpose to obtain a better view, and I did my best to ignore the proximity of Mira, who was taking advantage of the huddle to get considerably closer to me than decorum would normally permit with others present.

'I'm sure you recognise this,' the tech-priest began, in the reedy tones of a voxcaster in need of repair. Like many of his brethren, he'd apparently replaced his vocal cords, and a great deal else, with augmetic systems. As he spoke, he moved slightly, oscillating back and forth like a drunkard attempting to keep pace with the floor; after a moment or two I caught a glimpse of metal beneath his robe, and the coin dropped. The lower half of his body had been removed completely, leaving his torso resting on a metal plate, which in turn was supported by a thin steel tube, attached to a single, fat-tyred wheel. No doubt there was a gyroscope somewhere to impart stability, but, if so, it seemed barely adequate to the task, necessitating constant minor adjustments of balance to keep him from toppling over.

Everyone nodded as an image of the Viridian stellar system appeared, the planet we were standing on marked with the green rune which, somewhat optimistically, identified it as now being safely back in Imperial hands. Most of the significant offworld habs were similarly tagged. This was not surprising. The Reclaimers left behind on the *Revenant* had hardly been idle while the war on the ground was going on, and had retaken the largest rebel stronghold with an ease which had disinclined most of the others to make a fight of it, while the strike cruiser swatted any of the System Defence boats which failed to strike their colours as casually as it had taken care of the one which had been foolish enough to attack us when we'd first emerged from the warp. Only a few red icons marked die-hard dissidents, which quite effectively pinpointed the offworld sites where the 'stealers had managed to gain a significant foothold, and I was pleasantly surprised at how meagre they were.[1]

'A hundred and forty-seven years ago,' the tech-priest went on, apparently indifferent to our nods and murmurs, 'a flare of warp energy was detected in the halo.[2] Analysis at the time suggested an object of considerable mass had emerged, and a System Defence boat was dispatched to investigate. Perhaps fortunately for them, however, the object disappeared back into the immaterium before they were able to provide more than a few long-range sensor records.' Drumon did something at the control lectern, and the image changed to an indistinct blob which looked like nothing so much as a diseased tuber to me. There seemed to be nothing particularly threatening about it, but DuPanya's face had paled. Mira glanced at her father, looking concerned about someone else for the first time since I'd met her.

'The space hulk,' the governor said heavily, and that got a reaction, you can be sure. Gries's shattered visage twitched into the semblance of a frown, and he gazed at DuPanya like a schola tutor faced with a pupil stumbling over the catechism.

'You were aware of this?' he asked, his voice rumbling through the bunker like a distant earthquake.

DuPanya nodded. 'Of course,' he said, recovering fast. 'But as it was only in-system for a few hours, we felt the risk it posed to our security had been negligible. We kept the SDF on alert for a while, but with nothing to shoot at, there didn't seem much point in prolonging the watch.'

---

1. *It's actually not that surprising, as the genestealer cult would have been few in number to start with, and no doubt concentrated on expanding its influence planetside, where most of the institutions it wished to subvert were based. Most of the active rebels in the offworld habs would have been simple dupes of the brood mind, rather than members of it.*

2. *The belt of cometary debris which marks the nominal boundary of a stellar system.*

Concealing my surprise that he was apparently into his second century, which I suppose I should have expected, given what I'd already deduced about the nobility's fondness for juvenat treatments, I nodded judiciously. 'That's understandable,' I said, wondering for the first time if Mira was really quite as young as she appeared, and deciding I didn't much care either way. 'If there were greenskins aboard, I'm sure you would have noticed.'

Several of the Imperial officers smiled at the understatement, an ork invasion hardly being noted for its subtlety, but it seemed Gries had as little time for flippancy as he had for anything else which wasn't about slaughtering the enemies of the Emperor. 'Such complacency was negligent in the extreme,' he said.

DuPanya flushed. 'We could hardly remain on alert indefinitely,' he pointed out, a trifle defensively. 'The populace would have been panicked, to no positive effect. And it's not as if our defences were set up to counter this kind of insidious infiltration in any case.'

Gries didn't have to say 'Perhaps they should have been'. His silence was emphatic enough. To dispel the tension hanging in the air, and forestall any recrimination which was likely to be ripened by it, I stepped in to restore our unity, like the good little commissar I was supposed to be.

'All of which rather begs the question of how the 'stealers got planetside at all,' I said, as if I really wanted to know the answer. 'Magos, I'm sure a man of your erudition has been able to work it out?'

The wobbling half-man looked as pleased as it was possible to with a face composed largely of metal. The acolytes of the Omnissiah are supposed to be above petty human emotions, but I've noticed they seem as susceptible to flattery as anyone else.

'The balance of probabilities would seem to favour an opportunistic boarding by mineral prospectors in search of booty,' he piped, his thin tones in marked contrast to those of the Space Marine captain. 'The halo is full of small vessels, which the SDF crew would have found extremely difficult to distinguish at the range they were, given the masking effect of the hulk and the profusion of cometary debris registering on their auspex.'

That sounded plausible enough to me. It would only take a handful of people to be implanted for the taint to take root, growing stronger with each generation of hybrids, and the crew of a small vessel would do nicely for starters. Particularly if they had room aboard for a purestrain or two, to hurry the process along a bit.

'Which raises another alarming possibility,' I said. 'Given the amount of cargo entering and leaving the system, and the number of vessels carrying it, how sure can we be that some of these abominations haven't taken passage to other parts of the sector, intent on spreading their corruption as widely as they can?' The expressions of the senior officers surrounding me were all the indication I needed of just how much none of them liked that idea.

'That seems unlikely,' Drumon interjected, to everyone's visible relief, 'although it would be prudent to send an astropathic message to the appropriate authorities in the nearby systems.'

'I concur,' Gries agreed. 'Genestealer cults generally remain focussed on subverting one world at a time.' Well, I supposed he'd know, being the greatest local expert on the enemies of the Imperium, and the best way of scraping them off its collective bootsole.

'A more pressing concern is the hulk itself,' Yaffel put in, with the unmistakable air of a man dragging everyone back to the point. 'Wherever it goes, it will continue to infect inhabited systems.'

'Not to mention the ones it's already been through,' I said. I glanced round the bunker, finally managing to catch the eye of the senior intelligence analyst among the general staffers. 'We'll need to search the records, try to find other sightings that match–'

'We have already identified it,' Drumon assured me, the faint trace of amusement I recalled seeing aboard the *Revenant* during my convalescence surfacing briefly again. 'It's the *Spawn of Damnation*, first sighted in 447.M36, in the Spinward Drift. Or, at least, first sighted by anyone who survived to make a report. Its movements are as well known as any piece of warp flotsam.'

'Well, that's a comfort, at least,' I said, trying to sound as though I meant it, and hadn't been disconcerted by the name. Who chose it, and why they can't call these things something a little more cheerful, is beyond me.[1] 'It's a shame we can't warn whoever it's heading for next.'

'Unfortunately, given the nature of the warp, such a prediction cannot be made,' Yaffel said, not quite managing to inject an edge of regret into his mechanical monotone. 'However, it may be possible to follow the hulk to its next destination.'

'How?' DuPanya asked, quite reasonably under the circumstances, while Mira merely pulled a face at me, and made a surprisingly vulgar gesture indicative of mental derangement. Privately, I agreed with her, but if the Astartes were taking this nonsense seriously, the least we could do was hear the fellow out.

'By entering the warp at the same point the hulk did,' Yaffel said, 'and following the current. We've examined the logs of numerous cargo vessels which entered and left the Viridia System over the last century and a half, and the indications are that the flow of the immaterium in this region of space and time have remained reasonably stable.'

'Reasonably stable being something of a relative term,' Drumon interjected again, dryly. 'Following the wrong current will take us to a different system entirely. But we have a good Navigator aboard the *Revenant*, and he considers the gamble a reasonable one.'

'Not to mention the calculations I've made, which should narrow down the possibilities considerably,' Yaffel added.

'Then, forgive me if I'm wrong,' DuPanya said, 'are we to infer that you intend trying to track down the *Spawn of Damnation* in your own ship?'

'We do,' Gries said flatly. His head turned, sweeping his gaze across the assembled officers. 'The Imperial Guard should be capable of resolving matters on Viridia now the back of the rebellion has been broken. Once the operations we currently have under way are concluded, we will depart.'

'You'll be missed,' I said diplomatically, stepping in before any of the Guard officers could say something unfortunate that might

---

1. *Traditionally, space hulks are given their names by the Inquisition conclave responsible for the sector in which they first appear, and, as Cain points out, they do tend towards the melodramatic.*

lead to hurt feelings or worse. 'But we must all do our duty, wherever it leads.'

Looking back, I sometimes wonder whether if I'd just had the sense to hold my tongue at that point I would have avoided a great deal of unpleasantness, but somehow I doubt it. Gries had clearly made his mind up about the whole thing before he voxed me that morning, and a captain of the Astartes is a hard man to say no to. His gaze settled on me.

'Commissar. You may accompany us, if you wish. The *Spawn of Damnation* is a threat to the whole sector, and will continue to be so until it is neutralised. No doubt the higher echelons of the Imperial Guard would value your report of our actions.'

'I've no doubt they would,' I said smoothly, while trying desperately to think of a plausible reason not to get dragged into this lunatic quest. None came to mind, and, once again, I found myself cursing my unfounded reputation. How could I possibly refuse, with a roomful of generals and senior commissars staring at me, mostly with undisguised envy? I shrugged, determined to make the best of it. 'My orders were to liaise with you for as long as you deem necessary, so of course I'm happy to continue. I'll instruct my aide to make the arrangements for our departure.'

'Very well.' Gries nodded, turned and strode out of the bunker without another word, followed by the rest of the Astartes and the wobbling tech-priest. A babble of voices broke out, incredulity and outrage the predominant notes, and I became aware of Mira clutching my arm, her face set.

'Ciaphas,' she said firmly, 'we need to talk. About *us*.'

EIGHT

JURGEN TOOK THE news of our imminent departure in his usual
phlegmatic fashion, although I'm bound to say that I was less than
enthusiastic at the prospect of getting back aboard a starship so
soon after making planetfall. But then, for Jurgen, orders were
sacrosanct. I sometimes suspected that he believed the chain of
command to extend unbroken all the way to the Golden Throne,
so even matters as mundane as the appointment of the day's
latrine orderly were imbued with the unassailable authority of the
Emperor Himself. At any event, he simply nodded and busied
himself about packing my effects with no more than a simple 'Very
good, sir. Will you be wanting a bit of lunch before we leave?'

'I believe so,' I told him, after considering the matter. I'd lost
little time in requisitioning a comm-bead from the newly arrived
Guard contingent, to replace the one the necrons had vaporised
along with the *Omnissiah's Bounty*, so I was able to follow the
Astartes' preparations for departure without bothering Gries,
which probably came as a relief to both of us. Recovering their
active combat squads, who were scattered across half the system,
was going to take a little time, even for warriors of their formidable efficiency, and, true to the code of their Chapter, none of them

would be willing to break contact with a still-living enemy and leave the task they'd been allocated half-done.

Lunch would also be a good opportunity to take my leave of Mira (who I'd managed to detach myself from in the command bunker as quickly and tactfully as possible), on reasonably good terms. Her words had shaken me, which, given some of the perils I've faced in the Emperor's name, you might find surprising, but at least you know where you are with a charging ork. When a woman tells you she wants to talk 'about us', the one thing you can be sure of is that no amount of combat experience is going to get you out unscathed.

To my surprise, and, I must confess, relief, however, my invitation went unacknowledged, save by a sour-faced ladies' maid, who informed me with mingled relish and disdain that her mistress was 'not available.' Remembering the sulky expression on Mira's face as I'd prised her from my arm and found urgent business with the intelligence analyst I'd tried to speak to before, I could well believe it. It had been obvious to me from the moment we'd first got involved with one another that our liaison would be as fleeting as all the others I'd had over the years, my position and duty to the Commissariat making it inevitable that I'd be moving on to another war as soon as the situation on Viridia had stabilised, but Mira's little world had always revolved around her, and I was beginning to realise, somewhat belatedly, that she wasn't going to take kindly to my departure on anyone's terms but her own.

Oh well, too bad, I thought. Heiress to a planet she may have been,[1] but I couldn't see that having much weight with Gries if she tried to argue him into leaving me behind. For a moment the mental picture that conjured up, of the petulant young aristocrat haranguing the Space Marine captain, raised a fleeting smile, before I dismissed it and turned my attention to more pressing matters. 'See if they've got any of those little lizard things, and

---

1. *Which seems to indicate that Cain was never made aware of the existence of Mira's siblings, something most people would have thought to mention at some point under the circumstances: a small, but telling, confirmation of her self-absorption.*

some of that smoked fish pâté, in the kitchen,' I told Jurgen. The rations aboard the *Revenant* were adequate, of course, but fairly basic, the little comforts of life generally coming low on the list of priorities of a Space Marine, and I intended to make the most of the skills of the governor's chef while I still had the chance. 'Otherwise, use your initiative. And get something for yourself, too.'

'Very good, sir,' he said, and departed as quickly as he could without compromising the air of dignity he felt appropriate to someone in the exalted position of a commissar's personal aide, and which he endeavoured to maintain at all times, in blissful ignorance of the fact that it was completely invisible to everyone but him. He returned a short while later with a large covered tray, the contents of which he laid out for me, and a thermal bag leaking steam, which, to my unspoken relief, he bore off to his own quarters, there being few things in the galaxy more likely to curtail the appetite than watching (or listening to) Jurgen stuffing his face.

After concluding our meals there was nothing much else to do, since we had little enough kit between us, and Jurgen had already stowed it, so I found myself in the unwelcome and novel position of time hanging heavily on my hands. I busied myself with make-work, visiting the bunker for one final time to pass on what information I could about the state of affairs the Astartes were leaving behind (a lot of dead heretics, mainly), and pick up the latest news of the Guard campaign in case, in defiance of my expectations, Gries turned out to be interested. (I was right, as it happened; he wasn't. As soon as we'd left the Viridia System, his attention was focussed entirely on the pursuit of the space hulk, and I can't recall him ever mentioning the campaign there again.)

To my relief, I didn't run across DuPanya anywhere in the corridors of the palace, as I was by no means certain how much he knew of my association with his daughter, or of her recent displeasure. As it happened, I never set eyes on him again. I did find Orten hanging around in the command centre, marginalised by the Guard officers but gamely determined to do whatever he could to prevent them from making too much of a mess of his

home world, and made sure I said my farewells to him as publicly
as possible: I don't know if that made anyone take him a little
more seriously, but I hope so.[1]

Of Mira, I saw nothing before quitting the palace, which I must
confess to being ambivalent about. On the one hand, I couldn't
help feeling a certain sense of relief at having avoided a confrontation which would probably have ended in recrimination,
but on the other, I've never liked leaving unfinished business
behind. As Jurgen drove us out of the main courtyard and through
the wreckage of the gardens along the main causeway, which stood
out clearly as a straight strip of mud marginally less churned up
than its surroundings, I found myself glancing back over the
armour plate protecting the crew compartment of the Salamander
he'd requisitioned from somewhere to scan the hundreds of windows in search of a flash of blonde hair; but in vain. At last, as we
passed through the battered gate in the outer wall through which
Trosque had launched his attack on the besiegers, the palace disappeared from sight, and I directed my attention to our immediate
environment.

I hadn't seen much of Fidelis in the relatively short time which
had elapsed since our arrival. On the few occasions I'd ventured
out to compare notes with Guard commanders or Astartes in the
field it had been aboard a Rhino which my hosts had thoughtfully
dispatched, the arrival of which always seemed to excite a certain
degree of interest among Guardsmen and PDF loyalists alike. It
seemed the Reclaimers were still taking the matter of my personal
safety as seriously as the Terminator sergeant had intimated,
which was fine by me. The only downsides that I'd discovered so
far were an inability to see anything beyond the interior of the
APC, which was considerably roomier than the Chimeras I was
familiar with, and the fact that the bench seats were to the same

---

1. *Most Viridian histories of the war credit him with pulling the shattered remnants of
the PDF back into a credible fighting force almost single-handed, and playing a decisive part in finally ridding the planet of the genestealer taint, but we obviously have to
allow for a fair amount of bias and local chauvinism in these accounts. The Imperial
Guard records simply state that he was an effective mediator between them and the
PDF, which might charitably be interpreted as grudging approval.*

scale as the fittings aboard the Thunderhawk: fine for the super-human stature of a Space Marine in powered armour, but distinctly uncomfortable for us ordinary mortals. The upshot of which was that I'd only seen snapshots of the city, as it were, gen-erally a disputed part, where the amount of ambient noise and incoming fire made loitering to sightsee decidedly unwise.

Now, as Jurgen cannonballed us through the streets at his usual breakneck pace, swerving around those few obstacles too solid to bounce our tracks across, I found myself pleasantly surprised. The tide of war had evidently receded from the capital at last, only a few rockpools of unrest remaining to be dealt with, and the first signs of something approaching normality were beginning to appear, like shoots of green among the ashes of a forest fire. The road to the starport was clear of debris, the worst of the cratering marring its surface patched with raw rockcrete dressings, which I suppose was only to be expected given the amount of military traf-fic rumbling along it in both directions. What I hadn't anticipated was the number of civilian vehicles threaded in among them, overloaded cargo haulers for the most part, jammed with furnish-ings, possessions and grim-faced people clinging on for dear life among the detritus of their lives. They were, I suppose, returning to their homes, or the sites where once they stood, hoping to pick up where they'd left off, in defiance of all reason. Most of the ram-shackle transports were graced with icons of the Emperor, and a few meagre offerings had been left at the shrines beside the road, where, no doubt, they'd be purloined as soon as dusk fell, in defi-ance of the curfew.[1]

The side streets, which Jurgen eventually took to, impatient with the restrictions the density of traffic on the main thoroughfare placed on his natural inclination to open the throttle to its maximum and leave it there, were more cluttered, of course, but even here there were signs of returning life, which I found cheering. People were moving among the rubble of the sundered buildings, salvaging what they could, although if the emporium

---

1. *Probably not, in fact, given the average Viridian's tenacious faith in the Golden Throne, although I suppose there were the inevitable exceptions.*

I'd encountered the sentries of the brood mind in was anything to go by, I doubted that the looters would have left them much.[1] In a few places the smoke of cooking fires rose from within the ruins, where enough of the original structures remained to keep the rain off, occasionally supplemented with tarpaulins or other makeshift materials.

Few of the people we passed spared us a glance, with the inevitable exception of the children, who were playing amid the ruins with the total absorption in the concerns of the moment peculiar to the very young. They tended to glance up as we hurtled by, stones and chunks of pulverised rockcrete scattering from our treads, shouting or waving, before returning to their games.

As yet, there seemed little in the way of organised rebuilding, although we caught occasional glimpses of what might have been the beginning of a coordinated effort at returning Fidelis to habitability. A handful of tech-priests seemed to be abroad, roaming the city in ones and twos, making earnest notes in their data-slates or poking about in conduits, while a party of sappers from one of the Vostroyan regiments was erecting flakboard huts in a park Jurgen couldn't be bothered to circumvent, presumably intended to house the hopeful occupants of the lorries we'd seen earlier. The only building under active repair that we passed was a local temple, where ragged refugees were laying bricks under the supervision of an elderly ecclesiarch, no doubt in exchange for the promise of food and a bed for the night.[2]

A few moments later our progress began to slow again, and I poked my head over the armour plate surrounding the passenger compartment, reaching for my laspistol by reflex as I did so. Normally I liked to have the Salamanders I requisitioned fitted with a pintel mount, so I'd have something a bit more lethal to

---

1. *In fact they were probably more interested in searching for building materials than items of value.*

2. *As so often, Cain's habitual cynicism where members of the Ecclesiarchy are concerned may have led him to miss the point. Given the devout nature of so many Viridians, it's entirely possible that the labourers he saw were repairing the temple for spiritual rather than pragmatic reasons.*

hand if things went ploin-shaped, but Jurgen had just had to take what he could find in the vehicle pool, leaving me to make do with my sidearm if push came to shove. A Caledonian sergeant, in a mottled camo-patterned uniform similar to the one Orten favoured, was flagging us down, the squad of troopers with him regarding us with the wary eyes of combat veterans. They were keeping their lasguns trained on us, just as they should have done with so much PDF kit still in the hands of insurrectionists and troublemakers, and I was pleased to see that they kept them on aim even after my uniform had become visible.

'Commissar.' The sergeant nodded a greeting, no doubt wondering if he or any of his men were in trouble, but determined not to show it. Very few Guardsmen are pleased to see a red sash, which no doubt accounts for the inordinate number of my colleagues felled by friendly-fire accidents. 'We weren't told to expect you.'

'Probably because I had no idea any of our people were down here,' I said, noting the faint stirring of relief among the soldiers. 'My aide and I are on our way to the aerodrome.' I smiled at the troopers, who were still keeping us covered. 'You can stand down. We're not hybrids or 'stealer puppets.'

'Of course not,' the sergeant agreed, stepping forwards, a trifle nervously, with a portable auspex. 'But if you wouldn't mind indulging me, sir? I'm sure you wouldn't want us to neglect our orders.'

'By no means,' I agreed, reholstering my laspistol and climbing down to the roadway so he could take his genescan a little more easily. The unit beeped, and a rune flashed green, after which everyone looked a little more comfortable, particularly once Jurgen was confirmed to be a reasonable approximation of a human as well. 'You're to be commended for your caution.'

That went down well, as I'd known it would. There are far better ways of managing troops than simply putting the fear of the Emperor into them, as I try to convince the young pups in my care these days, in the vague hope that their careers will last a bit longer than their first night patrol.

The sergeant nodded. 'That's the worst thing about fighting 'stealers,' he agreed. 'You never know who might turn out to be a hybrid or an implant. Squadmate of mine turned on us on Keffia, just like that, no warning, been with us since basic. Had to shoot him myself.'

'I was there too,' I said, not wanting to remember too much about it. 'Similar thing happened. Bad business all round.'

The sergeant shrugged. 'I never liked him, mind. And I got his stripe. For showing initiative. So it could have been worse.'

I smiled again. 'You're a born optimist, sergeant. The Guard needs men like you.'

'Kind of you to say so, sir.' And, Emperor help me, he actually blushed. 'But you'll have to go round, I'm afraid. The street's impassable.'

'We'll get through,' Jurgen said, with quiet confidence, taking the statement as a challenge, as I'd known he would.

The sergeant shook his head. 'I doubt it,' he said. Jurgen might have been about to argue the point, but subsided, at a look from me.

'Impassable how?' I asked, and the sergeant shrugged.

'It's not there,' he said simply. Well, that sounded distinctly peculiar, so I left the Salamander with its engine running, and walked off down the rubble-strewn carriageway. For the first hundred metres or so, nothing seemed to have changed, the ravaged cityscape looming over me, and my bootsoles scraping against the smaller chunks of debris littering the 'crete.

Then the road ended, as sharply and abruptly as if excised with a knife. For a few metres the road surface became rippled, like a hardened lava flow, then simply dropped away into a broad pit, some three or four metres deep. It may seem incredible, reading this now, but my first thought was simply how lucky we'd been to have run into the troopers when we did; if they hadn't flagged us down, we might well have discovered the hole by falling into it. Then, as I began to take in the way the edges of the buildings around me had also melted and flowed like candle wax, realisation belatedly hit. This was where Mira and I had fought our desperate battle beneath the ground, and come so close to extinction before the Thunderhawk had torn the roof off to allow the Terminators to come to our rescue.

I can't be sure how long I stood there, reliving the horror and marvelling at the precision of our saviours, before a familiar odour brought me back to myself.

'That's a big hole,' Jurgen commented, materialising at my shoulder, his lasgun held ready for use as always.

I nodded. 'It is indeed,' I agreed, picking out the tunnel the pure-strains had emerged from at last. Nothing was left of the creatures which had attacked us, save a few greasy stains on the rain-streaked rockcrete below; some of the Terminators had carried flamers, and made sure that every last one had been consigned to the pyre before they broke off. I couldn't help wondering how many more of the xenos spawn still lurked beneath our feet, though, or how many apparent innocents still carried their taint. But that wasn't my problem any longer, thanks to Gries and the libratory tech-priest Yaffel.

'It'll take some filling in,' Jurgen added, after a moment or two of further deliberation.

'I'm sure it will,' I said, turning away at last, before my imagination could start playing tricks with the echoes. 'Can you find your way round it? We've still got a shuttle to catch.'

Jurgen nodded. 'Leave it to me,' he said.

THANKS TO MY aide's usual robust driving style, the unexpected detour didn't detain us overmuch: we reached the landing pad just as the Thunderhawk I'd arrived aboard, or its identical twin I'd noticed in the hangar bay, roared in over our heads and snuggled itself down between the blast walls like a raptor returning to its nest. Mine wasn't the only head turning to follow it: the scores of Guardsmen and Navy hands scurrying about the place were undoubtedly accustomed to the ceaseless arrival and departure of Valkyries, Aquilae and Throne alone knew how many other types of shuttle, drop-ship and combat craft, but the distinctive silhouette of the Astartes vessel grabbed their attention at once.

Jurgen, fortunately, remained as phlegmatic as ever, apparently considering it nothing more than a ship like any other, and weaved his way through the distracted ground crews with his usual aplomb, missing cargo haulers and foot sloggers by a typically narrow margin. Fortunately the noise of our engine, and the idling Thunderhawk, drowned out the comments which followed us, although the gestures which accompanied them were more than sufficient to convey their gist.

As he steered us through the slalom of blast walls surrounding the pad,[1] it became clear that Jurgen and I weren't the only guests of the Chapter intending to embark for the *Revenant* that afternoon. Magos Yaffel was there too, oscillating even more than usual in the backwash from the idling thrusters, accompanied by a handful of tech-adepts, and a couple of servitors, which were busily engaged in transferring an unfeasibly large collection of boxes and bundles aboard. As Jurgen coasted the Salamander to a halt, and began collecting our kit together, I hopped down and nodded a cordial greeting to the cogboys.[2]

'Magos,' I said, raising my voice a little to be heard over the screaming engines, 'I wasn't aware that you'd be accompanying us.'

'The Omnissiah directs our footsteps along the path of knowledge,' Yaffel replied, cranking up the volume of his voxcaster to overcome the din. Refraining from pointing out that in his case that would be singularly difficult, I merely nodded, as if the evident quotation[3] meant something to me. 'And the potential store of data to be reaped on this endeavour is incalculable.' At the time I thought his words to be no more than a simple figure of speech. If I'd known then what he was driving at, I'd have clambered back aboard the Salamander and told Jurgen to head for the horizon with all the speed he could squeeze from it (which I've no doubt would have been considerable). As it was, however, I merely

---

1. *Intended to reduce the sound of the vertical thrusters, which would always be loudest at takeoff and landing, and contain the worst of an explosion in the event of an accident.*

2. *A faintly derisive nickname for acolytes of the Machine-God, common among Imperial Guardsmen, apparently derived from the cogwheel symbol of their calling.*

3. *From* Soylens Viridians for the Machine-Spirit, *a populist work intended to make some of the principles by which the Adeptus Mechanicus operates comprehensible to the vast majority of us with little understanding or interest in technotheology: a no doubt laudable aim, which it signally fails to achieve, being too abstruse for the lay reader, and too simplistic for even the lowliest tech-priest. Its author, unsurprisingly, was Magos Yaffel, one of the handful of people actually to have read it.*

exchanged a few more reflexive pleasantries, before following my overloaded aide to the bottom of the boarding ramp, and dodging out of the way of a servitor on its way back for another load of whatever Yaffel and his cronies considered essential on the voyage.

As I regained my balance, another vehicle drew up smoothly alongside our abandoned Salamander, and I felt a strange unease descend upon me. It was a groundcar, long and sleek, its armour-crys windows polarised to the same glossy black as the bodywork. For some reason I was put in mind of the blank, reflective faces of the metal killers I'd fled from on Interitus Prime. Which I'd almost rather have faced again, if my sudden intuition about the car's passenger turned out to be right.

It was. A uniformed chauffeur, in a livery I'd come to know well since my arrival here, unfolded himself from the driver's compartment and glided round to the rear door. As he opened it Mira emerged, the sudden change in her expression a clear indication that the vehicle was soundproofed as effectively as it was shielded from the vulgar gaze of the hoi polloi, and waved cheerfully in my direction.

I waved back, masking my relief at her evident good humour with a faint smile meant to convey pleased surprise, and she came trotting over, grinning like a puppy who's just discovered how to open the meat locker. She'd evidently got tired of playing soldiers, as she'd discarded the dress-up uniform in favour of something a little more feminine: an indigo blouse, low-cut, like pretty much everything else in her wardrobe, and a crimson knee-length skirt, which, like the blouse, was fashioned from some material that shimmered slightly as the light caught it. In the turbulence thrown up by the Thunderhawk's idling thrusters it rippled constantly, so that Mira seemed to be clothed by a nimbus of rainbows. Her footwear was surprisingly practical: calf-high boots made from the hide of some local animal, although I doubted that their original owner had been quite so fluorescently pink.

'Mira,' I said, exhaling a little more strongly than I intended as she enveloped me in a hug which would have cracked an ork's ribs. 'It was kind of you to come and see me off.'

'I'm not.' She grinned again, and with a definite sense of

foreboding I belatedly registered the fact that the chauffeur was removing what looked like almost as much baggage as the tech-priests had accumulated from the car. 'I'm coming too. Isn't that a wonderful surprise?'

'Wonderful doesn't even begin to cover it,' I said truthfully.

NINE

Perhaps fortunately, the ear-splitting noise inside the Thunderhawk after it took off made further conversation impossible. There were the headsets Veren had drawn my attention to on the journey down, of course, but the last thing I needed was Mira vox-casting the details of our association across an open commnet, so I made sure the one I gave her just prior to our departure was switched off before handing it over. Though grateful for the aural protection it offered, I declined to activate mine, either: I had no interest in anything the tech-priests might have to say, and I knew from long experience that Jurgen would simply lapse into sullen silence the second our skids left the ground, too preoccupied with holding on to his last meal until we reached the turbulence-free zone beyond the atmosphere to respond to anything short of a life-threatening emergency. Or possibly an acute lack of tanna. In any event, he was hardly a sparkling conversationalist at the best of times, so I wasn't exactly left feeling deprived.

All of which left me with far too much time to brood. I'd had a few moments before we lifted to ask Mira what the frak she was doing here, although of course I was rather more circumspect about the manner in which I phrased the question, and she'd smiled in a manner I found distinctly disturbing. Before she could answer, though, the tech-priests had started trooping aboard, and Jurgen returned to inform me that our kit was properly stowed, so I'd had little option but to follow the herd and hope everything had a rational explanation. Mira certainly wasn't behaving in the usual fashion of people bidding farewell to their home world, gazing at it through the viewports as long as they could, trying to burn the image of it into their memories in the near certainty of never seeing it again, preferring instead to smile at me in a manner uncomfortably reminiscent of a bored eldar reaver looking for someone to torture to death to pass the time. Perhaps she simply lacked the imagination to grasp what embarking on a voyage through the warp actually meant. Even if she did return home, the chances were that decades, or even a century or two, were likely to have passed, and that she'd be as much of a stranger to the altered Viridia as an offworlder setting eyes on it for the first time.[1]

Predictably, I didn't get another chance to broach the subject until after the Thunderhawk had docked with the *Revenant*, after a journey Jurgen had probably found mercifully brief. The strike cruiser was still orbiting Viridia at a relatively low altitude, barely beyond the point where the first faint wisps of upper atmosphere would begin to drag at her hull, no doubt to facilitate the use of her teleportarium, or allow her weapon batteries to strike at targets on the surface in the unlikely event of her Space Marine complement requiring a little additional assistance. It still seemed long enough to me, though, and it was with a great sense of relief that I heard our engines throttling back, and the series of metallic clangs which preceded our arrival. What Yaffel and his tech-priests found to amuse them, I have no idea. Perhaps they conversed among themselves, in the peculiar manner of their kind, or just remained absorbed in communing with their data-slates.

I didn't have much opportunity to talk to Mira after we disembarked, either. To my pleased surprise Drumon was standing at the

---

1. *It was also possible, of course, that Cain's suspicions about her true age were correct, and that this wasn't the first occasion on which she'd boarded a starship.*

bottom of the ramp, and exchanged a few words of greeting with me, before striding on to confer with the tech-priests and begin examining the equipment they'd brought with them. By the time I'd completed the pleasantries and looked round for Milady DuPanya, she'd already snared a couple of faintly stunned-looking Chapter serfs, who'd evidently been incautious enough to wander within hectoring range, and was holding forth to them in great detail about the correct disposal of her luggage. I decided to leave her to it, and went to separate Jurgen and Gladden, the factotum who'd been assigned to look after me on the voyage here, who were already squabbling over the matter of who should be responsible for my kit with belligerent tenacity and icy politeness respectively. Apparently no one had expected me to bring my own aide, let alone one who looked more like a Nurgle cultist than a member of the Imperial Guard, so his arrival had caught them on the hop, rather.

By the time I'd sorted that one out, Drumon and the tech-priests had disappeared about whatever business they had together, and the pile of luggage Mira had brought with her had diminished to something approaching portable. I lingered while the last of it was thrown onto a trolley which looked as though it was more usually employed to rearm the Thunderhawks, and fell into step beside her. 'I give up,' I said lightly, contriving to look as though I was joking. 'What did you say you were doing here?'

'I'm the official representative of the Governor of Viridia,' she said, grinning impishly at me from under her fringe. 'My father's sent me to assess whether the space hulk remains any kind of threat to our system.'

'How can it?' I asked, no doubt looking and sounding as baffled as I felt. 'It's been gone for a century and a half, and it's hardly likely to come back.'

'But it could have left other threats behind, as well as the genestealers,' Mira said, in tones which made it abundantly clear that she didn't believe that any more than I did. 'We'd be failing in our duty to the Viridian populace if we didn't make every effort to ensure their safety, particularly now.'

'So your father asked you to come along on the hunt for the

Spawn?' I enquired, trying to keep my scepticism from becoming audible in my voice.

Mira grinned again. 'I sort of volunteered,' she said cheerfully, taking hold of my arm.

I nodded, being able to reconstruct that conversation all too easily. This had all been her idea, clearly, although I still found it hard to credit that she'd become sufficiently infatuated during our brief affair to be willing to wave goodbye to everything she'd known just to follow me through the warp.[1] 'How very dutiful of you,' I responded. 'No doubt the populace will be suitably grateful.'

'No doubt,' Mira agreed, clearly not giving a flying one what the hoi polloi thought, and attaching herself to me with a tight grip. 'So it looks as though we'll be liaising together for the foreseeable future.'

DESPITE THE FAINT sense of unease about the situation which continued to oppress me, particularly in the quieter moments when I had time to reflect on the potential ramifications, I had to admit that Mira's words in the hangar bay had cheered me at least as much as they gave me cause for disquiet. As I've said before, she was pleasant enough company, and I'd felt rather starved of companionship during the voyage to Viridia once I'd recovered enough to start taking notice of my surroundings. This time round, although the circumstances were somewhat bizarre, I had someone I felt I could converse with, as well as engaging in a variety of recreational pursuits, all of which promised to make my second sojourn aboard the *Revenant* a great deal more congenial than the first had been.

Then, too, I had Jurgen with me again, which fact alone eased my mind considerably. We'd been through a lot together since our first chance meeting on Desolatia (and were to go through even more in the years to come, although, perhaps mercifully, I had little inkling of quite how much terror and bloodshed awaited me

---

1. *I must say I find that all too plausible: Cain possessed considerable personal charm and was perfectly willing to use it to get whatever he wanted from people. A particular kind of woman would be extremely susceptible to that, especially if she wasn't overly bright to begin with.*

before I could sink into a relatively peaceful retirement[1]), and the prospect of facing whatever horrors awaited us aboard the *Spawn of Damnation* seemed far less daunting than they would have done without the knowledge that he would be watching my back as steadfastly as always. Not that I had any intention of getting within a thousand kilometres of the cursed piece of warp flotsam, of course, so anything lurking within the tangled mess of conjoined starships was of little interest to me; once we'd caught up with it, if we ever did, the shipmaster and his gunnery teams could carve it up at their leisure, and in the unlikely event of anything getting off before they did, it would have to be foolish in the extreme to try boarding a Space Marine vessel.

All in all, I suppose, I felt as happy about the fool's errand we were on as it was possible to under the circumstances, and resolved to make the best of things – an endeavour which Mira seemed determined to help with.

'I'm still not sure how you managed to persuade Gries to let you aboard in the first place,' I said, over a surprisingly palatable meal in my quarters, a few hours after we'd boarded. A fair proportion of her mountain of luggage turned out to have been delicacies of one sort or another, no doubt with my comments about the Spartan fare I'd subsisted on during our voyage to Viridia fresh in her mind. It felt odd to be eating a second breakfast when my body clock insisted it was late evening, but I'd hopped between enough worlds by now to be confident that I'd have readjusted to the *Revenant's* idea of chronology before too much longer. Gladden had got used to bringing my meals in to me here on the previous voyage, and resumed the arrangement without being asked; no doubt the serfs would have been as uncomfortable to see Mira and I in their mess hall as we would have felt about being there. What the Reclaimers did about meals, I had no idea, but if they ate together at all I was certain they'd find catering to the tastes and needs of ordinary mortals something of a trial. At any

---

1. *Which probably indicates that this portion of his memoirs was compiled before the tyranid incursions and the Black Crusade were to drag him back to reluctant active service in the closing years of the 41st millennium.*

event, neither Mira nor myself were ever invited to join them,
which I'm sure we found as much of a relief as our hosts did.[1]

Mira shrugged and bit into the florn cake she'd just spread with
ackenberry preserve. 'You know how it is,' she began, a trifle indistinctly, before swallowing and continuing more clearly. 'You can
get people to do pretty much anything, if you put your mind to it.
You just need to know how to ask.'

Which didn't really answer my question, of course, and being an
old hand at verbal evasion myself, I persisted, even as I admired
her technique. After a few more moments of verbal sparring,
which I have to confess I rather enjoyed, I eventually backed her
into having to give a straight answer.

'It was easy enough,' she admitted, licking a few stray traces of
the sticky preserve from her fingers with a coquettish glance in my
direction, to see if I'd be distracted by that old trick. (Which, I'm
bound to say, I might have been if I didn't already know her as
well as I did, so I just kept looking at her with an expression of
polite enquiry until she gave it up as a bad job and carried on.) 'I
simply told him it was my duty as a member of the ruling house
to confirm that Viridia was safe, just as it was his after having
pledged his aid to our people to make sure that the job was complete.'

'I see,' I said, contriving to look unimpressed, although if I'd still
been wearing my cap at the time I'd have taken it off to her.
Basically, she'd just told a captain of the Astartes that charging off
on a private quest before making sure that every single 'stealer,
hybrid and implant on Viridia had been tracked down and eradi-
cated[2] would be a gross dereliction of his duty, but he could do

---

1. *Astartes do, of course, eat, although most of them seem to regard doing so merely as
providing fuel for their enhanced metabolisms, taking little more pleasure in the act
than members of the Adeptus Mechanicus do. The real reason for the Reclaimers' reluctance to invite their guests to join them was probably that such gatherings are generally
regarded as providing spiritual as well as physical sustenance, being accompanied by
prayers to the Emperor and the Chapter's primarch, and readings from their own martial litanies. Doing so in the presence of outsiders, and thereby revealing some of their
Chapter's most sacred mysteries to non-initiates, would, of course, be anathema to them.*

2. *Which would have, and did, take years.*

what he liked without impugning the honour of his Chapter if he took her along too, as that would make it an extension of his original assignment. Had it not been for her complete self-absorption, she would have been an extraordinary asset to Imperial diplomacy.

'How long do you think it'll be before we catch up with the *Spawn*?' Mira asked, after her final recon sweep among the empty platters littering the tray had failed to turn up any further comestibles.

I shrugged. 'Hard to say,' I said, which sounded a little more authoritative than 'frakked if I know,' which was actually the truth of the matter. 'I suppose it depends on how good the Navigator is at reading the warp currents, and whether Yaffel has got his calculations right. Even if everything goes perfectly, which it never does, we'll probably be following the damned thing for months – if we ever catch up with it at all.'

'Sounds like we're in for rather a dull time, then,' Mira concluded.

'Yes, I'm afraid so,' I agreed, little guessing how far off the mark that was going to turn out to be, and just as well too for my peace of mind. 'We'll just have to amuse ourselves as best we can.'

'I'm sure we can think of something,' she said, before yawning spectacularly and stretching in a manner which emphasised her natural undulations in a decidedly pleasing fashion.

'Looks like you're ready for bed,' I said, chiming for Jurgen to come in and clear the debris of our meal. It seemed he and Gladden had reached the sort of compromise that only occurs or matters to underlings jealous of their status in colliding hierarchies, and that henceforth refreshments and their subsequent remains were to be handed from one to the other in the corridor leading to the guest quarters – which seemed like a pointless duplication of effort to me, but if it kept my aide happy, then good luck to him.

Mira grinned at me, the familiar mischievous expression on her face. 'I thought you'd never ask,' she said.

* * *

IN THE END, we weren't left to speculate about our mission for very long. After a few hours' sleep, which left me sufficiently refreshed to resume my duties, and left Mira somewhat cranky to say the least, Jurgen's distinctive aroma oozed into my quarters again, accompanied by the more fragrant one of freshly brewed tanna. 'Captain Gries presents his compliments, sir, and would like to see you on the bridge at your earliest convenience,' he informed me, busying himself with the tanna pot and a pair of tea bowls.

'What about me?' Mira asked, following him in from the direction of her own stateroom, still looking somewhat the worse for wear despite a change of clothes and a spraybath. It seemed she found the beds the Reclaimers provided for their guests a little too firm for comfort, although I found mine considerably more conducive to sleep than the overstuffed mattresses of the palace in Fidelis had been.

Jurgen nodded. 'I brought an extra bowl in, miss, in case you fancied one too.'

'Just get me a recaf,' she snapped. 'And that's not what I meant.'

The intransigent expression I knew only too well began to settle across my aide's grimy features, and I stepped in hastily to head off the inevitable clash. 'If you wouldn't mind, Jurgen,' I added.

'Of course not, commissar,' he said, his equanimity at least partially restored by the belated courtesy, albeit one that had arrived by proxy. The look he gave Mira's oblivious back as he left, however, made it abundantly clear that the slight wouldn't be forgotten easily or soon. 'And I've no messages concerning the young lady.'

'Thank you,' I said, as he disappeared down the corridor, the door hissing closed behind him. I picked up the drink he'd prepared and sipped it gratefully, regarding Mira gravely through the steam. 'Please don't treat Jurgen like one of your household servants,' I said, as soon as I was sure he was out of earshot. 'He's an Imperial Guardsman, and the aide of a commissar, with an exemplary record of courage in the face of the enemy. He deserves a bit of respect.'

Mira stared at me, her jaw working for a moment like a ruminating bovine, and the sullen expression I hadn't seen since the day of our first meeting smeared itself across her face. Then, as abruptly as the mist burning off from an early-morning hab spire, it had gone, displaced by another jaw-cracking yawn.

'Of course,' she said. 'Sorry. Not enough sleep.' Then the gamine grin was back. 'It was worth it, though.'

Perhaps fortunately I was spared having to find a reply to that by the return of Jurgen, who ushered the tray-bearing form of Gladden through the door, with an airy wave in Mira's direction. The odour of recaf began to mingle with the others in the room, which was beginning to seem decidedly cramped by now, despite the high ceiling. 'She's in there,' he said perfunctorily, then returned his attention to me. 'I found Gladden outside, sir, looking for the young lady, so I took the liberty of directing him in here. Seeing as she seemed in so much of a hurry.'

'Thank you, Jurgen,' Mira said, with a smile which surprised me almost as much as it evidently did my aide. 'That was very thoughtful of you. Especially as I'd been so unforgivably rude. I'm afraid I'm not at my best when I've just woken up.'

'That's all right, miss,' Jurgen said, fully mollified by the unexpected apology. 'You should see the commissar first thing in the morning.'

'Quite,' I said, while Mira turned away from him, suppressing a fit of the giggles with manifest difficulty. 'Was there anything else, Jurgen?'

'Not for the moment, sir,' my aide said, retreating from the room with an unmistakably self-satisfied air, while Mira fell on the recaf like a kroot on fresh meat.

Gladden coughed delicately. 'The brother-captain extends greetings to the Viridian envoy in the name of the Reclaimers, and suggests you may find a visit to the bridge informative, madam.'

'Then in the name of the Viridian Hegemony, I reciprocate his salutations, and will attend upon him with all due dispatch,' Mira responded, with a remarkably straight face.

'I'll be along too, as soon I've finished my tea,' I said, refilling the tanna bowl.

Gladden looked mildly disconcerted for a moment, but recovered quickly. 'Then I'll convey the news of your imminent arrivals,' he said, and left the room as quickly as he could without appearing to hurry.

Mira turned an accusing eye on me. 'Ciaphas, that was mean,' she said, not quite succeeding in hiding her amusement. 'He was only doing his job.' She lifted the lid from a side plate, next to her recaf, and studied the lumps of reconstituted protein thus revealed with a faintly suspicious frown, before stuffing one into her mouth with a resigned shrug.

'I suppose you're right,' I said, feeling as though I'd been somehow caught out by her. 'But I've never been comfortable with all that flowery protocol stuff.' I'd been getting a lot more used to it since being attached to brigade headquarters, of course, which had meant attending more tedious diplomatic functions than I'd ever thought possible back in my early days with the 12th Field Artillery, but I much preferred people to either say what they meant, or lie to me in plain, simple language. Still do, if I'm honest, although I suppose it was good practice for much later on in my career, when I found myself attached to the lord general's staff, and having to hack my way through thickets of polite obfuscatory verbiage on an almost daily basis. Luckily, by that time, my fraudulent reputation was so widespread I was able to sidestep the game entirely, playing up to my image of the bluff man of action, so I never had to learn to talk like that. Which was probably just as well, or my brain would have had to shut down in sheer self defence.

Mira shrugged, failing to offer me any of the nutritionally balanced whatever-it-was she was throwing down her neck, and washed the final lump away with a chug of recaf. 'How do you think I feel?' she asked rhetorically. 'I grew up thinking that sort of soil improver was plain Gothic.'

'Then I'm amazed you turned out as well adjusted as you did,' I said, wondering for a moment just how sarcastic I was being, but Mira appeared to take the remark at face value.

'It's not been easy,' she remarked complacently, and brushed a few crumbs from her inevitably exposed cleavage. 'Do you think this is a little louche for visiting the bridge?'

I examined the day gown she'd donned with a critical eye. It was cut from some shimmering gold fabric, which seemed to be held up by nothing more than willpower, and moulded itself snugly around whatever it touched.[1] The effect was certainly striking, particularly if the one you were after was that of a highly priced courtesan, but hardly suited to a military environment. I was sure the Astartes and the Mechanicus drones wouldn't be distracted at all, if they even noticed it, but the ship and its defences were in the hands of flesh-and-blood mortals, who might find their attention wandering at a critical moment, so pleasant as the view was in the abstract...

'Possibly,' I temporised. 'Perhaps something a little more businesslike would be better.'

'Why, Ciaphas Cain.' Mira grinned at me again, with a coquettish tilt to her head, which made her look more like a fifty-credit joy-girl than ever. 'I do believe you're jealous.' Then, before I could gather my wits to do anything more than gape in astonishment, she undulated out of the room.

---

1. *Probably static cling. I used to have a dress like that, but it was never quite the same after a firefight with some hrud; and concealing a weapon while wearing it was always extremely uncomfortable, so I never bothered to find a replacement.*

TEN

BY THE TIME Mira returned, rather more suitably attired in what she told me was one of her hunting outfits, I'd managed to convince myself that she'd been joking. After all, the very idea of me being resentful of other men appreciating her physical attributes was ludicrous enough to begin with, let alone the fact that most of the potential rivals for her affections aboard the *Revenant* would either have been tech-priests or Space Marines, and therefore out of the running. Which left only the serfs, who I doubted she'd even consider in that regard, given her typically aristocratic tendency to view the lower orders as little more than a refined type of servitor which didn't dribble lubricants on the carpet, and Jurgen, who was hardly the stuff a maiden's dreams were made of, unless she'd eaten too much cheese before turning in.

'Very suitable,' I complimented her, having had no idea until now that her wardrobe contained anything even remotely practical. It had definitely risen to the occasion this time, though, providing a jacket and trousers in muted colours, and a stout pair of boots, all of which lent her an air of businesslike efficiency, without overstating the effect. Fortunately, she appeared to have left the fowling piece that went with it at home.

Mira pulled a face. 'It's all a bit dowdy, if you ask me,' she said, examining the effect critically in a nearby mirror. 'Perhaps I should try again.'

'We're expected on the bridge,' I said, mindful of the length of time she'd already wasted rummaging through her luggage, and leaned in to straighten my cap in the looking glass she'd appropriated. Jurgen handed me my weapon belt. 'We can't keep our hosts waiting any longer,' I went on, checking the power levels in the laspistol and the chainsword's motivator cells, before fastening it into place. 'It wouldn't be polite or diplomatic.'

'Says the man who thinks "tact" means "nailed down",' Mira said, following me out into the corridor. At least she wasn't arguing about it, though, which I suppose was something.

'I'm a soldier,' I said, taking refuge behind my public persona. Something was getting to her, that much was obvious, but I couldn't for the life of me see what it was. 'That means I take my duties seriously.' Whenever there was a good chance that someone was watching me, anyway.

'You can be really pompous sometimes, do you know that?' Mira asked, in the tone of voice women use when they neither want nor expect an answer, and strode off ahead of me looking sulkier than ever.

I remembered enough of the layout of the *Revenant* to find my way to the bridge without difficulty, and fortunately, by the time we got there, either Mira's mood had improved, or she was practising her diplomatic skills again. As I'd expected, the warren of corridors had proven sufficiently daunting for her to have rejoined me without a word a few moments after her inexplicable burst of bad temper, and she seemed to be on her best behaviour as soon as we were in the presence of our hosts once more.

'Commissar. You are prompt, as always,' Gries greeted me, politely and inaccurately as we entered the bridge, and Drumon looked up from a huddle of tech-priests he was conferring with next to the hololith just long enough to nod a greeting in my direction. Mira gave me a sharp look, as though I'd somehow contrived to upstage her on purpose. 'Milady DuPanya. Your presence is appreciated.'

'But not that much, apparently,' she muttered *sotto voce*, apparently forgetting the preternaturally keen senses with which the Emperor had seen fit to endow his chosen warriors. If either of the Astartes present overheard her, however, they were too polite, or indifferent, to respond.

'Are the last of your combat teams aboard yet?' I asked, keen to show that I was taking an interest, and Gries nodded.

'They are,' he assured me. 'Squad Trosque completed the cleansing of the forge complex on Asteroid 459 while you were sleeping, and their Thunderhawk docked a few moments ago. Nothing remains to be done beyond the mopping up of a few isolated remnants of the infection and the restoration of good governance, both tasks for which the Imperial Guard seem admirably suited.'

'I concur,' I said, although being far more familiar with the way the Guard worked than he was, I felt rather less sanguine than the Reclaimers' captain about how easy the job would turn out to be.[1]

'Then it appears my people owe yours a considerable debt of gratitude,' Mira said, with a formal tilt of the head to the towering Space Marine, who turned his own to look at her as though one of the chairs had just spoken.

'Our service to the Emperor is reward enough,' he said, 'although your consideration is appreciated.'

'I'm pleased to hear it,' Mira replied dryly.

'Are we under way, then?' I asked, feeling faintly foolish at having to ask. The barely perceptible thrumming of the *Revenant's* engines had become so familiar to me in the course of our voyage to Viridia that I hadn't noticed it since boarding, although it was certainly there, a comforting presence in the background. They would have been idling while it was in orbit, of course, ticking over just sufficiently to provide power to feed the innumerable machine-spirits on whose health the vessel depended, and I listened hard, trying to determine if the note had deepened at all; but if it had, I wasn't able to tell the difference.

---

1. *Not without reason: almost a decade was to pass before the Ordo Xenos felt able to declare Viridia free of taint with any degree of certainty, and the local authorities remain vigilant for any sign of a renewed outbreak to this day.*

'We are,' the shipmaster informed me from his control throne.

I was a little surprised, but apparently questions regarding the functioning of the ship were delegated to him automatically by his masters, which was no bad thing; I'd hate to be aboard a vessel in combat whose captain had to refer every tactical decision to a higher authority. 'We'll be entering the warp at the designated material coordinates in approximately seven hours.'

'Six hours, fifty-four minutes and twelve point three one four seconds,' Magos Yaffel put in sharply from his position by the hololith. 'As I've explained, timing is absolutely crucial if we're to enter the warp currents in this particular region of space and time in precisely the right configuration to catch the fastest-flowing portion of the stream.'

'We'll catch it, magos,' the shipmaster assured him, 'Omnissiah willing.' Then, to my surprise, he made the sign of the cogwheel, which the tech-priests and Astartes present all echoed.

'Forgive my ignorance,' I said, approaching the hololith, 'but if we're merely going to be following the same current as the space hulk, how can we hope to catch up with it? Won't we be travelling at the same rate?'

'A very astute question,' Yaffel said, in the manner of a born didact pouncing on the opportunity to expound on his favourite subject. 'But the situation isn't as hopeless as you might suppose. Don't forget that the *Spawn of Damnation* is drifting, while the *Revenant* is moving under power. That means we can correct our attitude and orientation to the current, to optimise the flow around our Geller field.'

'And in simple language for the rest of us?' Mira muttered, then had the grace to blush as Drumon answered the comment she'd clearly believed to be inaudible.

'I gather the sport of waveboarding[1] is popular in some of the coastal regions of your world?' he asked, and Mira nodded, although Emperor alone knows how he discovered this. 'Then

---

1. *A peculiar form of recreation, practised in some form on many worlds, in which people attempt to balance on a plank being swept along by waves or water currents for as long as possible without falling off. Since they inevitably do, the appeal of the pastime escapes me.*

think of us as riding a waveboard, while the hulk just bobs about as the Emperor sees fit. Does that make things clearer?'

'I suppose so,' Mira said, as politely as she could. 'Thanks.'

'In addition,' Yaffel said, trying not to sound miffed at the interruption, 'the *Spawn of Damnation* will be returning to the materium at random intervals, for indeterminate periods of time, some of which will be in the order of years. We, on the other hand, can enter and leave the warp at will. As soon as we determine that it's not at a given exit point, we can re-enter the immaterium and continue our pursuit.'

'I see,' I said, vaguely surprised to find that I did. 'But how can we be sure we've found an exit point in the first place?'

The moment I'd finished speaking, I knew I was going to regret asking that particular question: Yaffel's gyrations increased markedly, as if he could barely contain his excitement, and he raised a hand to point at the hololith. Apparently divining what I'd just done, Mira kicked me sharply in the ankle, although I suspect my Guard-issue footwear made the gesture more uncomfortable for her than it did for me.

Fortunately, Drumon came to our rescue, intervening just before the magos could launch into the tirade of technotheological jargon I'd unwittingly come so close to unleashing. 'Essentially,' he said, 'the passage of so large an object between the two realms leaves a weak spot in the boundary between them, which our Librarian and Navigator believe they can detect.'

'How weak?' Mira asked, no doubt mindful that just such a spot now existed within her home system, and probably picturing a host of daemons flooding through it to lay waste to Viridia.

Yaffel nodded reassuringly at her, no doubt having had to assuage the fears of sufficient numbers of lay listeners by now to be aware of what she must be thinking, and grabbing the chance to display his expertise after all. 'Not enough to allow any of the warp's denizens access to the materium,' he said, his flat monotone sounding oddly sure of itself. 'The weakness is more akin to a deformation of the interface than a breach of it.'

'I see,' Mira said, managing to sound as if she meant it. 'But if you can predict where the weaknesses are, can't you just tell which systems are at risk and warn them by astropath before the hulk gets there?'

'Things are less simple than that,' Drumon said, drawing our attention to the hololith again. A moment's perusal was enough for me to recognise an astronomical display of the sector and a few of the systems surrounding it. 'Here is Viridia.' The system flared green. 'And these are the boundaries within which the *Spawn of Damnation* could have travelled.' A translucent tube began to extend itself from the green dot, the mouth of it widening the further it extended, so that by the time it reached its fullest extent, well over two dozen systems had been swallowed by the flickering funnel.

'It would take a lifetime to search all those systems,' I said, obscurely relieved at the realisation of just how impossible a task we were taking on. After a few months I'd find an excuse to leave them to it, and return to my desk, secure in the knowledge that whatever foolhardy undertaking General Lokris had been planning to drop me into the middle of would be safely over.

'Fortunately, we won't have to,' Yaffel told us, looking smugger by the second. 'Each emergence point we find will reduce the potential volume of space in which our quarry could be, and refine our predictions. After the first few have been plotted, we should be closing in on it nicely.'

'I'm glad to hear it,' I said.

'If they can find any weak spots in the first place,' Mira muttered beside me.

'How can we know until we try?' Drumon said, leaving everyone else looking faintly baffled.

After that, the briefing was clearly over to all intents and purposes, although I made sure I asked a few supplementary questions to show a proper concern for what we might be getting into. By this point Mira had given up even pretending to be interested, simply standing as close to me as she could in a grim silence I began to find increasingly oppressive.

As we eventually left, to let the shipmaster and his crew get on with whatever it is that starship bridge officers do, I felt it politic to pause for a moment in passing and pay our respects to Gries. To my surprise, he acknowledged my salute and nodded to me. 'I trust you have everything you require, commissar?'

Ignoring Mira's smug expression, I nodded. 'Your hospitality is as generous as I remembered,' I told him truthfully. 'But I was wondering, if it's no imposition, whether you had a little free space somewhere I could run through my combat drills every day. I rather neglected them while I was convalescing, and I almost paid the price for that in the 'stealer nest.' Shaken a little by the narrowness of our escape, I'd resumed my regular practice sessions with the chainblade forthwith, and I had no desire to forego them again if I could avoid it, although my quarters were rather too cramped for much in the way of physical exercise which didn't involve Mira.

'Of course.' Gries looked at me approvingly and nodded. 'I would expect nothing less from a warrior of your renown. I'll see to it that you're given access to one of our training chapels.'

'Thank you,' I said, only too aware of the magnitude of the accolade he'd so unexpectedly bestowed on me. All I'd been expecting was a corner of a cargo bay somewhere; this was tantamount to a senior ecclesiarch throwing open the door to the sepulchre of a saint and asking how many bones I'd like to take home.[1] 'I'll try to prove worthy of the honour.'

THE RECLAIMERS CAPTAIN was as good as his word. We'd barely made the transition to the warp when Jurgen knocked on my door with the news that the tertiary training chapel had been put at my disposal for an hour a day. I've no idea what the other two were like, but this one turned out to be an airy chamber about the size of a scrumball pitch, floored with metal mesh, and with luminators in the ceiling which could be adjusted to replicate any light level, from the glimmering of stars on a moonless world to a

---

1. Though Cain is clearly exaggerating a little here, he's quite right in the essence of his assertion: if there's an Astartes Chapter which doesn't regard its training areas as hallowed ground I've yet to hear of it, and granting access to an outsider is an honour seldom conferred.

dazzling glare. Much of the equipment ranged about the walls was either unfamiliar to me, or intended for users a great deal larger and stronger than I was, so I left it alone, preferring to run through the complex patterns of attack and defence with the chainsword which years of familiarity had made instinctive beyond conscious thought.

It's probably no exaggeration to say that those hours of solitary sword drills aboard the *Revenant* were among the happiest of my life. Throne alone knows I'm no Emperor-botherer, but centuries of use by His finest warriors had imbued the very walls of the place with a sense of dedication and reverence for tradition which made me feel as if everything I did there was part of something greater than myself. Not a sensation I'm used to, or particularly comfortable with in the normal course of events, but I couldn't deny it at the time.

If I'm honest, I also found the periods of solitude I spent there becoming an increasingly welcome respite from Mira's company. Which isn't to say that her companionship had become wearisome, exactly, but with very little to do herself, she seemed to want to spend every minute I wasn't attending to my duties attached to me like a Catachan faceeater. For a man as used to his own society as I was, that was a very mixed blessing indeed: so much so that, from time to time, I found myself inventing errands in order to delay my return to my quarters. On one occasion I even went so far as to ask Magos Yaffel for some further details of the techniques he was using to track the space hulk through the immaterium, which I dutifully transcribed into the report I knew full well General Lokris wasn't going to bother to read anyway when I eventually completed it, despite not having understood more than one word in twenty.

We all experienced a brief flurry of excitement about ten days into our voyage, when Gries announced that the Reclaimers' Librarian had sensed the deformation of the membrane between the warp and the material universe which Yaffel had predicted, but when the *Revenant* popped back into the real galaxy for a quick look round we turned out to be drifting through the silent void between the stars, with nothing on the auspex for light years in any direction except for the occasional gas cloud. Nevertheless, the Reclaimers and the tech-priests were all greatly heartened by this confirmation that the theory was sound, and since no one had seriously expected to bag the infernal relic on the first try anyway, we resumed our progress at once with high morale all round, except for Mira, who told me in no uncertain terms that she was bored stiff, and that this was all somehow my fault for persuading her to come along on this absurd junket in the first place. I can't deny, though, that when she finally calmed down enough to apologise, her idea of making things up to me was definitely worth it.

Our second emergence in the wake of the *Spawn* found us in a stellar system, which meant several days of frantic activity as we analysed auspex returns and sent the Thunderhawks scurrying around to check out anything which looked promising, but in the end we drew a complete blank. Fortunately, by luck or the grace of the Emperor, the star at its centre was a sullen, shrunken dwarf, husbanding the post-nova embers of a blaze which would have consumed anything in its habitable zone aeons before, and was now orbited by nothing more than barren chunks of scorched rock, which meant that the 'stealers would have found nothing or no one here to contaminate. So with a quick prayer of thanks to the Golden Throne, we were off again, casting ourselves adrift on the currents of the warp once more.

It must have been a day or so after we resumed our journey that I arrived in the training chapel at the appointed time to find it already occupied. I'd barely taken a couple of steps inside when I noticed Drumon in the middle of the chamber, surrounded by whirling cyberskulls, which he was fending off with the sword I'd noticed him wearing in the bunker under the palace in Fidelis, his plasma pistol gripped in his other hand. The blade was surrounded by a nimbus of crackling energy, like the claws I'd seen the Terminators use to tear apart the insurrectionist artillery pieces, although he must have moderated its strength in some way, as the tiny airborne servitors simply bounced away from each strike as though dazed by the impact rather than being sheared asunder. In a similar fashion, his plasma pistol had evidently been modified to unleash the merest fraction of its charge, as instead of being vaporised, each of the bobbing skulls he shot was only thrown aside for a moment, before returning to the attack.

The speed and precision of his movements were astonishing. I'm a pretty fair duellist myself,[1] but I'd never seen anything to match the flurry of stroke and guard the Techmarine was displaying. Not only that, he was somehow able to employ his sidearm with undiminished accuracy too, and even divert a little of his attention to swat at any cyberskulls trying to attack him from behind with the servo-arm grafted to the back of his armour, which he employed with the same casual expertise Felicia had displayed with her similarly sited mechadendrite back on Perlia.

Much as I'd have liked to linger and enjoy the spectacle, I began to edge away towards the door by which I'd entered. It seemed to me that Drumon had a far stronger claim on the training chapel than I did, since the demands of his duties must of necessity supersede the convenience of his Chapter's guests, and that by my very presence I was intruding on something private and personal. (By this point, although I still felt I had little in common with the superhuman Astartes, I'd got to know a few slightly better as a result of the honour their captain had seen fit to bestow on me, and I'd gathered that there was little a Space Marine regarded as more important than honing his combat skills.) I must have betrayed my presence in some way, however, because Drumon broke off his exercise to look in my direction, while the darting cyberskulls stopped moving, other than to correct their positions slightly in the air currents issuing from the recirculators.

'Commissar. My apologies.' He inclined his head, and made safe his weapons, before sheathing his sword and holstering his pistol. 'I recently made some adjustments to my wargear and wished to assess their performance. I regret the trials have taken far longer than I believed they would.'

'Time flies when you're having fun,' I said, intending to reassure

---

1. *In fact he was a great deal better than that, being one of the finest swordsmen I've ever encountered, which in my line of work is quite something.*

him that no offence had been caused, then found myself wondering if I'd sounded too flippant; after all, it was almost tantamount to joking about the sacraments with an ecclesiarch. To my relief, though, Drumon smiled.

'It does indeed,' he agreed, dismissing the cyberskulls with a gesture: they hummed away to one corner of the room, like ossiferous grox-flies, and the Techmarine followed them, pausing in front of one of the control lecterns whose purpose I'd been unable to guess at before now. 'Would you like me to leave the sparring drones active?' he asked, one gauntleted hand poised above the runes of the display.

'I think they'd be too much for me,' I told him honestly, remembering the rapidity and precision with which the Reclaimer had moved, unencumbered by the bulky armour he wore.

Drumon looked down at me, his head tilted quizzically to one side. 'You can vary the speed and number of the attacks from this lectern,' he explained, demonstrating the procedure, his fingers moving deftly around the dials despite their thickness and the ceramite gauntlets in which they were encased. 'Use these controls to activate and deactivate the system. If you wish to avail yourself of it another day, I can teach you the correct incantations of awakening.'

'Thank you,' I said. It was a tempting offer. Much as I'd enjoyed the last few weeks of what my old schola duelling instructor Myamoto de Bergerac always referred to as shadow practice, it wasn't the same as working with an opponent, and although it wasn't quite the same thing, the sparring drones would make an acceptable substitute. 'Are you sure my laspistol wouldn't damage them, though?'

'A good point,' Drumon said. 'I will obtain a practice powercell to fit it and reduce the power of your shots to within the limits of the drones' structural integrity.' So that was how they'd been able to keep bouncing back from hit after hit that should have pulverised them. 'In the meantime...' He powered down the system, and the cyberskulls settled onto their storage shelf like roosting birds.

'I'll look forward to trying them out,' I said. 'Running through the drills is all very well, but there's nothing quite like sparring with a partner to maintain your edge.'

'Indeed not,' Drumon agreed, and looked at me speculatively. 'I have a little time before I need to resume my duties. If you consider me a suitable match, I would be honoured to assist a guest of our Chapter to hone their skills.'

'More than suitable,' I said, wondering if I'd live long enough to regret accepting the offer. But I could hardly refuse without insulting him, and, by extension, the rest of my hosts. Not for the first time I wondered why I'd ever been persuaded to leave the 12th Field Artillery, where life had been relatively straightforward, but my snowballing reputation had finally attracted the attention of people of influence, and that had been that. If I'm honest, I'd thought a long and tedious career behind a desk, and a long way from anything lethal, had awaited me at brigade headquarters. The reality of being an independent commissar with a reputation for reckless heroism, and therefore a magnet for every hazardous assignment which came along, had been rather an unpleasant surprise.

'I suggest blades only to begin with,' Drumon said, drawing his and pressing the activation rune. The powerfield around it crackled into life, and a flicker of dubiety must have appeared on my face, as he added, 'the intensity of the field has been reduced to non-lethal levels.'

I smiled, with every appearance of being at ease. 'Non-lethal for an Astartes, or for a mere mortal like me?' I asked.

'Both, I assume,' Drumon replied, returning the smile. 'It should feel no more uncomfortable than a glancing blow from a shock maul.' Which, on its own, would be enough to return me to Sholer's domain if he wasn't careful, so he wasn't being quite as reassuring as he evidently thought he was. It was too late to back out now, though, so I drew my own weapon and started the teeth rotating.

'I'm afraid I can't return the favour with this one,' I said. 'If it hits, it hits.'

Drumon took up a guard position, which seemed familiar enough, and beckoned me on. 'If you can strike through my armour,' he pointed out reasonably, 'I deserve a few nicks.'

We began cautiously, feeling out each other's style and favoured strategies, but as we began to get the measure of one another the rhythm of our strikes and parries began to increase in tempo. I was conscious that he was holding back, giving me a chance, and although I continued to work at it, I didn't put everything I had into the combat either, content to pace myself instead of burning off all my energy in a single burst of do-or-die endeavour. He was blindingly fast, of course, as I'd already seen, but I trusted my reflexes rather than trying to think too hard about what I was doing. In my experience of close-quarter fighting, which is far greater than I'm comfortable with, it's usually better to wait for your opponent to make a mistake than it is to go charging in and suddenly find yourself on your hands and knees looking for your head. On the whole, it seemed to be paying off: I took a couple of jolts from his sword's power field, but held on to my own, and seeing a sudden opening drove in at Drumon's chest. The teeth of my blade had just started to skitter off his torso armour when his own reflexes cut in, and he parried my attack with a speed and precision which left me breathless.

'Very good,' the Techmarine said, with more animation than I'd ever seen from him (or any of the others for that matter). 'First blood to you, commissar.'

'I hope I haven't damaged your armour,' I said, knowing how precious it would be to him, but Drumon shook his head.

'I will leave that mark as a reminder,' he said, 'never to underestimate an opponent.'

'I'm full of nasty, underhanded tricks,' I said, truthfully enough, but inflecting it like a joke.

Drumon nodded. 'In my experience, survival is honour enough for the battlefield. Would you care to continue?'

Well, I would, and we did, although I never got through his guard again; even though he still held back, he was always more than a match for me. By the time we'd finished we found ourselves agreeing to meet again the next time his duties permitted, and over the next few weeks we managed to train together several times. I've no idea what his fellow Space Marines made of our arrangement,[1] but many of them seemed to be making more of an effort to be friendly around the time Drumon and I started training together.

All in all, the growing undercurrent of tension between Mira and I notwithstanding, I was beginning to slip into a fairly comfortable routine aboard the *Revenant*; so much so that I began to take it for granted that the voyage would continue uneventfully until we either caught up with our quarry, or abandoned the search. But, of course, I was about to receive a salutary reminder of just how dangerous our quest was, and that the galaxy contained far more perils than the one we pursued so diligently.

---

1. *If anything, Techmarines tend to be regarded as somewhat eccentric at best by most Chapters, which affords them a fair amount of latitude in their behaviour. In fact, judging by Cain's account, Drumon seems to be more accepted as an equal by his battle-brothers than would normally be the case, perhaps because of the Reclaimers' unusually strong ties to the Adeptus Mechanicus.* -

ELEVEN

OUR THIRD ATTEMPT to locate the hulk in the material universe was almost the death of us all; not that we had any premonition of the fact as we prepared to make our latest transition back into the realm of the real. If anything, I suppose, by now we were growing a little complacent, confident that Yaffel's calculations could be relied on, and that the Librarian's abnatural talents would be sufficient to drop us into the materium more or less on top of the space hulk we sought – or, more likely, where it had been at some time in the past.

Accordingly, when Gries invited me to the bridge to observe the transition, my immediate expectation was of a repeat of our previous attempts: merely a wilderness of the void, the details probably a little different from those we'd investigated before, but essentially no more than another dead end to be discounted before moving on. Mira had been invited too, of course, as protocol demanded. But, no doubt to everyone's relief, she'd declined to drag herself out of bed, the summons having arrived in what she and the ship's chronographs insisted was the middle of the night.

I, of course, was enough of a seasoned campaigner to have hauled myself upright, yanked my laspistol out from under the pillow (provoking a tirade of most unladylike language in the process) and clambered into my uniform within moments of the message being delivered by a bleary-eyed Jurgen. Fortified by the mug of tanna he'd waved in my general direction as I made my exit, I arrived on the bridge a mere couple of minutes after the surge of nausea which generally accompanied the transition from the warp to the realm of reality had swept over me.

'Any luck?' I asked, and the crewman manning the sensorium display nodded in my direction.

'The system's teeming with life. If the 'stealers are here, or have been, there's a lot for them to infect.'

'What kind of life?' I asked. It couldn't have been an Imperial system we'd arrived in, or our vox receivers would have been flooded with comms traffic, and challenges from the local SDF, by now. 'Where in the Throne's name are we?'

'Processing the starfield data now,' Yaffel assured me calmly, gazing into the hololith. 'After correcting for parallax errors, our most probable location would be here, give or take approximately eight light-seconds.' One of the stellar systems inside the green funnel, which had been reduced substantially since the first time I'd seen it, flared more brightly, and the translucent cone obligingly shrank a little more.

'Anything on auspex?' I asked, and the operator raised his head to glance at me.

'I've got thousands of contacts,' he reported. 'It'll take a while to narrow them down.'

'Thousands?' I asked, as he returned to work, my palms itching worse than ever.

'Void shields to maximum. All gunnery stations stand to,' the shipmaster said, pretty much confirming what I most feared, before looking across at me as well. 'Many of them appear to be under power and closing on our position.'

'Wonderful,' I said, before realising that sarcasm wasn't quite what was expected of the dauntless warrior everyone here fondly imagined me to be, and plastering a smile on my face which I hoped would seem sufficiently insouciant. 'Always something to be said for a target-rich environment. Any idea whose day we're about to spoil?'

'Still scanning frequencies,' the vox operator reported, his voice almost as calm as Yaffel's mechanical one. 'Getting something...'

'Put it on the speakers,' Gries ordered, and a moment later an overlapping babble of harsh, guttural voices burst into the room.

My stomach knotted, and I took a deep breath, stilling the instinctive surge of panic which swept over me. I recognised that sound all too well, was even able to pick out a word or two I knew. 'Orks,' I said.

'Undoubtedly,' Gries agreed, no doubt familiar with every enemy of the Imperium I'd ever heard of, and a double handful of ones that I hadn't. 'And eager to welcome us in the manner of their kind.' He looked across at the shipmaster. 'Engage them at your leisure.'

'By your command,' the shipmaster responded, with a grave inclination of his head. 'All batteries, fire at will.'

I moved across to the hololith, where Yaffel had thoughtfully brought up a tactical display which enabled me to see just how frakked we were. Innumerable greenskin vessels were swarming in on our position, evoking a curious half-memory of Drumon surrounded by the sparring drones, before the full seriousness of our position elbowed the whimsical image aside.

The Chapter serf gunners were disciplined, I have to give them that, holding their fire until they were sure of a target,[1] before unleashing the full fury of their awesome destructive power in a single concentrated salvo which gutted the ramshackle greenskin vessels they'd targeted. For every one they brought down, though, ten surged forwards to fill the gap, and had they been able to concentrate their fire it would all have been over within moments. Fortunately, however, they were as disorganised as ork mobs

---

1. *Hardly surprising, since they were probably aspirants to membership of the Reclaimers who'd narrowly failed the rigorous selection process.*

always are, blazing away in our general direction without seeming to aim, and only a few of their shots struck home. I felt the faint tremor of their impacts through the fabric of the hull with an answering quiver of apprehension, before forcing away the memory of the greenskin attack on the *Hand of Vengeance*, which had come so close to taking my life.

'Thunderhawks away,' the auspex man reported a moment later, and a cluster of smaller echoes[1] took up station around the blip which marked our position, doing a very nice job of keeping the greenskin fighters and occasional torpedo volley off our backs. 'Still no sign of our primary target.'

'Then it's probably not here,' I said, mainly to Gries, but pitching my voice so that my calm, reasonable tones would carry across most of the bridge. 'And even if it is, it'll take more than one ship to get to it through this much resistance.'

'I concur,' the Space Marine captain rumbled after a moment, much to my well-concealed relief. The overhead luminators flickered, plunging us into momentary darkness, broken only by the eldritch glow of pict screens and lectern lights, before flaring up again.

'Void shields holding,' one of the bridge crew reported. 'Generators two and nine down. Damage control responding.'

Gries turned to Yaffel, ignoring the clear implications which seemed to me like an unwise degree of single-mindedness. 'Your assessment, magos?'

'The probability of finding the *Spawn of Damnation* still within this system is now approximately seventeen per cent, and falling,' Yaffel said, after conferring with a couple of his junior tech-priests. 'Analysis of the auspex echoes can only go so far, however; the five per cent of anomalies requiring further investigation we found last time would appear to be something of an irreducible minimum.'

'Then we remain until the probability drops to five per cent,'

---

1. *Clearly more than the two Cain mentions seeing in the hangar bay earlier in his narrative; perhaps they were docked elsewhere, or simply engaged on other duties on the occasions he embarked and disembarked.*

Gries said, 'before proceeding to the next emergence point. If none exists, we will have to return in numbers sufficient to secure this system while we investigate the remaining anomalies.'

Well, good luck with that, I thought, resolving that if we got out of here in one piece I'd kiss a gretchin before allowing myself to be dragged along on so patently suicidal an endeavour. Which reminded me... I tapped the comm-bead in my ear. 'Jurgen,' I said, 'the ship's under attack by greenskins. Don't alarm Miss DuPanya unduly, but if you can persuade her to get dressed, and ready to move in a hurry, it might be wise.'

'Very good, sir,' my aide responded, in his habitual phlegmatic manner. 'Don't want to get caught on the hop again, like we did off Perlia, do we?'

'No, we don't,' I agreed, not envying the task I'd inflicted on him. Mira would probably have just got back to sleep, and wouldn't take at all kindly to being roused again. Better cranky than dead, though, in my view, and if the ork gunners' aim improved in the next few minutes we could all be breathing vacuum if we weren't light on our feet. (Not an experience I'd recommend, or wish to repeat.)

The deck shook under my feet again, and we were plunged into darkness, for nearly two seconds this time. When the luminators rekindled, they had a red tinge to them, which made the bridge look uncomfortably as though someone had sprayed it with blood.

'Starboard shields down,' the man at the enginseer's station reported dispassionately. 'DCT[1] reports reconsecration will take at least ten minutes.'

'That's too long–' I began, just as the auspex man glanced up from his pict screen.

'Mass torpedo barrage incoming,' he said, a blizzard of contact icons erupting into the space between us and the orks.

'Throne on Earth!' I breathed, horrified. There was no way in the galaxy that the Thunderhawks could intercept that many

1. *Damage Control Team, a term also in use by the Imperial Navy.*

missiles, but they gave it their best shot, managing to whittle them down by about ten per cent before they struck. Which only left enough to tear the guts out of the cruiser instead of vaporising it.

I braced myself for the ripple of impacts, but instead of the explosions I'd expected, I felt no more than the faintest of tremors through the soles of my boots, as the fast-moving projectiles impacted without detonating against the adamantium hull plates. 'They didn't go off!' I said, buoyed up by a sudden surge of relief, which dissipated almost at once as the obvious explanation occurred to me. 'They must be–'

'Prepare to repel boarders,' Gries voxed through the ship's internal speakers, confirming my conclusion before I could voice it. He turned back to Yaffel. 'Magos?'

'The probability of a successful detection is down to eight point five per cent,' the tech-priest informed him, his voice as uninflected as ever. It might have been my imagination, of course, but I was sure he was oscillating more than usual, however.

'Then recall the Thunderhawks,' Gries said, 'and prepare to withdraw as soon as it falls to five per cent.'

The shipmaster nodded, and opened a vox channel of his own. 'Bridge to enginarium,' he said crisply. 'Prepare for entry into the warp.'

For the second time in as many minutes, my sigh of relief was choked off before completion. Instead of the acknowledgement we'd all been expecting from Drumon or one of the serf enginseers under his supervision, the speaker rang with the sounds of combat and the bellowing war cries of orks. The greenskins had breached the enginarium, and until they were evicted, we wouldn't be going anywhere.

I MUST SAY, we all took it remarkably calmly under the circumstances. Or, to be honest, everyone else did, responding to the unexpected reversal with a flurry of sharp, succinct orders, while I kept a panicky eye on the hololith for any further signs of a greenskin assault. They weren't slow in coming either, with several more waves of boarding torpedoes already inbound, although with the Thunderhawks out of the way, our gunners were reaping a rich harvest of them, having switched their aim from the larger warships. Fortunately, the apparent scramble to claim us as a prize meant that any more destructive incoming fire from the surrounding fleet was sporadic at best, and no more accurate than you might expect, so all in all we were still getting off far more lightly than I would have believed possible. It also probably didn't hurt that several of the greenskin vessels were now exchanging fire with one another, the instinctive aggression of their kind finding a more immediate form of expression now that the battle for the *Revenant* had reached something of a standstill from their point of view.

'Squad Trosque is *en route* to the enginarium,' Gries informed the shipmaster, and a sudden sense of foreboding seized me in its talons. I was standing in the middle of the prime target for a boarding party, with Emperor alone knew how many orks charging towards it as fast as their malformed legs could carry them.

I tapped my comm-bead again. 'Jurgen,' I said, 'the greenskins have boarded the *Revenant*. Numbers unknown. Any sign of them where you are?'

'Not yet, commissar,' my aide responded, sounding a trifle disgruntled if I was any judge. Clearly, Mira had proven to be as acrimonious as I'd anticipated. At least he'd be able to take it out on the orks, though, which I'd no doubt he would, with as much relish as any Valhallan finding a greenskin in his sights.[1] 'Would you like me to go hunting?'

'No, better stay where you are,' I told him, 'and keep an eye on the Viridian envoy.' I'd never hear the last of it, I had no doubt, but the idea of Mira on the loose with a shipful of orks to run into hardly bore thinking about. The mood she was in, she'd probably challenge one to a head-butting contest.

---

1. *Valhallans have an intense loathing for this particular xenos breed, dating back to the unsuccessful ork invasion of their homeworld, and will engage them with scarcely less ferocity than the greenskins themselves. But with rather more tactical sense.*

'Oh,' Jurgen said, in the tone I knew all too well was the precursor to telling me something I really didn't want to know. 'I'm afraid the young lady isn't here at the moment, sir. She told me she was coming up to the bridge to see you.'

'Did she?' I said, my stomach plunging to somewhere in the region of my boots. There was no point asking him why he hadn't accompanied her. I'd ordered him to wake her up, and that he'd done, as punctiliously as he fulfilled every other order he was given. And, if I'm honest, in his place I'd have been as pleased to see the back of her as he'd undoubtedly been.

'Would you like me to go after her, sir?' Jurgen offered.

'No, stay in the guest quarters,' I told him, after a fractional pause for thought. They were about as far removed from anything strategically important as it was possible to get aboard the strike cruiser, and although orks weren't exactly renowned for sophisticated tactical analysis, their brutish instincts were often a reasonable substitute. It was still possible that a party of them might blunder in there anyway, of course, but on balance it was as close to a safe refuge as we were likely to find. 'Do whatever you can to make them defensible, and wait for me there. I'll go and retrieve Miss DuPanya.'

I could turn this to my advantage, I thought, as I filled Gries in on this development as succinctly as I could. 'I'm about as much use here as a heretic's oath at the moment,' I concluded, almost in the same breath as Yaffel reporting that if the blasted space hulk was anywhere in the system we weren't going to find it now, so we might as well move on as soon as the little ork problem in the enginarium had been dealt with,[1] 'and we can hardly leave her wandering around on her own under the circumstances. If you've no objection, I'll go and escort her back to her quarters.' Which ought to leave me well out of the way if the greenskins attacked the bridge, as I still expected them to at any moment.

'Of course,' Gries said, apparently taking my evident eagerness to get out there for a thinly disguised desire to bag a few orks.

---

1. *But probably not in quite those terms.*

'May the Emperor walk with you.' He made the Mechanicus cog-wheel gesture again and turned away to discuss the tactical situation with the shipmaster, no doubt relieved to know that Mira wouldn't be blundering in to distract everyone at some crucial point in the battle if I could get to her first.

I left the bridge as quickly as I could and trotted down the main corridor leading away from it, my weapons in my hands. I was pretty sure I knew which route Mira would take from the guest quarters, and was confident of being able to intercept her without too much difficulty. As I reached the first junction of the corridor, I found a contingent of the ship's crew setting up a lascannon on a tripod, while others settled behind a makeshift barricade with lasguns in their hands, and I began to wonder if my decision to leave the bridge had been a trifle hasty, but there was nothing to be done about that now; and at least I had another bolthole to run for if the greenskins turned out to be between me and the relative safety of the guest quarters after all. Feeling mildly reassured by that, I moved on, after exchanging a few words with the petty officer in charge.

They were the last people I saw for some time, however. The corridors seemed eerily silent, the Chapter serfs I was used to seeing passing to and fro on errands of their own absent about more urgent business, and my footfalls echoed on the deck plates more loudly than they normally did, unmuffled by the ambient sounds of other activity. It seemed to be taking an inor-dinate amount of time to find Mira, and I was on the point of giving up and retracing my steps, in the belief that she must have got lost in the labyrinth of interconnecting passageways, when I finally became aware of the sound of footsteps other than my own.

I tensed, taking a firmer grip on the hilt of my chainsword, and flattened myself against the metallic wall of the corridor. I was close to one of the maintenance hatches, which riddled them at intervals. Pointless attempting to seek refuge in one of the utility areas in this case, though, as the hatches were all kept securely locked, and I hadn't yet found a plausible pretext to ask for the access codes. After listening intently for a moment I was able to reassure myself that the footsteps were too light to be those of orks, and, in any case, if the voices in my comm-bead could be relied on, the greenskin boarding parties were all being successfully engaged elsewhere around the ship.

Thus reassured, I stepped out of concealment in the recess containing the utility hatch, just as Mira strode past, her expression grim. She was not, I surmised, pleased to see me.

'I suppose you think this is some kind of joke,' she began, before registering the weapons in my hands and moderating her voice a little. 'What are you carrying those for? You can't just open a window and take a shot at the enemy.'

'I won't have to,' I told her shortly. 'They've boarded us. Where's your gun?'

'Still in my portmanteau, of course.' She scowled pettishly. 'Your rank little imbecile didn't bother to mention that particular detail, just the attacking ships.'

'He didn't know anything about the boarders until I told him a couple of minutes ago,' I said shortly. Her description of Jurgen was undeniably accurate, but it irked me nonetheless. 'Come on.'

'Where to?' Mira, it seemed, wasn't about to let the trivial matter of a horde of greenskins on the loose divert her from the more pressing concern of her irritation with me and my aide for disturbing her rest. 'Shouldn't you be off shooting orks or something?'

'Maybe I should,' I said, on the point of turning away and leaving her to it. After all, I could always tell Gries I hadn't found her in time if the orks caught up with her before we eliminated them all. 'I just had this rather strange notion of making sure you were safe first.'

'Did you?' Her expression softened, and for a moment I remembered why I'd liked her, until her corrosive personality began to leak out around the edges. 'So what did you have in mind?'

'Getting you back to the guest quarters, to start with,' I said, beginning to move off in the direction from which she'd come. It seemed she had enough sense to follow me without urging, for which I was grateful; the last thing I needed under the circumstances was a further round of bickering.

We hurried back through the eerily deserted corridors, our footfalls ringing loudly despite all we could do to muffle them, and Mira glanced at me with a trace of the bravado I remembered from the day we'd first met. 'Remind you of anything?' she asked, and I nodded.

'We do seem to be making a habit of this,' I agreed, just as the shipmaster's voice suddenly burst into my earpiece, effectively dispelling any inclination I might have had to swap further banter.

'Incoming. Brace for impact.'

'Hang on to something,' I said, and it seemed Mira trusted my judgement enough to do so without further argument. She took hold of the handle of another of the ubiquitous utility hatches, and looked at me quizzically. 'Another wave just got past the guns.'

Before she could formulate a reply, the deck trembled a little beneath our feet, a faint vibration barely perceptible through the soles of our boots. Mira let go of the metallic protuberance and took a step towards me, her testiness evidently intensified by the anticlimax and the sense of having been made to look foolish. 'Well, that was hardly–' she began, just as a deafening clangour of brutally maltreated metal assaulted my ears, drowning out whatever else she might have been about to say. The deck rippled beneath my bootsoles, and a section of the ceiling appeared to decide it would be happier as a wall, swinging down to meet the deck plates in a shower of sparks and trailing conduit.

'You were saying?' I asked mildly, as Mira scrambled to her feet and glared at me as though the whole thing was somehow my fault.

'A gentleman would have helped me up,' she told me witheringly.

'Hands full. Sorry,' I replied insincerely. Only an idiot would relinquish either of the weapons I was currently holding under the circumstances. Now don't get me wrong, I've as much time for chivalry as the next man when there's something to be gained by it, or at least nothing to lose, but an impact that big must have meant that a boarding torpedo had hit no more than a deck or two from us, which put the greenskins far too close for comfort so far as I was concerned. I tapped the vox in my ear. 'Cain to bridge, hull breach in Section K, deck fifteen or thereabouts.'

'Acknowledged,' a calm voice replied, conspicuously unaccompanied by any sounds of combat, and I began to regret my impulsive decision to leave there even more strongly. 'Your current position?'

'K fifteen,' I said. 'Escorting the Viridian envoy to safety.' Which sounded a lot better than putting as much distance as I could between me and any greenskins who might have been aboard the projectile. It never occurred to me to question whether they'd survived an impact which would have reduced a human to a small, unpleasant stain.[1] I'd seen more than enough of their ability to shrug off almost as much damage as a power-armoured Space Marine on Perlia to be certain that some at least would be pulling themselves out of the wreckage even as I spoke. I glanced at the tangle of collapsed and twisted metal which effectively barred us from our original objective now, and gestured to Mira with the hand holding my laspistol, back the way we'd come. 'This way,' I told her. 'We'll have to get round it.'

'Right.' She nodded, decisively, the clear and present danger we were in obvious enough to forestall any further frivolous objections, and beginning to display some of the fortitude which had sustained her in the tunnels under Fidelis. 'At least that should be as much of a barrier to the orks as it is to us,' she added, with a final glance at the collapsed ceiling before moving to join me.

Hardly had the words left her mouth, though, than the utility hatch she'd been leaning on just a few moments before suddenly bulged perceptibly, the thin sheet metal from which it

---

1. *Something of an exaggeration: orks are considerably more robust than humans, but not quite to that extent.*

was formed twisting under the impact of a blow which rever-
berated between the corridor walls like the tolling of a cathedral
bell. 'Run!' I shouted, as the sound was repeated, but before I
could take my own advice the flimsy hatch popped from its
hinges, framing a sight I'd hoped never to see again (but which
I continued to see more often than I can count over the years):
the head and shoulders of a snarling, blood-crazed ork, which
bellowed in exultation the second it saw us, and charged.

TWELVE

Luckily for us, and unluckily for the greenskin, my weapons were already in my hands, and with reflexes sharpened by paranoia I cracked off a couple of las-bolts the second I saw it. Both rounds hit their mark, inflicting wounds which would have crippled or killed a human, but which only seemed to annoy the ork. Not for the first time, I found myself marvelling at their resilience even as I cursed it. The shots did serve to distract the brute, however; as it pushed its way through the narrow gap, the frame of the hatchway deforming to admit the full width of its shoulders, it staggered from the impact, catching its foot against the threshold. Pivoting adroitly out of the way of the toppling slab of bellowing, spittle-spraying malevolence, I decapitated it neatly with a single stroke of my chainsword, and turned to run before either segment of the creature had hit the deck plates.

'What are you waiting for?' I shouted, finding my way blocked by Mira, who, to my amazement, was trotting towards the downed ork with an expression of grim determination on her face.

'I need a weapon,' she said, stooping towards the outflung hand which still clutched a huge, crudely made pistol.

'Not that one!' I shouted, knocking her out of the way just as the cadaver's terminal muscle spasm tightened its finger on the trigger, and the spot she'd been standing on abruptly became a hole in the deck and a blizzard of razor-edged metal shards. Even if she could have prised the ork's hand open, a dubious proposition at the best of times, grabbing the gun wouldn't have helped her much in any case: she'd have had trouble even lifting the thing, and any attempt to fire it would simply have dumped her on her well-padded aristocratic arse, probably breaking her arm in the process.[1] Now was hardly the time to be explaining all this, though, so I simply pointed at the howling, frenzied mob of greenskins fighting one other to get through the gap in the wall, while the brighter ones began to dismember their erstwhile comrade in an attempt to get past the obstructing corpse to reach us. 'Run!'

Stubborn and argumentative she may have been, but Mira was no fool. She was hard on my heels as I pelted along the corridor, intent on nothing more than opening up as big a lead as I could before the orks could force their way past the cadaver, and one another. A brief burst of gunfire behind us spurred me on, indicating as it did that the question of precedence had now been settled in the traditional orkish fashion, and that the vanguard was probably already in pursuit. 'What's your plan?' she panted.

'Don't get eaten,' I said. I'd be the first to admit it wasn't much of one, but it had always worked up until now. I activated my comm-bead. 'Cain to bridge, contact confirmed, hostiles engaged.' (Which I thought sounded a lot better than 'run away from after a lucky hit.') 'Oh, and the Viridian envoy's still with me.'

'Acknowledged.' The Astartes captain sounded a little distracted, even given the current emergency. As he paused, the faint sounds of combat drifted through the tiny vox receiver in my ear. It seemed the orks were assaulting the bridge, just as I'd feared, but had yet to break through the defences I'd seen being erected on

---

1. *Cain is speaking with some authority here, as he had considerable experience of captured ork weaponry on Perlia.*

my way out.[1] 'All units are currently engaged.' In other words, good luck, you're on your own.

'May the Emperor protect,' I said as I signed off, which he was welcome to interpret as encouragement if he liked. I had someone a little closer in mind for His attention, and couldn't help wishing He'd had a few spare Astartes to make the job easier.

'I'm on my way, commissar,' a new voice cut in, and I'd be lying if I didn't admit to feeling a sudden surge of relief at the familiar sound of Jurgen's phlegm-thickened tones. Here, at least, was aid I knew I could rely on, even if it was going to take a while to get here.

'We'll save a few greenskins for you,' I assured him. No Valhallan Guardsman would relish sitting on the sidelines while there were orks to be shot, and I was certain he'd been chafing under my orders to remain where he was. 'Any sign of them down there?'

'Not even the sniff of one,' Jurgen said, his faintly resentful tone confirming my guess.

'Then we'll meet you halfway,' I told him. It appeared I'd been right about the guest quarters being as close to a safe refuge as anyone could find aboard the *Revenant* under the circumstances, so it seemed a pity not to take advantage of the fact. Jurgen may have lacked my affinity for three-dimensional mazes, but his straightforward mental processes would more than make up for that. I'd have bet my pension (which, like every other commissar in the field, I never really expected to be claiming in any case) that he'd simply head for K fifteen by the shortest possible route, and Mork[2] help any greenskin standing in his way.

'Meet who, halfway to where?' Mira demanded, only having heard one side of the conversation, and I filled her in as rapidly as I could.

'Jurgen, the guest quarters. There's fighting going on all over the ship, so it seems the best place to keep you safe.' There were always

---

1. *Hardly surprising, as they were being contested by a Space Marine captain and his command squad, as well as the armed crewmen Cain had previously noted.*

2. *One of the greenskins' principal deities, a piece of xenological trivia he'd presumably picked up during his hectic sojourn on Perlia a few years before.*

the saviour pods, of course, but taking to them would definitely be the last resort: our chances of surviving in a system crawling with orks were negligible. The *Revenant*, on the other hand, was our home ground, albeit infested with greenskins. If they weren't reinforced again too quickly, we might yet turn the tide.

As if to mock my hopes, the voice of the auspex operator rang in my comm-bead almost as soon as I'd completed the thought. 'Incoming torpedo volley. Stand by to repel more boarders.'

'Like we're just going to ignore them,' I muttered irritably, receiving a sharp look from Mira, who probably wondered if I was finally cracking under the strain. Before she could distil her disquiet into a typically acidic comment, however, the rather more welcome voice of Drumon crackled in my ear.

'Enginarium purged. Transiting now.'

Hardly had he finished speaking than the synapse-wrenching sensation which usually accompanied entry to the warp swept over me, more strongly than I could recall ever having felt it before; clearly, whatever the Techmarine had done, he'd done in a hurry, without time to complete all the necessary rituals. As the wave of nausea pounded through my body, I still found it in me to thank the Emperor that he'd managed it. The wave of reinforcements the auspex op had just detected would be passing harmlessly through empty space by now,[1] instead of injecting another dose of poison into our reeling vessel, and the balance of the battle had just tipped decisively in our favour. Now it would just be a matter of tracking down the ones who'd already made it aboard, and eliminating them.

'What the hell was that?' Mira asked, her face preternaturally pale after depositing her supper on the deck plates.

Checking the impulse to respond 'Looks like it used to be florn cakes,' I shrugged. 'We're back in the warp. Drumon got us out in the nick of time.'

'Well he could have been a bit more careful,' Mira shot back. 'I feel awful.'

---

1. Or, more likely, dragged into the warp in the wake of the Revenant, to be preyed upon by whatever daemons happened to be around at the time.

'You'd have felt a lot worse with another wave of greenskins rampaging through the ship,' I pointed out, perhaps not as tactfully as I might have done, but I still wasn't feeling too good myself, don't forget. Hardly had the words left my mouth than a bellow of triumphant rage behind us reminded me that there were still more than enough orks aboard to be going on with. 'Run!'

'Run? I can hardly walk!' Mira snapped back, clearly well on the road to recovery. She turned her head, and apparently decided she could run quite well after all, as she caught sight of the mob of orks rounding the last turn we'd taken in the corridor. There were five of them, the two in front filling the passageway from side to side, all brandishing *shootas*[1] like the one I'd dissuaded Mira from picking up in one hand, and equally crude axes in the other.

The one in front had a metal jaw, which I'm bound to say hardly improved his appearance, and more scar tissue than Gries. Clearly the most dangerous, and therefore the new leader. The rest were little better, particularly the one who seemed to have taken a bath in acid some time in the past, who glared at the world through a single, red-rimmed augmetic eye, and whose stance at Metaljaw's shoulder was enough to tell me that the two of them had fought together long enough to watch each other's backs as effectively as a greenskin could.

Before I could get a decent look at the rest, bolts and solid slugs began making a mess of the wall near where we stood, but fortunately they appeared to be no better shots than most of their kind. It could only be a matter of time before they got lucky, though, so I ducked down the nearest cross passage, Mira at my heels.

'Why didn't you shoot back?' she demanded, with a single glance over her shoulder to see if the greenskins had reached the junction yet. I didn't bother, secure in the knowledge that a renewed fusillade would announce their presence as soon as they could see us again, and turned into the first cross corridor which would take us back towards our original route. The last thing I needed now was Jurgen missing us because of the impromptu diversion.

---

1. *An orkish word for firearms in general. They have nothing more specific in their vocabulary, and, like many nouns referring to pieces of wargear, it appears to be a corrupted Gothic loan word.*

'Because I'd have to be damn lucky to bring one down, and the rest would be on us by the time I did,' I explained, reminding myself that she'd never seen the creatures before, so she wouldn't have anything like the hard-won appreciation I did for their resilience and ferocity.

No doubt recalling the exaggerated stories she'd heard about my exploits on Perlia, Mira nodded briskly. 'Can we outrun them, then?' she asked.

'I doubt it,' I said. We might stay ahead of them for a while, but their superior strength and endurance would tell against us in the end.

'Then we need an edge.' She slowed, and looked speculatively at the nearest of the ubiquitous access panels, to which a prayer slip had been affixed by a wax seal, the freshness of both mute testament to the diligence of the *Revenant's* enginseers. 'Can you get one of these open?'

By way of an answer, I swung my chainsword, chewing through the thin metal in seconds and a shower of sparks. No doubt the tech-priests would be horrified by so casual a desecration of even this minor a shrine to the Omnissiah, but it was nothing compared to the damage the orks would do to the ship if left unchecked. Or to us, come to that, which I must admit was of rather more pressing concern to me. 'What have you got in mind?'

Mira smiled, for the first time since I'd run into her. 'An old hunter's trick,' she said, starting to pull wires from the gap between the walls.

I have to admit I'd had my doubts about the wisdom of going along with this, every second we delayed eroding our hard-won lead, but I stayed to cover the corner around which I expected the orks to come at any moment while Mira busied herself with the cables she'd extracted. It seemed that despite my earlier scepticism in the bunker below the palace in Fidelis, her hunting trips had indeed endowed her with some knowledge and skills which might be of use to us in the present emergency. Her marksmanship, quite exceptional for a civilian, I already had good reason to be grateful for, so it seemed worth the risk to tarry a moment or two to see what else she had up her sleeve. Besides, I was confident that I could run faster than her if push came to shove, and our pursuers got too close.

'Finished,' she said, after a tense few moments, and not before time, as the clatter of iron-shod feet against deck plates was beginning to reverberate through my spine. 'Can I borrow this?'

Before I could even ask what 'this' was, she snatched my cap from my head, and reached up to hook it on a length of wire she'd thrown over a pipe running along the centre of the ceiling. My purloined headgear swung in the middle of the corridor, a little above my head and about face height for an ork. I didn't have the faintest idea what she intended to achieve by it, other than drawing their fire perhaps, but my neck seemed a great deal more important than my hat, so I simply started running again.

'Not too far,' Mira said, laying a hand on my arm. 'You'll be round the next corner before they can see us.' Well, that sounded fine to me. She seemed to have some idea of what she was doing though, so I slowed my pace a little and took refuge behind the next junction, levelling my laspistol back the way we'd come. Letting them see us was one thing, but I wasn't stupid enough to stand out in the open where they'd have a clear shot. Even an ork can hit the target occasionally.

They burst into view in a clump, jostling for position as they always did, which no doubt had slowed them down considerably and bought us enough time for Mira to do whatever it was she'd been doing. I flexed my finger on the trigger, tightening it to the point where the slightest movement would be sufficient to fire. My hours of practice against the hovering cyberskulls in the training chapel had paid off handsomely, my grip on the weapon as assured and instinctive with my new augmetic fingers as it had ever been with my original ones; even more so, if anything, as I'd found it easier to remain precisely on aim without the faint tremors no amount of training and discipline can quite eliminate.[1] I held back, though, wanting to be sure of a target. I still hadn't the

---

1. *Given that the main cause of perturbation in a hand holding a pistol on aim is the heartbeat, which affects the entire body, Cain's apparently unshakable conviction that his augmetic fingers increased his accuracy with such weapons may have been psychological rather than physiological in origin.*

faintest idea what Mira had been up to, and the last thing I wanted to do was throw away whatever advantage she'd brought us by precipitate action.

The first thing the greenskins saw was my hat, of course, all of them staring at it with expressions of vague confusion, which is the closest their kind can come to any form of cerebral activity. Their headlong rush slowed, and they began to move down the corridor towards us, grunting and barking in their barbarous tongue, which I was familiar enough with to gather that the one I'd killed had indeed been their leader, and that his successor was still attempting to impose his authority on the others.[1]

'If you wouldn't mind shooting them?' Mira asked irritably, so I took careful aim at Metaljaw, since he was the one shouting the most, which is usually a reliable indicator of status among greenskins, and squeezed the trigger. I'd only intended getting their attention, which was presumably what Mira had in mind, but I succeeded beyond my wildest expectations: I fired just as my target opened his mouth to bellow at a recalcitrant subordinate, and by great fortune my las-bolt hit him in the back of the throat, exiting through his skull and taking most of his brain with it.

For a fraction of a second the surviving greenskins stood in stupefied astonishment, watching another leader topple to the deck plates, then as one they reacted, charging forwards with a roar of 'WAAAAAAAAAAAAGH!' Despite this, I felt a faint surge of optimism. I'd seen many times on Perlia that once a group of orks falls below a critical proportion of their original number they tend to lose heart for the fray, breaking off to seek out another mob to join instead of pressing their attack. If I could just pick off another, that might be enough to shake the resolve of the rest.

But before I could squeeze the trigger again, the space beyond my sights was suddenly devoid of ork. The whole group of them had fallen, sprawling across the deck plates like drunkards in a drinking den, thrashing and bellowing with rage as they tried to rise, hampering each other as they flailed around like tantrum-throwing toddlers.

---

1. *Which probably accounted for at least some of the gunfire Cain noted earlier, orks having a fairly basic way of resolving most arguments.*

Mira looked at them with a faint air of disappointment. 'I was hoping they'd drop their weapons,' she said.

'That was your brilliant idea?' I asked, with a touch of asperity, getting ready to flee again. There was about as much chance of an ork dropping his weapons as deciding to take up flower arranging. 'A tripwire?' Which explained why she'd needed my hat, of course: the first principle of setting a booby trap is to direct the victim's attention elsewhere.

'Mostly,' she admitted.

'Then shouldn't we be running again?' I asked, with a hint of impatience. The only point of a tripwire would be to delay our pursuers, and standing around while they stood up and dusted themselves off would throw away that momentary advantage.

'Maybe,' Mira said, still looking back down the corridor with an air of vague expectation, and showing no signs of movement. Acidface had scrambled to his feet by now, bellowing imprecations at the others, and swatted at my dangling cap with the axe in his hand, no doubt relieving his feelings in the most direct fashion he could.

As the crude weapon smacked into my headgear, a blue-white arc of energy sparked across to the metal blade, and the ork spasmed, roaring and bellowing as he suddenly completed a circuit with the cable Mira had strung across the corridor. His comrades were caught in the discharge too, thrashing on the metal floor like fish on a griddle, their own ululations echoing loudly enough to pain the ears.

'That went about as well as could be expected,' Mira said, her expression now smug in the extreme.

I looked at her, then back to the twitching pile of smouldering orks. 'Why didn't you barbecue yourself while you were setting that up?' I asked, in some perplexity.

Mira shrugged. 'Rubber-soled boots,' she said. 'Saves time rigging the shock fence round a camp. It's an–'

'Old hunter's trick,' I finished for her. 'Next time you see that old hunter, thank him for me.'

Before she could reply, the abused power feed finally shorted out, and the standing greenskin collapsed on top of his comrades, with a faint clatter of falling weaponry. A fresh odour, pungent and familiar, forced its way past the stench of charring ork, and I turned to greet my aide.

'Jurgen,' I said. 'Prompt as always.' I indicated the feebly stirring mound of incapacitated greenskins behind me. 'If you wouldn't mind?' I could quite easily have put a las-bolt through each of their heads myself, but I'd promised to save him a few, and he'd only have sulked if I didn't.

'Of course, sir,' he said, and trotted off to administer the *coup de grace* to the fallen with every sign of enthusiasm. A few moments later he returned, bearing my cap, which he handed to me with a faint air of puzzlement. 'I'll have to see what I can do with this,' he said, 'but I'm afraid it's a little singed.'

THIRTEEN

As I'D SURMISED, now they'd been deprived of the almost infinite number of reinforcements they'd surely been counting on to take the *Revenant*, the remaining greenskins were easy meat for the Reclaimers. Tracking them down took a little time, of course, given the size of the vessel, but a fully-grown ork isn't exactly hard to miss, and the Astartes were extremely adept at xenos hunting. By the time Gries called a meeting to discuss the situation, the shredded remains of the last one had been hauled away to the taxidermist,[1] and the ship's enginseers were inhaling through their teeth[2] at the damage all those bolter shells had done to their nice clean bulkheads. Mira had, of course, been invited, but to no one's surprise elected to return to bed instead. Before doing so she disinterred her laspistol from the bottom of her luggage and tucked

---

1. *It's unclear here whether Cain is being literal, or merely making a flippant reference to Mira's use of her hunting expertise. Many Space Marine Chapters do indeed display the bodies of their defeated enemies, but given their profusion tend to be rather more selective about it.*

2. *A traditional artisan's benediction while assessing a repair job; its origin now lost, although some scholars speculate that it's a symbolic communion with their materials, infusing themselves with their essence before commencing work. At any event, the tradition persists throughout the Imperium.*

it under her pillow, as I habitually did. Better late than never, I supposed, but just in case there was still a *kommando*[1] lurking somewhere in the bowels of the ship, I'd asked Jurgen to keep an eye on the corridor. Needless to say, his vigil was a vain one, but he took the disappointment as stoically as he did everything else.

Which left Gries, Drumon, Yaffel and me arranged about the hololith, while the ship's crew scurried around us tidying up the bridge. The damage in here appeared remarkably slight, although the number of holes, scorch-marks and disquieting stains in the surrounding corridors bore mute and eloquent testament to the ferocity of the battle to preserve it. Hard to tell if I'd have been better off remaining here after all, or whether, despite my misadventures, I'd been prudent to get out while I could, so I gave up speculating about it in favour of the discussion.

'Damage to the enginarium was severe,' Drumon reported, 'but the guardian spirits of the circuit breakers responded promptly, preserving the core systems from harm. Our enginseers are performing the rites of reactivation, and have already honoured the guardians. The warp engines are performing as well as one might expect after a cold start, but will need shutting down for complete resanctification after we next emerge into the materium.'

'That sounds like a long job,' I ventured cautiously, not liking the sound of it at all. If our next port of call turned out to be a fire-wasp nest like the one we'd just escaped from, the last thing we needed was to find ourselves stranded there with no line of retreat.

'Roughly nine days standard,' Drumon replied promptly. 'Half that if we put in to a void station with a Mechanicus shrine, but we might as well wish for a forge world this deep into the Gulf.'

'I'll happily settle for a system free of orks,' I told him, while Gries and Yaffel reflexively meshed their fingers in the cogwheel gesture of the Adeptus Mechanicus, in response to the passing reference to one of the hallowed worlds devoted to the works of the Machine-God.

'Under the circumstances, so will I,' Drumon agreed.

---

1. *Orks unusually skilled at infiltration and sabotage.*

'Then we must trust to the Omnissiah to provide the respite our systems require,' Gries said, in a voice which made it clear he'd take a dim view of it failing to honour the request, and moved on to the main topic on the agenda. 'Though your resourcefulness saved our vessel, it may have put the success of our mission at some hazard.'

'Quite so.' Yaffel nodded, oscillating a little as he always did, and went on. 'The conditions under which we enter the warp are crucial to our ability to follow the right current. Being somewhat distracted at the time,[1] I was unable to complete the relevant calculations before we made the transition, which in turn renders our ability to detect the next emergence point problematic at best.'

'What's the worst-case scenario?' I asked, to show I was paying attention, and trying not to seem visibly pleased that this fool's errand sounded likely to be coming to an end before too much longer. There was bound to be a Guard presence on any Imperial worlds in the vicinity, to discourage opportunistic raiding by our recent hosts, so if I made myself known, I should be able to find a ship heading back to Coronus without too much trouble. Mentioning this prior to my departure might get back to Mira, however, so I kept my own counsel, wary of finding her turning up at the bottom of the boarding ramp again.

'That we fail to find the emergence point at all, or any clue as to its whereabouts,' Yaffel said, looking at me as though I was a simpleton.

'And what are the chances of that?' I asked, refusing to be deflected. If I could get them to realise the mission was hopeless for themselves, it would circumvent any amount of arguing later on.

'Somewhere on the order of three per cent,' the wavering magos told me, looking as perturbed as though that was a real possibility.

'Why so high?' I asked, before reflecting that perhaps sarcasm wasn't particularly sensible under the circumstances, neither Gries

---

1. *According to the log of the* Revenant *he was fending off an attacking ork with his mechadendrites and a convenient chair at the moment the vessel entered the warp.*

nor Yaffel having shown much of a sense of humour about our quest. If either was offended by my flippancy, or even noticed it, come to that, they gave no sign, however. Yaffel merely gestured to the hololith, where the glowing green funnel was still projected over the starfield.

'We've been able to refine our estimates,' he said, 'but only so far. Given the flow of the current we're now in, our destination could be any one of these three systems, with a probability of seventeen, twelve and thirty-two per cent respectively. Other, less likely, destinations are here.' A rash of icons appeared throughout the cone, a few in planetary systems, the vast majority in the deep gulf between them. As I regarded these, I felt a faint shiver of apprehension; if we ended up in the void between the stars, and for some reason the warp engines failed to respond to Drumon's ministrations, we would all surely die in the fathomless dark, centuries from succour even at the best speed our vessel was capable of in the material realm.

'What if we return to the orkhold and re-enter the current after your calculations are complete?' Gries asked, as calmly as if committing suicide like that was a perfectly reasonable proposal.

To my horror, Yaffel nodded. 'I've considered this,' he said, his tone so even that they might merely have been discussing the weather, rather than condemning us all to certain death. All of a sudden, making a run for it in a saviour pod was beginning to look positively attractive. 'My estimate of a ninety-seven per cent probability of success was predicated on us having done so.'

'We'll have to lay over and resanctify the system before we try that,' Drumon said firmly. 'A lot of the machine-spirits are still traumatised, and need to be healed before we can take the ship into combat again.'

'So it looks as though we'll just have to carry on looking for the *Spawn's* next emergence point for the time being,' I said, trying not to sound too relieved. If we found it, all well and good; either the hulk would be there, or we'd carry on searching, and either way there'd be no reason to return to an ork-infested hellhole. On the other hand, if we didn't, at least I'd have nine days or thereabouts to find a plausible excuse to leave them to it – and failing that, there was always the pods. 'What are our chances of success under the present circumstances?'

'No more than seventy-two per cent,' Yaffel said gloomily, and I resisted the temptation to throw the nearest heavy object at him, with what I still consider a heroic feat of self-control. I'd come out ahead on considerably longer odds than that, on innumerable occasions, and said so. If I'm honest, I was almost giddy with relief, but still in sufficient control of my faculties to refrain from telling the desiccated tech-priest precisely what I thought about his willingness to sacrifice the lot of us just to tidy up his sums.

'Let us hope your confidence is justified, commissar,' Gries said dryly, and on that encouraging note the meeting came to an end.

WITH SO MUCH at stake, it was hardly surprising that the next few weeks were more than a little tense. I whiled away the time as best I could with one piece of makework after another, relishing my daily exercise with the practice drones, and a couple of sparring sessions with Drumon, who seemed as relieved to get away from his duties as I was. Though he never said so directly, I soon inferred that the orks had left a considerable legacy of damage behind them, and the task of coordinating the repairs was an onerous one. Despite my best efforts to ignore them, Yaffel's words had left me feeling unsettled, and although I knew the chances of being dragged back to the orks' domain on a suicidal attempt to make his calculations come out right were remote (practically non-existent if I had anything to do with it), I couldn't shake a nagging sense of disquiet, which refused to leave me entirely except when I was engaged in physical exercise.

Perhaps as a result of this, or perhaps because electrocuting a mob of orks seemed to have put her in a better mood, I found myself spending more time with Mira again. I can't claim to have enjoyed her society as much as I had done back in Fidelis, but her enthusiasm for mine seemed undiminished, and as I've noted before, my opportunities for social interaction aboard the *Revenant* were somewhat circumscribed. To be honest, I'd been a little wary of renewing our association at first, a faint voice at the back of my mind still insisting that this was a bad idea, for reasons

I couldn't quite articulate, whenever I could be bothered to listen to it. But as the days passed, and she kept the virago side of her personality under better control, I began to feel a little more comfortable around her. Perhaps too much so; otherwise I'd certainly have paid more attention to the itching in my palms, which continued to flare up from time to time in the middle of apparently innocuous conversations.

There was one in particular which sticks in my mind, although the full significance of it didn't really occur to me at the time. Spurred on by our recent encounter with the greenskins, I'd been telling her a few colourful lies over a leisurely supper together about my supposedly glorious campaign to liberate Perlia from their kindred, and been duly rewarded by oohs and aahs of wide-eyed credulity in most of the right places – then she looked at me over the rim of her goblet as though taking aim.

'Haven't you ever thought about doing something else with your life?' she asked, in the studiedly neutral fashion she tended to adopt when trying to pretend she didn't care about the answer. I shook my head, in some perplexity, completely taken aback.

'Haven't you?' I asked in return, knowing that my question was equally ridiculous. Mira had been born into the ruling family of an Imperial world, destined since birth to take a hand in the governance of it, and her education and upbringing had no doubt been predicated on that assumption; she was no more in control of her own destiny than I was. From the day I'd been earmarked as a future commissar by a schola progenium functionary with a twisted sense of humour,[1] my destiny had been set in stone, just as surely as Mira's, but without the limitless wealth which had no doubt made her adolescence a great deal more comfortable than mine.

'All the time,' she said, to my surprise, an unexpected air of wistfulness entering her tone. Then she smiled, as if to make light of the revelation, and shrugged, setting up interesting oscillations in the clinging gold fabric of her favourite gown – which still made

1. *Or remarkably good judgement, given the progress of Cain's subsequent career.*

her look like a joygirl if you asked me. (Not that I considered that aspect of her appearance much of a disadvantage.) 'But I've never had the chance.' She glanced slyly at me. 'Not until now.'

'Being offworld, you mean,' I said, managing to look as though I was interested without too much difficulty. This was a happy knack I'd acquired early enough in life to make my time at the schola more tolerable than it might otherwise have been, and which had served me well in my subsequent career.

Mira nodded. 'Partly,' she agreed. She had a conspiratorial air about her now, as though she were about to impart some intimate confidence and feared being overheard by eavesdropping servants. Although since Jurgen was still the closest thing either of us had to domestic staff, and his presence was pretty noticeable even if he was out of sight, I didn't think she had too much to worry about on that score. 'It opens up a number of opportunities.'

'Does it?' I asked, unable for the life of me to see what she was driving at.

She nodded again. 'It does,' she confirmed, as though I'd grasped whatever she was blethering about, and tacitly agreed to it. 'With the right consort beside me, my father is bound to confirm me as his heir. Viridia will need strong leadership once the mess there has been cleaned up, and I mean to provide it.'

'Well, good for you,' I said, trying not to smile as I finally grasped the real reason she'd manoeuvred her way aboard our ship of fools. She was positioning herself to fend off any rival claimants to the throne, and wanted to prove she'd go to any lengths to protect her home world. And if she could bag herself a Space Marine to marry along the way, so much the better: the idea was quite ludicrous, of course, but somehow quite charming in its naivety.[1] 'I can't think of a safer pair of hands.'

'I was hoping you'd say that,' Mira replied, smiling at me in a way I hadn't seen for a long time. I returned it in kind, reflecting that

---

1. *As is Cain's at this point. It seems quite astonishing that he should miss what Mira was so clearly driving at. In his defence, however, it must be pointed out that his experience of women prior to this particular liaison had been rather more broad than deep, so to speak, and that he'd had very little contact with the nobility of the Imperium, so lacked a context for her dynastic ambitions.*

this augured well for the subsequent progress of the evening, and I'm bound to say that I was far from disappointed.

FOURTEEN

I DIDN'T HAVE long to enjoy the sudden change in Mira's demeanour, although she certainly became more pleasant company after that. It was almost like reliving the earliest period of our association back on Viridia, and although I couldn't help wondering now and again just what lay behind it, particularly on the occasions I noticed her staring at me like a kroot at some choice piece of carrion, for the most part I was simply grateful for the improvement. So marked was it, in fact, that I was taken by surprise when a momentary flash of her old petulance surfaced one morning, just after Jurgen had knocked on the door of my quarters to inform me that Gries had requested my presence on the bridge at my earliest convenience.

'Do you really have to go rushing off like a lackey every time someone sends you a message?' she asked, as I scrambled into my uniform, considered the state of my cap, which, despite Jurgen's best efforts, was still looking the worse for wear, and decided it would just have to do. 'He said at your convenience, not right this minute.'

'It's the same thing,' I told her, tilting it to hide the worst of the

damage and checking the effect in the mirror. 'You might be able
to keep people waiting as long as you like, but I can't. That was just
a polite way of phrasing an order.' Deciding I was now as present-
able as I was ever going to be, I turned back, to find her expression
softening again.

'That won't be the case for ever,' she said, and I smiled back,
touched by her evident faith in the upward trajectory of my future
career. (Which has indeed left me in a position to keep people
waiting as long as I care to, and has done for some decades now,
although the realities of my job mean that it's still generally
impolitic to indulge the impulse.)

'I'll be back as soon as I can,' I promised, and left as briskly as
protocol demanded. It was pointless asking if she wanted to
accompany me; even if she could be persuaded to get moving,
which with Mira was always problematic at best, the summons
had been for me alone. It was entirely possible that a separate message had been dispatched to her own quarters, of course, in the
interest of diplomacy, but she was so unlikely to respond that it
wouldn't have surprised me to learn that Gries had simply given
up even the pretence of attempting to include her in whatever
decisions needed to be made.

'Commissar.' The Space Marine captain nodded an affable greeting to me as I strode onto the bridge, before returning his
attention to the shipmaster, with whom he was in animated conversation about matters which meant nothing to me.

If I'd had any lingering doubts about what I was doing here they
were dispelled almost at once, as my eye fell on Yaffel and
Drumon, who were standing by the hololith, examining the star
chart with every sign of satisfaction. I ambled over to join them,
and the Techmarine glanced up as I approached.

'Commissar,' he said, standing aside to allow me an unimpeded
view of the display. 'Just in time.'

'So I see,' I replied, taking in the familiar star chart in a single
glance. One of the three systems Yaffel had pointed out at our
previous meeting was illuminated more brightly than any of the
others, and the green funnel had shrunk again, to leave the icon
apparently stuck in its narrowing throat. I nodded an

acknowledgement to Yaffel. 'Congratulations, magos. It seems your calculations were as reliable as ever.'

'By the grace of the Omnissiah,' the tech-priest agreed, contriving to project an impression of smugness despite the monotone in which the words were delivered, and the impassive expression generally considered appropriate to one of his calling. 'We've detected another weakness in the interface between realities, consistent with those we recorded earlier in the voyage.'

'Which should put us about here,' Drumon added, prodding at the icon I'd already noticed with his servo-arm. 'The Serendipita System. Within the usual margins of error, of course.'

'Of course.' I nodded, to show I was paying attention, and tried not to reflect that predicting an emergence point from within the warp was always little more than an exercise in wishful thinking; although our Navigator had proven remarkably able in that regard, which no doubt accounted for the fact that he or she had been engaged by a Space Marine vessel in the first place.[1] Then something else struck me. 'We've always emerged blind before. How can you be so sure this is the system we're coming out in?'

I should have known better, of course, and spent most of the next ten minutes nodding politely while Yaffel sprayed technical terms around, and wondering if his augmetic enhancements really had left him without the need to inhale, or whether it simply sounded like that to my reeling eardrums. Eventually he ground to a halt.

'Something of an oversimplification,' Drumon observed sardonically, 'but accurate in its essentials.' Then, apparently to ensure I realised he was joking, he added, 'It seems the most likely candidate, given the flow of the currents our ship has been following.'

'I see,' I said, wondering why Yaffel couldn't have been equally succinct. 'Is it an Imperial system?'

'Absolutely Imperial,' Drumon assured me, with one of the faint smiles I'd grown more adept at noticing since we'd become

---

1. *The exact ratio of male to female Navigators contracted out by the Navis Nobilite is a matter known only to them, although both sexes seem equally able practitioners of their arcane craft, and we can infer that only the most skilful would be accorded the honour of serving aboard a vessel of the Adeptus Astartes.*

sparring partners. 'One primary world, seven others supporting settlements, and thirty-eight void stations. Two of which are starports with dockyard facilities.' Which clearly accounted for his buoyant mood. I began to feel a sense of growing disquiet.

'That implies a sizeable population,' I pointed out. 'Which means it's the perfect place for the 'stealers to spread their taint.'

'Quite so,' Gries agreed, turning to look in our direction, and reminding me once again of the phenomenal hearing with which the Emperor had seen fit to endow him. 'You can rest assured we'll be prepared for any acts of treachery.'

'I'm glad to hear it,' I replied, though I felt a lot less easy than I tried to sound. We'd been ambushed almost as soon as we'd arrived in the Viridia System, and although the *Revenant* had shrugged off the attack easily enough, Drumon had made it abundantly clear that she was in no fit state to go into battle again. And Viridia had probably been infected by no more than a handful of implanted hosts; if the entire brood aboard the *Spawn of Damnation* had been roused, and able to rampage through the population virtually unchecked, the Serendipita System could already be lost to humanity. If that were the case, as my increasingly pessimistic imaginings were halfway to convincing me, then it would be like our arrival in the orkhold all over again.

So, as you'll readily appreciate, as we all turned to the pict screen which relayed an image of the universe outside the hull, the lingering nausea of our transition to the materium was the least of my worries.

In the event, I must confess, I found it something of an anticlimax. Instead of the marauding warships I'd steeled myself to expect, there was nothing to be seen in any direction but the reassuring glow of the stars. None of the pinpricks of light appeared to be moving, which came as a further relief; if they had, they could only be vessels of some kind. Of course the auspex operator had far more sophisticated senses to rely on than my eyes, and a moment later he confirmed my immediate impression.

'All clear,' he reported, in the same clipped monotone the whole ship's crew appeared to affect while on duty. 'Commencing detailed scan.'

'How far out are we?' I asked. My paranoia was as acute as ever, leaving me convinced that the system was going to turn out to be another firewasp nest sooner or later, and I wanted to be sure we'd have plenty of warning if trouble came looking for us. None of the speckled lights seemed any brighter than the others, but I was a seasoned enough traveller not to find that strange: at the kind of distances starships usually entered and left the warp, the local sun would be so far away as to appear no larger than any other star in the firmament.

'A little beyond the main bulk of the halo,' Drumon said, a thoughtful expression crossing his face, as he no doubt reached the same conclusion I just had. Innumerable pieces of cosmic flotsam would be clogging our auspex receptors, which meant an attacking flotilla would be all but undetectable at a distance – at least if they had the sense to power down and coast, igniting their engines only for the final attack run.

'That seems a bit far,' I said, determined to seem at ease despite the apprehension gnawing away at me. Starships would usually shoulder their way back into the real galaxy as close to a system's primary as they dared, to minimise the amount of time required to coast in to their destination; something I'd come to appreciate on the long, slow journey Jurgen and I had made from the halo to Perlia aboard a saviour pod.

Yaffel didn't actually shrug, but he contrived to give a passable impression of having done so as he leaned across the hololith table, oscillating slightly in his usual fashion. 'The hulk is drifting randomly, and we simply followed it through to the materium at the point from which it emerged,' he pointed out, in the manner of one of my old schola tutors wearily explaining the blindingly obvious to an indifferent cadre of progeni for about the thousandth time in his career. (A sensation I'm beginning to sympathise with, now I'm the one trying to get the young pups to pay attention.)

'Which might mean it hasn't been in-system long enough for the genestealers to infect anyone,' I said, feeling the first faint stirrings of hope since our arrival. Yaffel looked at me blankly, so I went on to explain. 'All those ork ships were clustered around the last emergence point, weren't they?'

The tech-priest nodded. 'I suppose so. What of it?'

'It must mean the *Spawn* was there just before we were,' I pointed out, conscious of the irony of the sudden reversal of our positions. 'A flotilla that size couldn't have been mobilised to intercept us that quickly. Those ships must have been going after the hulk, and arrived too late – just in time to target us as we emerged from the warp in its wake.'

'A sound inference,' Gries agreed, and Drumon nodded.

'Which means we should be concentrating our search efforts in this area.' He manipulated the controls of the hololith, muttering incantations under his breath, then hit the display three times with the heel of his hand to stabilise the image. The long-familiar starfield disappeared, to be replaced by a simulation of the stellar system we'd arrived in. A scattering of crimson dots picked out the Imperial population centres, confined for the most part to the moons of the largest gas giant, while a single gold rune marked the position of the *Revenant*. A three-dimensional grid fanned out in front of it, reaching almost halfway to the sun in the middle of the display.

Yaffel studied it for a moment, then nodded. 'I concur. If the commissar's deduction is correct, which seems extremely likely, the probability of finding the *Spawn of Damnation* within the demarcated volume is approximately ninety-nine point two seven per cent.'

'I'm pleased to hear it,' I said, moving aside to make room for Gries, who, like all Astartes, required a considerable amount of space to stand in. I liked the sound of that a great deal more than the tech-priest's last set of sums. Even more cheering, from my point of view, was the fact that the gas giant and its attendant cluster of icons was on the far side of the sun, way beyond the area of space Drumon had picked out, and even the closest outpost of civilisation[1] was well outside its boundaries. It was still possible

---

1. *A promethium refining facility in the upper atmosphere of the outermost gas giant, with a population of around thirty thousand.*

that a scavenger vessel of some kind had stumbled across the hulk, of course, as had appeared to be the case on Viridia, but even that worst-case contingency could be contained if we were quick enough. Despite a lifetime's experience that such feelings were merely the prelude to the discovery of a hitherto unsuspected greater threat, I found myself smiling confidently. 'It seems things are going our way at last.'

DESPITE THE PERSISTENT little voice at the back of my head which continued to insist that things could only be going this well to lull us into a false sense of security, I must confess I found myself beginning to relax over the next few days. The search for our quarry was as painstaking and time-consuming as on every previous occasion, with the obvious exception of the time we were being distracted by orks – the sheer amount of debris in Serendipita's halo was hampering our auspexes just as much as I'd expected it to do. This time, however, I had something productive to get on with, and threw myself into the work with an enthusiasm which surprised me a little.

We had, of course, transmitted the news of our arrival to Serendipita,[1] and the presence of a Space Marine vessel within their borders had created about as much excitement as you might expect, especially once the coin dropped, and the upper echelons of the System Defence Fleet realised that our mission meant a clear and present danger to their home world. Accordingly, a delegation of local worthies had been dispatched to meet us; and since diplomacy was hardly Gries's strong point, I'd found myself called upon to liaise with them in his stead.

To my faint surprise, however, Mira didn't seem to share my enthusiasm for this development, seeming, if anything, positively put out by it. 'I don't see why you have to do all their work for them,' she said, echoes of the pettishness I remembered all too vividly colouring her voice for the first time in weeks.

I shrugged, and sipped my tanna, while she tore a chunk out of

---

1. *Cain appears to be referring here to the primary world, rather than the system with which, in accordance with Imperial tradition, it shared a name.*

a freshly buttered florn cake with her teeth and masticated it sav-
agely. We were enjoying what I sincerely hoped was about to
become a rare quiet interlude, before the heavy shuttle bearing the
Reclaimers' latest guests arrived, and I felt it best to keep the peace
if I could. 'I don't really have a choice,' I pointed out reasonably,
transferring one from the salver to my plate while I still had the
chance, and topping it with a spoonful of ackenberry preserve. I'd
had ample opportunity to observe that Mira's consumption of
foodstuffs gained momentum in direct proportion to how
affronted she felt, and experience inclined me to safeguard my
own provender. 'My orders were to liaise between the Reclaimers
and the Imperial Guard, and since there's a Guard garrison on
Serendipita, I'd be derelict in my duty if I hadn't contacted them
at the earliest opportunity.' And thereby laid the groundwork for
my passage back to Coronus, as soon as I could detach myself
from this increasingly pointless assignment, although no one
needed to know that just yet.

'I can see that,' Mira conceded, with a conciliatory tilt of the head
and a faint spray of crumbs. 'I just don't see why you have to waste
your time with the rest of them.'

'I'd rather not,' I told her truthfully. 'But they're all arriving
together. Splitting them up isn't really an option.'

'No.' She shook her head, and I began to realise she probably
understood the situation better than I did: after all, she'd grown
up surrounded by competing factions jockeying for position, all
needing to be kept working together for the common good. 'It'd
create too much division, and if we're going to keep the genestealers from overrunning Serendipita, we all need to be singing
from the same psalter.'

'You'd make a good commissar,' I said, only half-joking, and she
smiled at me across the table.

'You'd make a good regent,' she said. Then she turned her head,
the smile sliding from her face, as the familiar odour of my aide
thickened the room, followed a moment later by its source. 'I told
you we weren't to be disturbed.'

'Pardon the intrusion, sir,' Jurgen said, addressing me directly,
with the exaggeratedly formal tones he tended to employ while

sticking rigidly to protocol in the faces of irate officers, then turning his head slightly to add a perfunctory 'miss,' before returning his attention entirely to me. 'Captain Gries would like you to join him at the ventral docking port. The diplomatic shuttle from Serendipita's due in about ten minutes.'

'Thank you, Jurgen,' I said. 'Please convey my respects to the captain. I'll meet you down there in a moment.'

'Very good, sir.' He saluted, no doubt to underline that this was military business which superseded whatever Mira might think about his unexpected arrival, and marched out in a vaguely martial slouch.

I turned back to Mira, whose expression now looked about as warm as a Valhallan winter, and whatever quip I'd been about to make to lighten the mood scurried back to the safety of my synapses unvoiced. 'Are you serious?' she asked, in incredulous tones. 'What in the name of the Throne do you want that malodorous halfwit with you for?'

'Because he's my aide,' I pointed out, with a little more asperity than I'd intended. 'Protocol demands it. And he diverts attention from me.' Which meant I could size up the new arrivals while they were nicely distracted, instead of being gawped at like a sideshow mutant because of my ridiculous reputation.

'I can believe that,' Mira conceded, and the frost in her tone began to thaw. She rose and began to make her way towards the door. 'I'd better leave you to your preparations.'

'I'm pretty much prepared already,' I admitted, picking up my much abused cap and sticking it on my head without further thought. I'd given up trying to position it to minimise the damage, and if any of the Serendipitans didn't like the look of it, they'd just have to lump it.

To my surprise, Mira turned back, reached up and adjusted the position slightly, then regarded the effect with a faint smile. 'That's better,' she said. 'Makes you look dangerous, rather than just knocked about a bit.'

I glanced at the mirror to see what she'd done, and found myself staring at the reflection of a hard bitten warrior who'd borrowed my face. 'Thank you,' I said, astonished by the transformation. 'How did you do that?'

Mira smiled, all trace of her previous bad mood gone. 'It's not what you wear,' she said, 'it's the way you wear it. Every woman knows that.' Then she turned and resumed her progress towards the door. 'Now if you'll excuse me, I need to take my own advice. See you in the docking bay.'

'You're going too?' I asked, and her smile spread.

'You said it yourself,' she told me. 'Protocol demands it.'

THE HANGAR BAYS used by the Thunderhawks were all positioned on the flanks of the ship, where they could best be covered by the broadside batteries when deploying under fire, so this was my first sight of the ventral docks protruding from the *Revenant's* keel. There were two bays in all, set back to back and separated by heavy blast doors, which Drumon told me could be retracted to combine the two chambers if required. I had no idea when this was likely to be, having seen no sign of anything the size of an Imperial Guard drop-ship in service with the Astartes, but was happy to take his word for it.[1] I suppose if I'd cared I could have asked him for more detail, but he was engaged in conversation with Gries and his bodyguards for most of the wait, and it wouldn't have been polite to interrupt.

At any event, both bays were accessed from open space by the usual arrangement of airtight doors, thick enough to be rammed by a Chimera without taking a dent, which closed off the end opposite the bulkhead separating them. From the observation gallery running along one side of both, and protected from decompression by a handswidth of armourcrys, it was pretty obvious which one was soon to receive our guests: the mighty portal had been cranked open, revealing the star-speckled velvet of

---

1. *Accommodating larger vessels would be one such occasion, of course, but combining the two bays would also allow what the Navy refer to as through-deck operation, allowing fighters and shuttles to arrive at one end and depart from the other, reducing the time required to rearm and re-equip them during combat. Somewhat hazardous, with the hangar open to vacuum, of course, but Space Marines and their vassals tend to be a bit blasé about that kind of thing.*

eternal night beyond, while the other chamber was still sealed and pressurised.

'Impressive,' Mira commented quietly in my ear, her perfume beginning to displace the earthier scent of Jurgen, and I started, having remained unaware of her approach.

'Very,' I agreed, turning to look at her. 'Every millimetre the diplomat.' To my unexpressed relief she'd dispensed with the joy-girl outfit, replacing it with a formal gown of indigo hue, which was echoed by the soft slippers she'd employed to sneak up on me. But then, I suppose, matching her appearance to the occasion was a skill she'd grown up with, not unlike my own talent for dissembling.

'I'm glad you approve,' she said, with every appearance of sincerity. 'Have I missed much?'

I shook my head. 'Not yet,' I assured her, with a nod towards the vacant hangar bay. Something was clearly going on down there though, void-suited Chapter serfs scurrying about on the deck plates, so the arrival of the shuttle was undoubtedly imminent. A fresh burst of movement caught my eye, and I nodded. 'Oh, nice touch.'

Gries and the other Astartes were entering the chamber through an airlock almost directly below us, and beginning to take up their positions, ready to greet the new arrivals, completely untroubled by the lack of anything to breathe down there. The impression made on the delegates, watching through the viewports of their transport while the chamber pressurised, would undoubtedly be a strong one, reinforcing the air of superhuman invulnerability Space Marines tended to project as a matter of course.

'He's more of a diplomat than he thinks,' Mira agreed, as the shuttle finally appeared in the rectangle of star-spattered darkness, and coasted inside as silently as a nocturnal raptor swooping on a rodent. It was larger than I'd expected, closer in size to a bulk cargo lifter than the Aquila I'd anticipated, and I began to realise that perhaps Gries had had the right idea in keeping as far away from its passengers as possible.

'Looks like a bit of a crowd,' Jurgen observed, and I nodded, calculating rapidly. You could have fitted a platoon inside it quite

Sandy Mitchell

comfortably, along with their Chimeras, but if I was any judge a vessel that extensively ornamented would have been designed with its passengers' comfort a far higher priority than the efficient use of space. Even allowing for individual staterooms and a fairly commodious common area, though, there would still be room for a couple of dozen at least.

'About thirty, I would think,' Mira said, and it suddenly dawned on me that she was probably a great deal more familiar with this type of vessel than anyone else on board. She pointed to a detailed mosaic of thermal tiles wrapped around the blunt nose of the ship. 'That's the governor's personal heraldry, so we can expect that whoever's on board has a fair bit of pull.'

'Wouldn't we have been informed if the governor was coming?' I asked, and Mira shrugged, which I always found agreeably diverting.

'Not necessarily,' she said, 'but I doubt it. He's probably running round in little circles back on Serendipita, making sure any obvious signs of corruption or misgovernment are tidied away before the Astartes arrive.' Then she smiled, in a self-deprecating fashion which quite suited her. 'It's what I'd do.'

'But he put his personal shuttle at the disposal of the delegation,' I said. 'How very generous of him.'

Mira smiled again, either at my apparent naivety, or the thinly veiled sarcasm. 'Generosity has nothing to do with it,' she said. 'It shows he's taking the Reclaimers seriously, and willing to get involved, but keeps him conveniently distanced from any decisions made here which might cause trouble at home.' Her voice held a faintly admiring edge. 'He plays the game well.'

'Let's hope you get the chance to tell him that, before the genestealers eat his system out from the inside,' I said. We were certainly off to a good start, but my innate pessimism, forged in the crucible of far too many unpleasant surprises just when we thought we'd got on top of things, was refusing to let go of the conviction that the situation was hardly likely to remain as straightforward as it had been.

Jurgen nodded. 'Doesn't do to turn your back on them,' he said, no doubt mindful of our experiences on Keffia.

'I don't imagine we'll be doing that,' Mira said.

'Certainly not,' I agreed. A chill mist was beginning to drift against the armourcrys by now, as the thickening atmosphere in the docking bay was chilled to the temperature of space, and a barely perceptible thrumming was growing audible, as the air became dense enough to transmit the sound of the pumps feeding it into the cavernous chamber. I began to lead the way towards the staircase leading down to the airlock. 'Our first priority has to be assessing the threat, and the best way to combat it with the assets we have in-system.' I'd timed it nicely, the outer doors of the airlock grinding open to admit the diminishing howl of the shuttle's engines,[1] as the pilot powered them down.

'Commissar. Commendably prompt,' Gries rumbled, as the boarding ramp began to descend. If he was surprised to see Mira with me, his helmet hid it, and he acknowledged her presence with a simple 'Envoy.'

'Captain,' she responded, with a perfunctory curtsey. 'Whose company are we to expect the pleasure of?'

Pleasure wasn't exactly the thing I was anticipating, I must admit. I wanted to talk to the real soldiers among the delegation, which basically meant the Imperial Guard officers, along with the PDF and SDF representatives for their local knowledge. I was already certain that the vast majority would turn out to be Administratum drones and members of the local aristocracy instead, though, keener to boost their position by association with the Astartes than to make any meaningful contribution to the defence of the system.

Gries evidently felt much the same way, judging by the curtness of his reply. 'Omnissiah knows,' he said. 'Or how many of them will have something relevant to say.'

'Then if I may make a suggestion,' Mira said brightly, 'perhaps Ciaphas should just liaise between you and the military people, like he's supposed to, while I keep the hangers-on out of the way.

---

1. *Which implies that both sets of doors were being left open, to expedite the disembarkation of the passengers: not the safest thing to do, but, as previously noted, Space Marines tend not to be too concerned at the possibility of exposure to vacuum.*

I've nothing practical to contribute to the strategic planning in any case, but I do know how to talk to politicians without yawning.'

'That would be helpful,' Gries agreed, and I nodded, concealing my surprise as best I could.

'It would indeed,' I concurred, wondering what would be in it for her, and deciding that right now I didn't really care. The important thing was to stop Serendipita from going the way of her home world, and too many others along the Eastern Arm for comfort.

'Good.' Mira smiled at me. 'Then let's try to look as though they're all welcome, shall we?'

Editorial Note:

As usual, though he mentions a few of the astrographic details in passing, Cain is vague at best about conditions in the Serendipita System. Accordingly, I've inserted the following extract here, in the hope that it may make things a little clearer.

From *Interesting Places and Tedious People: A Wanderer's Waybook*, by Jerval Sekara, 145.M39.

SERENDIPITA IS WELL named, for it does indeed come as a delightful surprise to the warp-weary traveller; a small constellation of habitable worlds, though, it must be said, with varying degrees of comfort, orbiting a single gas giant of quite prodigious size. So large, indeed, that it radiates light and warmth in the manner of a small star,[1] rendering its half-dozen planet-sized moons tolerable for the hardy folk who make their homes here. The most favoured

---

1. *Unlikely as this may sound, Sekara isn't exaggerating. According to Mott, my savant, such protostars are hardly uncommon in the galaxy, although it's extremely unusual to find one circled by even one habitable world, let alone the multiplicity of them described in this account.*

of these is Serendipita itself, which enjoys a temperate climate, abundant oceans and two small polar caps. Rendered the capital world of the system by virtue of supporting the bulk of its population, and having been the first orb settled by humanity, it's a pleasant enough sphere to tempt even the most jaded wayfarer into lingering for a while.

Should its charms pall, however, the other moons of this singular primary are also worth visiting, with the exception of Tarwen, the industrial centre of this curious conglomeration of worlds. Tarwen is as aesthetically unpleasing as its inhabitants, who, like their home, are grimy and dour, and the best that can be said for the place is that its existence allows Serendipita itself to remain charmingly unspoilt, save for those little comforts of civilisation which only seem important when unobtainable. In a similar fashion, much of the agriculture supporting the far-flung population is relegated to other moons, although Serendipita does boast some tolerably picturesque rural hinterlands serving her larger cities.

It should be noted in passing that other centres of population exist in the wider stellar system, but contain nothing of interest, being devoted entirely to mining, commerce or other such occupations of the artisan class, while a remarkable number of ne'er-do-wells continually ply the magnificent ring system and innumerable lesser moons around Serendipita in search of exploitable resources and other plunder; not the least of which are the ramshackle vessels generally employed in this pursuit, and which come to grief about as often as one might expect given the inordinate number of hazards to navigation in so thick a belt of debris. From the surface of the habitable worlds, however, the ring is most notable for the breathtaking spectacle it affords those seeking diversion after nightfall.

FIFTEEN

OVER THE NEXT few days, I must confess, I had good reason to be thankful for Mira's intervention. The delegation had proven to be every bit as overrun with time-serving bureaucrats, Emperor-bothering ecclesiarchs and inbred imbeciles from the local aristocracy as I'd feared, far too many of whom wanted their picts taken with honest-to-Emperor Astartes, the Hero of Perlia, or both, to keep my temper in check without the considerable exertion of willpower. Fortunately, the prospect of having to ingratiate themselves with Jurgen in order to gain access to me deterred all but the most persistent, and the few who persevered had no more luck getting past him than anyone else I didn't want to see; but it couldn't be denied that Mira was doing an excellent job of keeping the majority occupied, and I was duly grateful. Quite what she did with them I had no idea, and cared even less, but it was bound to have fewer repercussions than my favoured option of shoving the lot of them out of the nearest airlock and leaving them to walk home.

At any event, her willingness to suffer fools gladly, or at least to tolerate them without giving way to the impulse to violence, left the way clear for me to assess the threat with the aid of General

Torven, the overall C-in-C[1] of the Guard units garrisoning the system against the possibility of an attack by the orks we'd run into on our way here, Planetary Marshal Kregeen, his opposite number in the local PDF (who, to my relieved surprise, seemed both to take her responsibilities seriously, and understand them, neither of which could normally be relied on when, as here, the senior command staff of the local standing army was drawn from the ranks of the local aristocracy), and Admiral Duque, whose stewardship of the SDF fleet may have lacked the swashbuckling panache of a Horatio Bugler,[2] but seemed solidly competent at least. All of them had brought aides, adjutants and advisors with them, of course, but the ones who sat in on the meetings generally had the good sense to keep quiet unless they had something useful to contribute, and I must say we made pretty good progress between us. Gries was, of course, far too busy directing the hunt for the space hulk to participate himself, but that was the whole point of my liaison job, and I made sure he had a cogent summary of our deliberations at the end of every session.

The good news was that we seemed to be pretty well prepared to counter the genestealers if they were foolish enough to show their hand (or talons, to be a little more accurate) openly. The existing threat of the orks meant that Serendipita was in a constant state of vigilance anyway, and everyone present had been involved in seeing off a raid or two in recent years. I had no doubt that the Serendipitans, and their Guard allies, were more than capable of holding their own against even a full-scale incursion, but the more insidious long-term threat posed by 'stealer infiltration required more subtle counter-insurgency measures which simply hadn't seemed necessary up until now.

'We've got a couple of regiments with that kind of experience,' Torven said, one of which turned out to have acquired theirs on Keffia, which was a considerable bonus. 'They can take point on

---

1. *The usual Imperial Guard abbreviation for commander-in-chief.*

2. *An Imperial Navy officer of some renown in the Damocles Gulf. Although he and Cain were both involved in the Adumbria incident of 937.M41, there's no evidence that they ever met face to face.*

this, and bring the others up to speed.' As always, he spoke quietly, but with the deliberate emphasis of someone who didn't need to raise his voice to be sure he was being listened to – an assumption which, given his wealth of experience in the field against the enemies of the Emperor, he was perfectly entitled to make. His appearance was as unassuming as his voice; despite his rank he still dressed for the field, in fatigues and body armour, although few of the men under his command would have either which fitted so well, or were kept so scrupulously clean. Unsurprisingly, he was popular with the common troopers, who regarded him as one of their own; and he'd certainly done his time in the field, if the burn scar which still marked the left side of his face (the result of a nearby plasma burst, if I was any judge) and the worn condition of his pistol grip was anything to go by.

'My people could benefit from some instruction in that area too,' Kregeen added, 'if we could arrange to liaise on that.' She was astute enough to know that the PDF were regarded as something of a joke by the Guard contingent, but never acknowledged it, always speaking to Torven as an equal; and he was sensible enough not to resent it, or show the fact if he did. Despite betraying her aristocratic lineage by sporting a dress uniform even Mira might have regarded as a little over-ornamented, she paid close attention to our deliberations, and such interjections as she made were always cogent. Now she rested her elbows on the table, supporting her chin on her hands, and looked at the general as though she'd requested nothing more significant than a fresh mug of recaf.

'That would be prudent,' Torven agreed, and two sets of aides peeled away from the table, to go into a huddle in one corner of the conference room which had been set aside for our use. Given that the long table and the padded benches were a comfortable size, instead of being scaled for the more massive frame of the Astartes, I assumed that some of the crew were even now cursing us quietly for the disruption to their regular messing arrangements – an impression strengthened by a stain in the grain of the tabletop not far from where I was sitting, which looked uncannily like gravy.

Kregeen nodded, meeting the general's light brown eyes with her own, which were the same flinty grey as her hair. Although she presumably had the same access to juvenat treatments as anyone else of her status, she'd evidently chosen to fix her biological age at around the mid-forties, as a visible reminder of the significance of her office. 'I'll open some channels with the Arbites as well,' she said. 'I'm sure they'll have some useful advice about what to look for.'

'That sounds like a good idea,' I agreed. Like most civilised worlds, Serendipita had a small staff of resident arbitrators to oversee the local law enforcers, and I'd been vaguely surprised not to find one of them included in the delegation.[1] 'They've had more practice at rooting out clandestine activity than anyone else, so if a 'stealer cult does get established, they're almost certain to be the first to know.'

'If they know what they're looking for in the first place,' Torven added.

I nodded. 'Good point. Perhaps you could use the marshal's contacts to make sure they get the benefit of your Keffian veterans' experience.' Not a desperately subtle way of making sure the Guard and the PDF were working together, rather than following their natural inclinations to ignore one another as much as possible, but it seemed to do the job: Torven and Kregeen both nodded, a pair of aides next to them made eye contact and brief entries on their data-slates, and we were onto the next item for discussion.

'It's all well and prudent,' Duque said, having listened to the exchange without commenting, 'to be prepared to fight the genestealers if we have to, but surely it would be far more sensible to eliminate the threat entirely before things get to that point.' He had the pale complexion and ectomorphic build of a void-born, and no doubt felt more comfortable aboard a vessel in space than on the surface of a world, which was quite ironic given the unusual degree of choice his home system offered in that regard.

---

1. *It seems that there were only three, an arbitrator senioris and two assistants, none of whom were on Serendipita itself when the Governor's shuttle was dispatched.*

'It would,' I agreed, 'if that were possible. Do you have any suggestions as to how we go about achieving it?'

The admiral nodded, his pale face bobbing above a midnight-blue uniform which seemed even darker than it actually was by contrast. 'I do,' he assured me, with quiet confidence. He gestured to one of his staff, a junior lieutenant who bore a faint resemblance to him, a niece or a cousin perhaps, and took the data-slate she proffered. 'Given the progress of the search so far, we can assume that the *Spawn of Damnation* will be located within the week, and most probably a great deal sooner.' He consulted the display, then glanced around the table. 'I've already given orders for the majority of our System Defence Fleet to rendezvous with the *Revenant*, in the expectation that by the time they arrive, the hulk will have been found.'

'Well done.' Kregeen was nodding in approval. 'If we can keep it blockaded, nothing will be able to get on or off. All we'll have to do is wait for it to fall back into the warp, and blast anything which gets too close or tries to leave in the meantime.'

'Blockaded?' Duque looked surprised for a moment, then smiled, in what looked to me like honest amusement. 'You misunderstand me, madam marshal. I intend to destroy it.'

'With respect, admiral,' I said, 'I think you may be underestimating the sheer size of the thing. I'm given to understand that previous encounters recorded its mass as being on the order of a small planetoid, rather than a spacecraft as we'd normally understand the term.'

'Quite so.' The pale man didn't seem too put out at the interruption. 'But we'll have plenty of time to shoot at it. If the estimates the Astartes have given us are accurate, it will be at least a month before the *Spawn* passes close enough to any human habitation to pose a threat. We can reduce it a piece at a time if we have to, but reduce it we will.'

'Won't that create an even greater danger?' Torven asked, looking troubled. 'That amount of debris will pose a significant hazard to navigation throughout the system.'

'Not for long,' Duque assured him. 'The *Spawn of Damnation* is currently heading almost directly for the centre, and will end up falling into a cometary orbit about the sun within the next two to three years. It won't take much to time the attacks to nudge it a little, so that the bulk of the debris will pass close enough to be vaporised. Some of it will escape, of course, but that won't be passing close to Serendipita, or any of the other habs, on this orbit, and by the time it comes round again it'll be the middle of M43; time enough, I would have thought, to take any reasonable precautions against it hitting something.'

'It sounds a bit chancy,' I said, 'but I'd rather have a cloud of junk to deal with than a space hulk full of 'stealers.' After all, there was no telling how long it might take for the *Spawn* to drop back into the warp again; according to Yaffel they sometimes stayed in the real galaxy for decades, and the thought of thousands of genestealers drifting around a densely inhabited system, just waiting for some idiot whose greed was stronger than their sense of self-preservation to come dropping in looking for loot, made my blood run cold. After all, that's what appeared to have happened on Viridia, and the blasted hulk had only been in-system for less than a day. Duque's SDF could mount a blockade, of course, but the longer it went on, the higher the chances of a 'stealer or two somehow managing to infect a host and sneaking off to wreak havoc.

I nodded judiciously. 'In the absence of a more effective plan to preserve the security of the Serendipita system, I'll recommend we carry it out.'

'OUT OF THE question,' Gries said flatly. By now I'd got to know him well enough to realise a statement like that was effectively the end of the matter, but I have to admit I was taken aback by the speed and vehemence of his reaction.

Accordingly, I merely nodded in response, masking my dismay with the instinctive ease of a man who'd bet heavily on an inordinate number of promising-looking tarot hands in his time, only to realise shortly afterwards that everyone else's were better. (A reflex which had enabled me to scoop rather more pots than I'd otherwise have been entitled to, nevertheless.) 'Might I ask why?' I enquired, as though the answer were merely of academic interest.

I couldn't deny that Duque's scheme was chancy, to say the least, but it still seemed to me that the balance of risk was marginally in its favour.

'Because the *Spawn's* value is incalculable,' Drumon put in, glancing across the bridge towards the hololith, where Yaffel and a cadre of his red-robed acolytes were twittering away to one another in Binary, as they studied a three-dimensional image of what looked to me like the circulatory system of a diseased heart. 'A space hulk that venerable is a repository of archeotech almost beyond imagining.'

With a sudden sinking feeling, I realised that the diagram the tech-priests were studying so intently must be a schematic of the hulk's interior, no doubt reconstructed from generations of sensor scans culled from the archives, and therefore so out of date as to be worse than useless.[1] 'Don't tell me you're planning to board it?' I protested, too startled to give a frak for protocol.

'We are,' Gries said, in a voice which brooked no argument. It's probably a measure of how startled I was that I tried arguing anyway.

'The potential rewards may well be worth the risk,' I conceded, secure in the knowledge that someone else would be taking it, and determined to at least be diplomatic about my reservations, 'but surely our highest priority has to be the security of Serendipita?'

Clearly, Gries wasn't used to having his decisions called into question, at least by anyone outside his own Chapter,[2] but fortunately he seemed willing to make an exception in my case. If anything he seemed surprised, rather than irked, which was fine by me; my sparring sessions with Drumon had left me well aware of the speed and precision with which an angry Astartes could strike down anyone provoking their wrath, and I had no desire to provide a bit of practice.

---

1. *Or perhaps not. The configuration of the internal spaces would be unlikely to change much over the centuries, other than the occasional structural collapse as overstressed materials finally gave way.*

2. *Or, probably, within it. Space Marine units tend to operate autonomously for years, even decades, at a time, and officers of Gries's rank and status would have little opportunity or inclination to refer matters to a higher level of the command chain.*

'Our highest priority is our duty to the Emperor,' Gries told me, looking down to meet my eyes, and I saw in his the kind of complete and utter conviction that I'm more used to seeing in madmen, inquisitors and members of the Adepta Sororitas.[1] 'And I will determine where that lies.' He didn't have to add, 'and not you,' because I heard it quite clearly in any case.

'Quite so,' I agreed, inclining my head in a respectful nod. I wanted him to continue to think of me as a trustworthy ally, rather than a potential problem. 'Given your wealth of knowledge and experience, I wouldn't have thought otherwise for a moment. But I'm afraid it's my job to keep the Serendipitans on side, and the only thing they seem concerned about is the clear and present danger to their home world.'

'Of course.' Gries nodded, apparently mollified. 'Then you must assure them we remain committed to that objective.'

'I'll make them see sense,' I promised, although to be honest that was something which seemed in very short supply aboard the *Revenant* at the moment. Gries and Drumon seemed to be buying it anyway, looking down at me in a faintly approving fashion which reminded me of my old schola tutors when I parroted the answer I knew they wanted to hear. 'Blockading the hulk seems a rather more practical option in any case.'

'Considerably more,' Drumon agreed. 'And the presence of an Astartes strike cruiser should dissuade anyone from trying to run it.'

'It would me,' I agreed. 'But I'm not a scav barge skipper who thinks the Emperor just dropped a fortune in his lap. Anyone stupid enough to risk boarding a hulk full of genestealers isn't going to be put off by the near certainty of being blown to bits on the way in.'

For a moment, as my brain caught up with my tongue, I wondered if I'd risked offending my hosts again, but apparently neither Astartes thought my remark about the idiocy of attempting

---

1. *Hardly flattering to see inquisitors among the list, but considering the one Cain had the most to do with apart from myself was Killian, a Radical renegade mass-murderer, and barking mad to boot, I can't say I'm all that surprised.*

to board the *Spawn of Damnation* applied to them. But just to make sure, I thought I'd better draw a distinction. 'I'm sure your operation over there will be rather better planned and resourced than a scavvy raid,[1] however.'

'Indeed,' Gries said, nodding again. Then, to my surprise, he strode to the hololith, scattering tech-priests as he went, and gestured to me to follow him.

I looked at the tangle of passageways laid out by the faintly flickering three-dimensional image, my underhiver's instinct translating the intersecting streaks of variously coloured light into an almost physical sense of the space they represented. (Something I was to be all too grateful for later, as it turned out, but which at the time seemed no more than a convenient aid to interpreting the briefing.)

'Our first entry point will be here,' Drumon said, indicating a chamber somewhere on the outer skin of the complex weave of ducts and corridors. 'A relatively undamaged docking bay, which seems large enough to accommodate a Thunderhawk, and defensible enough to provide a beachhead. The Terminators will suppress any resistance and secure the perimeter. Once that's been done, Magos Yaffel and myself will lead a working party here...'

He did something with his servo-arm which caused the image to zoom in on the sector he'd first indicated, separating the beachhead and the objective by almost a metre instead of just the millimetre or two they'd occupied of the overall schematic. As the area depicted enlarged, so did the detail, and a further tangle of intersecting capillaries grew around the veins and arteries we were already looking at, leaving the whole hololith just as crowded as it had been before. For the first time I began to appreciate just how vast and complex the leviathan of the warp we were pursuing really was, and wished the boarders every bit of luck the Emperor could spare; I was certain they were going to need it.

---

1. *A slang term common to many hive communities, referring to those both literally and figuratively at the bottom of the social heap, who scrabble a precarious existence out of what they can salvage of the detritus falling from the higher levels. Cain alludes repeatedly to an early life spent in an underhive, but as yet his world of origin remains obscure.*

'…and attempt to recover the cogitator core of this vessel,' Drumon concluded.

'Why that one?' I asked.

'Because it has the most directly accessible cogitator banks of any of the derelicts making up the hulk,' Gries said, as though that should have been obvious from a cursory glance at the pile of virtual string hovering in front of my face.

'And because it's been tentatively identified as a Redeemer-class vessel, none of which have been in service for over five thousand years,' Yaffel put in, positively salivating at the prospect. 'The maintenance logs alone should yield untold blessings of the Omnissiah which have been lost to posterity.'

'A prize indeed,' I said evenly, which was far more tactful than verbalising my real thoughts would have been. It seemed to me that if the galaxy had been getting along perfectly well without these lost blessings for the last five millennia in any case, losing the 'stealers along with them would have been better all round. But it wasn't my call, so that was that. I'd just have to break it to Duque that he wouldn't be able to knock any lumps off the hulk, at least for the time being, and ride out the ensuing recrimination. Come to that, Torven and Kregeen would be far from thrilled too. At least I had Gries to blame, and I'd been a commissar for long enough to know how to use their common resentment to get them cooperating a bit more effectively than they otherwise would have done, so all in all, things could have been worse. Then something else occurred to me. 'This is probably a stupid question,' I asked, 'but what happens if the *Spawn* falls back into the warp while your sca… retrieval expedition is still aboard it?'

Yaffel gave me a faintly superior look, like an eldar deigning to notice one of the lesser breeds of the galaxy (which they consider to be everyone except them). 'That can't happen,' he said, with an airy confidence which left me far from convinced.

Drumon nodded. 'The hulk is coasting in towards the sun,' he reminded me. 'And natural warp fissures can only occur outside a gravity well. Even a starship with a properly focussed Geller field can only force its way between the realms on the fringes of a system.'

'So it's stuck here until it drifts out past the halo again,' I said, grateful as always for his pared-down summary of the situation.

Magos and Techmarine nodded in unison, apparently equally delighted at the prospect. They'd have years to poke around in the wreckage for technosorcerous trinkets, with nothing more to worry about than Emperor knew how many ravenous genestealers lurking in the dark.

Which also meant that, far from coming to a close as I'd expected, my assignment here looked like being prolonged indefinitely. Someone would have to liaise between the Reclaimers, the Serendipitans and the Imperial Guard, and, for better or worse, I'd been stuck with the job.

I considered the implications. It wouldn't be too hard to convince everyone that the best place to work from would be Torven's HQ on Serendipita, where I'd have ready access to system-wide intelligence, the PDF and SDF command structures, and, most importantly, all the little comforts available on a civilised world, instead of being stuck aboard a starship where the chances of finding a decent tarot game were about as high as Jurgen becoming the next lord general. And while I was getting on with looking busy, I'd be a long way from brigade headquarters on Coronus, along with anyone intent on roping me in to whatever suicide mission they happened to have to hand. All in all, I thought, I could live with that.

I RETURNED TO my quarters in a distinctly cheerful mood, to find Mira waiting for me while Jurgen laid out a tolerably pleasant supper, and lost no time in sharing the good news with her. She'd have found out anyway, soon enough, and I felt it prudent to be the one to tell her. That way, whatever else she might take exception to, at least I couldn't be accused of deceit.

Despite whatever forebodings I may have harboured, however, she seemed almost as pleased at the prospect as I was, which I suppose shouldn't have come as that much of a surprise. She'd clearly found life aboard the *Revenant* even more tedious than I had, and would no doubt seize the chance to relocate to more salubrious surroundings with equal alacrity.

'In fact,' she said, a forkful of smoked salma from her hoard of delicacies halfway to her mouth, 'I suppose my little errand here is pretty much over too.'

'I suppose so,' I agreed, taking a mouthful of my own and washing it down with an inoffensive vintage I strongly suspected was the best the Space Marine vessel had to offer. 'The hulk definitely isn't going to present any kind of threat to Viridia from now on.' When it eventually did drift back into the warp, I had no doubt that the Reclaimers and the Adeptus Mechanicus would go right along with it, as reluctant to let it go as a kroot with a bone; and their eagerness to carry on looting the hulk wherever it ended up would prevent it from posing a threat to any Imperial system it happened to arrive in, which was all to the good.

Mira smiled, as though I'd just said something witty. 'Quite,' she agreed. 'But I did have other motives for coming along, you'll recall.'

'Of course,' I said, dredging my memory. Something about strengthening her claim to the throne back home, and finding a consort able to help her grab it. 'I'm glad they seem to be working out for you too.' She seemed to have given up on the ridiculous idea of persuading a Space Marine to elope with her, and for a moment I wondered who else she'd found who looked like a suitable candidate. One of the Serendipitan delegation, presumably – they can't all have been as pointless as they looked.

Her smile spread. 'For both of us, surely.'

'Well, yes,' I agreed. It wouldn't take much to turn my liaison job into a sinecure guaranteed to keep me comfortably out of harm's way for years to come, which was pretty much as good as it ever got for someone in my position. I raised my goblet, in a slightly ironic toast. 'Here's to both of us getting what we want.'

'To both of us,' Mira said, her glass clinking against mine, and I found myself genuinely wishing her well, which for someone as focussed on my own concerns as I usually was, came as a bit of a surprise. Her cheeks coloured slightly, and as she lowered her drink, she looked at me in a manner I found a little odd. 'Are you sure about this?'

'Of course I am,' I said, touched by her concern. The sooner I could feel a world beneath my feet again the better.

'Good.' She became businesslike again. 'Serendipita doesn't do much trade with us, but there's a Charter ship or two linking the systems, with only a couple of intermediate layovers. We should be able to get passage within a few months.' She looked at me speculatively. 'Unless you've got some strings you can pull? We might as well use them while we can.'

'While we can?' I echoed, feeling oddly like a character in a ball-room farce.[1] Her words were undeniably Gothic, but the meaning behind them kept eluding me.

Mira nodded. 'While you still have some influence with the Munitorum,' she elucidated, as though that made perfect sense. 'Could you get us berths on a military ship?'

'I suppose so,' I said, falling back on the card player's instinct which generally helped me out at moments like this. Time and again I've found that if you appear to understand what's going on, and don't panic, sooner or later you'll get a clue. Everything will fall into place, and no one will ever know you were out of your depth. It's an important skill for a commissar, too, come to think of it, as we're supposed to look calm and in control whatever happens. It's remarkably difficult to rally troops under fire when you're dithering about screaming 'Frak, oh frak, we're all going to die!' So I nodded judiciously, as though she'd just asked a perfectly reasonable question. 'If you wanted to hurry back, of course.'

'Good point,' she rejoined, smiling at me again, in a manner I can only describe as curiously cloying. 'Let's enjoy ourselves for a few weeks while we can. Serendipita's quite a pleasant world, apparently.'

'Something to do with the ring system, I suppose,' I said, having

---

1. *A popular form of theatre on several worlds in the sector, in which a large cast of characters continually misunderstand one another to comedic effect. They're generally set in an aristocratic milieu, allowing the general populace a bit of harmless amusement at the expense of a stratum of society that's barely aware of their existence in any case, and culminate in some dramatic contrivance to bring everyone together at the same time. For obvious reasons a ball is a frequent choice of the lazier playwrights, hence the name.*

picked up a little bit about conditions there from Torven and the others. 'I hear it's quite spectacular.'

'Then you've talked me into it.' Mira's smile became coquettish. 'We might as well enjoy the honeymoon before we have to get down to work.'

'Exactly,' I heard my mouth say, the pieces finally dropping into place, and our earlier conversation taking on an entirely new meaning which had escaped me at the time. She hadn't been out to bag herself an Astartes at all. The Liberator of Perlia would do perfectly well as a consort, particularly as I seemed to be a hero on Viridia as well.

A chill prickle of panic chased itself down my spine. I can't deny that, in the abstract, the notion of continuing to enjoy Mira's more obvious charms indefinitely, along with the material comforts formalising our relationship would provide, had its appeal, but the idea was utterly preposterous. The Commissariat wasn't like one of the confection-box regiments[1] my would-be fiancée and her aristocratic cronies amused themselves by playing at officers in, which would cheerfully accept a resigned commission whenever more pressing or diverting business presented itself. If I abandoned my assignment to return to Viridia with her I'd be branded a deserter, and the only question left open about my future would be whether the ensuing tribunal had me shot by a firing squad, or packed me off to a penal legion to let the enemies of the Emperor save them the ammo. No doubt Mira believed that being the consort of a planetary governor would be sufficient protection from the wrath of my erstwhile colleagues, but I was under no such illusion: once you put on the scarlet sash, it's there till they bury you in it (assuming they can find enough bits for the ceremony, which in our vocation is never entirely certain). Even if you make it through

---

1. *On Viridia, not to mention many other worlds where a period of service in the PDF is considered an acceptable way of keeping young members of the nobility relatively harmlessly occupied, the rather more flamboyant than practical uniforms of the units so favoured are a perennially popular subject for such packaging. Why any confectioner would consider their wares enhanced by such images we can only speculate, but the hope of selling a few boxes to rich idiots would be my guess.*

to retirement intact, you can still be yanked back into the field pretty much on a whim, as I've found out only too well these last few years.[1]

Even so, I hesitated before speaking. Mira was clearly under the impression that I'd not only divined her purpose, but somehow signalled my agreement to her absurd proposal. I knew only too well how she was likely to react to being disabused. I'd seen the lurking virago erupt from behind the refined facade over matters so minor they'd barely registered with me, and now I was about to take a chainsword to her most cherished ambitions. Worse still, of course, would be the blow to her vanity. Most women like to think they're irresistible, and discovering that she wasn't wouldn't sit well at all. Add to that the fact that I'd seen her kill people without turning an immaculately groomed hair, and my wariness becomes even more understandable.

All this being so, it can come as little surprise to hear that I remained paralysed by indecision, nodding and responding with automatic platitudes, while Mira prattled on about her grandiose plans for Viridia once we'd consolidated her grip on it, most of which seemed to consist of score-settling with people I'd never heard of. Whether I would eventually have found the courage to speak out, or just jumped on the first transport ship back to Coronus while her back was turned, I'll never know, however. I was just on the point of pouring myself the largest amasec I thought I could get away with, when Jurgen returned to my quarters, his face composed in the faintly dyspeptic expression he tended to adopt whenever he felt an air of gravitas was required.

'Sorry to interrupt your meal, sir,' he said, 'but your presence is requested on the bridge. They seem to think they've found it.'

---

1. *A clear reference to his involvement in the defence of the sector against the tyranid hive fleets at the turn of the millennium, the details of which, though fascinating, need not detain us at this juncture.*

SIXTEEN

Seizing gratefully on my aide's timely intervention, I lost no time in hurrying to the bridge, leaving Mira happily planning her *coup d'état*[1] with all the enthusiasm most women of her rank reserve for cotillions. Though my mind continued to reel with the shock of the realisation of what I'd blundered into, I must confess that the bustle of activity which met my eyes the moment I entered the nerve centre of the *Revenant* was almost sufficient to drive it out entirely.

'Contact confirmed,' the auspex operator was saying as I stepped through the doors, which were still showing faint traces of orkish small-arms fire despite the best efforts of the shipboard artisans to restore the devotional images adorning them, and the air of expectation suffusing the chamber became so dense I almost had to resort to hacking through it with my chainsword. 'It's definitely a

---

1. *Despite Cain's highly subjective characterisation of her as both ruthless and selfish, there's no evidence at all that Mira intended deposing her father by force of arms. His earlier assertion that she was intent merely on strengthening her position against rival claimants when the governorship eventually fell vacant seems far more likely.*

hard return,[1] refined metals by the signature.' For the first time I heard a tremor of suppressed excitement in the even tones I'd grown used to hearing from the Chapter serfs manning the bridge, and, despite my own concerns, felt an answering flicker of it within myself.

If this truly was the end of our quest, it could hardly have come at a more propitious time. It meant I'd be on my way to Serendipita almost immediately, and once I was there, I'd be able to avoid Mira far more effectively than I possibly could in the cramped confines of the *Revenant*. A faint flicker of optimism even dared to raise the hope that, once we were back on *terra firma*, and she was again immersed in her own social environment, she'd begin to see the huge gulf between our respective milieux for what it was, and abandon the absurd project she'd conceived of her own volition. (Not that it seemed particularly likely. When she made her mind up about something, she pursued it as tenaciously as a gaunt scenting blood.) It was possible, however, that I could get off the ship before she noticed I was gone, citing orders and duty, which would at least buy me a breathing space.

'Could it just be a vessel?' Gries asked, leaning forwards a little, as though he could force the pict screen to greater magnification purely by willpower. 'The SDF flotilla should be nearing the rendezvous point by now.'

'Unlikely,' Drumon told him. 'None of the System Defence boats would be that far out of position.' He loomed over the auspex operator and made some minute adjustments to the dials set into the surface of the control lectern, pinching them delicately between the fingers of his gauntlets, like an ogryn trying to pick up a porcelain tea bowl. 'Displacement reads in the gigatonnes.'

'Then it's the *Spawn*,' Yaffel said, sounding rather more excited than was strictly commensurate with his position. He wasn't exactly hopping up and down, which would have been difficult given his lack of legs, but he was definitely oscillating more violently than usual. 'It's the only reasonable inference.'

---

1. *By which he meant that the object the auspex was scanning was dense enough to register strongly, and was therefore probably not a natural phenomenon.*

'And right where you predicted it would be,' I reminded him, which wasn't exactly true, as he'd only been able to narrow it down to a pretty wide volume of space, but he didn't seem inclined to quibble about it, merely nodding sagely in agreement.

'The Omnissiah leads us down the path of logic to a sure destination,'[1] he said, with the comfortable certainty of a man for whom the universe not only ran like clockwork, but chimed the first few bars of 'Throne Eternal' on the hour.

'Boosting the gain on the long-range imagifers,' Drumon said, doing something I couldn't see to the back of a nearby lectern with his servo-arm, and Yaffel trundled over to the hololith, where he began to poke around in turn.

'Then if the interociters hold together,' the tech-priest added, 'we should be able to... Omnissiah be praised.' The three-dimensional display flickered into life, and the image of what looked like a jagged piece of scrap metal began to tumble gently within it, growing larger with every passing minute, until it filled the space almost entirely. It wavered a bit, as such representations generally do, but Yaffel seemed to know what he was about, and with a few muttered benedictions, some fiddling with the controls, and a well-placed thump of his fist, he steadied the image.

'The *Spawn of Damnation*,' Drumon said, his voice remarkably hushed for a Space Marine. Gries nodded, apparently too overcome to speak at all, and his battered half-face relaxed into an expression I found hard to interpret, but had certainly never seen there before.

I studied the image, seeing nothing that made much sense at first. I was aware of the scale of the thing intellectually, of course, but it wasn't until I suddenly recognised a small blemish on the surface as a Galaxy-class troopship that something of the awe clearly felt by everyone else present transmitted itself to me. 'Throne on Earth,' I found myself saying. 'It's vast!'

Even that involuntary exclamation barely began to cover the sheer size of the hulk. It was big the way a small moon is, beyond any sense of scale a human can grasp or relate

---

1. *Another quotation from* Soylens Viridiens for the Machine-Spirit.

to.[1] Despite knowing the effort was pointless, I began to try to pick out more details, but any attempt to impose order or understanding on the tangled lump of wreckage was doomed to failure. Even trying to estimate the number of vessels which had fallen victim to this reef of space, only to become part of it in their turn, was impossible; at least for me, although I was sure Yaffel would have been able to take a shot at it. Drawn together by eddies in the warp currents, their physical structures had become combined and mingled, twisted around and within one another as they collided, rather than shattering and fragmenting as they would have done in the materium. It was as if a vast hand had scooped up a random selection of starships, and kneaded them together like a pastrycook with a fistful of dough. And it wasn't just ships: I was sure that here and there I could make out the harsher lines of pieces of natural debris, rocks and asteroids, drawn in by the gravitational field of the hulk during its periodic transitions through realspace, to become inextricable parts of it in the crucible of the warp.

The worst thing about it, however, was the sense of menace it radiated, an almost palpable threat, like the snarling of an ork just before it charges.

'Where are you planning to board it?' I asked Yaffel, and he indicated a semi-intact hull about three-quarters of the way round the lump from the wreck of the Galaxy I'd previously recognised.

'The docking bay here,' he told me, and I was orientated at last, my underhiver's synapses instinctively overlaying the internal structure I'd seen before on the exterior view. 'The sensor records we recovered from the archives are some centuries old, of course, but they seem to indicate that it could be made functional again with little effort.'

'So long as a 'stealer brood hasn't set up home there in the interim,' I said, not entirely sure how serious I was being.

'We'll take precautions,' Yaffel assured me, sounding blithely unconcerned; but I'd seen purestrains up close too often, and too recently, to dismiss the threat they represented so casually.

---

1. *In actual fact it was only four or five kilometres across in any direction, but that's quite big enough under the circumstances.*

'Then you'd better hope to the Throne they're sufficient,' I coun-selled, perhaps a little more sharply than I'd intended. It may have been this which drew Drumon to join us, or perhaps he just wanted a better view of the space hulk. At any event he was sud-denly at my side, looming over me like a well-disposed promontory.

'They will be,' he promised. 'By the time we get over there, we will know where the bulk of the brood is.' His demeanour was calm, and despite the improbability of his claim, I found myself reassured. After all, he was one of the Emperor's chosen, and he'd probably been facing 'stealers or worse since my great-grandfather was tracking bounties in the sump (or trying to outrun the would-be collectors of his own, most likely),[1] so he ought to know what he was doing.

'How soon will that be?' I asked, conscious of my responsibili-ties to Torven and the others. If I was going to make a good case for transferring my liaison post to the Imperial Guard headquar-ters on Serendipita, I'd better have some juicy titbits to throw to them.

Drumon considered the question a moment. 'Around twelve hours,' he said. 'The cats should have dispersed enough to locate any active genestealers by that point.'

'Cats?' I echoed, baffled. Plenty of Guard regiments use animals for one purpose or another on the battlefield, generally as cavalry mounts or attack beasts, but I'd never heard of Astartes doing so; and even if they did, felines would hardly seem the most likely creatures to give a genestealer a run for its money.

'See ay tee,' Yaffel elucidated, no doubt divining my confusion. 'Cyber-Altered Task units. Like very simple servitors, without the biological components.'

'Then how do they work?' I asked, even more puzzled than before. I might not have been a tech-priest, but even I knew it was

---

1. *A rare direct reference to Cain's own family history, although, as noted elsewhere, anything he says in this regard must be treated with considerable caution. Many of these fragments of information are clearly contradictory, particularly those which occur in his reported conversations with others.*

the living brain which allowed a servitor to remember and process simple instructions.

'Quite satisfactorily,' Drumon said, with a momentary smile at his own wit, before continuing. 'They require no cognitive functions; just a simple vox circuit to relay picts and other environmental data. Once released, they just keep moving in a straight line until they reach an obstacle.'

'Of which,' I said, equally dryly, 'I suspect the *Spawn of Damnation* has more than its share.'

'Undoubtedly,' Yaffel agreed, apparently as constitutionally incapable of recognising sarcasm as the majority of those in his vocation. 'But the CATs have a simple mechanism attached to their tracks. When they reach an obstruction they can't negotiate, they simply rotate ten degrees on the spot, before moving forwards again. If they're still impeded, they repeat the process, and so on. Eventually they find a direction they can progress in.'

'They sound ingenious,' I said, wondering which of them had come up with the idea, and suspecting it was probably Drumon; the devices Yaffel was describing seemed to fit his practical turn of mind rather better than the tech-priest's analytical one.[1]

'They should serve their purpose,' Drumon agreed. 'We plan to teleport thirty of them across to the hulk, around the area we intend operating in. If there are enough genestealers around to pose a threat, we'll know about it long before the Thunderhawk arrives.'

'That sounds like a wise precaution,' I agreed, nodding judiciously. If I'd been going off to loot a derelict, knowing there was

---

1. *In fact CATs have been in service with the Astartes and the Adeptus Mechanicus for centuries, if not millennia. Few Space Marine Chapters make much use of them, however, preferring to rely on the expertise of their scouts under most circumstances, while the Mechanicus finds the more versatile servitor better suited for most practical purposes. Nevertheless, the construction and modification of CATs remains a popular pastime for a considerable number of tech-priests, who claim to find the activity meditatively calming and beneficial in advancing their understanding of the blessings of the Machine-God, so that it's a rare visit to a Mechanicus shrine which isn't likely to be interrupted by the erratic progress of one or more of these ambulatory devices. Despite these pious assertions, and though true servants of the Omnissiah would vigorously deny the fact, to outsiders they seem less like recreational construction projects than pets.*

a 'stealer brood lurking somewhere aboard, I'd feel a lot happier knowing where they were too – or, at least, that they weren't in the immediate vicinity of where I planned to be. 'Can you stick a bolter on them as well?'

Yaffel shook his head, failing to recognise the joke. 'That wouldn't be a practical option,' he began. 'The power-to-weight ratio–'

'Pity,' I said, little realising how prescient I was being. 'That might save everyone a lot of trouble.'

As I'd ANTICIPATED, Torven and the Serendipitans were less than enthused by the tidings I bore, and the atmosphere around the makeshift conference table was distinctly frosty by the time I concluded my briefing. It was plain that all three of them shared my misgivings about the wisdom of boarding the *Spawn of Damnation*, and, as I'd expected, it was Duque who first put them into words.

'So what you're telling us,' he said slowly, 'is that not only are we prevented from destroying the thing by the presence of friendly units in the target zone, we can expect the genestealers to be handed a potential vector of contamination on a platter with a salad garnish?'

'Essentially, yes,' I told him, noting the restive fashion in which Torven and Kregeen shifted their weight on the benches as I did so. 'But I'm sure our gallant allies in the Astartes will take all due precautions.' Not for the first time, I found myself treading a delicate path between the conflicting agendas of the Reclaimers and the defenders of Serendipita. If I was going to turn this assignment into a comfortable refuge from a galaxy apparently hell-bent on killing me, I needed to keep both factions feeling I was more in sympathy with their point of view than the other.

'No doubt,' Kregeen said, in a voice which oozed dubiety.

'They should know what they're doing,' Torven said. 'They're Astartes after all. It's the cogboys that worry me. They seem so obsessed with the prospect of getting their hands on a stash of archeotech they're incapable of assessing the risk objectively.'

I couldn't argue with that, and I didn't have the heart to tell him that so far as I could see the Reclaimers were equally keen to go dashing off on a treasure hunt, so I simply nodded judiciously. 'They believe they can, of course, but I've yet to meet a 'stealer that'll back down and run away if you tell it its presence is a statistical fluke.' That lightened the mood, of course, as I'd hoped it would, as well as reminding them that I'd faced and fought the creatures on more than one occasion, and I followed up the advantage with a little careful morale-boosting. 'At least if anyone does fall prey to them, the damage ought to be self-limiting,' I added. 'Astartes and Mechanicus tend not to go in for large families.'

This time the witticism produced visible smiles, even from some of the aides, who generally seemed to feel that their chances of promotion depended on behaving as much like servitors as possible without a lobotomy.

'Quite so,' Torven agreed evenly. 'But the bulk of the *Revenant's* crew are ordinary men. If any of them should become tainted, and make their way to Serendipita, they'll start spawning hybrids almost at once.'

This was true, of course, and I nodded reassuringly. 'Then it's fortunate that only Astartes and members of the Adeptus Mechanicus will be included in the boarding party. None of the Chapter serfs will be exposed.'

'Not initially,' Torven said. 'But you said it yourself, they intend to continue exploring the hulk for as long as it remains in the materium. That could be anything up to a decade, and a lot can happen in that amount of time.'

'And what happens if one of the Astartes does get implanted?' Kregeen asked. 'They don't have to father children to act in the interest of the brood mind, do they?' For a moment the image of the tainted PDF troopers who'd turned against Mira and I in the tunnels beneath Fidelis rose up in my mind, and I tried not to contemplate the havoc a similarly compromised Space Marine could wreak. Not to mention the prospect of an implanted Thunderhawk pilot smuggling a few purestrains on board, to cut a swathe through the crew, thereby seeding the nucleus of another genestealer cult in the heart of Serendipitan society.

'No, they don't,' I agreed, my resolve to get as far away from the *Revenant* as quickly as possible even stronger than before. 'I'll raise the possibility with Captain Gries at the earliest opportunity and let you know what precautions he'll be taking against it.' If nothing else, he was a realist, and I was sure he had contingency plans in place, even if they were just the same as the ones we had in the Guard: summary execution and burn the body. (Which was in fact the case: when I did eventually get the chance to raise the subject he became as close to agitated as I ever saw him, which I found strangely reassuring. Clearly he regarded the notion of losing one of his own to the brood mind as abhorrent as any mortal commander would have done.[1])

'That's all very well,' Duque said, 'but I'd rather take precautions of my own.' In the absence of a hololith, or pict screen large enough for us all to look at, he passed round a data-slate, on which a cluster of illuminated dots appeared, annotated with icons identifying them as the hulk, the *Revenant* and a dozen or so System Defence boats. 'I'm deploying the blockade in this pattern. Individual ships will rotate in and out, of course, according to operational requirements, refit and resupply, but the total number will never drop below this minimum.'

'It looks pretty tight,' I said, although my grasp of three-dimensional tactics was tenuous at best; one of the first things a good commissar (as opposed to the by-the-book martinets who'll execute a trooper at the drop of a hat, and like as not end up on the wrong end of a negligent discharge[2]) learns is when to dispense a few words of quiet encouragement. 'But won't committing so many vessels to this operation leave you overstretched elsewhere in the system?'

'We'll manage,' Duque said. 'We won't have much of a strategic reserve left, admittedly, but we can still respond to a greenskin

---

1. *If not more so: this would irrevocably contaminate the gene-seed carried by the host's progenoid glands, passing on the taint to any later recruits implanted with it.*

2. *An Imperial Guard term for the accidental firing of a weapon.*

raid effectively enough if we have to. And the genestealers are here now, so that's where I'm putting my ships. If the worst happens, we can still keep them from causing any harm.'

'Well, let's hope you don't have to,' I said, taking his meaning and nodding almost imperceptibly to let him know I'd done so. He'd positioned his ships where they could combine their fire against the *Revenant* if the worst came to the worst, and enough of the Reclaimers and their vassals were taken over by the brood mind to seize control of the cruiser. If it ever came down to it, the fight would be a bloody one, but the SDF would almost certainly prevail by sheer weight of numbers. 'I take it everyone else has been considering the worst-case scenarios?'

Torven and Kregeen glanced at one another, then nodded in unison, and I was pleased to see that they appeared to be working together reasonably well on this. 'We have,' Torven confirmed. 'The marshal and I are agreed that the existing contingency plans against an orkish invasion will prove sufficient if required.' So it seemed we were as prepared as we could ever be to defend ourselves against a strike force of implanted Space Marines spearheading a genestealer swarm: another possibility I devoutly hoped would remain purely theoretical.

'The trouble is,' Kregeen said, 'we've got no real idea of the scale of the threat. Best case, the Astartes and the Mechanicus really are as on top of things as they like to think, and we can let them get on with it knowing the admiral's blockade will be enough to do the job if they fumble. Worst case, it's all going to the warp in a sabretache, and we need to be ready to mobilise in a heartbeat.' She shrugged. 'So which is it?'

I adopted an expression intended to convey sober reflection. 'I don't suppose we'll know for sure until they've been over there,' I said, after pausing just long enough to give the impression I'd been mulling it over.

'Exactly,' Torven agreed. He leaned across the table towards me, as though about to impart a confidence he'd rather not have overheard. 'Which is why we'd all feel a lot happier if there was an objective observer attached to the boarding party.'

Duque and Kregeen nodded their agreement, and with a

sudden thrill of horror uncannily reminiscent of my conversation with Mira, I realised what they were driving at. Nevertheless, I nodded again, as if I was seriously considering it.

'I could ask Captain Gries to let me tag along,' I said, which was perfectly true, I could; but I had about as much intention of doing so as going back to the orkhold to challenge the local warboss to an arm-wrestling match. 'How he'd feel about it, though...' I shrugged, to show I had no idea. Hardly a subtle piece of misdirection, I'm sure you'll agree, but it did the job. Everyone relaxed visibly, and although no one went so far as to pat me on the back, I was left in no doubt that a warm welcome awaited me on Serendipita.

'We couldn't ask for more,' Torven said.

I smiled, playing up to my reputation for modest heroism, as though being asked to take an insanely dangerous risk was merely routine (which, come to think of it, it more or less was by this point in my career), and glanced around the table. 'Then perhaps I'll have some more news for you when we meet on Serendipita,' I said. Whatever happened, this would be our last meeting aboard the *Revenant*: it seemed the parasites Mira had been herding had had enough of the Reclaimers' hospitality by now, a sentiment which I was certain was heartily reciprocated, or perhaps the governor just wanted his shuttle back. At any event, the delegation was due to depart the following day, and the military personnel along with it. (Apart from Duque and his people, who were hopping over to his flagship aboard an Aquila it had dispatched for the purpose, and which was rather pointedly timed to arrive several hours before the boarding party set off for the *Spawn*.)

Of course, despite the impression I'd gone some way to foster, I hadn't the slightest intention of attaching myself to what I was convinced was little more than a suicide mission. But, once again, I'd reckoned without Mira.

I'D TAKEN THE precaution of voxing Jurgen before leaving the conference room, to ensure that my quarters were currently free of my self-appointed helpmeet, so I must admit to feeling a little cheated by fate when she popped out of a cross corridor close to the guest quarters as abruptly as a villain in a mystery play.[1] Seeing her in the flesh again, aesthetically pleasing as it was, disconcerted me considerably, and the dilemma I'd managed to push to the back of my mind under the pressure of more recent events came flooding back, seemingly as intractable as ever.

'Ciaphas.' She smiled, evidently still in a good mood and apparently pleased to see me. 'This is a pleasant surprise.'

'I could say the same,' I returned, donning a smile of my own and wondering if I'd be able to head off the inevitable confrontation for a while longer, or whether I should simply get it over with as quickly as possible. I carried on walking in the direction of my stateroom while I spoke, in the vague hope that she had urgent business elsewhere, or that at least if it all went ploin-shaped she'd be less inclined to try to kill me with Jurgen in earshot. To my distinct lack of surprise she fell in beside me, chattering brightly as she undulated along the corridor.

'I've just had some excellent news,' she informed me, and despite the faint itching in my palms which these words provoked, I nodded, as if I couldn't wait to hear the details.

'Good,' I said, not entirely inaccurately. 'I could do with some.'

Mira smiled, looking for a moment as if I'd just complimented her on her finger painting. 'I've been talking to the seneschal,' she said brightly, as if I knew or cared which of the inbred drones among the delegation she meant, 'and he said not all the military people are going back to Serendipita on the shuttle tomorrow.'

'That's right,' I said, wondering how some gretch-frotting civilian had found out about this, while making a mental note to remind everyone in the SDF party what 'need to know' meant, and put the fear of the Throne into them until it stuck.

---

1. *A form of festival entertainment popular on a number of worlds in the Eastern Arm, in which incidents from the lives of the saints or the Emperor are mingled with the crudest kind of knockabout humour. Far from being considered sacrilegious, these are generally regarded with indulgent approval by the Ecclesiarchy, on the grounds that they're bringing the word of the Emperor to the masses, and a few flatulence jokes is a small price to pay for actually being listened to for once.*

'Duque and his people are joining the blockade.'[1]

'Oh, you knew.' She looked faintly disappointed, as if I'd guessed the punchline of a joke she was telling before she'd reached it. Then she brightened again. 'So you know what that means, right?'

'A little more leg room for the others?' I hazarded, although from what I remembered of the shuttle's arrival, that didn't seem much of a consideration.

Mira smiled at me, unsure whether I was joking, or genuinely didn't get it. Correctly divining the latter, she grinned more widely. 'Room for more passengers,' she said. When I still didn't jump around punching the air, she amplified further. 'Us.'

Emperor help me, she was serious. I stopped moving and stared at her in perplexity.

'Mira, I can't just up and leave on a whim.' The first thunderclouds started to gather over her perfectly groomed eyebrows, which were moving together over deepening frown lines, and I carried on as though I'd always meant to, hoping to head them off. Now it was looking like a distinct possibility, I decided I really couldn't deal with a confrontation today. 'However much I'd like to. I have duties and responsibilities to consider. There are just too many people here counting on me to do my job.'

'Do they mean more to you than I do?' she asked, and I could hear the first rumble of the approaching storm, like distant artillery, in her voice.

'What I want doesn't come into it,' I said. That had been true, one way or another, from the first day I tied my sash, and lent verisimilitude to the rest of my words. 'What I'm doing now could be crucial to protecting Serendipita from the genestealers. If I could turn my back on that, would I really be the man you want beside you on Viridia?' To my relief, the first faint flicker of doubt was beginning to show on her face, as she began to think about it. I followed up the advantage. 'If I got on that shuttle with you now, you'd regret it. Maybe not today, or tomorrow, but soon, and for

---

1. *Ironically, despite his ambivalence towards her, Cain still seems to consider Mira more officer than civilian at this point – unless he's deferring to her diplomatic credentials.*

the rest of your life. You'd never know if I was there for you, and the good of Viridia, or for my own selfish reasons.'

'I'd know,' she said confidently, but the flicker of doubt in her eyes told a different story.

'If I could go with you, I would,' I said, truthfully enough; I had precious little idea what a governor's consort was supposed to do, other than supply an heir or two, which I was confident I could manage given the amount of practice we'd had, but I was sure they got shot at rather less frequently than I was used to, and the food and accommodation were certainly far superior to anything the Imperial Guard had to offer. 'But I'm needed here. The boarding party's going across in the next few hours, and the Guard and the Serendipitans need my reports. The security of the entire system might depend on it.' I don't mind admitting I was laying it on with a trowel by now, but the results were undeniably satisfying: Mira was looking at me with a kind of awed respect I hadn't seen before, and which, I must confess, I rather liked.

'You're going over to the space hulk?' she asked, all trace of her incipient tantrum gone, and I nodded, milking the moment.

'I've been asked to, at any rate. I was just on my way to discuss it with Captain Gries when I ran into you.' Too late, I realised the trap my tongue had laid for me. Mira could no more keep a juicy morsel of gossip like that to herself than she could give up breathing, and it was carrots to credits it would be all round the parasites she was herding before the hour was out. Which, in itself, didn't matter that much, except that Torven and Kregeen would be on the shuttle with them, so certain to hear all about it, and my chances of retaining their good opinion once they realised I'd been nowhere near the *Spawn* would be somewhere between slim and negligible.

'Then I'd better let you get on with things,' Mira said, disengaging from my arm as we arrived at the door to my quarters. As I opened it, Jurgen's distinctive aroma billowed out into the corridor, and she turned away quickly. 'Good luck.'

'Thank you,' I responded, stepping inside and hoping I wasn't going to need it.

'Are you all right, sir?' Jurgen asked, rearranging the grime on his face into an expression of puzzled concern. 'You look a bit peaky, if you don't mind me saying so.'

'I've felt better,' I admitted.

'I'll get some tanna on,' Jurgen said, slouching away in search of a kettle.

'Thank you,' I said. 'Then, if you wouldn't mind, can you arrange a meeting with Captain Gries?'

The situation wasn't entirely lost, I told myself, as the welcome scent of brewing tanna began to permeate the room. After all, he could always say no.

SEVENTEEN

I SHOULD HAVE known better, of course. Gries was all for it; he didn't go quite so far as to pat me on the back and say 'Wish I was going with you, bag a 'stealer or two for me,' but he probably would have done if that sort of thing hadn't been unseemly in an Astartes of his rank and seniority. As it was, he simply nodded, said 'That would be acceptable,' and got one of the Chapter serfs to scurry off and make the arrangements before I could think of a plausible excuse for changing my mind.

The only bright side to the whole sorry mess was that Mira was so impressed with my apparent heroism she insisted on spending the few remaining hours before my departure in a protracted and strenuous farewell, which came close to making my imminent demise seem almost worth it. As I trudged across the hangar floor to our waiting Thunderhawk, though, the prospect of taking a few happy memories to my grave with me did little to offset the leaden weight of dread now freighting my stomach.

'Commissar,' Drumon greeted me as I approached. 'Good news. The vox relays with the CATs are functioning well, in most cases, and there appears to be no genestealer activity in the vicinity of our landing point.'

'Excellent,' I said, trying to appear relaxed, enthusiastic and quietly confident, and probably failing dismally in every respect, before the full import of his words filtered through my trepidation. 'What does "in most cases" mean, exactly?'

'Three of them are failing to transmit any data,' Drumon expanded. 'We infer that they materialised too deeply inside the derelict for the vox signal to reach through the hull.'

'Definitely not ripped apart by genestealers, then?' I asked, trying to sound as though I was joking.

'That seems most unlikely,' Yaffel assured me, scooting across to join us, and I found myself wondering how well he was going to fare if the *Spawn of Damnation* was as chewed up as wrecked ships usually seemed to be.[1]

Drumon nodded. 'If they were disabled by enemy action, they would have transmitted some data back before we lost the link,' he pointed out, and, somewhat reassured, I echoed the gesture.

'One did,' Yaffel said, with perfect timing, and my burgeoning confidence wilted again like a Tallarn salad. 'But I can confidently rule out aggression by a genestealer as the cause.'

'I'm delighted to hear it,' I said. 'And the reason for your confidence would be...?'

Yaffel quivered a little, although whether it was from suppressed indignation at my manifest scepticism, or the vibrations set up in the deck by the synchronised plodding towards the Thunderhawk of our Terminator escort, I couldn't rightly have said. 'The CAT in question was equipped with motion sensors,' he said. 'Nothing could have approached it within twenty metres without registering, and nothing did. So, unless you're aware of a genestealer capable of travelling in excess of ninety metres a second, in order to overwhelm the response time of the auspex to movement within its vicinity, simple mechanical failure seems far more likely.' He seemed genuinely put out by the

---

1. *Cain's experience of damaged ships was generally as a result of combat, of course, so he may well have been picturing the kind of structural damage inflicted by torpedoes or lance batteries, which would have indeed made it difficult for the tech-priest to get around.*

admission, which I suppose was only to be expected, having noted on previous occasions how loath tech-priests generally were to admit that anything might go wrong with their precious contraptions.

"Stealers are hellish fast,' I agreed, 'but not that quick.' Another thought struck me, and I seized on it eagerly, seeing a last, faint hope of avoiding this ridiculous enterprise. 'I don't suppose any of your mechanical moggies were able to tell if there's anything fit to breathe over there?' The Reclaimers wouldn't care one way or the other, of course, and for all I knew everyone in the tech-priest contingent had been fitted with augmetic lungs, but I most definitely required something with a dollop of oxygen in it to keep me going. I'd tried breathing vacuum once before, and that was novelty enough for one lifetime.

'They were,' Drumon assured me. 'Both composition and pressure are well within tolerable limits for an unmodified human.'

'Well, that's nice to know,' I said, as the air in my immediate vicinity became marginally less wholesome, announcing the arrival of my aide.

'Sorry to keep you waiting, sir,' Jurgen said, with a salute-like wave in the general direction of Drumon, a compromise he generally fell back on when unsure precisely where someone connected to the military stood in relation to his own somewhat nebulous position,[1] and a businesslike nod to Yaffel. 'I was preparing a flask and a few sandwiches, in case you got a bit peckish later on.'

'Thank you, Jurgen,' I said, and although it would have taken a lot more than a quick slurp of tanna to perk me up at that point, I felt my spirits beginning to revive nevertheless. As I've

---

1. As Cain points out at several points in the course of his memoirs, Jurgen, though effectively seconded to the Commissariat, and therefore outside the Imperial Guard command structure, was technically still a serving Guardsman, and subject to its rules of conduct. In his usual forthright fashion, Jurgen tended to deal with this contradiction by ignoring it completely, except when there was clearly something to be gained from deciding one way or the other, which he did on a case-by-case basis.

remarked before, his phlegmatic demeanour and apparently
boundless confidence in my leadership, however misplaced,
was curiously heartening. His lasgun was slung from one
shoulder, in an apparently casual fashion which belied the
speed with which he could reverse and use it, and, as ever, he
seemed perfectly willing to follow me on this absurd escapade
with no more thought for the risks involved than he would have
employed on a foray into the kitchen in search of a snack.

His flak armour was partially obscured by a tangle of pouches
and webbing, containing Emperor alone knew what (apart
from a flask of tanna and some sandwiches, of course,
although their precise location was anybody's guess), but by
now we'd served together for so long that something would
have seemed seriously amiss if he was prepared to venture into
the field without it. 'Your timing's impeccable, as always.'
Which wasn't exactly true, but no one else seemed quite ready
to leave either.

'We might as well board,' Drumon said, leading the way up
the ramp and into the bowels of the Thunderhawk. Seeing no
further reason to delay, I followed suit, Jurgen trotting at my
heels. Yaffel stayed where he was, hovering anxiously, while a
couple of loading servitors with the Adeptus Mechanicus sigil
proudly displayed on their tabards plodded towards the
Thunderhawk bearing brass-bound boxes, for all the galaxy like
an apprehensive habwife watching the family porcelain being
heaved into a pantechnicon by carters. What they contained I
had no idea, and cared even less, beyond inferring that they
had something to do with the tech-priests' scavenging expedition.[1]

The interior of the passenger compartment seemed rather less
commodious than I remembered, around a dozen Terminators

---

1. *It's hard to be sure from Cain's vague description, but it's possible that these were
portable cogitator cores, intended to download the data from the venerable archives
aboard the derelict prior to attempting to salvage the system physically. That way, the
information would survive, even if the mechanisms themselves proved too fragile to
remove intact.*

taking up quite a lot of room,[1] but we found seats with little difficulty – and this time I made sure that I got hold of a headset
before strapping in. The seat Drumon had steered me to, before
settling into his own, between the looming bulk of the
Terminators and the red-robed tech-priests twittering away to one
another in Binary, had a clear line of sight to a nearby viewport,
through which I watched Yaffel directing the stowage of the last of
his baggage before scooting up the ramp to join us.

No sooner had he done so than the boom of the closing hatch,
felt rather than heard over the rising racket of the engines, echoed
through my bones, and the suffocating sense of apprehension I'd
fought so hard to dispel swept over me once more. Like it or not,
I was committed, about to set foot aboard a warp-spawned deathtrap, and however devoutly I might wish it, there could be no
turning back.

I DON'T SUPPOSE the short hop from the strike cruiser to the *Spawn
of Damnation* took more than a handful of minutes,[2] but it seemed
an eternity to me, my apprehension growing with every passing
second. To distract myself, I flicked through the frequencies the
headset could pick up, but none of the conversations I overheard
made much sense: the Mechanicus contingent seemed content to
continue warbling at one another in their own private language,
the Terminators were absorbed in one of the pre-battle litanies
peculiar to their Chapter and Drumon seemed to be meditating,
no doubt praying to the Omnissiah to provide a sufficiently juicy
stash of archeotech to make the absurd risk we were running

1. Since the Codex Astartes specifies an upper limit of ten men to a Space Marine
squad, including Terminators, we can infer that either two smaller squads were present,
or a single one had been reinforced by attached specialists of some kind. Since the most
likely individual to have been accorded the honour of a personal suit of Terminator
armour would have been a Librarian, who would undoubtedly have reacted to Jurgen's
presence in a noticeable fashion, we can be reasonably confident that the former alternative was the case; which ties in with Cain's earlier description of a specialised assault
squad working in concert with a regular formation of Terminators. If, of course, his
habitually vague estimate of their numbers can be relied on.

2. Around a quarter of an hour, according to the official mission logs.

worth taking. Since Jurgen was never exactly a sparkling conversationalist at the best of times, I was effectively thrown back on my own company, with nothing to occupy my mind apart from the ominous view through the panel of armourcrys facing me.

Until our Thunderhawk left the docking bay, I'd had no idea how close to the space hulk the *Revenant* had moved; but almost as soon as the sturdy gunship moved out of the shadow of the hangar doors, the vast derelict was filling the viewport, like a misshapen metal asteroid. As our pilot boosted us away, on a parabolic trajectory towards the shattered hull of the Redeemer-class vessel somewhere on the far side of the vast conglomeration of scrap, the strike cruiser shrank rapidly, diminished by distance, while the dimensions of the space hulk seemed largely unchanged. I found myself reminded of the tiny fish that accompany oceanic leviathans,[1] then, rather less comfortably, of the lesser bioforms which swarm about the massive bulk of a tyranid hive ship.

Though I tried to pick out some of the more identifiable features I remembered from the hololithic image Drumon and Yaffel had shown me, the effort was futile. I'd seen spacecraft from the outside before, of course, but in every case their hulls had been limned by a myriad of light sources, from the huge luminators guiding shuttle pilots into the hangar bays to the sputtering sparks of the welding torches in the hands of the void-suited tech-adepts pottering about on the hull, not to mention the warm, welcoming glow seeping from uncountable viewports. The immense bulk of the *Spawn of Damnation* was utterly dark, however, as bleak and inhospitable as the void itself, so that despite its size and solidity it seemed an insubstantial phantom, appearing only as a hole of greater darkness against the glittering backdrop of the stars.

After a few moments the glowering shadow had expanded to encompass the entire viewport, and I felt an overpowering sense of vertigo, as though we were falling down an infinite abyss ripped into the fabric of the universe. I gripped the armrests tightly and

1. *Something he may have witnessed for himself during the battle for the floating hives of Kosnar.*

listened to the hammering of my heart, which for a moment or two seemed to drown out the perpetual howl of the Thunderhawk's engine.[1] It was only at this point, perhaps because we were so close by now, that I finally began to pick out patterns in the darkness, deeper shadows which spoke of fissures in the accretion of detritus below us, and the faint gleam of reflected starlight striking highlights from peaks and promontories in the horizon of twisted metal.

'Magnificent!' Yaffel breathed, apparently in all sincerity, and I found myself reflecting that there was never a heavy object around to throw when you really needed one.

'Let's hope you still think that when you've got a pack of genestealers snapping at your heels,' I said, momentarily forgetting that he didn't have any, and with a touch more asperity than politeness and protocol would normally have allowed.

'Our Terminators should be able to keep them at arm's length, at least,' Drumon commented wryly, rousing himself from his trance in time to forestall whatever riposte the tech-priest might have been about to make.

'Bolter range would be better,' I said, inflecting it like a pleasantry, and nodding to convey my gratitude to him for helping to smooth over a potentially awkward moment.

'Better for some,' the nearest Terminator put in, raising a hand to display the fearsome claws I'd last seen ripping apart an artillery piece. His helmet swivelled in my direction, the voice issuing from it imbued with the calmness which comes from unshakable confidence. 'Arm's length suits me.'

'I'm pleased to hear it,' I replied politely. 'In my experience, the one thing you can say for genestealers is that there are always enough to go around.'

'Well said,' the sergeant I'd last seen in the ruins of Fidelis put in. 'If they turn up, we'll be ready.'

'They're not going to turn up,' Yaffel said, with an edge to his voice which might have been irritation if tech-priests hadn't been

---

1. More likely the engine had been throttled back, allowing the gunship to coast, while the pilot corrected its attitude in preparation for docking.

supposed to be above such things. 'The corridors around the beachhead are completely free of the creatures. None of the CATs has registered any movement.'

'Then where the frak are they?' I asked, not unreasonably.

'In hibernation, probably,' Yaffel said. 'If there are any left alive at all.' Though he wasn't exactly built for shrugging, he made a creditable effort, which his shoulder harness effectively neutralised. 'We're only inferring their presence, after all, from the infiltration of Viridia. It's possible the infestation came from another source entirely.'

'Possible,' Drumon conceded, 'but hardly probable.'

'Be that as it may,' Yaffel said, effectively conceding the argument, probably because if he did bother to work out the odds as he usually did it would have demolished his own position,[1] 'there's no reason to suppose that there was ever more than a handful of the creatures on board.'

'Can I have that in writing?' I asked, once again allowing something of the agitation I felt to imbue the words with rather more testiness than I'd intended. 'If there really are 'stealers aboard the hulk it's because the tyranids put them there, and they never bother with just a handful of anything when a few hundred will do.' As it turned out, even that was a woeful underestimate, but as I was still in blissful ignorance of that particular fact, my initial guess worried me more than enough to be going on with.

Any further debate was cut short by a few uncomfortable moments as the engines fired again, and the Thunderhawk pitched abruptly, its nose coming up as the pilot aligned it with whatever was left of the old Redeemer's docking bay. Then the gunship's external floodlights came on, throwing the wilderness of metal outside into clear visibility, and an audible gasp rose from the little coterie of tech-priests, despite most of them no doubt

---

1. *Quite. The probability of the genestealers in the Viridia System having originated somewhere other than the Spawn of Damnation is in the order of 0.35%, according to my savant Mott, who has a considerable aptitude for this kind of statistical analysis. Or any other kind, come to that, which is why he's been barred from innumerable gaming establishments, particularly when accompanied by Cain.*

feeling such blatant displays of emotion were a trifle *infra dig* in the normal course of events.

Not that I could blame them for that. In its own way, the metallic landscape was quite awe-inspiring, though undeniably bleak. It spread out below us, filling the viewport to the jagged horizon, a wasteland of bent and buckled hull plates, sheared structural members and what looked to me uncomfortably like the wreck of a utility craft of a similar size to our Thunderhawk. Whatever it was had impacted too quickly for much to remain identifiable, but there was a wrongness about the proportions of the pieces of tangled wreckage which made me suspect it had been of xenos manufacture. Before I could draw Drumon's attention to it and ask his opinion, however, it had passed out of sight, and our descent had become even more precipitous.

Having been through more docking runs than I could count, even in those days, I gripped the armrests of my chair just as the pilot rolled us vertiginously around, the on-board gravity field fluctuating uncomfortably for a second or two as it synchronised with the local one and established a subtly different direction for down. Now, instead of descending, we appeared to be approaching a solid wall of fissured metal, and, despite knowing intellectually that our pilot was more than competent, I tensed involuntarily for an impact my hindbrain insisted was about to come.

It didn't, of course. No sooner had Jurgen's muttered imprecation about the flight crew's parentage faded into the echoes around us than the exterior of the derelict disappeared, to be replaced by the walls of a docking bay.

'This appears to still be functional,' Yaffel said, his tone adding an unspoken 'I told you so.'

'It does indeed,' Drumon agreed, 'but appearances are often deceptive.'

'Quite so,' Yaffel agreed. 'But we should be able to get the doors closed and the chamber pressurised without too much difficulty.' The hull-mounted luminators were reflecting brightly back from walls of age-dulled metal, their buttresses more slender and finely wrought than those I was used to seeing aboard Imperial vessels, and the arcane mechanisms scattered about the periphery of the docking bay seemed somehow simpler and more compact. What this meant I had no idea, beyond a vague notion that our intrepid hunters of archeotech had been pipped to the post, and that anything useful had probably been salvaged by others generations before; but Yaffel and the others didn't seem in the least bit downhearted, chirruping away to one another nineteen to the dozen, and pointing things out with fingers and mechadendrites like juvies in a confectionery store.

A final impact jarred against my spine, and the shrieking of the engines died back to a pitch which enabled me to remove the headset. Jurgen shook his head, scattering dandruff, as he followed suit.

'Well, that didn't take long,' he commented, checking his lasgun as he hopped down to the floor from the Astartes-sized chair he'd been sitting in. 'Better bring a footstool next time.'

'Good idea,' I said, flexing the pins and needles out of my legs, and wondering why I hadn't thought of that myself. A faint tremor was transmitting itself through the deck beneath my feet, which seemed a little odd, and I found myself looking around for the cause.

'Amazing,' Yaffel said, staring out of the viewport for a moment, before turning to Drumon with a self-congratulatory air. 'The autonomic relays appear still to be functioning.'

I didn't have a clue what he was talking about, of course, but the gist of it was clear enough: the ship's machine-spirit must still have been watching over the hangar bay, even after all these millennia, because the massive doors were sliding closed, with a smoothness and precision quite eerie to behold. Back on the *Revenant* it had taken a dozen void-suited crewmen to supervise the equivalent mechanism, and the same number again to begin pumping the atmosphere into the chamber once it was sealed. Here, it seemed, the ship was capable of doing the job for itself.

'Who's closing the hangar doors?' Jurgen asked, hefting his lasgun as he peered out of the viewport, evidently expecting hordes of ambushers to rush the Thunderhawk at any moment.

'The vessel's machine-spirit,' the tech-priest told him, no doubt relishing the chance to expound on the miracles of the Machine-God, despite my aide's manifest inability to grasp the finer points of technotheology. (Not that mine's all that great either, I must confess. Either something works or it doesn't so far as I'm concerned, and if it doesn't it's an enginseer's problem. That's why we have tech-priests in the first place.) 'It's clearly aware of our presence.'

'Then let's hope it's the only one,' I said, scanning the shadows for signs of movement. I had no idea if genestealers could survive without air,[1] but I learned a long time ago that it never pays to underestimate an enemy.

Drumon glanced in my direction, a data-slate in his hand, and nodded reassuringly. 'None of the CATs are registering movement,' he said, 'so it seems a reasonable inference.'

'So far,' I said.

'So far,' Drumon agreed, and donned his helmet. When he spoke again, his voice was flattened a little by the external vox speaker. 'I'll let you know the moment anything registers.' He began to make his way to the nearest airlock, no doubt intent on doing whatever was necessary to provide us with something outside we could breathe, but before he could enter it, I became aware of a faint tendril of mist wafting past the viewport.

'I think you've just been saved another job,' I said, beginning to understand why he and Yaffel were so keen to recover the ancient technologies which made marvels like this possible. Once they were understood, they could undoubtedly be used for the benefit of the Imperium in ways I couldn't even imagine. However great the hypothetical gains may have been, however, the threat of the genestealers was both real and immediate, and I resolved not to let my guard down for a second.

'So it appears,' the Techmarine agreed. He gestured towards the boarding ramp, including us all in the general invitation. 'Shall we

---

1. *They can't tolerate vacuum indefinitely, like some of the void-adapted creatures of the tyranid hive mind, but they can certainly remain conscious and dangerous for considerably longer than an unprotected human would; so even depressurising a section of a ship or void station harbouring them may not be enough to subdue them entirely.*

take advantage of the fact?'

'By all means,' I agreed, determined to at least look as though I felt confident of surviving the next few hours, and fell into step beside him.

EIGHTEEN

MY INITIAL IMPRESSION, as my boots first echoed on deck plates half as old as the Imperium,[1] was, surprisingly, one of peace. The venerability and size of the cavernous hangar bay lent it something of the air of a cathedral, and although I've never had much time for the songs and pongs,[2] I must admit to finding such places pleasantly tranquil on the few occasions I've had reason to enter them. The ceiling was high and devoid of the curving buttresses I'd have expected to see supporting it aboard a Navy vessel, but the bas-relief aquila on the far wall, looming over everything, was reassuring enough, even though it had been rendered in a fashion which made it look as though

---

1. *In fact they were probably a great deal more ancient than that; according to the surviving records, the Redeemer-class heavy cruiser was first commissioned during the lifetime of the Emperor, and used extensively in the great crusades predating the Horus Heresy. Along with so much else, the secrets of their construction were lost in the course of the centuries following that cataclysmic upheaval, and although they continued to serve with the Imperial Fleet, the inevitable losses were never able to be replaced. The last known example was destroyed by renegades attempting to force passage through the Cadian Gate early in M35.*

2. *A flippant reference to the liturgical chants and votive incense generally employed by the Ecclesiarchy.*

it was floating without sufficient support for its weight. The air was musty, of course, but no worse than one would expect to find on the lower levels of the average hive, and I found the spurious sense of familiarity which that imparted to our surroundings was also helping to put me at my ease a little – at least as much as was possible under the circumstances.

'This isn't so bad,' Jurgen said, producing a luminator from somewhere among his collection of utility pouches, and snapping it onto the bayonet lugs of his lasgun. The external lights of the Thunderhawk were still burning brightly enough to render our immediate surroundings clearly visible, but he swept the shadows in the corners methodically nevertheless, and I nodded, commending his caution.

'So far, so good,' I agreed, unfastening the flap of my holster and loosening my chainsword in its scabbard. The Terminators trotted forwards to secure our beachhead, their weapons at the ready, and I relaxed a little; nothing was going to get past them without being noticed, and raising an unholy racket in the process. To my surprise, however, instead of taking up firing positions to cover the door leading from the hangar to the stygian gloom of the corridor beyond, the hulking figures passed straight on through it and disappeared.

'Where are they off to?' Jurgen asked, sounding about as puzzled as I felt.

'Fanning out to cover our line of advance to the cogitator banks,' Drumon said, looming over us as he approached. 'There are a number of cross corridors intersecting with our optimum route.'

'Good idea,' I agreed, remembering the tangle of ducting and passageways projected in the hololith. There were far too many opportunities for ambush for my liking, and it made sense to plug as many of them as possible with sentries before the main body of the expedition departed the hangar bay. 'Wouldn't want to find a horde of genestealers charging up your... aah, magos. Got everything you need?'

'I believe so,' Yaffel confirmed, rolling up with his servitors, and a gaggle of red-robed acolytes, in tow. Most of them were lugging more junk than Jurgen, although what purpose it served was way beyond me. The only thing I recognised for certain was the bolter Drumon was carrying, and, with a sudden thrill of apprehension, it dawned on me that, apart from the Techmarine, Jurgen and I were the only people in sight holding weapons. 'We won't know for certain until we reach the sanctum, of course, but we've been able to anticipate most contingencies.'

'Apart from having to fight your way out,' I said. 'Don't you think a few guns might be advisable?'

'The risks are negligible,' Yaffel assured me airily. 'We're still getting no sign of movement from the CATs, and in the unlikely event of a dormant genestealer or two reviving inside our perimeter, I'm certain the Terminators will be able to keep them away from our party.'

'Our party?' I echoed, masking my horror as best I could. 'I was under the impression Jurgen and I were along merely as observers.' A responsibility I'd been intending to discharge from the safety and relative comfort of the Thunderhawk's passenger compartment, well away from any genestealers that might be lurking in the vicinity.

'What better opportunity to observe, then?' Yaffel asked, as though bestowing an enormous favour. 'You can monitor the communication channels just as effectively through your commbead while you accompany us, and see the recovery operation at first hand while you're about it.'

'A chance not to be missed,' I agreed, masking the sinking feeling in the pit of my stomach with the ease of a lifetime's dissembling. He still seemed dangerously sanguine about the chances of a genestealer attack to me, but at least we'd have a squad of Terminators to hide behind, and from what I'd seen of the ease with which they'd cleansed the nest under Fidelis they wouldn't be got past easily. I could still have refused to go, of course, but that would have meant sacrificing a measure of Drumon's regard, and with it my undeserved standing among the Reclaimers. So, as ever in that kind of situation, I resolved to simply make the best of a bad job, and be prepared to make a run for it at a moment's notice.

As it turned out, though, my fears appeared to be unfounded, at least to begin with. After leaving the docking bay we made surprisingly good time, the corridors free of clutter and detritus for the most part, although the occasional ceiling panel had fallen, and some of the deck plates were sufficiently corroded to present a trip hazard to the unwary. In one or two places there were signs of more serious obstruction, but these had been removed from our path by the vanguard of Terminators, and no serious obstacles to our progress remained.

The only other sign that our companions had come this way before us was the channel of disturbed dust along the centre of the passageway, and the occasional cyclopean footprint, picked out by Jurgen's luminator. His was the only one kindled, leaving the echoing darkness to wrap itself oppressively around us. I had no problem with this: our environment was sufficiently close to the underhives I'd grown up in for all my old instincts to have returned, the way sounds rebounded from the surfaces surrounding us and the feel of stray air currents against my face more than compensating for the lack of light, and I was perfectly happy not to be making myself an obvious target by carrying one. Drumon, I was sure, had no need of a luminator to find his way in any case, his helmet being stuffed with artificial senses to supplement his own, and no doubt the tech-priests had sufficient augmetic eyes and the like between them not to bump into things and each other too often.

We came across one of the Terminators within a few moments of setting off, his back to the corridor, facing one of the side passages, his twin-barrelled bolter aimed down it in a reassuringly steady grip. As we carried on past him, Drumon pausing to exchange a few words with his comrade, I realised for the first time just how bulky the heavy armour was; even the Techmarine looked relatively slight standing next to it. The Terminator, by contrast, filled almost the entire width of the narrow passageway, the hunched shoulders rising up behind his helmet brushing against the ceiling, and for the first time I began to wonder if perhaps we'd have been better off with a lighter, more nimble escort. If the worst came to the worst, these lumbering behemoths would block the constricted corridors like corks in a bottle. I don't mind admitting that chills of apprehension chased one another down my spine at that thought, my morbid imagination being able to picture the consequences of being unable to shoot past our guardians, or dodge round them to flee unhindered, all too well.

'Any signs of movement?' I asked, as I came abreast of his back, and the Terminator responded at once, his voice echoing slightly in my comm-bead as it overlapped with the one issuing from the external speaker of his armour.

'A few faint auspex returns, very tenuous,' he told me. 'No visual contact.' Which pretty much confirmed my earlier guess about the sensorium links in his helmet.

My palms began tingling again. 'How distant?' I asked.

'They're reading at about three hundred metres,' he told me, apparently quite unconcerned. 'If they're there at all.'

'Just auspex ghosts,' Yaffel said confidently. 'Nothing to worry about.'

'Ghosts?' Jurgen asked, sounding mildly curious, and no more perturbed than usual. 'Are the wrecks haunted?' He swung his luminator around for a moment, as if hoping to find the shade of some long-deceased crewman dripping ectoplasm on the bulkheads.

'It's a theological term,' Yaffel explained patiently, 'for a false reading, which looks like a genuine trace. Even the most conscientious of machine-spirits will sometimes be mistaken, or perhaps be moved by a sense of mischief inappropriate to the sanctity of their task.'

'Or perhaps there really is something out there,' I said, drawing my laspistol. The gesture may have been futile, but the weight of the weapon in my hand felt comforting, and I stretched my senses, listening intently for sounds of scrabbling in the dark.

'If there is, it'll just be vermin,' Yaffel assured me easily, with a faintly supercilious glance at my drawn sidearm, 'or cables moving in the air current from the recirculators.'

'Vermin that's spent countless generations exposed to the warp?' I wondered aloud. 'Emperor alone knows what that'll have evolved into.' Or what it lived on, come to that. Foraging wouldn't exactly be easy in an environment composed mainly of metal, which was why the genestealers tended to hibernate between systems. (At least according to the archives Gries had authorised my access to, and remarkably thin they'd turned out to be, considering this particular space hulk had first been reliably identified almost two thousand years ago.[1])

Yaffel subsided, looking a bit less sure of himself, although I had little enough time to enjoy my minor victory. I voxed Drumon, sure that he'd been paying at least partial attention to the conversation. 'Any change in the readings from the CATs?' I enquired.

'Still no sign of movement in their immediate vicinity,' the Techmarine responded at once, confirming my guess. 'But another one just ceased transmission.'

'In the same way as the first?' I asked, feeling a sense of vague disquiet.

'Precisely,' Drumon confirmed. His helmet swivelled towards Yaffel. 'It should be recovered for examination. So high a failure rate may point to an unforeseen environmental factor.'

'That may be the case,' the tech-priest conceded, sounding more than a little unhappy at the possibility. 'But our highest priority has to be the recovery of the cogitator core.'

I craned my neck to catch a glimpse of the data-slate Yaffel had produced. A deck plan, familiar from the hololith aboard the *Revenant*, was displayed on the tiny screen, our position marked precisely where I'd expected us to be, and a speckling of icons around us picked out the cordon of Terminators. A wider scattering of coloured dots a little way beyond them, most of which were moving slowly and erratically, just had to be the CATs; the one nearest to us was both stationary and limned in red, indicating that it had just malfunctioned.

---

1. *Or perhaps not quite so remarkable, considering the relative rarity of the occasions on which it had both popped out of the warp in an Imperial stellar system, and someone had been on hand to take auspex readings. If anyone had tried to board it before the Reclaimers, they left no record of the attempt; not even in the rather more comprehensive archives maintained by the Ordo Xenos.*

'That goes without saying,' I said, thinking rapidly. If Jurgen and I branched off at the next cross corridor, always assuming we could squeeze past the Terminator guarding it, we'd reach the downed mechanism in a handful of minutes. It wouldn't be hard to manhandle it back to the Thunderhawk, and we could spend the rest of the time before our departure with several centimetres of ceramite and a reassuring amount of firepower between us and the genestealers infesting this deathtrap, instead of roaming around a pitch-dark labyrinth waiting for something to pounce on us. 'But Drumon has a point too. If there is something about the hulk affecting our devices, there's no telling what could fail next.'

'That's highly unlikely,' Yaffel said, with an air of studied unconcern, no doubt reflecting that for someone as dependent on augmetics as he was I'd just raised a rather disturbing possibility. 'But I suppose it would be prudent to look into it. What do you suggest?'

'Maybe Jurgen and I could recover the CAT,' I said, as if the idea had only just occurred to me, 'while you push on to the objective. We won't be much help with the theological stuff anyway, and everyone else will be needed to salvage the cogitators.'

'That would seem to be the most efficient use of our resources,' Drumon agreed. He indicated the icon marking the Terminator guarding the next junction. 'Brother Blain can accompany you, as that shouldn't compromise our perimeter. He can resume his post once you've picked up the CAT.'

'Sounds good to me,' I agreed, passing through a doorway into a roughly square chamber, where the clawed Terminator who'd conversed with us briefly aboard the Thunderhawk was on sentry go. Like the other portals we'd passed through on the way here,[1] it had been left open, presumably by the advance guard ahead of us; the door to the left as we entered was open too, the tracks on the floor of the exposed corridor confirming that it was indeed

---

1. *Another typically vague statement, although study of the deck plans would seem to indicate either two or three, depending on whether you counted the exit from the hangar bay or not.*

the route to our objective, while the pair directly ahead and to our right remained tightly closed.

Jurgen and I moved aside, into the far corner, clearing the way for the rest of our party to turn to the left and clatter off into the darkness, while Drumon and Blain exchanged a few words. If the Terminator was surprised or resentful of his sudden change of orders he gave no sign of it, merely beckoning to us to follow as he slapped the palm plate set into the wall next to the door opposite the one we'd entered the room by.

'This way,' he said, unnecessarily, as the thick steel plate moved smoothly aside, with none of the metallic groaning I'd become used to aboard the vessels I'd travelled on. Jurgen shone his luminator down the corridor thus revealed, picking out nothing more threatening than another identical portal closing off the end of it some ten or twelve metres away.

'After you,' I said, mindful of my earlier fears, and unwilling to find myself trapped between a jammed doorway and a lumbering ceramite giant if it all went ploin-shaped, something my well-developed paranoid streak kept insisting could only be a matter of time. Whatever the tech-priest might prefer to believe, there were definitely genestealers somewhere around, and that meant they were bound to show up sooner or later. 'Anything on the auspex?' It was also a pretty safe bet that, like the Terminator we'd passed on our way here, Blain had enough sensory gear built into his helmet to give us a useful head start if the 'stealers started moving in on our position.

'Nothing significant,' Blain said. 'I'm picking up faint signs of movement on the deck above us, but nothing on this level at all.' He led the way into the narrow passage, filling it almost completely, like a mobile wall, while Jurgen and I trotted in his wake, our weapons aimed back behind us in case of unexpected ambush. A moment later he stopped abruptly, almost provoking an undignified collision. 'It should be through here.'

Another pneumatic hiss, as air pressures equalised on either side of the opening door, and he stepped through into a wider pool of darkness. Jurgen followed, sweeping the luminator around the walls, and, reassured that there was nothing lurking in the gloom waiting to pounce, I took up the rear.

We were in another square chamber, I realised at once, the ambient echoes enough to tell me that even if the beam of my aide's luminator hadn't been bouncing off the walls, picking out another three doors, all closed. Blain was plodding towards the middle of the enclosed space, casually pushing aside a few scattered cargo containers which would have taxed a heavy-lift servitor, when he stopped and looked down. (Or, to be more accurate, his helmet tilted a few degrees from the vertical, which seemed to be about as much head movement as anyone wearing a Terminator suit was capable of.)

'It's over here,' he said, gesturing towards a tangle of twisted metal by his foot.

Jurgen and I hurried over to join him, the shattered mechanism pinned in the beam of the luminator. I activated my comm-bead, staring at the wrecked CAT in perplexity. Things had indeed taken a turn for the worse, but not quite in the manner I'd anticipated.

'Drumon,' I voxed, 'we've found it. And you were right about an environmental factor being to blame.'

'With respect, commissar,' Yaffel cut in, before the Techmarine was able to reply, 'that's hardly a determination you're qualified to make.'

'In this case I am,' I said, not too perturbed to enjoy the moment. 'Somebody's shot it. With a medium-calibre bolter, if the damage is anything to go by.'

There was a moment of stunned silence, broken only by the faint hissing of static, before Drumon replied. 'Genestealers do not use guns.'

'Hybrids do,' I said, with the unshakable authority of personal experience. 'I recommend you proceed with extreme caution.' Which was hardly necessary advice under the circumstances, but it wouldn't hurt to look as though I was taking the mission seriously.

'Noted,' Drumon replied, in the tones of a man intending to follow that advice to the letter.

I turned to Blain. 'Anything on the auspex within firing range?' I asked, suddenly conscious that what might have seemed a reasonably safe distance from a purestrain would be anything but from a hybrid with a bolter.

'Still nothing on this level,' he assured me, sounding faintly disappointed – but then he was walking around behind enough ceramite to shrug off a direct hit from anything short of a tank shell.[1] Not being similarly blessed, I was a great deal less sanguine, you may be sure.

I walked around the chewed-up mechanism, wondering how best to shift it. Up close, it seemed a lot larger, and considerably more unwieldy, than I'd anticipated. Jurgen and I should still be able to manage it between us, though, but it would mean having to stow our weapons, and for a moment I hesitated; but our journey back to the hangar bay would be protected by the cordon of Terminators, so the risk of doing that should be minimal, and the only alternative I could see was to admit defeat and catch up with the others. I'd promised Drumon I'd recover his toy, and scuttling back to the Thunderhawk without it would undermine my credibility with his Chapter, so it was either that or show willing by taking my turn as 'stealer bait. Something about the shattered CAT's position seemed subtly wrong to me, although I couldn't for the life of me see why.

'How do you think it got in here?' Jurgen asked, and I shrugged, my mind still mainly engaged with the more pressing matter of where best to get a grip on the blasted thing.

'The same way we did, I suppose,' I told him.

'Oh.' He frowned in perplexity. 'I just don't see how it got the door open, that's all.'

'It couldn't,' I said in some alarm, glancing at the open portal behind us, and the three others, all firmly closed. I brought my laspistol up and began backing away towards the door we'd

1. *Not quite; though phenomenally tough, even compared to conventional Space Marine armour, Terminator suits are just as vulnerable to a lucky shot as anything else. Which, given that they're also employed by the Traitor Legions, is probably just as well.*

come in by, trying to keep all the scattered cargo containers covered at once. Confident as always in my judgement, though Emperor knows why, Jurgen brought his lasgun up to a firing position and fell into place at my back, bringing a welcome sense of greater security and a blast of halitosis as he did so.

'Commissar?' Blain asked, sounding about as baffled as my aide usually did. 'Is something wrong?'

'The room was sealed when we arrived,' I said, chills of apprehension chasing one another down my spine. 'Whatever shot it could still be here.'

'If it was, it would have registered on the auspex before we entered,' Blain said, with what sounded suspiciously like a trace of amusement in his tone. 'And it would be dead by now.'

I should have found that reassuring, but for some reason it only increased my apprehension. I stared at the detritus surrounding the crippled CAT, and sudden horrified understanding burst in on me. 'The blips on the next level,' I asked urgently. 'How close are they?'

'A score or so metres,' Blain replied evenly.

'Out! Now!' I said, Jurgen responding instantly, as I'd known he would, while the Terminator simply took a couple of paces in our direction, no doubt wondering if I'd lost my wits. Suddenly the air current I'd assumed was coming from a grille above our heads took on far more sinister connotations, and I drew my chainsword, powering up the blade as I did so. 'Jurgen, the ceiling!'

'Commissar.' My aide complied at once, raising the luminator attached to his lasgun, and picking out a ragged hole in the roof of the chamber. The luckless CAT hadn't been sniped, as I'd first assumed, just struck by a single bolt from a whole burst, the rest of which had chewed up the floor plates around it badly enough to drop it through to the deck below. To my horror, the attenuated beam picked out something moving in the shadows beyond the gap, bounding forwards inhumanly fast, before flowing like quicksilver through the aperture above us.

'Blain!' I just had time to shout. 'Look out!' then the first of the purestrains was on him. I saw the crackle of arcane energies

I'd marked before in Fidelis playing about the blades at the end of his arms, as he parried the 'stealer's first blow, matching it slash for slash. It fell, bisected, while Jurgen and I opened up with our las weapons, secure in the knowledge that we could harm only our foes. Sure enough, another of the creatures fell, in the act of leaping towards us, while a few stray las-rounds expended themselves harmlessly against the reassuring bulk of the Terminator's ceramite.

Then I felt the breath constricting in my throat. Parallel grooves had been scored deeply into the surface of the impregnable armour, where the first genestealer had struck before being dispatched, and some thick, dark fluid was seeping from it, crusting like resin to seal the damage.[1] I hesitated, unwilling to risk felling an ally by friendly fire now his suit had been breached, but events were out of my hands by this time: as Jurgen and I began to retreat down the corridor, a third purestrain threw itself at Blain's unprotected back. He ducked forwards, lowering his right shoulder as far as the cumbersome armour would allow, trying to dislodge it in the manner of a wrestler attacked from behind, but to no avail; powerful talons tore into the ceramite as easily as a potter's fingers into clay, finding purchase where none should exist. Blain backed into the wall, hard, and chitin cracked. The 'stealer keened, an ululation of agony which made my teeth ache and pierced the space behind my eyes like a sliver of razor-edged ice, echoing off into the darkness, but held on regardless, distending its jaws as some foul-smelling ichor issued from the cracks in its carapace.

'Turn round!' I bellowed, forgetting in the terror of the moment that Blain could hear me perfectly well over the vox. 'Let us get a shot at it!' The Terminator stumbled in our direction, abused servos in his knee and ankle joints whining in protest, but before he

---

1. *Though Cain seems unaware of it, this was almost certainly Blain's blood, that of Astartes being modified to coagulate instantly on exposure to air in order to seal wounds which would incapacitate a normal man without impairing their fighting ability. That the Terminator had lost enough of it to leak out of his suit would indicate severe trauma, even by Space Marine standards.*

could comply the genestealer brought its head forwards over his own, and before my horrified eyes sank its teeth deep into the ceramite of his helmet. The deck plates shuddered as Blain fell to his knees, and the 'stealer on his back brought round a handful of wickedly curving talons, to plunge them into the joint where helmet and suit conjoined. The vox in my ear carried a small sound, somewhere between a cough and a sigh, and Blain collapsed, toppling towards Jurgen and myself, his torso clattering resonantly to the metal floor of the corridor.

The 'stealer raised its head and stared at Jurgen and I, apparently bemused, shaking its head as if it had been dazed by the impact.[1] Then it seemed to rally, fixing me with a gaze of pure malevolence. Its momentary hesitation was to prove its undoing, however, as Jurgen and I had taken advantage of the brief respite to centre it in our sights; before it could spring at us, we fired almost as one, tearing it apart in a flurry of las-bolts.

'Blain's down,' I voxed, 'dead, I think.' To my surprise, my voice sounded calm and authoritative, despite the panic rush of adrenaline hammering through my system. 'Three purestrains accounted for, but there are probably others close by.' The faint echo of scrabbling talons drifted to my ears. 'Correction, definitely others, moving this way.' One look at Blain's corpse, stretched across the threshold, was enough to dispel any hope of closing the door against the onrushing tide of talon and mandible; I could barely have moved his hand, never mind that mass of ceramite.

'His lifesigns have ceased,' Drumon confirmed,[2] after what was probably no more than an instant or two, but seemed considerably longer. This came as a relief; for a moment I'd feared having to attempt some kind of rescue, despite the manifest

---

1. *Or, perhaps, by Jurgen's proximity: although his peculiar anti-psychic talent had yet to be revealed, some time later on Gravalax, it could well have been disrupting the brood mind, isolating and disorientating any of the genestealers incautious enough to venture close enough to him to become affected.*

2. *That he was evidently monitoring the condition of the other Astartes in the boarding party can be taken as a fairly reliable indicator that he was in overall charge of it; unless, as the de facto artificer responsible for their maintenance, he was more concerned with the condition of the Terminator suits than their wearers.*

impossibility of success, in order to maintain my reputation.

'Then we're pulling out,' I said, backing away down the narrow corridor as quickly as I dared, reluctant to take my laspistol off aim for fear of the worst. And with good reason: an instant before Jurgen and I reached the opposite end, bursting arse-first into the chamber Blain had been guarding in a manner I've no doubt anyone observing our arrival would have found comical in the extreme, the head and shoulders of another purestrain erupted into the passage, the misshapen body behind it attempting to force its way past the obstructing cadavers. Jurgen and I popped off a couple of rounds each to discourage it, scoring a lucky hit or two, but the chitinous horror proved as resilient as most of its kind, merely ducking back as our las-bolts vaporised fist-sized chunks of its exoskeleton.[1] That bought us enough time to hit the palm plate, though, and before the 'stealer or any of its companions could recover, the thick metal slab slid back into place, sealing them in.

Or us, I suppose, as they still had the run of most of the hulk; and so far as I was concerned, they were welcome to it.

'What now, sir?' Jurgen asked. 'Should we catch up with the others?'

I shook my head. 'Back to the Thunderhawk,' I said, no longer giving the proverbial flying one what anybody thought. I'd come up with some kind of excuse before Drumon and the cogboys returned, if they ever did. We might have evaded them this time, but the brood mind was now aware of our presence aboard the hulk, and would be mobilising its genestealers against us as surely and dispassionately as antibodies against an invading virus. I exhaled, releasing the tension which had wound my body tight, trembling a little from the adrenaline comedown, and tapped my comm-bead. 'We're back at the sentry point. More 'stealers in pursuit, but we've sealed the hatch, so the perimeter's secure again.'

I should have known better, of course; a genestealer brood may be only a pale reflection of the tyranid hive which originally

---

1. *If true, one or both weapons must have been damaged in some way, in order for the las-bolt to be so widely diffused, instead of penetrating more deeply over a smaller surface area. Unless, of course, he's resorting to hyperbole again.*

spawned it, but its gestalt intelligence is a powerful one. The broods I'd encountered on Viridia and Keffia should have taught me that, but the individual purestrains behave so much like predatory animals that I'd fallen into the trap of believing them to be little more than mindless beasts – an error pointed out to me in the most stark and graphic manner possible, as the door slid smoothly open again, and an entire pack of the creatures boiled into the room.

NINETEEN

'PERIMETER BREACHED!' I yelled, opening up again with my laspistol, and wishing I'd replaced the powerpack while I'd had the chance. Jurgen flicked the selector of his lasgun to full auto, no doubt reflecting that if we didn't manage to check the creatures' headlong rush, running out of ammunition was going to be the least of our worries. The leading one fell under the hail of las-bolts, not a second too soon, still reaching out for me, and I swatted its wickedly taloned hand aside with the blade of my chainsword as I retreated.

To my horror, a babble of overlapping voices answered my warn-ing, and the distant roar of heavy bolters echoing through the corridors from what seemed like every direction immediately con-firmed my worst fears. It seemed the genestealers had merely been biding their time, building up their numbers at the limits of aus-pex range, before attacking in force.

'Multiple signals all round!' one of the Terminators confirmed. 'Closing fast.'

'Engaging,' another called, as I cracked off a fusillade of shots at the 'stealer bounding over the corpse of the group leader, seem-ingly fixated on ripping my spleen out. This time the las-bolts barely slowed it, and I parried the first slash of its talons with my

chainsword, feeling the screaming teeth bite deep into chitin. I followed up reflexively, stepping inside the reach of its quartet of
arms, and driving the tip of the blade up through its jaw as I did
so, to bury it deep in the creature's brain.

'Commissar!' Jurgen fired another burst, slowing the next one as
it lunged, and I pivoted aside, dragging the expiring 'stealer with
me to impede the progress of its fellow, as the chainblade ripped
free, bisecting its skull. 'This way!' He'd taken up a position
defending the door we'd first entered the chamber by, guarding
our line of retreat back to the Thunderhawk, and I made haste to
join him, shooting randomly into the middle of the pack as I
went. His lasgun barked again, then went silent. 'Sorry sir, I'm dry.'

Deprived of his covering fire I fell back on my duellist's reflexes,
retreating step by step, parrying by pure instinct each blow that
sought to eviscerate me. There was no time for thought, and if I
tried I'd be dead. A couple of times I fired my pistol again, once
downing another of the 'stealers with a lucky shot through the eye
socket, but relying in the main for my survival on the well-worn
blade in my hand. I've no doubt that the hours of practice I'd
spent in the *Revenant's* tertiary training chapel, and my sparring
bouts with Drumon, saved my miserable skin in those few frantic
moments, the keen edge they'd imparted to my fighting skills
making all the difference.

Out of the corner of my eye I noticed Jurgen's hand dip into one
of his array of pouches, but, to my surprise and consternation,
instead of the lasgun powercell I'd been expecting, he drew out a
frag grenade. Before I could shout a word of caution he'd already
primed it, only the pressure of his grip forestalling an explosion
which would undoubtedly kill us both in so confined a space.
Watching me intently, he retreated a step or two, into the corridor
behind him.

Well, grenade or no, it still seemed a healthier place to be than
the middle of a genestealer swarm, so I swung the chainsword in
a last desperate arc, driving my assailants back for the space of a
heartbeat, and scrambled through the portal myself, smacking the
palm plate as I passed it. Not that closing the door had helped
much the last time, but even a second or two's head start would be

better than nothing, and after more than a decade of serving together I thought I had a pretty good idea of what Jurgen had in mind.

I was right. The second I reached for the door control my aide lobbed the frag charge he'd readied, and the metal slab slid smoothly closed just before it detonated. The dull thump of the explosion was followed instantly by a metallic clatter, like someone dropping a tray full of tanna spoons,[1] as the hailstorm of razor-edged shrapnel shards pattered against the sheltering steel plate. (With any luck after passing through a considerable thickness of intervening genestealer.)

'Nicely done,' I congratulated my aide, and he nodded with quiet satisfaction. 'But what would you have done if they'd killed me before I got to the door control?'

'Hit the plate with my elbow,' Jurgen said, as incapable as ever of recognising a joke, and I nodded too, as if considering the matter.

'That would have worked,' I conceded. 'But I'm pleased I could save you the bother.'

'Me too, sir,' he agreed, snapping another powercell into his lasgun at last, and, sure that he was now able to keep the door covered in case of any more unpleasant surprises, I lost no time in following suit. According to the glowing runes in the butt which kept track of such things, the number of shots remaining were down to single figures, and I wanted a lot more than that in hand with 'stealers on the loose.

We waited tensely for a second or two, our weapons aimed at the blank metal slab, but if there were any 'stealers left on the other side capable of opening it to pursue us they had more sense than to try. When it became clear nothing was going to happen, I turned and began to lead the way back towards the Thunderhawk at a rapid jog. I must admit it crossed my mind to put a las-bolt through the palm plate, just to make sure we couldn't be followed,

---

1. *Small utensils, with a bowl roughly the size of a thumbnail, traditionally used to measure out the infusion. Among Valhallans, the consumption of this beverage, to which Cain's long association with regiments from that world left him inexplicably partial, has acquired a great deal of custom and etiquette, as baffling to outsiders as the appeal of the drink itself.*

but reason prevailed over the impulse. I'd hardly be able to maintain my good standing with the Reclaimers if anyone survived the genestealers' initial onslaught, only to discover that I'd sealed them in with a slavering horde of ravening purestrains, and there was no guarantee that damaging the controls would secure the hatch in any case. For all I knew, the machine-spirit which had nursed this wrecked vessel for so long would react to such casual vandalism by opening it again out of pique, and the last thing I needed was provoking it into siding with the chitinous horrors. As it turned out, I was going to be grateful for my restraint sooner than I expected.

'Pull back,' Drumon's voice instructed in my ear, and I realised that only a handful of seconds could have passed since my first panic-stricken warning. 'Form up on this position, and we'll punch our way through to the docking bay.' A chorus of assent answered him, which I ignored; I wasn't about to put myself in harm's way again with a safe refuge a mere few minutes running time away.

Or so I thought, until a marked increase in the noise ahead drew my attention, and I beheld a sight which chilled me almost as much as a Valhallan shower. The Terminator we'd passed on our way in was backing towards us, firing continuously as he came, almost filling the passageway with the bulk of his armour. There wasn't a heretic's prayer of getting past him, although given that the strobing muzzle flashes of his storm bolter[1] were affording lurid glimpses of a mass of genestealers pressing him hard, I'd feel seriously disinclined to try. They were falling in droves, as you might expect, but for every one which went down, another would appear, bounding over the corpses of its fellows to charge straight down the barrels of his gun. What they were hoping to achieve by this was beyond me, at least to begin with; like the 'nids that spawned them, genestealer broods seem to regard individual members of the group mind as essentially expendable, but in my

---

1. *The usual Astartes designation for the twin-barrelled variant Cain noticed before; presumably he picked this up in conversation at some point, probably with Drumon.*

experience they only did so in pursuit of an objective. This seemed
like a wanton waste of life, even by their standards.

'Back,' I told Jurgen, unnecessarily, as there was clearly nowhere
else to go; not even an air duct we could have squeezed down at a
pinch. He nodded, phlegmatic as always, and began jogging back
the way we'd come.

As I turned to follow, the purpose of the brood mind's strategy
became horrifyingly clear. The Terminator's weapon jammed,
probably overheated by the constant firing; for a moment he
struggled to clear it, then the leading 'stealer surged forwards,
slashing with its talons. The Terminator stood his ground, trying
to fend it off with the useless weapon, but the creature had an
unbreakable grip on his arm. As he tried to tear it free with his
other hand, a second one sprang out of the darkness, ripping open
the ceramite protecting his torso as though it were paper. Before I
could even think of trying to intervene, he was down, the tremors
of his fall vibrating through my bootsoles, and I turned and ran,
while the rest of the pack skittered and struggled to get past the
bulky obstruction to dismember my aide and I.

No doubt warned by the echoes of my sprinting footfalls, Jurgen
put on a burst of speed too, striking the door plate with his elbow
as he passed it, and diving through the widening gap without
slowing, his lasgun at the ready. No sounds of combat ensued, so
I followed without hesitation, cracking off a few shots as I turned
to close the hatch behind us. The bolts impacted on the snout of
a 'stealer which had managed to get past the deceased Astartes and
the tangle of its fellows still atop him, and got far too close to my
unprotected back for comfort. It reeled from the impacts and lay
thrashing on the floor of the passage, although whether I'd done
enough to kill it I'll never know. The door slid closed, hiding the
sight of the carnage beyond.

'We'd better get moving,' I said, picking my way through the
chunks of genestealer decorating the room, a rather satisfying
result of Jurgen's trick with the grenade. Now the creatures were
dead, there seemed to be fewer of them than I remembered,
although whether that was because the survivors had fled, or I'd

Sandy Mitchell

simply been too busy for an accurate headcount at the time, I couldn't be sure. 'They'll be through at any moment.'

'Down here?' Jurgen asked, flashing his luminator along the passageway Drumon and the tech-priests had taken the first time we'd passed through the chamber. I listened for a moment and shook my head. An all-too-familiar scrabbling sound was echoing out of the darkness beyond the range of the beam.

'No,' I said. 'The 'stealers are ahead of us.' No doubt they were intent on slaughtering the salvage party at the moment, but I was certain they'd devote some of their attention to us if we were foolish enough to attract it. I hefted my weapons and struck the control plate of the sealed door opposite; we already knew the other exit led straight to more genestealers, so to my way of thinking this one was the best card in a rather poor hand. Despite my trepidation, however, the darkness beyond was reassuringly silent, so I lost no time in hurrying through; a moment later an increase in the ambient light levels, and a small but perceptible thickening of the atmosphere, told me Jurgen was at my shoulder once more, and I closed the portal again.

'Where are we?' he asked, flashing the beam of his luminator around our refuge. It looked like all the other corridors we'd seen so far, but that didn't bother me; I'd recalled enough of the internal layout I'd seen on the hololith display to remain confident of finding our way back to the hangar bay without too much difficulty, so long as there weren't too many genestealers around to get in the way.

I shrugged. 'Only one way to find out,' I said, leading the way into the darkness.

How LONG WE'D been wandering through the passageways I couldn't be sure, but it was certainly taking a lot longer to get back to the Thunderhawk than I'd expected. My innate sense of direction seemed to be working as well as ever, so I was pretty confident that I knew roughly where both we and it were relative to one another, but there was no getting around the fact that connecting the two points was a lot less straightforward than I'd hoped. I could still recall the images I'd seen in the hololith in reasonable detail, but the reality of the maze of intersecting passageways we found ourselves negotiating was considerably more complex than the clear lines of the diagram suggested. Some routes were blocked by debris, or unsafe decking, forcing us into time-consuming detours, while other routes were blocked by the echoes of an ominous scrabbling, which betrayed the presence of more genestealers lurking in the darkness ahead. Needless to say, I avoided these passageways entirely, even going so far as to retrace our steps for a while before turning aside, just to make certain we'd given these pockets of activity a wide enough berth to evade detection.

Just to complicate matters, it wasn't long before I realised that we'd passed beyond the section of the *Spawn of Damnation* I'd seen enlarged, so most of the corridors, ducting and cable runs we followed hadn't appeared on the reduced scale of the main map at all: the only things I could be certain of were that we were deviating ever deeper into the core of the hulk, and that we'd passed from the relatively easy going of the derelict we'd first boarded to more decrepit surroundings entirely. On a couple of occasions I even felt a curious sensation of momentary vertigo, as level decks suddenly became slopes, or vice versa, while my eyes stubbornly insisted that nothing had changed.[1] As you can imagine, this was particularly disconcerting when we were traversing sections of the wrecks which were out of kilter with one another in any case; a couple of times Jurgen and I found ourselves picking our way through clumps of defunct luminators protruding from the floor like rusting undergrowth, and realised we were walking along what had once been a ceiling before the warp had claimed whatever luckless vessel this was, and on one particularly unpleasant occasion we traversed a section of ship turned at ninety degrees from its neighbours, where corridors had become abyssal shafts, plunging further than our luminator could plumb, forcing us to

---

1. *This kind of fluctuation in the local gravity field is apparently common aboard space hulks, and far from unknown on the larger naval vessels and charter ships, particularly when they've been cobbled together from salvaged hulls: it's apparently due to the misalignment of overlapping gravity generators, something which is almost inevitable when as many vessels as commonly make up a space hulk have been randomly thrown together.*

scramble around them on narrow ledges which once had been thresholds.

Everywhere we went there were doors, too, although once we'd left the environs of the ancient derelict and the venerable machine-spirit standing guard over it, these had to be manhandled open or closed, with a fair degree of sweat and profanity. (The former predominantly from Jurgen, and the latter from me, although I must own that we each contributed liberally to both.) In the main we left the portals we'd passed through open, unwilling to take the time and effort required to shut them again, and reluctant to cut off a known line of retreat, although I was more than aware of the risk this entailed; you may be certain I kept my ears well open for any suspicious sounds behind us, and we halted on innumerable occasions to listen more carefully and discount the possibility of being followed. Most of the corridors we wandered down were, of course, lined with doors too, but mindful of the effort required to get into them, and spurred on by the worrying possibility that the Thunderhawk would depart without us, we were disinclined to explore any of the side chambers.

Perhaps the most disturbing thing about our present circumstances was that I'd lost contact with Drumon and the surviving Terminators. My comm-bead was certainly continuing to function, if the faint wash of static in my ear was anything to go by, but the fragments of signal traffic I'd been listening to, hoping to keep track of their progress (and, by extension, the whereabouts of the greatest concentration of genestealers, or so I devoutly hoped), had been getting progressively fainter for some time. Now it seemed that the sheer mass of metal between us was preventing the relatively low-powered signals from getting through at all. I found myself wondering if any of our companions were still alive, and hoping so, although the last few garbled transmissions I'd heard had been less than encouraging. Certainly more of the Terminators had fallen, although some had linked up with Drumon by the time I'd lost contact. But from what I'd seen, their chances of making it back to the hangar bay through the labyrinth of narrow corridors were slender at best.

I was roused from my sombre reverie by Jurgen, who was

walking a few paces ahead of me, sweeping his luminator methodically across walls, ceiling and floor, paying particular attention to any areas of shadow cast by protrusions or recesses. We'd both seen enough by now to be well aware of how readily the purestrains could conceal themselves, and were by no means sanguine about the possibility of sudden ambush.

'Wait, sir.' He held up a warning hand and advanced a few more paces, the beam picking out a huddled mass on the deck plates ahead of us.

I drew my weapons as it came more clearly into view. 'Is it dead?' I asked. The genestealer remained inert, instead of bounding to its feet and charging us as I would have expected, but I remained alert nevertheless. I'd never seen one asleep before, if they even did, and the middle of the corridor seemed like an odd place to choose for a nap to say the least.

Jurgen pulled the trigger of his lasgun, and the 'stealer remained where it was, despite the fresh crater which appeared in its misshapen forehead. My aide shrugged. 'It is now,' he said, in a matter-of-fact tone.

I listened to the echoes of the *crack* of the weapon's discharge fade away into the distance, rebounding into the labyrinth, and hoped it hadn't attracted any attention; but the damage was already done, if any had been, and chiding him would have been pointless at this juncture. Instead, I merely nodded. 'So it would seem.'

Emboldened, I approached the creature and examined it curiously. The wound Jurgen had inflicted had penetrated its skull, neat as you please, but that wasn't what had done for it. Its thorax was ripped open from the inside, in a manner I could recognise all too easily.

'That's a bolter wound,' I said, wondering how in the warp it had managed to crawl this far from the attacking Astartes before expiring.

My aide nodded. 'Old one, too,' he added, his face twisting into a grimace of distaste. 'It's getting pretty ripe.'

'It is indeed,' I agreed, the stench of decay belatedly reaching my nostrils through the nearer and more familiar odour of Jurgen. As he widened the sweep of the beam, I began to discern a spattering of dried ichor and viscera on the walls and the grating underfoot. 'And it was shot right here.' I indicated the traces left on our surroundings by the explosive projectile's detonation somewhere within the creature's chest cavity.

Jurgen nodded thoughtfully. 'You think there's another group of Astartes on board?'

'I doubt it,' I said, after thinking it over for a moment. It was possible that Gries had dispatched another team without telling me, but it hardly seemed likely. Getting our own group together had been an unholy scramble, and I couldn't see that he'd have had the time, even if the Reclaimers did have some clandestine business they didn't want to share with the rest of us. 'Why would they shoot their own CAT?'

Jurgen shrugged. 'Beats me,' he admitted. 'But why would a hybrid shoot another genestealer?'

That didn't make much sense either, and I shrugged in turn. 'We're missing something,' I said, edging gingerly around the repulsive cadaver. But there was no point worrying about it now. The important thing was to get back to the hangar bay and safety as quickly as possible. I hesitated for a moment, reorientating myself, and selected the next right-hand turning I could see, a few metres further on from where we stood. 'This way, I think.'

For once, it seemed, I was in luck. The corridor I'd chosen was long and unobstructed, and we made good time, despite the caution with which we continued to move. Though I carried on listening as assiduously as ever for the sinister skittering sound I'd come to know so well, there seemed to be a remarkable absence of genestealers in this part of the hulk, for which I gave continual thanks to the Emperor under my breath. Welcome as this unexpected development was, I must admit I found it vaguely disquieting. The only explanation which occurred to me was that Drumon and the Terminators were continuing to make a fight of it, and keeping the brood mind distracted. I couldn't see that happy circumstance lasting for much longer, if it was indeed the case, however, and made as much haste as possible, to wring the maximum advantage from the situation while I still could.

After a while I became aware that our surroundings were growing a little more distinct, the shadowy forms of struts and girders
emerging out of the murk, and the outlines of piping and ventilator grilles becoming more clearly visible. I gestured to Jurgen. 'Kill
the luminator,' I said.

He complied at once, plunging us into a darkness which seemed
at first to be as profound as before. As our eyes adjusted, however,
I found I'd been right, a pale glimmer of illumination seeping into
our surroundings from somewhere up ahead. 'We need to go carefully,' I cautioned.

'Right you are, sir,' Jurgen agreed, holding his lasgun ready for
use, and we pressed on, alert for any signs of ambush. So far as I
knew, purestrain genestealers had no more need of light than the
Astartes did, but some hybrids at least seemed more comfortable
being able to see where they were going,[1] and I could conceive of
no other explanation of the lights ahead of us. We were a long way
from our own party, if there was anything left of it at all, and the
chances of a luminator system still happening to be functional
aboard one of the derelicts after centuries of drifting in the warp
without the ministrations of a tech-priest seemed vanishingly
small. All my instincts were to turn back and avoid whatever might
be waiting for us, but there was no sign of any immediate threat,
and the Thunderhawk wouldn't wait for ever. At least if something
tried to kill us now we'd be able to see what it was, which in my
experience is generally an advantage.

As I'd expected, the ambient light levels continued to grow as we
moved closer to the source, the brightening glow leaking around
corners and from side passages, until at last we came to a section
of corridor where the luminators were functioning normally. As I
stared around us, taking in our surroundings, a sense of disquiet I
couldn't quite account for settled over me like the ever-present
pall of choking dust. Wires were running from the glow-plates in

---

1. *A debatable point. Some, otherwise indistinguishable from humans at a casual
glance, seem to have inherited all the arcane senses of the abominations which polluted
the genes of their forebears, while others, much closer to purestrains in appearance, do
not. As with so much else where genetics is concerned, random chance appears to play
a major part in the distribution of these characteristics.*

the ceiling, linking them to one another, and down through a ragged hole in a nearby wall panel, beyond which they'd been crudely spliced into a thicker cable, which sparked and sizzled alarmingly.

'Tracks,' I said, stooping to examine them, but the dust had been kicked up too badly to discern anything other than the fact of considerable activity – something the repairs to the luminators had already been enough to tell me.

Jurgen edged past the hissing cable as though it might suddenly rear up like a serpent to strike at him, and I must confess I felt something of the same apprehension. This was clearly unsanctified work, with none of the amulets or prayers of protection a tech-priest would have put in place to make it safe, and the place positively crackled with the sour scent of danger;[1] I felt the hairs on the back of my neck stirring in response.

So pervasive, in fact, was the sense of some lurking threat in this unhallowed place, that the sudden sound of gunfire erupting from a nearby corridor came almost as a relief.

I HESITATED FOR a moment, torn, as so often in the course of my life, between the impulse to flee and the desire to discover precisely what threat I was facing. In truth, however, there was only one choice to be made, and I did so; on the battlefield it's the unexpected that kills you, and the best chance of safety I had was to find out what else was lurking in these corridors apart from me, a malodorous Guardsman, and an inordinate number of genestealers. I suppose I could have been influenced by the realisation that at least some of the shooting appeared to be coming from a bolter, which might mean the presence of more Reclaimers to hide behind, but in my heart of hearts I knew so convenient a development would be too much to hope for. Accordingly, I gestured for Jurgen to accompany me, and set off to discover what else the Emperor had placed aboard the *Spawn of Damnation* to make my life difficult.

Confident that the sounds of battle would mask any noise we

---

1. *Or possibly ozone from the electrical discharge.*

might make, Jurgen and I picked up our pace, grateful for being able to see where we were going at last. The roar of gunfire grew louder as we got closer to its source, and I tightened my grip on my sidearm, snuggling the grip reassuringly into my palm. My recently acquired augmetics felt like a natural part of my body now, the forefinger resting gently against the trigger needing the merest flexion to spit death at whatever enemy had the temerity to present itself. In my other hand I held the chainsword, my thumb poised to activate the whirling blades at a heartbeat's notice. All of which may convey a little of what I felt at the time; although I was as loath as ever to go looking for trouble, I was pretty confident of being able to deal with any we might come across, especially if we could sneak up on it from behind. A notion, I'm bound to say, which I was soon to be disabused of.

The roar of weapons had increased in volume by now, and I began to pick out the sounds of several different kinds. The unmistakable sibilant bellow of bolter fire I'd already recognised, as I said, but behind and around it was a syncopation of stuttering slug-throwers, and the sharp bark of a shotgun or two. Something about the cacophony struck me as vaguely familiar then, but I couldn't quite put my finger on it. There was another sound too, which surrounded and overlaid the others, an inchoate roaring like a deephive sumpfall,[1] which I felt sure I ought to be able to identify, but which somehow continued to elude me.

'We seem to be coming to a hold or something,' Jurgen said, and I nodded, surprised. We'd passed through a few open spaces in our erratic progress, but the last really vast chamber we'd seen had been the hangar bay in which the Thunderhawk had docked; and the deeper we'd penetrated into the hulk, the more constricted our way had seemed to become.[2] Now, though, the pattern of echoes

---

1. *A torrent of liquid falling into the sump, or lowest levels, from higher up in a hive; some last for years, or even decades. Given the enclosed nature of an underhive, the echoes they raise can be quite literally deafening if appropriate precautions aren't taken.*

2. *A consequence of the constituent vessels having been brought together by the warp currents, so that their physical structures had become intermingled rather than coterminous; a state of affairs rendered permanent by the hulk's periodic sojourns in the real universe.*

indicated an open space far larger than any we'd so far come across, and I began to move more cautiously again. The passageway we were following seemed to be coming to an end, a rough rectangle of brighter illumination growing ahead of us, although as yet I had no idea what we'd find when we reached it.

As we did so, the noise, no longer attenuated by distance, battered at us like a physical force. I edged forwards a final pace or two, finding the corridor ended in a vertiginous drop, and glanced down, flattening myself against the last metre or so of the metal wall. My breath seemed to congeal in my chest, and I muttered a few expletives, in a combination I'd only previously heard in a gaming establishment when one of the patrons turned out to be carrying a few of his own cards for luck.

Jurgen was, as always, more succinct. 'Orks,' he said, as though they might somehow have escaped my notice. 'Thousands of 'em.'

TWENTY

AT FIRST GLANCE, which was more than enough for me, my aide's estimation of the greenskins' numbers seemed depressingly accurate. Everywhere I looked, there seemed to be more of them. From our vantage point high on its sloping rim, we were able to look down into a vast hollow at the heart of the hulk, hundreds of metres across and almost as many deep, seething with activity. And everywhere my eyes fell there seemed to be more of the creatures, squabbling, hurtling around randomly in ramshackle vehicles, or busying themselves battering metal into new shapes, for purposes which eluded me. There were at least as many gretchin among the larger creatures, of course, scurrying around on errands for whichever ork offered them a measure of protection, being casually swatted out of the way by any others whose progress they impeded, or engaging in vigorous altercations of their own. A pall of smoke drifted over the section where the bustle seemed greatest, where the *mekboyz*[1] and their stunted servants

---

1. *An orkish word, referring to the greenskins' equivalent of tech-priests, although their rites are as primitive as the rest of their culture. Instead of propitiating the machine-spirits which serve them, in the manner of the Adeptus Mechanicus, the mekboyz appear to terrorise them into acquiescence.*

were busying themselves with the construction of new engines of war; but strain my eyes as I might to penetrate the choking shroud, it and the distance combined to obscure any useful details about what they might be up to.

For a moment or two I found myself wondering how a space this big could exist in such a densely tangled accumulation of derelict ships. Then my eye fell on the ragged edge of the deck plates I was standing on, and the answer came to me, as I registered the unmistakable marks of crudely wielded tools: the orks had created this steel cave themselves, hacking away at the metal surrounding them with all the brute force they were capable of, scavenging the pieces to construct fresh weapons and the other necessities[1] required to support their colonisation of the hulk. Now the reason for the armada which had met us on our arrival at the orkhold became horrifyingly clear. They'd been the stragglers, too late to board the hulk with the others before it returned to the immaterium, impelled by some innate drive deep in the orkish psyche to migrate with the warp tides wherever they led.[2]

'Holy Throne,' I breathed, as the full implications of this horrifying new development dawned on me. Serendipita wasn't just facing the possibility of stealthy infiltration by the genestealers; as soon as the *Spawn of Damnation* had drifted close enough, a torrent of orkish invaders would erupt from it like pus from a boil, intent on nothing but bloodshed and destruction. Duque's cordon of SDF boats would never be able to stem such a tide, and unless I found some way to warn them, the planet's defenders would be caught completely by surprise.

I reached for the comm-bead in my ear, then let my hand fall

---

1. *Actually, for orks, there are no other necessities to speak of.*

2. *This instinct, which has been observed many times over the millennia, is undoubtedly real, and deeply ingrained. Although, since orks are perfectly capable of constructing navigable starships, the question of why they should continue to trust their fate to the uncertain drifting of a space hulk remains unanswered. Whatever the reason, however, they remain one of the most common xenos breeds to be found infesting space hulks, second only to genestealers in frequency of sighting, and there is much anecdotal evidence that a few even manage to exert a modicum of control over the course of the hulks they occupy once they re-enter the materium.*

without activating it. There was no one close enough to hear the transmission, except possibly the greenskins, and the longer they remained unaware of our presence the better. I drew back a little further into our refuge, but none of the creatures so much as glanced in our direction, those close enough to have noticed our arrival completely absorbed in the source of the gunfire which had first attracted our attention. As happens so often among orks, a quarrel seemed to have broken out between two of the innumerable factions among the horde, and they'd promptly begun to settle their differences in the usual fashion of their kind. Around a dozen were firing weapons at their rivals, with the general lack of accuracy I'd had plenty of cause to be thankful for during my encounters with them on Perlia, while almost twice as many hacked and belaboured one another with a variety of blades and cudgels, and several hundred of their fellows called out encouragement or insult[1] from the sidelines, heedless of the danger of being felled by a stray round or two.

The opposing leaders were easy enough to pick out, being bigger than any of their compatriots, and brandishing the largest and most destructive weapons in sight. Each wore crude armour, decorated with the barbarous glyphs which the greenskins employ in place of both heraldry and script, and Jurgen nodded sagely. 'Clan leaders,' he said. 'Both used to being warboss.'[2]

That made sense. I'd seen on Perlia how different tribes would put aside their enmities in the pursuit of a greater conflict, but the old rivalries would remain simmering beneath the surface, leaving such alliances fragile at best. (A circumstance which had worked strongly in our favour, once I'd inadvertently killed the warboss keeping the others in line, and the whole invasion force had fallen apart as his would-be successors turned their guns on one another instead of the Imperial forces opposing them.) If I knew orks

---

1. *Which for orks are more or less indistinguishable.*

2. *Like many Valhallans, Jurgen was able to read orkish glyphs, a cultural legacy of the failed greenskin invasion of his homeworld several generations before. To this day, natives of that world retain a particular detestation for orks, and a strong tradition of knowing the ways of the enemy, the better to confound them, persists.*

(which I did rather more than I'd have liked since Perlia), neither would be willing or able to back down, for the fear of a potential challenger scenting weakness and attempting to usurp their position, which was fine by me: the longer the battle below kept the greenskins' attention diverted, while Jurgen and I slipped away quietly, the better I liked it.

I took a last look around the echoing steel cave, gauging its extent as best I could, and felt a faint shiver of apprehension. It would take us hours to circumvent, particularly if we did our best to remain at a safe distance from it to minimise the possibility of discovery, and the chances of the Thunderhawk still waiting in the hangar bay by the time we reached it were minimal. Not for the first time I reminded myself that minimal and non-existent were far from synonymous, and that crucial distinction had made all the difference between survival and death often enough by now to ram the lesson home. (Though not nearly as thoroughly as the ensuing decades were to do, as circumstance and ill-luck forced me to apply it over and over again.)

'Pull back,' I told Jurgen, *sotto voce*, although the cacophony from below was still enough to drown out a marching band. If anything it was growing louder, as another ork *nob*,[1] larger and more generally repulsive than either of the other two, and surrounded by bodyguards who at least matched them in physique, ploughed through the baying crowd, bellowing orders and threats. I would have surmised him to be the warboss of the entire *waaaaghh!* from this alone, even without the distinct resemblance to the late and unlamented Korbul.[2] 'Time we were leaving.'

'Right you are, sir,' Jurgen agreed, no doubt considering that the multitude below were rather too many to take on, ancestral vendetta or no. He indicated the warboss, who was restoring order with all the tact and subtlety of a Khornate berserker with a hangover, and patted his lasgun. 'Shame I can't get a clean shot from here, though.'

---

1. *An orkish word denoting status, one of the many phrases Cain appears to have picked up during his activities on Perlia, or from subsequent encounters with the creatures.*

2. *The orkish warboss Cain bested in single combat on Perlia, effectively breaking the back of the invasion in the process.*

'It'd make a good trophy,' I agreed, retracing our steps as quickly as I could consistent with caution, in case he was tempted to take a crack at it anyway. That would be all I needed, an army of hacked-off orks chasing after me, as well as playing dodge the genestealer. 'But I'm not sure there's room for it on the wall of your quarters.'

'Probably not,' Jurgen conceded, after a moment's reflection. Then he brightened. 'But at least we know who shot the CAT thing now.'

'I suppose we do,' I said, as we regained the welcoming gloom of the unlit tunnels at last. The indiscriminate hail of bolter fire which had blasted a hole in the deck as well as the target was certainly consistent with orkish ideas of marksmanship. But orks were looters by nature, almost as innately as they were fighters, and none of the greenskins I'd previously encountered would have abandoned a prize like that after disabling it, especially with a contingent of mekboyz around to barter for the remains once they'd dragged it home. The palms of my hands itched again, but whatever disquieting pattern my subconscious was recognising failed to elbow its way into my forebrain. Knowing better than to try forcing it, I turned my attention to a strategy for getting us back to the hangar bay; unfortunately, the best I could come up with was 'Keep moving and avoid the xenos,' which, although it seemed to have worked so far, seemed a little light on the essential details.

Jurgen nodded sagely. 'Better keep an eye out for perimeter patrols,' he cautioned, rekindling the luminator. 'Must have been one of those that got it. And the 'stealer back there.'

'More than likely,' I agreed. If my innate sense of direction was working as well as it usually did, the docking bay would be somewhere on the far side of the orks' encampment, and it was only too likely that they'd posted outer pickets there, one of whom had used the peripatetic automaton for a spot of target practice. Which meant getting to safety would mean eluding a greater concentration of greenskins from now on, as well as the roving fragments of the brood mind.

Then some of the sense of unease I'd been feeling crystallised suddenly into a hard knot of apprehension. 'If they've got sentries out,' I said slowly, 'why didn't we see any on the way in?'

Jurgen shrugged. 'Maybe the genestealers got them,' he said. 'They were quick enough to get through the hole the orks shot in the floor.'

'They were,' I agreed, the dark shadow still failing to lift from whatever my subconscious was fretting about. 'But we didn't see any of those close to the greenskin camp either.'

'Apart from the dead one,' Jurgen reminded me, pausing to put his shoulder to a corroded hatch cover blocking our progress any further. I kept the widening gap covered with my laspistol until we were reasonably certain nothing was going to leap out and attack us, then motioned him through, glancing back down the corridor for any signs of a hostile presence. Despite my obvious apprehension, I heard nothing like the scrabbling of talons or the ringing of iron-shod boots on the deck plates, although my imagination supplied movement enough in the shadows behind us.

'Shot with a bolter,' I mused aloud, and Jurgen nodded, no doubt taking the attempt to order my thoughts as a desire for confirmation.

'Looked like it to me,' he agreed. 'And at least a week ago. Could have been more. No way to tell how fast things rot in a place like this.'

'The orks have been here a lot longer than that,' I said, understanding beginning to sink in at last. 'So why hasn't the brood mind moved against them?' The genestealers had attacked us less than an hour after our arrival aboard the *Spawn of Damnation*. Yet the orks, who'd presumably been here for weeks on end, still seemed unaware of their presence.

'Just too many of them?' Jurgen suggested. Well, that was possible, of course, but according to Gries's datafiles a hulk as large as this one would normally have thousands of genestealers aboard it, and a battle on that scale would certainly have left far more evidence of itself than a single cadaver.

'I don't think so,' I said, with a shake of my head. The genestealers had been quick enough to react to the presence of the Reclaimers and the tech-priests, and if the orks were being left alone it had to be for a reason. Once again, I found myself forced to consider that the brood mind was a more subtle and dangerous enemy than the waves of animalistic genestealers it controlled made it appear. 'The 'stealers are up to something.'

Jurgen shrugged again. 'Of course they are, sir. They're xenos,' he pointed out reasonably. 'But if they're concentrating on the orks instead of us, good luck to 'em.'

Well, those were sentiments I could hardly argue with, so I nodded instead, but kept my weapons handy nevertheless. Both xenos breeds were utterly inimical to humankind, and they were welcome to take lumps out of each other until there were none of either left standing so far as I was concerned; but my finely tuned sense of paranoia was convincing me that whichever side won, we'd lose.

WORKING OUR WAY round the greenskins' beachhead took just as long as I'd feared, and more than once I had cause to be grateful for the tanna flask and ration bars Jurgen had secreted about his person before leaving the safe haven of the *Revenant*.

Though necessary, each of these pauses for rest and refreshment were anxious ones, punctuated by glances at my chronograph, until even my most optimistic estimates of how long the Thunderhawk would remain waiting for survivors to straggle back to it had been long exceeded. But there was nowhere else to go that I could think of, so the hangar bay remained our objective. Even if the entire expedition had been massacred by the purestrains stalking it, I was pretty sure the Reclaimers and their allies in the Adeptus Mechanicus would be unwilling to leave the treasure trove of archeotech aboard the *Spawn of Damnation* alone for long, and it would only be a matter of time before they launched another attempt to loot the hulk. Which meant rescue would simply be a matter of waiting, and hoping we didn't succumb to starvation, the blades of the orks or the jaws of the genestealers, before they stopped dithering and got on with it. True, there was no guarantee that they'd make for the same docking bay again, but that was a possibility I didn't allow myself to dwell on for too long.

By the simple expedient of keeping the faint glow of the

functioning luminators to our right, as it continued to seep through the labyrinth of passageways, ducts and conduits like the herald of dawn on some habitable world, we contrived to remain far enough from the main body of the greenskins to avoid ready detection, without deviating too far into the depths of the hulk again. On several occasions we were forced to seek refuge in some shadowy side turning, or behind some tumbled debris, by the approach of footsteps and the guttural barking of the greenskins' barbarous tongue, but orks and gretchin aren't exactly stealthy at the best of times, and Jurgen and I were able to conceal ourselves long before the risk of detection became a real possibility. Though all these parties were armed, the carrying of weapons being as natural as breathing to an ork, so far as I could see, without sticking my head out far enough to be noticed, they were being hefted in a distinctly casual manner, and I remarked as much to Jurgen, as the shrill squabbling voices of a gretchin scavenging party under the sullen supervision of an apprentice mek and a couple of bored-looking *boyz*[1] faded into the distance.

'I thought that too,' my aide confirmed, rekindling the luminator attached to the barrel of his lasgun once he was certain the greenskins were too far away to notice it. Although they were kind enough to let us know they were coming from scores of metres away, the genestealers were far less considerate, and neither of us felt particularly keen to be taken by surprise, the fate of Blain and his battle-brother still vivid in our memories. 'They can't expect to be running into any 'stealers this close to their camp.'

'I don't think they know about them at all,' I said, having had long enough to consider the matter to be fairly certain by now that my initial conclusion had been correct. 'They'd be moving a lot more carefully if they did.'

'Wouldn't whoever shot the one we found earlier have told

---

1. *Orkish warriors or footsoldiers; also used as a generic suffix to indicate a group with more specialised abilities, like mekboyz (ibid.), weirdboyz (the nearest greenskin equivalent to sanctioned psykers), painboyz (roughly analogous to medicae or chirurgeons, although their ministrations are only sought by most orks under the direst of circumstances), and so on. Largely synonymous with gitz, which is often applied to any group of boyz which doesn't include the speaker.*

them?' Jurgen asked, and I shook my head, forgetting for the moment that he couldn't have seen the gesture in the dark even if he hadn't been several paces ahead of me.

'They would if they made it back,' I said, having thought about this too, 'but I don't think they did. We only found one dead 'stealer, and they tend to hunt in packs. Look what happened to the Terminators.' If they'd been able to overwhelm such formidable warriors by sheer weight of numbers, a relatively unprotected ork would have had virtually no chance.

'Makes sense,' Jurgen agreed. 'If one or two went missing out of all that lot, no one'd notice.'

'I suppose not,' I said. If a recon patrol of Guardsmen disappeared, the entire garrison would be on alert within hours, and assiduous efforts made to either find them or determine their fate. But greenskins come and go on a whim, caring little or nothing for any of the others, and unless the genestealers' prey had been sent out on a specific errand by a nob further up the food chain,[1] it was indeed probable that their absence had gone unremarked. All of which merely confirmed the disquieting conclusion I'd already come to: the brood mind had a reason to keep the invaders ignorant of its presence aboard the space hulk. Try as I might, though, I just couldn't conceive of what that might be; and when I found out, I was going to wish devoutly that I'd remained in ignorance.

---

1. Not necessarily a metaphor in the case of orks.

TWENTY-ONE

DESPITE SEVERAL CLOSE calls with wandering greenskins, we eventually made it to the far side of their enclave without serious incident; and I must say I felt a strong sense of relief as the last lingering glow of its luminators faded into the darkness at our backs. True, we were forfeiting whatever protection from the genestealers we'd been deriving from its proximity, but every step we now took brought us closer to our goal. We were still some appreciable distance from the Redeemer-class wreck we'd first boarded, which meant I was having to find our way purely by luck and by instinct. But my old underhiver's affinity for environments like this seemed as reliable as ever, and I was fairly confident that another couple of kilometres would bring us to the area I'd seen magnified in the hololith on the *Revenant's* bridge. Brief as that glimpse had been, what now felt like a lifetime ago, I was sure that once we reached the area it delineated I'd be able to recall enough detail to accelerate our progress considerably, so I pressed on as quickly as seemed prudent, as anxious to reach it as you might expect.

I was still more than aware of the danger from genestealers, of course, and kept my ears open for any tell-tale scrabbling in the darkness, but the further we got from the greenskins the more my spirits rose. At the very least, it meant we could concentrate on one threat at a time.

'We'll have to go back, sir,' Jurgen said, from a few metres in front, sounding no more discouraged than if he was letting me know that my morning tanna was going to be a few minutes late. 'It's a dead end.'

'Frak,' I said, feelingly. We'd been making good progress over the last half hour or so, having hit on a relatively unobstructed passageway, but we'd passed few side turnings which looked passable, and none at all in the last ten minutes. To the best of my recollection, retracing our steps to a point where we could branch off with a reasonable chance of finding a parallel route would take us uncomfortably close to the orks again, not to mention losing rather more time than I felt we could afford.

I was about to turn away, when a faint, regular pattern flickered into view in the circle of light cast by Jurgen's luminator, all but obscured by the patina of rust and accumulated filth adhering to the metal wall in front of us. I moved closer and raised a hand to brush the worst of it away, rendering my glove almost as disreputable as my much-abused headgear in the process. 'Can you hold that light steady?'

'Of course, sir,' Jurgen replied, leaning a little closer to see what I was doing and bringing a strong blast of his unique aroma with him. Preoccupied, I barely noticed, tracing the faint Gothic lettering my efforts had made marginally more legible. 'What does it say?'

'Emergency bulkhead,' I picked out laboriously, in what had once been authoritative capitals, followed by a series of letters and numbers, presumably identifying the section of the vessel which lay beyond. 'It must have been tripped by whatever happened to the ship this once was.'

'Like the *Hand of Vengeance*,' Jurgen said, no doubt remembering the thick slab of metal which had slid into place to seal off the decompressing section we'd been trapped in when our transport ship had taken a hit off Perlia. I shuddered, the same recollection striking me. 'Can we get it open, then?'

'We can try,' I replied, a little dubiously. We'd manhandled plenty of obstructing hatches open on our unintended hike through the bowels of the space hulk already, but this one seemed heavier and more obdurate than most. I glanced around the litter of debris surrounding us. 'We'll need something to lever it open, though.'

Fortunately we found a metal bar some three metres in length, which seemed stout enough, after a few minutes of foraging, and I hefted it experimentally. 'This ought to do,' I concluded, returning to the obstacle, which Jurgen helpfully illuminated for me.

I examined the slab of metal carefully, searching for a suitable spot. There was no sign of a join down the middle, which meant it must have moved as a single piece. Not encouraging. I transferred my attention to the nearest edge, finding only the narrowest of grooves where the bulkhead met the wall. It must retract into this side then, which would mean levering it from the other.

'Frak,' I said vehemently, discovering exactly the same thing after a cursory inspection on the other side of the corridor. 'It must have come down from the ceiling.'

'We won't be shifting that, then,' Jurgen said gloomily.

Even though the same thought had occurred to me, I shook my head. The sense of disappointment which had washed over me was abruptly pushed aside by a surge of anger, almost childish in its petulance, a fact I can only attribute to the hunger and exhaustion I'd been keeping at bay for some time now by willpower alone. I was damned if I was going to let a lump of scrap metal get the better of me now we'd come so close to our goal. 'Wait a moment,' I said, my voice sounding surprisingly level under the circumstances. 'Let's not give up just yet.'

I examined our surroundings in more detail, my eyes having long since adjusted to the level of light supplied by the Guard-issue luminator. It goes without saying, of course, that the decking under our feet had changed innumerable times since we set out on our interminable hike through the bowels of the *Spawn of Damnation*, from solid metal to mesh grating and back again, occasionally varied by way of carpeting, the odd slab of wood and, once, what seemed uncomfortably like bone.[1] Now we were standing once again on metal mesh, suspended a few centimetres above a gully running beneath the floor, through which cabling and pipework ran to mechanisms Emperor knew where, and which had no doubt ceased to function generations before.

I bent down and tugged hopefully at the section of mesh closest to the bulkhead; finding it sealed immovably into place by the rust of centuries, I gave up the subtle approach and freed it with a couple of swipes of my chainsword. The adamantium teeth ripped through the venerable metalwork within seconds, with a shower of sparks and a shriek which set my teeth on edge. After a few anxious moments, in which hordes of genestealers and curious orks failed to erupt from the shadows, I sheathed the weapon again, marvelling at my folly, which I can only attribute to the fatigue which was still threatening to overwhelm me.[2] The utility gully was too shallow to squeeze through, of course, but I found what I was looking for, and smiled; the thick metal slab was resting in a groove cut into the floor, running from one wall to the other, lined by the decayed remnants of some flexible sheet material, no doubt intended to ensure an airtight seal. The rotting material had left a gap, into which I was able to thrust the end of the bar, and after a few moments of hopeful manipulation, I felt it catch against the underside of the lowered bulkhead.

'So far, so good,' I said, and the furrowing of Jurgen's forehead dislodged some of the grime adhering to it. (Although, to be fair, I can't have looked much cleaner myself by this point.)

'We'll never shift that with just the two us,' he said reasonably, illustrating the point by leaning his entire weight on the raised end of the pole. Beyond a faint, protesting creak from the edge of the mesh deck plate now acting as a fulcrum, his efforts had no discernible effect whatsoever.

---

1. *Possibly from an eldar vessel, or a long-deceased tyranid leviathan.*

2. *He must have been almost completely exhausted by this point to take such an uncharacteristically reckless course of action; although he does at least seem to have retained sufficient sense not to try cutting through the bulkhead directly, which would have taken a considerable amount of time and noise even if his chainblade had been able to penetrate it.*

'I know,' I said, leading the way back to the debris-choked side passage where I'd found the bar. Part of the ceiling had given way here, Emperor alone knew how long ago, and there were plenty of pieces of sheet metal, cabling and general clutter left lying beneath it. Nothing short of the arrival of a 'stealer swarm or an ork horde would have persuaded me to risk entering so obvious a death trap, but enough of the detritus was close enough to the main corridor to lay hold of without much danger to life and limb, and we'd soon accumulated a collection which would have netted us a small fortune if we'd been able to get it to a downhive trading post somewhere.

A few more moments of perspiration and profanity were enough to transfer our hoard to the barrier blocking our progress, and I looped some of the electrical cable I'd scavenged around the top of the bar, knotting it as securely as I could, before repeating the operation at right angles to the first. That left two loops crossing one another, hanging from the end, and I lost no time in wedging a flat sheet of metal into them, creating a short, but relatively stable, platform. After that, it was simply a matter of wedging the largest chunk of debris under the jutting pole, to create a higher fulcrum than before, and beginning to load the rest of the scrap onto the high end. I was just beginning to doubt that it would work after all when, with a heart-stopping groan, the whole thing shifted several centimetres, and I tensed, on the verge of leaping for my life. After an anxious second or two I became convinced that it wasn't going to collapse, and, somewhat nervously, resumed piling debris onto the makeshift counterweight.

'It's working, sir!' Jurgen said, unmistakably pleased, despite his habitual lack of excitement. But that was fine; I was anxious enough for the pair of us.

'Last piece,' I said, wondering if I was going to have to go back for more ballast, but the last lump of scrap was enough. With another shriek of ancient metal against metal, the whole mess tilted, raising the thick metal slab blocking our way about half a metre above the deck plates.

'It's open,' Jurgen told me, as though I might somehow have failed to notice, and ducked, to shine the beam of his luminator

through the gap. The bulkhead turned out to be around thirty centimetres thick, and I marvelled at our good fortune in being able
to shift it at all; had I realised quite how great its mass was, I suspect, I wouldn't have bothered even making the attempt. Jurgen
sniffed the air beyond it suspiciously. 'It smells a bit,' he reported,
as oblivious as ever to the irony, 'but it's breathable.'

'Good,' I said, dropping to crawl under the suspended slab of
metal in my turn. I must admit to a strong sense of apprehension
as I passed beneath it, but as I stood and surveyed our surroundings, that was replaced by a rush of elated relief. We'd overcome
the obstacle after all, and although doing so had cost us a fair
amount of time, it was still far less than we'd have squandered
retracing our steps and looking for an alternative route. To say
nothing of the risk of running into the orks.

The passageway here was just as clear and uncluttered as it had
been on the other side of the bulkhead, and I breathed a silent
sigh of relief. It seemed I'd made the right decision after all. As I
inhaled again, I noticed a faint tang in the air I couldn't quite
identify, but which made my palms itch nevertheless. Suddenly,
although nothing had changed, the shadows surrounding us
seemed deeper, more threatening, and I urged Jurgen into motion
again. 'Come on,' I said. 'The sooner we're out of here the better.'

IF ANYTHING, HOWEVER, my sense of unease grew ever stronger as
we pressed on, despite the fact that we seemed to be making good
progress. I started to hear the muffled scrabbling sounds I'd
learned to associate with prowling genestealers again, and urged
Jurgen to halt on several occasions while I tried to pinpoint the
source. Every time I did, though, the sinister susurration either
faded away entirely, or echoed so much that I found myself unable
to narrow it down. In the end I just determined to proceed as cautiously as possible, and trust my instincts to warn us of any
ambush up ahead. But when an attack did come, it was in a form
it had never occurred to me to expect.

'There's an open space up ahead,' I told Jurgen, as quietly as I
could, after another nerve-shredding half-hour or so had passed.
The echoes of our footfalls and the air currents against my face felt

different, and the odd, faintly acidic tang in the air seemed a little stronger now.

'The hangar?' my aide asked, and I shook my head.

"Fraid not. We're still a good couple of hours from that. Probably a hold.' I'm no expert on starship construction, of course, but I'd travelled on enough of them over the years to be fairly certain that the wreck we were currently picking our way through was a bulk cargo hauler of some kind – or at least it had been, before some catastrophe had overwhelmed it, leaving it marooned in the warp until the capricious currents of that hellish realm had washed it up against the *Spawn of Damnation*. The sounds in the dark around us were growing louder and more numerous now, and I drew my weapons again, tension winding tighter in the pit of my stomach. For a moment I considered ordering Jurgen to extinguish the luminator, but the 'stealers seemed to have no use for light, so I didn't suppose it would attract their attention any more than the sound and scent of us would.[1] As I've remarked before, I've generally found it helpful to be able to see anything trying to kill me.

'You're right, sir,' Jurgen told me, a few moments later, the beam of his luminator picking out an open door in one of the walls of the corridor. As we passed it the pervasive smell grew stronger, and I glanced through the portal, regretting the impulse at once; the space beyond was vast, and the floor so packed with the inert bodies of genestealers, their four arms curled protectively around their thoraxes, that not a millimetre of metal was visible.

'Are they dead?' Jurgen asked, and I shook my head, too shocked to speak for a moment.

'No,' I whispered at last, backing away fearfully, expecting the whole nest to rouse and tear us apart at any moment. I'd had merely the briefest of glimpses, but there must have been at least a thousand of the abominable creatures in there, probably more if

---

1. *Though Cain errs in the specifics here, he is correct in the essentials: like most tyranid organisms, the senses of the average genestealer (if there can be said to be such a thing, given the astonishing mutability of all such creatures) are extremely acute. Although they do indeed use vision as well as their other senses, their sight is by no means limited to the visible spectrum, extending well into the infrared and the ultraviolet.*

I could be bothered with a proper headcount. 'Just dormant.' I tried desperately to remember the files Gries had shown me. 'The ones who attacked us before must have been revived to protect the others.'[1]

Which meant we were in a very uncomfortable position indeed. I glanced round again, alert for any sign of movement, and withdrew to the far side of the corridor. We had to go on, there was no question of that, but the thought of those monstrosities at our backs was a terrifying one.

'Do we turn round?' Jurgen asked, and I shook my head slowly.

'No,' I said. The chances of running into an active 'stealer or two would be just as great whichever direction we took, and at least the hangar was a definite objective, as opposed to wandering around in the dark waiting to be torn to pieces.

'Very good, sir,' my aide replied, his matter-of-fact demeanour as obscurely heartening as it usually was in a crisis, and I felt a measure of confidence beginning to return. After all, the purestrains behind us were all dormant, so unless we did something catastrophically stupid to rouse them...

The distinctive *hisssss... crack!* of a bolter round impacting a few feet to my left, blowing a fist-sized hole in the metal wall beside me, galvanised me into action, and I brought my laspistol up in the direction it had come from, returning fire instinctively as I dived for cover. Jurgen responded too, the beam of his luminator picking out the distinctive lumpen profile of an ork as he brought his lasgun on aim. The greenskin ducked back behind a stanchion, as las-bolts peppered the metalwork around him, and I began to pick out other shapes moving in the shadows beyond.

'Pull back,' I ordered, trying to get an estimate of their numbers. This was hardly the best place to start a firefight, as I strongly suspected the genestealers would be rather cranky on first waking, and we were making a considerable amount of noise between us already.

'Right you are, sir,' Jurgen agreed, with a trace of reluctance, eager

1. *Or from a different nest; similar hibernacula would have been distributed throughout the hulk, allowing the brood mind to survive the loss of a group or two.*

as any Valhallan to be killing orks, but this was hardly the time or place to indulge him. There seemed to be a dozen or so greenskins lurking in the darkness ahead of us, and a couple more of them began to shoot as well, though fortunately with no more luck than the first one was already having. 'They're trying to keep our heads down.'

'And they're succeeding,' I said testily, as a couple of heavy slugs ricocheted from the edge of the shrine to the Omnissiah atop the tool locker behind which I'd found refuge.

'Getting ready to charge, most likely,' Jurgen reminded me, a tactic we'd become more than familiar with on our Perlian odyssey, and I nodded grimly.

'Wait until they move,' I told him, unnecessarily, given how conversant he was with the best tactics to use against the creatures, and he nodded too, flicking the fire selector of his lasgun to full auto.

Without any further warning, a staccato rhythm of metal-soled boots began ringing off the deck plates, and a small knot of greenskins charged, brandishing the crude axes so many of them tend to favour in close combat. As they bore down on our position, a sense of foreboding washed over me; something was definitely not right about this. (Apart from the obvious point of an enraged mob of orks wanting to hack us to shreds, of course.) Then the hairs on the back of my neck began to prickle, as realisation dawned: the greenskins were running towards us in complete silence, none of them having made a sound since the skirmish began. On every other occasion I'd encountered them, they'd bellowed warcries, threats and exhortations to one another even before combat was joined, not to mention yelling their lungs out for as long as it continued, and they remained in any condition to do so.

'Don't let them get near you!' I yelled, as if Jurgen had been planning to offer them tanna and a florn cake, and he opened up at the same instant I did, spitting a fusillade of las-bolts down the corridor. There was no point in worrying about the genestealers in the hold now; the brood mind already knew precisely where we were, a deduction confirmed an instant later by a barely perceptible shifting in the shadows behind the orks with guns. Expecting to see something of the kind, I recognised it at once for what it was: a purestrain 'stealer, observing the actions of its implanted puppets with dispassionate interest.

'Grenade!' Jurgen yelled, lobbing another of the frag charges down the corridor, where it landed just ahead of the charging greenskins neat as you please. Both of us turned to run as it detonated, the concussion echoing in the confined space like an Earthshaker firing, and the pressure wave slammed into our backs as we took to our heels. The onrushing orks faltered, the leading ones shredded by the hail of shrapnel, and those behind either sufficiently incommoded by it or impeded by the resulting mess to allow us to open up a lead I hoped would prove sufficient.

'There was a genestealer with them,' I panted, praying that it would be prevented from pursuing us immediately by the tangle of perforated orks blocking the passage. We stood a reasonable chance of staying ahead of the lumbering greenskins for a while, until their greater endurance started to tell, but I was under no illusions about being able to outrun a purestrain.

Jurgen nodded. 'Saw it too,' he confirmed, before another bolt detonated uncomfortably close behind us; the phenomenal resilience of the orks was already allowing at least some of them to recover from the explosion.

We both turned, directing another hail of unaimed las-bolts back in their general direction, with the vague hope of putting them even more off their aim than usual, and for a second the air in my lungs seemed to freeze solid. Most of the las-bolts were impacting on the thorax of another genestealer, which had just entered the corridor from the cargo hold. It was moving sluggishly, rather than with the blinding speed and agility I usually associated with the creatures, and went down without even an attempt at seeking cover, but I knew we wouldn't be so lucky again. Even over the sounds of combat, and the ringing of our bootheels on the deck plates, I was beginning to hear a rustling, faint at first, like the wind in a forest, gradually rising to a muted roar, which reminded me uncomfortably of the tidal bore which had almost swept me to my death on Rikenbach. (And taken the feet out from under the heretic Dreadnought I'd been running away from at the time, luckily for me; I'd eventually washed up half-drowned on a sandspit, while our Hydra battery chewed it to pieces before it managed to get up again.[1])

'The whole nest's reviving!'[2] I shouted, finding I could run a little faster after all. The distinctive *click-scratch* of talons on metal echoed all around us, and I risked a quick glance back, regretting it at once. The pursuing 'stealers weren't just racing along the floor of the passageway, they were moving just as fast along the ceiling and the walls, their claws ripping purchase even from apparently smooth surfaces. The resulting fast-moving constriction in the dimensions of the corridor, beyond which more purestrains and a few implanted orks could be intermittently glimpsed, made it looked uncannily as though Jurgen and I were being swallowed – an impression I found about as comforting as you might expect. The creatures were still moving a little more sluggishly than usual, true, but they were gaining nevertheless, and I found myself trying to estimate just how long it was going to be before I felt claws in the back of my neck. The only result I could come up with was not nearly long enough, which was hardly helpful. The side passages we passed were choked with debris, and attempting to find refuge in any of them would be futile, simply slowing us down enough for the horrors in pursuit to catch up even more quickly.

As the breath began to rasp in my throat, made even worse by the dust our headlong dash was raising from the metal mesh at our feet, I sent a few las-bolts into the darkness at our backs entirely at random. The chances of an effective hit were minimal, true, but I was almost bound to strike something among so dense a concentration of xenos flesh, and even a token effort to fend them off fostered the comforting illusion that there might still be some action I could take to avoid a fate which now seemed inevitable.

---

1. *Though Hydras are intended primarily for air defence, most Imperial Guard commanders are well aware of the damage their quad-mounted autocannon can do to a heavily armoured target or dispersed infantry formation, and aren't slow to take advantage of the fact when the opportunity presents itself.*

2. *A substantial proportion of it, at any rate; the number of genestealers Cain describes could hardly have fitted into so narrow a maze of corridors all at once.*

Then, just as everything seemed lost, I felt a sudden flare of hope rise within me, as the beam of Jurgen's luminator picked out the rust-pitted surface of the bulkhead we'd so laboriously levered open, no more than a couple of hundred metres ahead of us. If we could only buy ourselves a few more precious seconds to reach it, before the onrushing horde reached us instead...

I risked another glance behind, to find that the swarm had closed the distance more rapidly than even my most pessimistic estimate; the recently roused genestealers were clearly feeling rather more chipper now, probably at the prospect of breakfast. We'd never even make it as far as the barrier at this rate, let alone manage to wriggle through the narrow gap beneath it, before we were overwhelmed.

The recently kindled flame of hope guttered and subsided, but I refused to let it be extinguished entirely. 'Jurgen!' I bellowed, over the rising noise behind us, and for a brief, hallucinatory moment, tasted seawater again. 'Any grenades left?'

'A couple, sir,' Jurgen said, rummaging through his collection of pouches. 'Frag or krak?'

'Frag!' I shouted, hoping he wouldn't take it for stress-induced profanity.

'Right you are, sir,' my aide responded, imperturbable as ever, and produced one with the air of having performed a successful conjuring trick. In a single deft movement, he primed and lobbed it over his shoulder, not bothering to look or care where it landed. In truth, neither did I. I heard the casing clatter resonantly against the metal mesh of the deck, felt my shoulder muscles tense instinctively for the shock of detonation, and hoped to the Throne that we'd be out of its area of effect by the time the hail of shrapnel was released. A second or two later I was punched hard in the back by a large, hot fist, and risked a glance behind us, being rewarded with a confused impression of thrashing limbs and tails receding further with each footstep I took. There was no time to see more, as we'd reached the bulkhead at last, and, praise the Emperor, it was still precariously raised by our makeshift lever.

Hearing the renewed skitter of fast-approaching claws, I lost no time in scrabbling under the thick metal slab, while Jurgen did his best to discourage the swarm with a final burst of his lasgun through the firing slit the gap created.

'Through you come, sir,' he said encouragingly, grabbing my forearm and yanking me the rest of the way, like a recalcitrant cork from a bottle. I half-slid into the utility conduit, where we'd removed the covering mesh, before recovering my balance, barking my shin painfully on the edge of the next section of deck plating as I did so.

'Thank you, Jurgen,' I said, turning to swipe the blade of my chainsword at the excessively clawed arm groping through the gap after me. The limb parted and fell into the channel beneath the deck plates, but if I knew 'stealers that wasn't going to be enough to discourage its owner from following, let alone its brood mates, so I turned, and severed the length of pipe holding the bulkhead up with a single stroke of the whirling blade. The thick slab of metal fell with gratifying speed, and a thud which made the deck plates shudder beneath our feet, crushing the first purestrains which were trying to follow us in the process. A couple of heads, an assortment of limbs and a generous dollop of mashed torso slithered down into the gully in the wake of the arm I'd cut off, making an unholy mess of my boots as they did so.

'That ought to hold 'em,' Jurgen said, an unmistakable note of satisfaction suffusing his voice, and I nodded, drawing deep draughts of the foetid air into my lungs to slow my hammering heart. The narrowness of our escape finally sank in, and I sat on the pile of scrap we'd used as a counterweight a little more heavily than I'd intended, heedless of the damage it was doing to my greatcoat. Right now I could hardly look much more dishevelled than I already did in any case.

'For a while,' I agreed, as a faint rasping began behind the bulkhead, and I belatedly realised that creatures capable of ripping Terminator armour apart weren't likely to be held back for very long by a mere few centimetres of steel. I regained my feet, having got enough of my breath back to start running again if I had to. 'Come on.' I started to lead the way down the tunnel.

'Won't that take us straight back to the orks?' Jurgen asked, falling in at my shoulder, and I nodded.

'I hope so,' I told him, ignoring the familiar expression of puzzlement falling across his features like a waning moon. 'Right now, they look like the best chance we've got.'

TWENTY-TWO

THOUGH WE WERE retracing our steps exactly, it seemed to take far less time to get back to the enclave of the orks than it had done to cover the same distance in the opposite direction. Partly, I suppose, that must have been due to our familiarity with the terrain; heading away from it we'd been checking for unexpected hazards the whole way, whereas now we were able to place our feet with confidence, certain we weren't about to be pitched through some weakened section of flooring to the deck below, like the damaged CAT we'd got into this mess in the first place by attempting to recover. Mainly, however, I think it was due to us knowing all too well what we were heading towards.

As we passed the tunnel mouths I'd considered going back to in search of an alternative route when we'd first found our way blocked by the bulkhead, I had to exert all the willpower I possessed not to turn aside in the hope of being able to bypass the genestealer nest and attempt to reach the hangar again. The only thing that stopped me was the realisation that it would be impossible to evade the creatures now. The brood mind had become aware of our presence, and I was certain that the malignant mass of the creatures we'd stumbled across would be diffusing itself though every corridor, duct and passageway by this time, effectively isolating us from our goal, while hunting us down deck by deck. Our only chance, slender as it was, would be to give it something else to think about – which is where the orks came in.

Seeing the implanted ones among the swarm had pretty much confirmed the deduction I'd made about the brood mind's reasons for leaving the great mass of them in ignorance of the presence of genestealers aboard the *Spawn of Damnation*. The first few it had taken would have left it in no doubt of the single-minded viciousness of the species, and that any attempt to confront so many of them directly would have left the 'stealers in poor shape to continue spreading their blight through the galaxy, if any had survived at all. Far better to continue lurking in the shadows, picking off a few of the interlopers here and there, until the greenskins' warhost was thoroughly infiltrated and its ability to fight off the swarm had been critically compromised. In the meantime, it would get to invade Serendipita by proxy, through implanted and hybridised orks, who would spread the genestealer taint wherever they went, no doubt taking as many of the purestrains as they could along for the ride. And while they got on with that, the ork horde would be giving the defenders of the system more than enough to think about, allowing the 'stealers to start polluting the gene pool of Serendipita's human inhabitants unnoticed and unopposed.

The only way I could see to prevent that, and, more importantly, save my own skin, was to turn the brood mind's own tactics against it. Something easier said than done, of course, but my instinctive affinity for enclosed spaces and remaining orientated within them had given me the germ of an idea. A fairly nebulous one, it's true, the only part I was certain about being a great deal of running, but it was better than nothing. Thus it was, far too soon for comfort, I found myself skulking through the lit corridors of the section the orks had colonised again, hoping we were in the right area and that we wouldn't come across too many of the inhabitants before we were ready.

However, it seemed that the Emperor was with us once more, the creatures' habitual bellicosity and flatulence combining to produce more than enough audible warning of their presence for Jurgen and I to find concealment in time to escape notice. Before too long we found ourselves looking out for the second time over the vast metal cavern which their relentless energy and destructiveness had wrenched from the fabric of the space hulk.

Fortunately, my sense of direction hadn't let me down, and we'd arrived more or less where I'd hoped we would, overlooking the smoke-shrouded section where the mekboyz toiled, creating weapons and ammunition to lay waste to Serendipita. Even at this distance I could feel the heat from the roaring forges, and hear the clank of tools from the decks below us where gangs of gretchin riggers were scavenging fresh raw material for the furnaces. Between the murk and the heat haze it was hard to make out much detail, but the little I could was more than enough.

Almost immediately below us was an area devoted to the construction of battlewagons: mobile weapon platforms bristling with weapons, which I recognised from Perlia. No two were alike, of course, but I'd faced them often enough to know how hard they could be to knock out without armour support, and hoped Torven and Kregeen would be able to scrape up a fair number of tanks between them. There were plenty of smaller trucks about as well, armed too, of course, but for the moment at least being used to shift supplies about from one end of the cavern to the other. (And for all I knew, the orkish mindset being what it was, back again, just for the fun of charging around at life-threatening speeds.) In the middle distance was a latticework of scaffolding, where the minuscule figures of innumerable gretchin were swarming over a vast pile of scrap, which looked alarmingly like a half-completed gargant; but that, at least, would be a problem for later, and preferably somebody else.

'Those look like promethium tanks,' I said, nudging Jurgen and pointing to a cluster of domed cylinders on the periphery of the vehicle assembly area. 'Can you read the glyphs?'

My aide nodded and squinted a little, trying to bring the crudely daubed symbols on the sides of the tank into focus through the smoke-stained air. 'Looks like a warning,' he said at last. 'Fire, or burn, and *zogoff*.'[1]

'Excellent,' I said, my guess confirmed. 'Do you think you can hit it from here?'

'I reckon so,' Jurgen said, peering through the sights of his lasgun. 'It's a long shot, but at least there's no windage to worry about.' He steadied his breathing, lining the shot up carefully, and fired once. I strained my eyes, but the distance and the obscuring murk were too great, and I could see no sign of the impact. 'Bit to the left.' He repeated the process, to no apparent effect, then tried a third time. I was just on the point of giving up and trying to find an alternative target, when my aide grunted with satisfaction. 'That ought to do it.'

'Did you hit the tank?' I asked, still waiting for some kind of visible effect with a sense of vague disappointment. I suppose I was hoping for something like the inferno which had engulfed the refuelling station in Prosperity Wells,[2] although that had been sparked by a krak round from a rocket launcher rather than the feeble punch of a lasgun fired from far beyond its normal effective range.

Jurgen shook his head. 'The tank?' he echoed, looking puzzled, although that was nothing new. 'I was shooting at the outlet valve.' Squinting in the direction of the blocky cylinders, I was just able to make out some minute protrusions where a cluster of pipes joined the assembly. It may have been my imagination, but the haze seemed a little thicker there, and I thought I could make out the shimmer of liquid gushing from the nearest one, to form an ever-growing pool.

---

1. *An orkish word, which translates roughly as 'go away', but which may also mean, 'leave it alone', or 'I doubt your veracity', according to context. Clearly the second of the three meanings is intended here.*

2. *The township on Perlia where Cain's celebrated March of Liberation began. It was subsequently renamed Cainstead, to his mingled amusement and embarrassment; even after taking up residence on that world, as a tutor at the schola progenium there following his retirement, he continued to refer to the place by its original name.*

'That would work much better,' I assured him, marvelling, not for the first time, at his standard of marksmanship. To hit so small a target at this range would have involved a fair degree of luck as well, of course, but I wasn't going to turn up my nose at that either. 'Well done.'

'You're welcome, sir,' Jurgen said, allowing a faint air of satisfaction to enter his voice, then nodded judiciously. 'Just give it another moment to let the fumes build.' He sighted down the lasgun again. 'Only needs a little spark...'

He squeezed the trigger, and I stared at the fuel dump, hopeful anticipation narrowing my eyes. Where the shot hit, I had no idea, but the las-bolt must have struck metal, producing the spark Jurgen had wished for. For the briefest of instants nothing seemed to happen, then a bright orange flare blossomed from nowhere, racing through the air as it expanded, to engulf the entire complex.

'Good shot!' I started to say, then everything was drowned out by a thunderclap which left my ears ringing, the sound rebounding and redoubling in the confined space. A lake of liquid fire poured through the assembly area, washing over the newly completed battlewagons, immolating orks and gretchin by the hundred in the process. A couple of trucks on the fringes of the mekboyz' compound turned and raced away, trying to outrun the spreading flames; one made it to safety, while the other was overtaken and engulfed, its own fuel combusting in a miniature echo of the main fireball, all but lost in the general conflagration.

'That went well,' Jurgen said, sounding distinctly pleased with himself, over the rolling boom of a succession of secondary explosions, as the ammunition aboard the burning battlewagons began to cook off. I found myself wondering where the main munitions dumps were, and whether we'd perhaps overdone it a little. I'd been hoping to get the orks' attention, not wipe them out entirely.

Well, that wasn't going to happen, of course. Despite the vista of destruction spreading out beneath our feet, the greater part of the greenskins' colony had been left untouched. Tearing my

eyes from the inferno we'd unleashed, I was gratified to see
them charging around in even greater disarray than usual, while
bellowing nobz[1] attempted to restore order with about as much
success as you might expect. The warboss we'd seen before was
forging his way through the milling throng, cracking heads and
roaring at anything unfortunate enough to cross his path, and I
gave Jurgen a nudge. This was too good an opportunity to miss.
'Isn't that the one you wanted to take a crack at the last time?' I
asked.

'Looks like it,' Jurgen agreed, taking the hint and lining up
another shot. It was too much to hope that he'd be able to drop
the leader of the host from here (although given the devastation
he'd already managed to wreak with just a few las-rounds I
wouldn't have been all that surprised if he took the brute cleanly
between the eyes), but I had another objective in mind in any case.
'Frak. Just winged him.'

The warboss looked up, snarling, as Jurgen's las-bolt impacted
on the left shoulder plate of his armour, adding another barely
visible dent to the impressive collection already decorating it, to
glare furious hatred in our direction. Which was precisely what I'd
hoped for. I stepped to the very brink of the vertiginous drop at the
end of the abbreviated corridor, heedless of the suffocating heat
rising from the inferno below, and flourished my chainsword,
locking gazes over the intervening distance. It was a gesture I knew
no greenskin would be able to interpret in any manner other than
a challenge, and I was right; with a bellow of rage, inaudible over
the roaring of the flames, and the cacophonous collapse of the
partially completed gargant as the supporting scaffold softened in
the furnace heat, he began running in our direction, skirting the
inferno as closely as he could. His bodyguard came with him, of
course, and, true to the mob mentality which seemed to govern all
these creatures' actions, every other ork in the vicinity trailed along
behind. Even from this distance, and over the deafening clamour
of the destruction we'd unleashed, I could hear the rising
communal shout of 'WAAAAAAGGHHHHHH!' which betokened
their unleashed bloodlust.

---

1. *Orks in a position of authority.*

'Time we were going,' I said, estimating how long it would take for them to reach us. Several minutes, at least, but they wouldn't be expecting us to hang about either. As they climbed the intervening levels they'd be fanning out through them too, hoping to get ahead and cut us off. Which might even have worked, if there hadn't been a swarm of genestealers on our heels already, no doubt hoping to repeat the trick in the other direction.

For want of any better idea, I hurried back in the direction of the branching corridors which had attracted my attention on our way in, hoping the genestealers wouldn't have advanced that far by now. I was fairly sure they'd continue to avoid the orkish enclave, as penetrating its perimeter would reveal their presence, effectively frakking up their plan to use the greenskins for their own ends; but the orks must be spreading out too by now, maddened by bloodlust and the desire for revenge, and with any luck the two groups would encounter one another before either caught up with us. Of course that raised the interesting question of how we were going to slip through a minor war without being caught in the crossfire, but I'd worry about that when the time came.

In the event, however, it wasn't the 'stealers or the orks which found us first. We were still well inside the illuminated area when a pattering of running feet on the deck plates behind us snatched at my attention, and I whirled round to find the corridor choked with gretchin, charging towards us with shrill squeals of malevolent glee, urged on by the roaring bulk of their orkish overseer. Just our luck: they must have been foraging in this part of the wreck when we blew up the fuel dump, noticed the commotion, and got caught up in the general bloodlust.

'I'll take the big one!' I shouted, placing a couple of las-bolts from my pistol in the centre of the ork's chest, which, given how much he towered over the grotz[1] was hardly a difficult test of my marksmanship. He staggered, but rallied, and would probably have charged me if it hadn't been for the milling mass of smaller greenskins clustered around his feet. Jurgen thinned them out nicely with a couple of bursts from his lasgun, leaving the rest to

---

1. *The usual orkish word for their smaller cousins.*

decide they were more scared of us than the ork, and scatter squealing. Finding the way unexpectedly clear, the ork began to charge forwards, a club the thickness of my forearm raised to strike; but I was ready for him, and ducked under it, the edge of my chainsword chewing through his torso in a rising horizontal cut. Bellowing in surprise and outrage, the hulking greenskin tried to turn for another go, before the realisation that he'd been almost bisected finally sank in, and he toppled to the deck plates, staring in stupefaction at his widely distributed entrails.

'That was easy,' Jurgen remarked, and I nodded, flicking the speed setting of the chainsword back to idle. I suspected I'd be needing it a lot more in the next few hours, if I managed to last that long, and didn't want to find the powerpack depleted when I did.

'Better make the most of it,' I advised. 'Things are going to get a bit trickier from now on.'

In that expectation, I was far from disappointed. By the time we'd reached the relative sanctuary of the darkened corridors again, we'd seen off another half-dozen orks, in twos and threes,[1] the first few of the mob hunting us to make it into these upper levels. But I knew there were bound to be more, hard on their heels, and I began to wonder about the wisdom of the course of action I'd begun.

Well, it was too late for second thoughts, of course. By now we were almost at the first of the side tunnels I'd been making for, and I picked up my pace a little, conscious that the genestealers would almost certainly have ripped their way through the bulkhead by this time, and could be skittering towards us from out of the darkness as fast as their six limbs could carry them. If they hadn't already got this far, and were now lurking in ambush, of course, or others of their kind hadn't found their way here by another route. I listened carefully, alert for any hint of scuttling in the gloom around us, but what I could hear over the hammering of my heart was too faint and diffuse to pinpoint.

No point worrying then, I told myself, before a barely

---

1. *Clearly not a literal half-dozen, then...*

perceptible change in the quality of the darkness enfolding us started tickling at the edge of my awareness. 'Kill the luminator,' I instructed Jurgen. Responsive as ever to orders he complied immediately, and I realised at once that I was right. There was a faint glow behind us, growing in intensity moment by moment, and as I strained my ears I was able to make out the irregular drumming of a large number of fast-moving feet. A moment later it was joined by the timbre of guttural voices, quarrelsomely raised, which dispelled any possible doubt there might have been about who they belonged to. 'This way! And try to stay quiet.'

The last admonition may not have been strictly necessary, I suppose, as the oncoming orks would almost certainly have drowned out any noise we might be making with their interminable bickering, but it never hurt to be careful. Besides, I hadn't forgotten that the genestealers were somewhere around too, and were probably listening out for us with just as much energy and interest as I was for them. Fortunately I'd memorised the position of the cross corridor we'd been aiming for before our luminator went out, and a few strides were sufficient to take me there; my nose enabled me to fix Jurgen's location just as easily, and guide him in the right direction too, so that by the time the diffuse glow behind us separated into a score of distinct light sources, the pair of us were comfortably ensconced behind a large lump of rust a few metres into the passageway, which looked as though it had once been a pump of some kind. From there we had a good view of the corridor we'd just left, so I hunkered down, my laspistol at the ready, and peered round the defunct mechanism, hoping to see enough to get an estimate of the size of the group behind us.

In the event, I was to see a great deal more than that. As the orks approached the junction, and Jurgen and I steadied our weapons, preparing to drop any which split off from the main body to explore our refuge, the light around us grew brighter with every step closer the greenskins took. As yet, although they were more than audible, the pursuing orks had still to become visible; the pump behind which Jurgen and I were lurking was on the side of the passageway they were approaching from, so the view we had of the main corridor was up towards the genestealer nest we'd stumbled across what felt like a lifetime ago, but which my chronograph stubbornly insisted had been barely an hour and a half.

I centred the junction of the two passageways in my sights, and blinked, thinking for a moment that fatigue and stress had finally caught up with me. The shadows were shrinking and deepening as the luminator-bearing greenskins approached, but one had appeared to ripple, moving in the wrong direction, before settling again, somewhere in a tangle of pipework depending from the ceiling.

My breath froze. "Stealer,' I whispered, almost inaudibly, not daring to raise my voice any louder in case the chitinous obscenity heard me. 'In the main passage.'

'I make it three,' Jurgen responded, equally *sotto voce*, an instant after I spotted the others, clinging to the wall beside a ventilator grille a little above eye level, and lurking in the utility channel beneath the mesh deck plate. Then more shadows rippled, and a whole swarm of them was suddenly there, blocking the passageway entirely, just as the vanguard of the orks came pounding into view from the other direction.

I suppose humans in that position might have hesitated, paralysed for a moment by surprise or indecision, but both xenos breeds were governed by an instinctive aggression which generally served them well in such encounters. With a bone-rattling yell of 'WAAAAAGGHHH!' the greenskins surged forwards, firing their crude bolters and swinging their axe blades, and the purestrains flowed to meet them, meeting firearm with mandible, edged steel with claw. Blood and ichor flowed, neither side willing or capable of giving quarter, each equally determined to annihilate the other.

'Come on,' I instructed, leaving them to it and hurrying down the passageway as quickly as I could without breaking an ankle on some unseen obstruction. After barking my shins on pieces of scrap littering the place a couple of times, I told Jurgen to rekindle the luminator; after all, the orks were using them too, and wouldn't be able to tell us from allies at a distance, and I was already convinced the 'stealers would be able to find us just as easily whether we were using one or not. The noise of the skirmish behind us was drowning out any warning my ears might have given of purestrains lurking in ambush, so, like it or not, we had no option other than relying on our vision in any case.

'Sounds like they're all at it,' Jurgen observed, sounding no more concerned than if he'd been informing me that rain was expected by evening, and I nodded in agreement. Sporadic shooting and orkish war cries could be heard echoing down the shafts from every direction now, and it became clear to me that perhaps we wouldn't find a way out after all. My gift for remaining orientated in environments like this still seemed as reliable as ever, but it appeared the way back to the hangar was now blocked by two hordes of inimical xenoforms hell-bent on knocking the proverbial nine shades out of one another. If there was anything at all positive about the situation, I supposed, it was that the greenskins were now well and truly aware of the genestealer presence, which meant neither would have much time or attention to spare for launching an attack on Serendipita any time soon. This may have been gravy for the Serendipitans, but wasn't much help to me.

'Let's try this way,' I said, spotting lights moving up ahead, and turning aside down a passageway which looked, if anything, even more decrepit and dangerous than the one we'd just left. A flicker of motion caught the corner of my eye, and I turned, bringing up my chainsword instinctively, powering the teeth up to combat speed. Yet again, my duellist's reflexes saved my life, as the blade sliced cleanly through the arm of a genestealer millimetres from closing its claws around my head, and I pivoted out of the way of its rush, decapitating it neatly on the backswing. As it fell I looked around for more, but this one seemed to have been alone, much to my relief.

Any respite could only be temporary, however; I had no doubt that the brood mind was aware of our location now, and would be sending more of the creatures after us. All we could do was keep moving, and hope the orks were keeping the rest of the 'stealers in the vicinity occupied. At which point I became aware of the lights in the distance again, following us down the side passage we'd taken. It seemed they'd noticed us at the same time we'd seen them.

'Keep moving,' I said urgently. 'As fast as possible.'

'Right you are, sir,' Jurgen said, suiting the action to the word and breaking into an ungainly trot. It seemed we'd passed into yet another section of the hulk, in greater disrepair than the old freighter and whatever vessel the orks had been cannibalising had been. The corridor was narrow, and the floor plates badly corroded. The ubiquitous dust being kicked up by my hurrying footsteps was stained brown with rust here, and flakes of the stuff came off the walls every time my shoulders brushed against them. Loops of cable hung like jungle vines from the ceiling, where the brackets holding them in place had worked loose, or fallen away entirely, and for a moment I found myself wondering if we could somehow emulate Mira's trick with the power lines back on the *Revenant*, but the generators which used to feed them had ceased to function centuries ago, if not millennia, and even if they hadn't I'd probably just have ended up electrocuting myself in any case.

'It's a dead end,' Jurgen called, flashing his luminator round a rubble-choked chamber, which, judging by the control lecterns and the glass-fronted dials set into the walls, had probably once been a monitoring chapel for the ship's power core. There was no other way out that I could see, and I expressed my disappointment in several short phrases I think it best not to record for posterity. 'Can we go back the way we came?'

'If we clear the orks out of the way first,' I said, indicating the brightening glow some way off down the passageway.

Jurgen took cover behind a chunk of fallen ceiling, his lasgun aimed at the narrow entrance. 'Not a problem,' he assured me.

'Glad to hear it,' I said, hoping he wasn't being overly optimistic. It sounded like a fair-sized mob to me, and, although they could only enter the chamber one at a time, I'd fought greenskins too often to be sanguine about our ability to drop them all as they came in. I'd seen orks shrugging off lasgun wounds which would have killed or incapacitated a man, and it would only take a few of them to rush us in so confined a space before we were overwhelmed. 'Got any grenades left?'

'Sorry, sir.' Jurgen shook his head dolefully. 'We've used the last one.'[1]

'Oh well,' I said, trying to sound casual. 'Can't be helped. We'll just have to do the best we can.' I popped off a few speculative las-bolts down the passageway, hoping to delay our pursuers, or goad them into doing something rash, but all I received for my pains was an answering flurry of bolter rounds, which punched holes in the metal walls surrounding us with a ripple of overlapping detonations which made my ears ring. That sparked another idea, and I scurried over to the walls, examining the damage. If the metal was thin enough, I might be able to cut us an exit with my chainsword, while Jurgen kept the greenskins at bay.

The hope was a forlorn one, though; a brief inspection was enough to convince me I'd never be able to slice through it in time, even if the teeth of my weapon didn't break in the attempt. What really made me decide against trying, however, was the flicker of movement I glimpsed through the nearest hole. I sprang back reflexively, as a claw a good thirty centimetres long poked through the aperture and wriggled around experimentally. After a moment it withdrew, then reappeared again, along with its four companions, punching through the metal as though it were cardboard. Slowly they drew together as the 'stealer beyond the wall closed its fist, the metal crumpling like the foil of a ration pack, then withdrew, ripping away an entire handful, to leave a hole roughly the size of my head.

'The 'stealers are coming through the walls!' I warned Jurgen, as a mouth with far too many fangs snapped at the gap, just failing to force its way inside. I fired my laspistol at it from point-blank range, and it withdrew in a spray of foul-smelling ichor, but the respite was only short-lived. The metal of the wall began to buckle and tear in several other places, and with a thrill of pure horror I realised there was an entire group of the monstrosities ripping their way through to us.

'The orks aren't getting out of our way either,' my aide

---

1. *Presumably in one of the minor firefights Cain glossed over a few pages ago.*

responded, phlegmatic as ever, sending a burst of automatic
fire down the corridor as he spoke. Another burst of bolts
responded, hissing over our heads, to impact against the wall.
The 'stealers reeled from the multiple detonations, but rallied
quickly, renewing their attack on the weakened barrier; at this
rate they'd be through in a matter of seconds.

I backed away another couple of paces, swinging my
chainsword in a defensive pattern, and waiting for a target of
opportunity for my laspistol. I'd only have time for one or two
shots, and I intended to make them count.

Then a flicker of motion caught my attention again, half-
hidden by the shadows at roughly the height of my shins, and
I whipped round to face it, bringing the pistol to bear. My
finger began to tighten on the trigger.

'Commissar! Is that you?' The voice in my comm-bead was
attenuated and hazed with static, and for a moment I was too
taken aback to respond. 'The pict link is considerably
degraded.'

'Drumon?' I slackened the pressure on the trigger, just in time
to avoid blowing a hole in a CAT, almost identical to the one
we'd found shortly before Blain had gone to report to the
Emperor. It trundled out from behind a sagging console, which
had concealed it from view when Jurgen and I first entered the
room. 'Where are you?' I fired a couple of las-bolts at a genestealer which had ripped a hole in the wall while I was
speaking, sufficient to poke its head and shoulders through,
and which was reaching out to grab me. It dropped, most of its
head now missing, to dangle grotesquely, halfway through the
aperture, like a badly mounted trophy.

'Aboard the *Revenant*,' the Techmarine replied, sounding
faintly surprised. 'We thought you were dead.'

'I soon will be,' I replied, with a degree of brusqueness, cutting
at another 'stealer, which had burst through the wall as though
emerging from some nightmare chrysalis. It retreated, leaking
fluid from its thorax, and prepared to charge again. 'The hulk's
crawling with 'stealers and greenskins.' As if to emphasise the
point, Jurgen fired again, eliciting a bellow of orkish rage, and

abandoned his post to join me. 'We're boxed in between them.'

'Sorry, sir,' Jurgen reported, yanking the luminator from the barrel of his lasgun and dropping it unceremoniously to the deck, where it rolled around, casting grotesque shadows across the monsters hemming us in. He drew his bayonet and snapped it into place where the light had been. 'I'm completely dry.'

'Hold your position,' Drumon advised, and cut the link.

'Like I've got any choice!' I snarled, ducking under a scything blow from the rallying 'stealer, and laying it open from thorax to head before it could recover its balance. It dropped, and I turned to face the next, snapping off a shot at the first ork to enter the chamber as I did so. He staggered, then recovered, and began to charge, his clumsy axe raised for a killing blow, while the genestealer I was facing lunged, too fast for me to counter...

Then something seized me, crushed me and tore me inside out. For a timeless, blinding instant I lost all sense of who, what and where I was, overwhelmed by more pain and terror than I knew it was possible to experience. Then I felt another wrench, like that of a starship's transition from the warp back to real-space, and fell, feeling cold metal beneath my face.

'Commissar. Are you well?' It was Drumon's voice again, but real this time, not issuing from the tiny transceiver in my ear. I blinked my blurry vision as clear as I could, and felt huge ceramite gauntlets lifting me to my feet.

'I'll let you know,' I said, wondering vaguely why gretchin were hammering spikes into my temples, and no one was doing anything about it. 'Where are the 'stealers?'

'And the orks,' Jurgen added, looking about as healthy as I felt, which is to say not noticeably different from his usual demeanour.

'Back on the *Spawn of Damnation*,' Drumon said, as though that should have been obvious.

'Then where the hell are we?' I asked, trying to focus on our surroundings. We were in an echoing metal chamber, lit by functioning luminators. Arcane mechanisms were everywhere, being tended by solemnly-chanting tech-adepts, and the air was thick with incense and ozone. Everything I looked at made my headache worse, so I gave up trying to make sense of it.

'Aboard the *Revenant*,' Drumon said, in the same tone of voice. He indicated the automaton we'd stumbled across, which for some reason was still with us, and pottering around the echoing chamber at random. 'Fortunately the CAT's teleport homer was still functioning, so we were able to bring you back along with it.'

'You mean you could just have teleported the one we went to fetch back aboard any time you felt like it?' I asked, feeling foolish and angry in roughly equal measure.

The Techmarine shook his head. 'It was deactivated,' he reminded me.

'So it was.' And if I'd known then what I knew now, I'd have cheerfully left it to rot. I glanced at the doorway, as another towering figure strode through it with a nod of greeting. 'Apothecary Sholer. A pleasure to see you.'

'I imagine so,' Sholer said. 'An unprotected teleportation can have unpleasant effects on the system.'

'Indeed it can,' I agreed. 'But, all things considered, a decided improvement on the alternative.'

TWENTY-THREE

I SPENT THE best part of a week under Sholer's care, recuperating from the effects of being yanked through the fringes of the warp by the scruff of my neck,[1] and feeling vaguely resentful that I was suffering the worst hangover of my life without having had the fun which should have preceded it. Jurgen, to my surprise, seemed none the worse for the experience, recovering in little more than a day,[2] and busied himself as usual with fending off unwelcome visitors and sorting out the administrative trivia I felt too groggy to deal with. Some things I couldn't avoid, of course, Gries among them, and I filled my time between sleeping and gradually diminishing bouts of nausea with compiling as complete a report as I could of our wanderings aboard the *Spawn of Damnation*, and the unpleasant surprises I'd found there.

Feeling I ought to make a show of taking my position of

---

1. *The actual mechanisms of teleportation are a little more complex than that, involving the linkage of two discrete physical points through a precisely focussed Geller field, but Cain's typically forthright description is close enough for most purposes.*

2. *Possibly because his peculiar gift cushioned him from the worst effects of exposure to the warp, although Cain would have had no way of knowing that at the time.*

Imperial Guard liaison officer seriously, I got Jurgen to forward copies of my evasions and excuses to Torven, who passed them to Duque and Kregeen in turn, and all three passed the information down the line of their respective commands; the inevitable upshot of which was that rumour and exaggeration soon began to outpace the factual summaries, so by the time I was up and about again practically everyone in the system was convinced I'd seen off a greenskin invasion, and a swarm of genestealers, pretty much single-handed.

'It's no wonder the governor wants to see you,' Drumon told me, on his last visit to my quarters aboard the *Revenant*. Now that the immediate crisis was over, and I was feeling a lot more like my old self, I'd lost no time in arranging my transfer to the Imperial Guard garrison on Serendipita. I'd had more than enough of spacecraft for the time being, and just wanted to be somewhere away from metal corridors and shadows that might turn out to harbour a genestealer or two. True, it would have to be a very foolish 'stealer indeed to try boarding an Astartes strike cruiser, but every time I glanced out of a viewport, the ominous mass of the space hulk could be seen looming over us, and the further I could get from it the better so far as I was concerned. 'You seem to be the only man in the system more honoured than he is.'

'So long as he doesn't want to challenge me to a duel,' I jested, surprised, and a little touched, that he'd bothered to come and see me off.

Drumon smiled faintly. 'Small fear of that,' he said. 'The way the locals are talking about you, I think he would rather take on the brother-captain if he had a grievance.'

Jurgen fell into step behind us, hefting my kitbag along with his own, as we made our way through the corridors towards the hangar bay where our shuttle was waiting. As befitted the impression of modesty I endeavoured to cultivate, I'd asked for an Imperial Guard Aquila to collect my aide and I, rather than putting the Reclaimers to the inconvenience of dispatching a Thunderhawk – which meant I'd be able to sleep in peace, or catch up on some reading, without having to don the clumsy ear-defenders. As I'd saved him the bother of fending off a greenskin invasion, and the simultaneous infiltration of the system by ravening genestealers, Torven had been more than happy to indulge my whim, and I have to admit to feeling a warm glow at the sight of the sturdy little utility craft nestled in between the Thunderhawks like a fledgling among adult raptors.

At first, however, I barely noticed it, being too astonished at the sight of an honour guard of Reclaimers, their freshly burnished armour resplendent in the light from the overhead luminators, lined up between the doorway and the lowered boarding ramp of the Aquila. Gries himself was at their head, and he took a pace forwards as Drumon and I drew abreast of his position.

'Commissar. Your assistance has been appreciated,' he said, inclining his head to look down at me. Somehow he seemed to have got the impression that I'd been keeping the genestealers busy on purpose, buying the time for the boarding party to fight its way back to the Thunderhawk with the data Yaffel had managed to salvage from the Redeemer's cogitator core, and I wouldn't have felt comfortable disabusing him.

'The honour's all mine,' I told him, truthfully enough. 'Is the situation aboard the hulk stable enough to resume salvage operations?'

'Not yet.' He shook his head regretfully. 'But the conflict between the orks and the genestealers is diminishing slowly, along with their numbers. When reinforcements arrive, we should be able to cleanse the key areas at least.'

'I'm sure the magos will be delighted to hear it,' I said. 'As will the governor, when I report to him.'

I don't mind admitting to feeling a flicker of apprehension as Jurgen and I climbed the boarding ramp. Even though I knew Mira had left the *Revenant* aboard the governor's shuttle, along with the parasites she'd been herding, part of me still expected her to turn up at the last minute, as she had done before, ready to disturb my hard-won equilibrium again. She didn't, of course, and I took my seat with a faint sigh of relief, finally daring to hope I'd seen the last of her, and wondering why that thought came with a faint pang of regret. Despite everything, life with her around had been far from dull, I had to concede that at least.

I felt no such ambivalence about my last sight of the *Spawn of Damnation*, though, bidding the cursed vessel a hearty good riddance as it gradually diminished to a speck, and finally vanished completely among the stars.

MY FIRST SIGHT of Serendipita was every bit as spectacular as I'd been led to expect, the lush blue-green globe silhouetted against the mottled ochre hues of the gas giant around which it orbited, while the ring system laid a glittering diamond pathway beneath the Aquila's keel. I couldn't tell you how long I simply stared out of the viewport, while the world grew large enough to eclipse its primary, then occult it entirely, gradually growing to fill my field of vision. Eventually all I could see was the curve of a horizon, and the sprawl of a continent, encroaching on a cloud-flecked ocean; then the land expanded to encompass the whole viewport, its mottled surface slowly resolving into forests, plains and signs of habitation. Towns and cities became visible, roads appeared linking them, and the regular outlines of field boundaries began segmenting what, from higher up, had seemed to be nothing more than patches of foliage.

'That must be it,' Jurgen said, pointing to an expanse of parkland in the distance, its artfully natural landscape betraying the hand of human intervention. Before long he was proved correct, by the appearance of a palace, set on the shores of a lake which might once have been real before someone decided to tidy it up a bit round the edges. It was low, and well proportioned, as such buildings go, constructed of some local stone of a faintly pinkish hue, which echoed the colours of the gas giant about which the whole world orbited. The pilot brought us down neatly on a landing pad fringed with the same material, which partly obscured the more utilitarian rockcrete necessary to support the weight of a shuttle, and bordered with flowerbeds stuffed with some local variety of flora.

'And this must be the governor,' I agreed, as the boarding ramp descended and a distinguished-looking fellow in a formal robe, his neatly curled waist-length beard embellished with a bow of yellow silk, stepped forwards to meet us. The style here was evidently informal. If he had household troops or bodyguards with him, they were tucked somewhere discreetly out of sight.

'Commissar Cain?' he enquired, as if there might be some doubt as to my identity, and I nodded once, in acknowledgement.

'Governor Metrelle. My compliments on your garden – a real tonic to the spirit after so long in space.'

The man smiled faintly. 'I'm the governor's majordomo, commissar. His Excellency is waiting for you in the tea garden. If you'd care to walk this way?' He turned and began leading the way across a neatly clipped lawn towards a topiary arch in a head-high hedge.

'If I walked that way,' Jurgen muttered, in a voice I devoutly hoped was inaudible, 'I'd be singing soprano.'

Our guide stopped by the gap in the foliage and motioned us through. 'Commissar Cain, your Excellency, and...' his gaze rested on Jurgen for a moment, while his brow furrowed with the effort of attempting to formulate an adequate description, 'another person.'

'My aide, Gunner Jurgen,' I said, stepping through the arch. Beyond was a pleasant formal garden, scattered with comfortable chairs and small tables, at the largest of which sat a young-looking man of athletic build with a chin you could have used to chisel granite. He stood, smiling, and shook me firmly by the hand.

'Of course. Your indispensable right arm.' To the astonishment of both of us he shook Jurgen's hand too, wiping his own surreptitiously on the leg of his crisp white trousers as he returned to his chair. 'I've heard a lot about you.'

'All exaggerated, I'm sure,' I said, slipping easily into the modest hero routine. There were four place settings at the table, I noticed, although no other guests seemed to be here yet.

'Not in the least,' a warm contralto voice said, and my spine turned to ice. I'd have recognised it anywhere, even before

Jurgen said 'Good afternoon, miss,' and I turned to see Mira smiling at me through the gap in the hedge.

I like to think I rallied quickly, responding with a formal incli-nation of the head, and returned the smile, as noncommittally as possible. I had no idea what she was doing here, and thought it best to bide my time until I saw how the land lay.

Metrelle smiled at her too, in the faintly simple-minded fash-ion of a man besotted with a member of the opposite sex, and not quite sure what to do about it. 'My betrothed is a great admirer of yours, commissar. You seem to have made quite an impression on her while you were travelling together.'

'How gratifying,' I replied automatically, before the full import of his words sank in, and I raised an eyebrow at Mira. 'Betrothed?'

'Since last night.' She smiled at the governor in a manner I remembered all too well. Then she turned to my aide. 'Jurgen, I wonder if I could impose on you for a minute? I managed to get hold of some of that Valhallan drink you're both so fond of, but our kitchen staff are a little unsure of the correct method of infusion.'

'You managed to get some tanna?' I asked, the full extent of the governor's wealth and influence starting to become clear to me. It was all I could do to maintain a small personal supply of the stuff, with the access my position gave me to the vast resources of the Munitorum. Emperor alone knew how Metrelle had managed it, at just a few days' notice, or how much it had cost him.

He nodded. 'Mira said you'd appreciate it,' he said.

'If your servants don't frak it up,' Jurgen said, oblivious as ever to the niceties of non-military protocol, but our hosts didn't seem to take it amiss. Mira was used to him, after all, and I was pretty sure Metrelle would go along with whatever seemed to suit her. 'I'd better go and show them how it's done.'

'Thank you,' Mira said, and smiled at the governor again, seeming as gooey as an éclair in a heatwave. 'Would you mind pointing him in the right direction, dearest?'

'Of course.' Metrelle heaved himself out of the garden chair, and led Jurgen through the archway. His voice diminished in the distance. 'Just down here, past the toad pond and across the courtyard...'

'I know what you're going to say,' Mira said, switching off the simper and watching me through narrowed eyes, 'but what did you expect? You went gadding off to that drifting mausoleum and let everyone think you were dead.'

'And why bother fighting for a throne back home when there's one here you can just help yourself to with a smile and a quick proposal?' I added.

'Precisely.' Mira nodded, looking more aristocratic than ever, even if she was still spilling out of her gown like a joygirl desperate for custom. 'Viridia's going to be a complete mess for years after all the fighting, and it's a lot more comfortable here. Besides, Metty's quite sweet really. I could do a lot worse.'

I smiled, feeling a rush of relief so strong it left me breathless.

'Then I suppose congratulations are in order,' I said.

Mira watched me narrowly, sifting my words for any hint of sarcasm. 'I take it you're not going to make a scene, then?' she asked at length, sounding vaguely disappointed.

'No,' I said gravely, trying to look as though I was holding my emotions in check, and firmly suppressing the impulse to start doing handsprings round the garden. 'I won't spoil it for you. Best man won, and all that.'

Her expression softened again, so I assumed I'd got away with it. 'That's very sweet of you,' she said, although she must have known me better than that by now. 'And speaking of the best man, I've got a little favour to ask...'

'By all means,' I said, distracted by the mingled odours of Jurgen and freshly brewed tanna. He and the governor were returning, with a small comet tail of retainers, all bearing trays. Things were definitely looking up.

'Can you find some excuse to frak off back to Coronus before the wedding?' Mira asked. 'You're not exactly low profile around here, and I don't want to be upstaged on my big day, do I?'

'Consider it done,' I agreed. In truth, I'd already made up my mind to leave as soon as I could, the idea of living on a planet under Mira's capricious and pudgy thumb being far too uncomfortable to contemplate. I raised the tea bowl Jurgen had passed to me in a toast to the happy couple. 'The Emperor protects.'

Well, He'd definitely come through for me today; it was only polite to say thank you.

[On which note of uncharacteristic piety, this portion of the Cain Archive finally meanders to an end.]

ABOUT THE AUTHOR

Sandy Mitchell is a pseudonym of Alex Stewart, who has
been writing successfully under both names since the mid
1980s. As Sandy, he's best known for his work for the Black
Library, particularly the Ciaphas Cain series. Currently, he's
in the final stages of a two year MA in Screenwriting at the
London College of Communication, which has left far less
time than usual for having fun in the 41st Millennium, but is
continuing to chronicle Cain's progress at every opportunity.
His most recent project as Alex was the short film *Ruffled
Feathers*, a comedy about a catastrophic hen night, which
premiered in July 2010.

WARHAMMER
40,000

CIAPHAS CAIN
HERO OF THE IMPERIUM

This omnibus contains *For the Emperor, Caves of Ice* and *The Traitor's Hand*

SANDY MITCHELL

SURVIVING THE 41ST MILLENNIUM, ONE BATTLE AT A TIME

ISBN 978-1-84416-466-0

WARHAMMER 40,000

CIAPHAS CAIN
DEFENDER OF THE IMPERIUM

gly roguish hero,
mbat at both
d very personal
Military SF!'

es bestselling
Drake

SANDY MITCHELL

DEATH OR GLORY • DUTY CALLS • CAIN'S LAST STAND

UK ISBN 978-1-84416-882-8   US ISBN 978-1-84416-883-5